24.95

COVER TO COVER

COVER TO COVER

robert craig

Weidenfeld & Nicolson
LONDON

First published in Great Britain in 2003
by Weidenfeld & Nicolson

© Robert Craig 2003

A CIP catalogue record for this book
is available from the British Library.

ISBN 0 29782898 3

Typeset by Deltatype Ltd,
Birkenhead, Merseyside

Printed in Great Britain by
Clays Ltd, St. Ives plc

Weidenfeld & Nicolson

The Orion Publishing Group Ltd
Orion House
5 Upper Saint Martin's Lane
London, WC2H 9EA

For Anthony and Aiden

With immense thanks to Laura
for her work on the book and for making my dream,
the chance of a career as a writer, a possibility.

PROLOGUE

I am content. Then the phone rings. It's Friday at 9.25 p.m. and he doesn't give me a chance to speak, nor does he say his name or even hello.

'Dave's marrying Rachel tomorrow.' Richard blurts out these names as if they should mean something to me. To keep him on his toes I pretend I do not know who is speaking.

'It's me. Richard. Who did you think it was? We're invited, Tanya. If you fancy coming.'

'Are they friends of yours?' I ask carelessly because I'm racing to finish Patrick Suskind's *Perfume* before an American sitcom I like begins on Channel 4.

'*Dave*,' Richard stresses in an outraged tone, which implies Dave is my closest friend. When I repeat it to myself the name is vaguely familiar; I think Dave went to school with Richard, or they used to work together, or used to go watch Spurs together. Something uninteresting.

'And this wedding is tomorrow? Did you just find out about it today, Richard?'

He clears his throat without taking his mouth from the telephone. I'm almost deafened.

'I thought it was for the best if I waited until the last minute before I asked you to come, in case I changed my mind about going, or we broke up before the day. So do you fancy coming then? I won't be offended if you say no.'

Why should he be thinking we might break up? In the last few weeks I've actually had concerns over whether he's been hinting we should live together. He's been leaving more of his possessions here than is necessary, as if moving in surreptitiously, by instalments.

I keep Richard exclusively for the sex, even though – oh dear – I do not have sex exclusively with him. I'm pleased to be compelled to have someone for sex otherwise I might

I

easily drift into never needing other people around. Then, having acquired the habit of being entirely alone, it might only be a question of time before I completely withdraw from every other pursuit where people are involved. I don't have the resources to finance a hermit madness like Howard Hughes's; mine would have to take the more common form of never leaving the house except for food or books, waddling around the streets in clothes I have owned for twenty years and being totally oblivious to my moustache and greasy hair. I first knew for certain there could never be a prolonged relationship with Richard when we were on our second date, in an Italian restaurant, the first time I saw him eat. Sitting opposite him, looking straight into his face, I noticed how as he chewed his eyebrows moved up and down in conjunction with his jaw, as if connected by a muscle.

'Tanya? Don't you want to go? I should have given you more notice – is that the problem?'

Still with the telephone receiver in my right hand and *Perfume* in my left, stalling so amateurishly anyone more astute than Richard would have hung up, I ask him:

'It's tomorrow, you say? What time is the ceremony?'

'Eleven in the morning. St John's.'

This is my second reading of *Perfume* and since Wednesday I have been rationing pages so I would finish today. If I lose the chance to shop for books tomorrow I will then have to shop on Sunday, or reread another book – which is seldom the same thrill, not even with such brilliance as *Perfume*. I consider how best to tell him this diplomatically.

'I don't know, Richard.'

'Jesus, I wish I'd never asked you now.'

This settles it, I can't let him get away with that.

'I'd love to come.' I'll show him. I'll get drunk and start a fight. I'll grab the groom's cock. I'll heckle during the ceremony.

'Can you come and pick me up at ten-thirty?' he asks in a conspicuously different tone from his 'Jesus, I wish I'd never asked you now'.

Saturday morning and I have hatched a simple schedule entirely dependent on speed. I do not hesitate in getting out of bed, I rush my bath and do the food shopping strictly to the list. So far so good. From then on, however, the plan collapses. Choosing something to wear takes double the amount of time I had allotted. Wardrobes and cupboards are emptied in a frenzy. This strategy finally works: I rediscover a dark blue crushed-velvet dress I had long since forgotten. It has languished in the darker reaches of my wardrobe and as a consequence – if I push the fabric into my nostrils and inhale deeply – smells a little fusty, though nothing that cannot be disguised by a severe shaking and a heavy dose of scent. I put my hair up, eventually reassuring myself how the few defiant strands that scar my face actually look sexy. I attempt to gain back lost time by applying make-up in a rush – the classic error. If I go looking like this the bride will donate her veil. It has to be wiped off and applied again and as a consequence of all this I am ready to go, but it is ten-thirty-five. It's worth this delay, though. I want Richard's friends to approve of me. If they do not he might be persuaded to dump me and I don't want that. When the time comes it has to be me who dumps him. I have my dignity.

Richard does not live too far away so I arrive within ten minutes. It is times like this – meeting him out of routine, seeing him almost as if for the first time – when I remember the reason I first fancied him. As he gets into the car the first words he speaks are a reminder of why he is doomed.

'This aftershave is making my balls sting.'

'Why did you put aftershave on your balls?'

'I dab it everywhere that sweats. So I put it on my balls because they sweat.'

'I have to go to a bookshop first,' I tell him immediately, so as to allow him plenty of time to lose the argument.

He looks at his watch, then moves his hand up to his hair as if to rub his fingers through it, stopping only when he remembers the crust of gel. The church is not too far away and his calm mood is consolidated by the anticipation of a long day of alcoholic consumption.

'Have you always been this boring?' he jokes. I thump him on the leg.

Through the bookshop window I can see Richard still in the passenger seat. Though I am browsing aimlessly, and it is

3

ten-fifty-two, he remains impeccably patient. It was by sheer chance we stumbled upon this second-hand bookshop with, remarkably, a vacant parking space right in front.

Ten-fifty-five. Richard sounds the car horn. I panic and reach out at random, then finger-walk until I am drawn in. The book I pick up is *The Counterfeit Confetti* by Tanya Stephens. I give a shrug of the shoulders and laugh because Tanya Stephens – of course – is my name. The book is a hardback, with no dust jacket, olive green with silver lettering. There are no publishing notes, nor any biography of the author. I turn to page one. For me it is the most compelling opening for a novel I have ever read.

Her father had prostate cancer and died aged just forty-three. This death warned her off marriage; to rely on other people inevitably means being let down.

She had already moved out of her parents' home – so returning and staying there through the last three days of his life was uncomfortable. She stayed in her old bedroom, now alien. It had wallpaper still punctured with drawing-pin holes from her old posters and a carpet stained brighter where furniture had gone. An ancient mahogany wardrobe had been moved here rather than being destroyed, because her father hated waste. Her brother Gary had come up from his final year at Oxford to attend the death and

Richard sounds the car horn three times, prolonging the final blast into a scream. I see him get out of the car. It is ten-fifty-seven. I have to buy the book.

This is why:

My father died of prostate cancer, age forty-three. My brother Gary went to Oxford University. My mother still has the old mahogany wardrobe even though it was she who always hated it. The only part that is inaccurate is when the book says it was my father's death that warned me off marriage. I reached that conclusion on my own.

4

ONE

I am not sure of the route to the church and Richard is having to shout repeated warnings of upcoming left or right turns. He is forced to repeat the warnings as often as four times before they register.

My mind, understandably, is on *The Counterfeit Confetti*. I have hidden the book from direct view, safe in the glove compartment, in the shop's plain white bag. I remember those three nights leading up to my father's death. My room smelt cold, it lacked life. I have not thought about that room for ten years, not until I read that opening paragraph. Curiosity is compelling me to speculate on other coincidences the book might hold. My lack of concentration forces Richard to grab the steering wheel when, without noticing, I veer out to the other side of the road, unconsciously playing chicken with an HGV.

'For fuck's sake, Tanya!' he bellows. 'Wake up!'

When we finally reach St John's it is seven minutes past eleven. I watch Richard from the corner of my eye. He is shaking his head. He snaps his seat belt off and jumps out of the car, making a deliberate point of slamming the door. I watch him walk towards the church. He is forced to wait when he realises I am not following. Instead, I take out *The Counterfeit Confetti* and open it at random, approximately one third of the way through. The obstacle that prevents me from skipping over the first open page and moving to the next is the register of one word. A name. Martin. Seeing that name forces me to read the full paragraph.

Martin was her only boyfriend, friend, lover who ever meant more than the simplest fulfilment of those words. Now, so many years after he has gone, there is no constructive way for her to navigate through the confusion she suffers whenever she wonders how she can so often dwell for hours upon him: his face, his character; his reactions to her. No one has ever known how to react to her as accurately as Martin. She knows how those many differing, subsequent biographies of him she has composed for her own comfort, all are fiction; none could be the truth because all include her.

'For fuck's sake, Tanya!' my current boyfriend yells again, exasperated. He has returned to the car and is looking through the driver's window. I return the book to the glove compartment.

I think about, remember, Martin's first ever present to me, a copy of Budd Schulberg's *The Disenchanted* with the four-word inscription, 'Tanya. Love. Always. Martin.' If I had kept the book it would remain my only souvenir of him that features his writing. He never wrote me a letter because until it ended we were never apart. The one letter he wrote after we had separated, I returned. Also, when I finished with him I packed *The Disenchanted* in with his possessions.

As we walk towards the church Richard calms himself enough to ask:

'What can be so damn fascinating about another book?'

We enter the church. Because a hymn is in progress our entrance causes little disruption. To be safe, we sit at the back. To me, strangers always look as if they know how to attend marriages expertly, routinely, and this seems especially true of this congregation. We pick up a hymn book and, having to share and joining in too late, open it at random and make silent goldfish-like movements with our mouths, as if afraid of being denounced for hymn evasion. The hymn ends and we sit.

Even before the vicar has a chance to speak he has lost me. I am not thinking about *The Counterfeit Confetti* or the character of Martin in that book, or even the paranormal coincidences of those matching names and circumstances. I am thinking of the real Martin I know. Though it is nine years since I last saw him I remain determined to avoid using the past tense. I do not want it to be finished. Yet I no longer sense he is still alive; or maybe it is truer to say I find it too sickening to accept he could have existed through all those nine years without me. To make a detour around these thoughts I speculate how he might be spending his Saturday morning. This ploy fails insomuch as I am unable to imagine anything plausible, though it succeeds in reassuring me how logic demands he must sometimes think of me and wonder about my life. In these nine years he must have thought of me, even if his thoughts are rare and dismissive.

I think about, imagine, a future where we stayed together. One day, as we prepare to move to another home, I discover some of our old, forgotten possessions in a trunk in the loft, amongst which is the copy of *The Disenchanted*. I call Martin up to remind him of the book and ask if the inscription has remained true. This is in my imagination – very much under my control – so of course he assures me the sentiment remains exactly as true as ten years previously.

I do not wish to be younger and do not believe in regret, yet I want the past back. I want to be living ten years ago, living that life again, with *him*. Even if it means being aware of all the misery yet to come – Dad dying, Martin leaving, me becoming this sombre, bad-tempered version of myself, which knows love cannot exist again – it would not matter. I could once more be happy.

We were both nineteen when we met; my experiences of boys until then had been fickle and fleeting, whilst Martin deliberately believed he was too cynical, too dark for love. However, when we fell we could no longer fool ourselves. Like all new converts our faith was all the more evangelical; we took every opportunity to be together. If we attempted to stay apart, even for just a few hours, it failed and we would end up walking the two miles that separated our parents' homes just to kiss, talk a while, then part. The eventual remedy to our separation was for me to move into my own small flat. Martin stayed most nights. I was never troubled by the basic conditions – my time there was and remains the happiest, most fulfilling period of my life. Our time together was filled with talk, sex and subversive domesticity, cooking for each other as if fulfilling vendettas. Martin would often sprawl around my flat for hours upon end, an arm out like a fishing rod, gripping an open book. I read whatever books he recommended, wanting to discover how accurate was his judgement of my taste and personality. I soon developed a greater appetite as I began to follow authors and genres.

Richard drives us to the wedding reception because I am still too distracted. When we arrive there is a great deal of activity as guests say hello to all those other guests they know. The reception is the traditional fixed-budget event: upstairs in a pub, amateur DJ, buffet food, relatives in groups so strictly segregated it makes apartheid seem like Woodstock. We can't even buy a drink, the bar is so busy. Eventually some stranger hands me a drink. It's sherry but tastes like meths-flavoured jam. Richard finally grows tired of my complaints and fights his way to the bar. He brings me a Pils, pleading for me to drink from a glass and not the bottle.

'I gave you a lift here, I did as you asked,' I tell him as I pour. 'Now I'm in the mood to get drunk. I'll get a taxi home and collect my car tomorrow.'

I hand him the empty bottle. Richard gazes longingly over to his mates who have formed a large scrum in front of the bar. They are there in abundance and Richard can now only wish he had not invited me. The females of this tribe have formed their own coven, annexing two tables at the side of the tiny dance floor.

Richard escapes our silence by contriving reasons to abandon me. Within the first hour he visits the toilet twice, the bar three times and once feigns illness so as to spend a few minutes downstairs in the main pub. I do not want to be here. I could be reading about Martin. Reason dictates I have to be here, though – Martin has long since gone and *The Counterfeit Confetti* is fiction.

On one of the occasions I am alone, an idiot comes up to me yelling, 'Whoa! Gail warning! . . . So you're back with Richard?' I say nothing. He answers this by telling me, 'You're not Gail,' as if I have been trying to deceive him. He leaves. I am not very impressed by Richard's friends.

By now I am on my fourth or fifth Pils and Richard has relented, letting me drink straight from the bottle after deducing this is slower than drinking from a glass. As a result of this concession I become less hostile. In a moment of weakness I consider the consequences of allowing Richard to drop me behind enemy lines. He sees me looking over to the women and seizes the opportunity:

'You know, they're all very nice. You'll like them.'

I have recognised one of the women. The reason I did not identify her earlier is that I have not seen her for five years and she has dyed her hair dark ginger. She still wears it in a bob and the combined effect is as if she is wearing a copper crash helmet. Caroline started at Ill Will (the greetings card company I still work for) eighteen months after me and we worked together for the following two years.

'I've seen someone I know,' I tell Richard. 'An old friend.'

Richard is with his mates before I have chance to elaborate.

I stand still in front of Caroline. She is too involved in talking to the woman next to her to notice me. I am forced to repeat her name several times before it attracts her attention.

'Caroline? . . . Caroline? . . . Caroline. Hello.'

Caroline is unhappy at being interrupted and freezes the exaggerated gesture she is using to accompany her story. I consider turning on my heel, pretending I have made a mistake. After all, speaking to Caroline holds dangers. My friendship with her had been a relapse: a return to wanting to be out and with people. With Caroline I was the Tanya from pre-Martin. Frankly, on reflection, I don't care much for that Tanya. She was too young.

To my embarrassment Caroline's eventual recognition of me begins with my dress, only then followed by my face.

'Tanya! Oh wow!' She shouts this so loudly the women at both tables turn and stare, wondering what possible quality I could have to inspire such affection. This is why I sincerely like Caroline – she sincerely likes me.

'This is fantastic! Unbelievable!'

Though cheered by this fuss I am also self-conscious, like a celebrity causing a traffic jam. I edge in next to her.

'Small world, eh?' I ask.

'Bollocks! If it was a small world it wouldn't have been such a long time before I bumped into you again. So come on, explain yourself, why did you stop calling me, you bitch? Oh – hold on – hell – shit – I remember now. It was when I was in *luuurrrvvv*, wasn't it? What a dopey twat I was. So what are you doing here, who do you know?'

I point to Richard.

'Boyfriend. He's a friend of the groom.'

'You're with Richard? Oh, I know Richard. My God – it *is* a small world. So, come on, is it serious with him?'

'We've been seeing each other for five months.' I am pleased with this answer; it implies a certain amount of commitment without actually being a lie. 'And who are you here with?' I ask back.

Caroline has one of those grins I remember from the past; an anecdote is about to follow. Nothing is ever straightforward in Caroline's life. She first reminds me of how our friendship faded away: she had met someone and fallen in love, became engaged and consequently had less time for me or anyone else. It turns out her ex-fiancé is Dave, today's groom.

'Er, well, I guess at least it's nice that you managed to stay friends,' I offer.

'It isn't quite like that. I was still engaged to David when he started seeing Rachel. Rachel was actually married! Married to Clive. And guess what? Clive's here, too, over by the fruit machine. Aren't we all very civilised?'

I am annoyed at Richard. Here is all this exciting sexual history behind today's wedding and he has told me none of it.

'It's OK, everything's settled now,' Caroline continues. 'There were a few months of animosity – I took great joy in throwing a brick through his car windscreen, for instance – but then I began to realise I was let off the hook.'

She smiles broadly when she says this and I judge the remark to be sincere. Though never having been in a comparable situation, I have empathy because it is how I would be if Richard did the same to me: dismayed but relieved.

I tell her about everything I have been up to since I last saw her – this takes seven seconds. I tell her the news of Ill Will, of all the changes that have happened since she worked there. We then reminisce about our time together at Ill Will when we were the youngest there and felt like children in the teachers' common room. We recall the many incidents from our frequent nights out together. When Caroline asks me if I miss those days as much as she does, I squeeze her hand to show her, the best way I can, how pleased I am to have met up with her again.

It is Caroline's turn to tell me about her recent life. After Ill Will she changed jobs even more frequently than she changed flats. Eventually she settled for working for an advertising agency, drawing storyboards for TV adverts. Big fat smirk on her face now, for some reason. She began to see one of the copywriters, Kenneth, who in his spare time wrote a children's book.

'*The Stink Monsters* the book is called. Heard of it?'

'Of course I've heard of it. The characters are on T-shirts, toys, games, everything imaginable.'

'Right! The merchandising rights alone are worth a fortune. The book has sold phenomenally, including the two follow-ups; it went down a storm in America. And now they're making an animated series –'

'But I'm not interested in what someone you once went out with has been doing. Not unless he's dead and has made you his sole benefactor.'

The way Caroline looks at me now, straight, serious, I wonder if I have made the worst kind of faux pas: a joke about something that has really happened.

The flat above me is occupied by an elderly couple I only knew as Mr and Mrs Davies. Earlier this year I bumped into Mrs Davies as she was collecting the mail from the hallway. I noticed she held a stack of mail, all greetings cards, so I made the assumption it was her birthday and wished her a happy one. 'You must know,' she said. In spite of her obvious distress I kept the smile on my face. 'Mr Davies has died.' They were cards of sympathy.

But Caroline is not disgusted by my response, she is simply feigning innocence, milking her oversight for maximum effect.

'Oh, didn't I say? Didn't I tell you it was me who illustrates *The Stink Monsters* books? Didn't I say that I agreed to take a percentage of the profits rather than a fee? I think what I'm trying to tell you, Tanya, is that I am now officially – and by any reasonable measure – loaded. So what do you think of that then?'

'That's fantastic, Caroline. Congratulations.'

The summary of my recent years had been: 'Still at Ill Will, same desk, same job; still in the same flat; but the car is new and the boyfriend – as you know – is different.' After hearing of Caroline's success I am degraded even to the degree where I am grateful for the existence of Richard. As pointless, condemned and redundant as he is, I can still understand how others might regard having him as my only achievement. No one would be impressed if I told them I own thousands of books; no one would present me with an accomplishment award if they knew I had spent a decade of my life reading. I have been reading whilst Caroline has been experiencing. To make amends and try to gain some of Caroline's respect, I begin to boast about Richard. It actually surprises me how easy this is. He has more qualities than I imagined. Other qualities I simply invent.

'To be frank,' I lie, 'the sex is sometimes too passionate. I mean, he's so easily aroused that it's a bit of a problem. He can get a hard-on just from watching the Channel 5 newsreaders. What he really needs is a new pill to be developed, something like an anti-Viagra.'

'What! You lucky lucky bitch. God, you're spoilt for it if that's your biggest worry. Myself, I'd settle for a one-off quickie at the moment. It's been two fucking months – two *non*-fucking months – since I last saw any action.'

'Who was that with?'

She shudders. 'An ex-boyfriend. And he's married nowadays. It was awful. Oh, before I get any drunker,' Caroline continues, 'I'll give you my phone number so we can arrange for me to show off my home.'

One of Caroline's friends lends her a pen and she peels the print off a beer mat to write her number down. I am about to do the same before I realise it is unnecessary. My phone number has not changed and she still has it.

Through the rest of the afternoon and into the evening we continue to talk as if our friendship had never been interrupted. Much later, when the alcohol has kicked in with a vengeance, the talk becomes less about reality and more about abstracts. In spite of her new wealth she has fewer

happy days, she tells me, and wonders why this is. My 'Don't
know' is not particularly helpful.

'What do you think life is about, Tanya?' Her voice is tired
and I suspect she means the question to be rhetorical. This
doesn't prevent me making a reply; I've had an answer for
this for some time, never expecting to be actually asked. I tell
her my firm conviction that life isn't about anything; it has no
grand purpose.

'We live for moments of happiness. We live from one
moment to the next; the best you can hope for is that the
moments aren't too far apart.'

'Fucking hell, Tanya! And is that it? Is that all there is to
hope for?'

Whilst she meditates on this she takes a sip from her drink.
A sip proves inadequate so she empties the glass.

'What it is – I admit it – what the problem is . . . A half-
decent man is the only thing missing from my life at the
moment. I want a man. A good, nice, friendly, funny, strong,
odd, sexy man. Why can't I have one, Tanya? You've got
one. It's not fair.'

Good. Nice. Friendly. Funny. Strong. Odd. Sexy. Richard
would – yes – pass a rudimentary test for all of these epithets,
but not in the right ways. He is good without possessing
virtue, nice without being pleasant, friendly without being
fun, funny only insomuch as he gets my jokes, strong but too
easily manipulated, odd without being enigmatic, sexy
without inspiring infatuation. I am currently content to have
him but would not be miserable without him.

Caroline mumbles, 'Did I tell you I went to see a Tarot
card reader?'

I close my eyes and smile wearily, hoping this will convey
amused scepticism. It fails.

'Tanya? Are you asleep?'

I open my eyes. 'Caroline – come on! Tarot cards?'

'I wasn't convinced myself until I went. I wanted to know
if I had anything to look forward to. I'll tell you what, she
was really good.'

'It's nonsense. I don't believe in any of that crap: star signs,
UFOs, ghosts. The only things worth believing in are those
things you can actually touch and see.'

My vehemence dissuades Caroline from adding anything else about Tarot cards. I did not mean to become irritated. I am pleased it is getting late as I have reached the threshold of my tolerance. Conclusive evidence of a late hour is the display of men returning to women. Richard sits and puts his arm around my shoulders. He kisses my ear. Caroline watches.

'This is your friend?' Richard whispers to me.

'I've mentioned Caroline to you.'

'I never realised it was *this* Caroline,' he smirks. 'What I mean is – this Caroline. You know – erm – Dave's ex.'

'And by the way, who's Gail?' I ask. He goes as red as a spanked arse.

Caroline laughs, pointing at me. 'Oh God, yes! I never thought about it – you're the spitting image.'

'She's just an ex ... You don't look like her,' Richard adds, looking away. Then he kisses my cheek and neck. I feel a cold stroke, which might be a dribble of his spit. 'Back to my flat – huh?'

'OK.'

My departure from Caroline is a prolonged recap of how great it has been to see her and how much I enjoyed our talk, and a promise to phone her the following week, unless she phones me first.

In the fresh air outside the pub I finally comprehend just how drunk I am. A taxi waits, and Richard walks to it. I go, instead, to my car to fetch *The Counterfeit Confetti* from the glove compartment. It's a struggle for me to work out the complexities of opening the car door. Richard makes the taxi driver sound his horn. Though I intend to read the book tomorrow, if I stay at Richard's, a dictating curiosity forces me to open the book immediately. Again I open it at random and this is all I read:

After marrying, Martin then settled into fathering two children. He continued to live in Swansea, working for the DVLA, and continued to be happy.

Seeing me throw up, Richard comes over to collect me. I am

14

bundled into the taxi. *The Counterfeit Confetti* is left in my car.

TWO

I am awake in Richard's bed, keeping perfectly still because I do not want to test the severity of my hangover. I know it is day from the strong light seeping round the edges of Richard's thick curtains. Earlier this morning Richard woke and, believing I was asleep, attempted to dress in silence. This process was so slow I became bored with pretending to be asleep and made a performance of waking: I stretched and blinked and made Skippy noises.

'I fell asleep last night, didn't I? Before we could do anything,' he confesses.

'I was too drunk anyway,' I answer, though I have a hazy recollection of thumping him in the back and demanding sex.

He brushes my fringe, straggly with sweat, away from my forehead; then brushes my cheek with the back of his hand.

'I agreed to work today. But I'll stay and look after you.'

It is when I am ill that I most passionately want to be alone. Alone, I never have to explain the symptoms of my illness, nor give updates on my recovery. I don't have to exaggerate weak speech or make slow movements, or alternatively I don't have to put on a brave face. I can just make my own schedule for self-pity and let nature take its course.

'No, you work. I'm OK. It's just a hangover, I'll sleep it off.'

'OK. If you want. I won't go in my car. I'll phone Pete on his mobile and tell him to collect me on the way to his next job. That way when we've finished he can drop me off at St John's and I can bring your car back here for you.'

Pete is the man Richard works with. They fit carpets. Though most of their jobs can be done single-handedly, working together makes it easier and quicker; plus, being a team gives their customers a reassuring impression of professionalism.

'Maybe . . . you know, if I'm feeling better when you come back home, maybe we can . . .'

'You're staying here till then, are you?'

I nod yes.

'You're staying here?' He stresses each word and I smile at his repetition. He has become aware, like me, of this new, exciting situation: him at work, me here; him returning, me waiting. For the first time in almost half a year one of us would be *returning* to the other. This is a significant development in most relationships; in ours it seems as monumental as an exchange of rings.

I wait until I hear him leave the flat, the sound of the outside door closing, before I attempt to masturbate. All goes well through the early stages: the warm-up, the building of a momentum, the complicated scenario writing. At first, from a misplaced sense of loyalty to Richard, I visualise variations of him – older, foreign, richer. These repeatedly fail and so I revert to Martin, my reliable masturbatory standby. Sometimes I manufacture elaborate stories of a reunion, or a world where we never parted and in that long-lasting relationship we have devised an elaborate sex schedule. The latest edition to these scenarios is one where I win the Lottery and track him down; we meet and it's as if we've never been apart. My problem this morning is, after reading a sentence in *The Counterfeit Confetti*, I have learnt all these scenarios are impossible. There can be no future.

For a couple of hours I drift from one oasis of daydreams to others of conscious abstraction without ever achieving deep sleep – I am trying too hard. Exhausted, I now force myself out of bed. The moment I plod into Richard's bathroom and set the shower going I feel lively enough to examine myself in the mirror. I am yellow ochre; my hair is set in contorted horror. All this is remedied by a shower and a clean of the teeth. My hair problem is remedied by gel. Richard owns a selection of gels any hair-care trade show would be proud of. I choose the most expensive.

I eat a bowl of Coco Pops – it's worth mentioning how Richard has three boxes of Coco Pops because God forbid he should run out of Coco Pops! – then decide to use the great freedom of having nothing else to do to look around Richard's flat and judge the kinds of books he reads, that's if he owns any. I quickly assess that there are no books in the living room. I tick off every other room where I know for certain there are no books: the bedroom, the kitchen and the bathroom. The only other possible place is the hallway cupboard, which Richard ludicrously describes as the utility room. It is the 'utility' room only because it is where the gas and electricity meters are, plus it is also where he stores his vacuum cleaner. Before I had even met him Richard had removed the plug from the vacuum cleaner to use on his Sony playstation. Consequently there are areas of the living-room carpet, specifically an exclusion zone around the armchair, which actually crunch underfoot. There are no books in the utility cupboard. There are plant pots, a disassembled wine rack, empty coffee and jam jars, a tool box, a shoe cleaning kit, a fake white Christmas tree and shelves of blankets. Yet also, promisingly, alongside the blankets is a cardboard box whose flaps have been folded in on each other simply begging to be opened. Inside, there are bundles of documents: insurance, tax, purchase agreements and so forth. An A4 envelope full of photographs at first also seems promising but provides only one surprise. The photographs are mainly of Richard and his mates, in various pubs, or at various social functions, crowded together, saluting the photographer with their raised pints. The last photograph I look at is in a fold-out cardboard frame: it is of Richard sat at a table at a party of some kind, with his arms around and cheek pressed against Caroline.

So Richard went out with Caroline?

I dial Caroline's number. I have taken the beer mat out of my handbag. This is why being friends with Caroline is a danger. Her friends unexpectedly find out things about her. Trouble happens when she's around. I will use this new information as a pretext for keeping my distance – we will be friends again, but not close – and I will not be dragged out to nightclubs or into undignified incidents.

The information might also be handy to ditch Richard. He

18

has deceived me, I will tell him. I won't be melodramatic but I'll be vicious.

Caroline is pleased to hear from me, which momentarily disarms me.

'I just thought I'd phone you and ask . . .' Oh, sod this, I have no need for diplomacy, I have done nothing wrong, so I decide to go for it – 'ask how long you went out with Richard for.'

This question comes out wrong. My intention had been to sound casual but instead I sound threatening – it is a surprisingly thin line.

'Oh. You know? Well . . . Look, Tanya . . . Erm. When I was talking to you yesterday I soon realised Richard hadn't told you about us yet . . . When it happened – about ten months ago, I'd say – I was on the rebound, still, from Kenneth, and Richard – well, he wasn't on the rebound from anyone but men always behave as if they're rebounding, don't they?'

'Maybe he was rebounding from Gail?'

'Hardly. He split from her three or four years ago. Oh Christ, are you angry with me, Tanya?'

'No.' I have a desire to add a qualification, a no *but* . . . but I cannot think of one. I settle for demanding details.

'Did you sleep together?'

'We went out for two weeks. Of course we slept together. But I was just a fling to him, and him to me. The thing is . . . And I wouldn't tell you this normally because you'll think I'm a prat, but the thing is, even though we split up a year ago I still love Kenneth. You know – who writes *The Stink Monsters*? I mean, I like Richard, I do; and I hope he likes me, but us having gone out with each other only makes him as inconsequential as every other one of my ex-boyfriends. I feel less for them than I do for my cat.'

'You've got a cat?'

'One at the moment. I'm thinking about getting him a friend.'

Cat ownership is a measure of how single women have slipped into madness. One cat is a manageable symptom – like sending Get Well Soon cards to soap opera characters in hospital; two cats – especially if they've been given quirky, amusing names – and alarm bells should peal around her street; three cats mean the fight for rationality has been lost.

'Are we fine then, Tanya? Richard and me – it was nothing. It has nothing to do with you and him, or me and you. OK?'

I have no genuine grievances about a past fling she had with my current boyfriend. I have no reason or desire to torment her – I can save that for Richard.

'What are you going to do with your cat when you're away in America?' Caroline told me yesterday of a trip she is making to America to supervise the making of the TV animated version of *The Stink Monsters*.

'I usually fob him off onto my mother. It works out OK – it gives us a subject of conversation that doesn't inevitably lead to an argument. Though she refuses to use its name. It's called Rotten Egg, by the way.'

'Rotten Egg?' Oh dear. This is more serious than I first thought.

'Rotten Egg – you know? From *The Stink Monsters*?' she asks.

'Oh – right. Got it.' It sounds as if Caroline expects me to have read one of the books. I'll have to buy a copy in case she quizzes me.

Happy that our dispute is resolved, Caroline asks which night I might be free to come and tour her flat. Any night would suit me, but wishing to keep on the smart side of caution and also to give the impression of a busy schedule, I tell her I can only give a definite date when I am in my own home and able to consult my diary. The telephone conversation ends with reassurances of our renewed friendship and Caroline complaining about having to keep her regular Sunday appointment with her mother.

'With all my money I'm considering employing somebody to go in my place,' she jokes.

With no books to read I turn on Richard's TV, lie on his settee and settle. I drift into sleep, led there by my wondering just exactly how well-off Caroline is these days. Sleep allows me to indulge in a fantasy of my own increased wealth. It is many hours later when I wake, just as Richard returns. He thinks I am watching an episode of *Columbo*.

'It's a good one, is this,' he tells me. It is; I've seen it many times before. The most accurate definition of the concept of infinity is the number of times the BBC have repeated *Columbo*. I am sleepy and immobile on his settee. I say nothing to him yet because I am preparing myself for a confrontation about Caroline. I should change out of his old T-shirt and back into my dress, in case I wish to make a hurried, indignant exit.

Richard crouches down to ask if I am still suffering.

'I feel much better,' I assure him.

'Good, because I have bad news.'

'Oh?'

'Your car.'

'Oh?'

'Has been stolen. It wasn't at St John's where you left it. I'm sorry, Tanya.'

Earlier this year I was without my car for a fortnight whilst it was being serviced. Although getting to work was slightly troublesome I was freed from the daily stress of London driving, then having to find a parking space. My only sense of loss regarding this theft is that *The Counterfeit Confetti* was in the car. Reading the whole book would have been interesting.

Richard stands by the phone as I ring the police. Afterwards he hugs me with the depth of compassion felt only by someone who loves cars for the objects they are and not, like me, someone who owns one only for its practicality.

'Shall I drive you home? Whatever you want to do – it's up to you, I'll understand.'

I have no book to read.

I get back into his bed. I hear the shower. Seconds after the shower is turned off Richard is in the bedroom, drying himself. He tosses the damp towel aside and gets into the bed from the base, head first. I feel his wet hair on my ankles, then his chin on my legs. He was in too much of a rush to shave.

The sex took longer than anticipated as we went through all procedures: the routine, the unnecessary and even one or two new items on the agenda. Straight after, even before I fully get my breath back, I ask about him and Caroline.

'She told you?'

'I talked to her on the phone today.'

'It happened ages ago.'

'It was less than a year ago, Richard.'

'Before I met you. You don't care about it do you?' This is a smart way for him to phrase the question. The only response that will preserve my dignity is to affirm that *of course I do not care.*

'I just don't understand why you didn't tell me,' I say. 'That's all.'

Richard goes to the kitchen and returns with spaghetti hoops and miniature sausages on toast. I like that Richard is not a 'New Man', and I also like the fact that he believes doing things like warming up a tin of spaghetti makes him one. Tonight, as he eats, even his trampolining eyebrows do not bother me. When we finish eating we place the plates on the floor and lie back. I dare not stay another night. If I do, tomorrow I will have to return to my flat, wash thoroughly, change and eat, then get to work on time – all without a car. Richard folds himself around to rest his head on my chest, above my breasts. I feel so drowsy that I know I will sleep if I do not fight.

'I have to go, Richard,' I mumble.

'Huh?'

'I . . .'

Hours later I wake under his dead weight. I force him off me, using a strength that comes out of my determination to leave. I use an aggression that would easily wake most other people.

'Come on, Richard. You're driving me home.'

'In a minute.'

I get dressed. It takes longer than his requested minute. I shake him again, this time with all the violence of an interrogator.

'In a minute!'

Today I liked Richard. He was kind, considerate, tolerant. The sex was at its best due to aroused expectations and a change of circumstances. Now he has reverted to his worst. I phone for a minicab, then go straight outside to wait. The cold increases my bitterness. So very late on a Sunday night the noise of traffic is negligible, enabling me to clearly hear Richard tapping on his window. I even hear him calling for me to wait.

THREE

The short journey home is occupied with fighting off sleep. Though the journey and the cold fail to lift my tiredness, when I am in the building and climbing the stairs towards my flat one sound scares me wide awake. I hear Mrs Davies's door, on the floor above me, being unlocked. Dreading that she has been waiting for me, I increase my pace, taking two steps at a time, simultaneously rummaging through the clutter in my handbag for my keys. The key glides effortlessly into the lock, an easy turn and . . .

'Tanya?' she calls, still out of view.

I ignore her. I am exhausted – this entitles me to be rude. She cannot possibly have anything urgent or important to tell me as nothing important ever happens to her. The death of her husband is the only eventful tale she has to tell, and it's a story I've now heard many times. I cannot face such torment tonight.

'I've been waiting for you to come home, Tanya,' she says, still out of view. I am done for.

'Hello, Mrs Davies,' I say when she completes the journey down the stairs. Her movements are artificially slow, her expression theatrically distressed. She looks older than ever before. The hall lighting and the late hour do not suit her.

'I wanted to warn you to make sure you locked your door properly. I've been burgled, you see.' Tears. Tears as readily as if there were talk-show cameras trained on her. 'It happened this morning. When I was at church. You don't expect to be burgled on Sunday, do you?'

Why? Because burglars are known for observing the Sabbath? Because they have a strong union, which has preserved their two-day weekend?

'They took my photograph frames, my ornaments, but worst of all . . .' Please God – spare me from this! '. . . they

24

took all my jewellery, all the jewellery Clement bought me over the years.'

I have never seen Mrs Davies wearing any jewellery other than an awful brooch, which is either a butterfly or a vagina, and I am hoping Clement was Mr Davies and is not one of her cats. My eyes sting with tiredness and boredom. I ache for sleep.

Mrs Davies shivers. The house has no main heating and the landing can become icy. She looks vulnerable, shivering and tearful; she is old. She is alone without wanting it nor ever having anticipated it. The police aren't interested and my main concerns are my own fatigue and the cold. Her most treasured possessions have been taken and no one is concerned. She must even suspect that if they were not regularly fed even her cats would desert her. She is unburdening herself on the only available set of ears. Mine. She was once somebody; she once lived a life of work and sex and busy days. She had a lover and a constant companion. Now she is ferociously alone and to her it's a form of death. She invested her love and her life in one other person, then was amazed by the inevitable betrayal of his dying.

'Would you like a coffee, Mrs Davies?' I cannot accept any credit for making this apparently selfless offer – I am secretly praying she will decline.

'You're so kind to me. I've sat in alone all day brooding on it and just getting myself more and more upset.'

I leave her in the living room whilst I make the drinks.

'I won't stay long, Tanya,' she calls to me when I am in the kitchen. 'I know you have to get up for work in the morning.'

Though this is encouraging, I still take the promise with a pinch of salt. Time is relative to the elderly; they can talk of the 1950s as if they were recent years and when she says 'I won't stay long' it could just as easily mean from now on we will be co-renting this flat. When I bring the drinks into the living room I am delighted that she remains standing and more so when she begins to gulp the coffee. I put in plenty of milk to keep it cool. As a bonus to this, the prospect of more tears seems to have completely diminished. She compliments the way I have decorated the living room. She comments on all the books I have, my two cuckoo clocks and the two bronze statues of storks I have at either side of the fireplace. These remind her of her stolen ornaments and – *hey presto!* – we are back to talking about her burglary.

'Do you know who I think might have done it, Tanya?'

'No,' I say because how the fuck could I know?

Her main suspect is Trevor from downstairs. He lives opposite Alison's old flat. (Alison has stubbornly remained my friend despite moving out of this building and despite my best attempts to avoid continuing any contact with her.) I do not know Trevor's surname – incredibly he never seems to receive mail – even though he has lived here since before Alison moved out. For Mrs Davies the heavy metal music he plays is an open insult; it is Devil worship.

'Who else could it be?' she asks. Her grounds for prosecution are weak; her hatred of the music is the only evidence she has to implicate him in the burglary.

'I don't know,' I answer carelessly. My attention has been drawn to the light flashing on my answerphone. The most likely candidates for the caller are my mother, possibly Caroline, or maybe even Richard – he might have phoned after I left him, to apologise. I interrupt Mrs Davies to tell her I have a message, implying it may be urgent. She has finished her coffee, yet grips the cup as if it is her permission to stay. The single message is from the police. They have found my car on an industrial estate. The fire brigade reported it after putting the fire out. The thieves must have torched it, the policeman says. Clearly he is detective material. Though I had already dismissed any idea of having the car returned intact, I had still naively hoped *The Counterfeit Confetti* might somehow have been retrieved. I use the message as a pretext to lie to Mrs Davies – I tell her I have to immediately dig out insurance documents. Offering me sympathy, she leaves.

So *The Counterfeit Confetti* has gone.

In spite of the Horlicks and my exhaustion, I sleep badly. My face is sore from Richard's stubbly face.

Carless and bookless, I leave home at 7.37 a.m., determined to find a good newsagent – one that sells books – before reaching work. I know the choice of books offered will be limited and obvious best-sellers but this might work out OK. I might be led to an author I have never read before who is better than I imagined, which then presents me with their whole back catalogue. Not many people would understand this acute craving for a book. Carl understands.

Though the postman hasn't yet been, at least I escape from the house without an unprovoked attack by Mrs Davies. As I pass his door I notice – faintly, but it's there – music coming from Trevor's flat. So, long-haired, heavy metal freak that he is, nevertheless he still does play his music at a lower volume and show concern for his neighbours. I may tell Mrs Davies this, and she might reduce his sentence or even find him Not Guilty.

I have slept with Carl twice. I first met him near my street. I was reading Jonathan Coe's *What a Carve-Up!* as I was walking home and had to dip it to negotiate myself around Carl's trolley. Carl sweeps roads. He smiled at me – I smiled back, politely.

'Are you enjoying it?' Carl asked about *What a Carve-Up!* I did not immediately answer. Carl then produced the same book from a pouch in his overalls.

Confession time. The reason I hesitated from beginning a conversation was because of a snobby concern about being seen talking to a road sweeper. I was appalled at myself for this thought. Richard is a carpet fitter – that's hardly like being a lawyer or doctor. Road sweeper or not, Carl is more my type than Richard. He knows about books and discussing them. Now that I know him I always look forward to seeing him. Though Richard is more obviously good looking, Carl is attractive in a boyish, happy way. The reasons I keep Richard are that he is easygoing, undemanding. He's there when I need him and he's seldom intrusive. I do not want more; I have Richard for sex and if I want obsessive love I am fortunate to have the memory of Martin – although that has now been violated by the intrusion of rationality.

'I am enjoying it,' I told Carl about *What a Carve-Up!*, 'though I was a little confused by all the family names at first. But that's settled down now.'

To redeem myself for my snobbishness I asked him which book he intended reading next. The book he mentioned was one I had read, which I told him I didn't recommend. He asked me to tell him some titles I did recommend and this began a discussion that lasted for half an hour. To further compensate, and because by then I was genuinely interested in him, I arranged to meet him on the same street the next day. Which we did. For the next fortnight we began a routine of meeting, talking and exchanging books. The progression from simply talking to . . . er . . . Well, it was my turn to lend him a book. Unable to think of one suitable, I invited him home to look through my collection. Don't ask me to explain the psychology of how we set off to my flat with only the thought of books on our minds, yet less than an hour later ended up in bed together. All I can do is report the sequence of events.

Before even removing my coat I took Carl into my bedroom. It's where I store the majority of my books.

'This is going to be hard to explain to your boyfriend if he should turn up unannounced,' Carl joked. I explained how such a scenario was unlikely to happen. I can't remember why I wasn't at work that day. It may have been attributed to illness, more likely I was on holiday. Carl asked if he could wash his hands and face. I showed him the bathroom. When he returned he had removed his overall. He was in jeans and a plain, dark-green T-shirt. On his right arm he has a tattoo of a quill pen piercing a human skull with the motto *Ars Longa Vita Brevis* underneath. Having taken off my coat and removed my shoes, I was sitting on the floor, resting against the bed. Carl sat next to me and rubbed his hands together in delighted anticipation.

'Before I start looking, you don't have *King Jesus*, do you? Robert Graves.'

'I have a few of Robert Graves's books. Not that one though. I don't think I know it.'

'I had it at college but never got around to reading it. After I left college I sold all my books.'

'I would never sell my books,' I answered, though I was thinking: *You* went to college? You're a road sweeper; which course is required? Sometimes, just sometimes, I'm smart enough to resist my constant temptation to be rude.

Carl had read many of the books in that first box, so we

discussed these – again finding our verdicts to be often very similar. When I sat down next to him with the second box I inadvertently sat closer. I stayed there, connected. He leant across to take a book from the box and his bare arm brushed against my breast. He apologised and shuffled away. The next time he leant across I noticed how his neck was connected to his chin, the outline of the muscle and the strength of the curve. He had been speaking and looked at me to emphasise a point. When he stopped speaking I had to force my attention away from his neck. He was studying me, now.

'I like the tattoo, incidentally. I don't usually like tattoos.'

I had instinctively reached out to indicate where his tattoo was – as if he wouldn't know! I stopped when I realised my foolishness. Then I changed my mind and touched his arm anyway. He slightly nodded his head, as if agreeing to something. From my eyes he looked down at my lips. I locked on his eyes hard so as to force his gaze back. Except he kissed me. It was a second longer than a peck. He withdrew by inches, to test how I would respond. I responded by doing nothing – keeping silent, no facial expression, no movement away. He kissed me again.

'I've told you I have a boyfriend,' I said when our lips separated.

'Yes.'

His yes wasn't an acceptance of any rejection, it was a mild disappointment about something else. I am sure I was telling him how kissing me was wrong and how it should certainly progress no further.

The main pleasure of the sex was its unexpected tenderness; and of course this was enhanced by the act being illicit, unplanned and taking place in the daytime. Its conclusion had no clumsiness, no embarrassment nor recriminations. We made love, then carried on talking as we dressed. He decided against taking all the books I wanted to lend him – there was no practical way for him to get them home. He selected just three: *Complicity* by Iain Banks, *Lost in Music* by Giles Smith and *The Road to Wigan Pier* by George Orwell. As I let him out of the flat he gave me a friendly kiss and said he hoped I would track him down when I wanted the books returned. I was happy to believe this was a one-off. I had been seeing Richard for only a couple of months.

The second time was again at my flat, and again on the same pretext – I had invited him to look at my books. That second time, however, we were in bed within minutes. Though the actual sex was even more accomplished, afterwards the conversation was uneasy, too formal, as if we were fooling ourselves. Again he kissed me when he left, readily accepting the rules I had made the previous time. No woman in the world wants such complacency after making love. He should have ignored my relationship with Richard and demanded we meet up again soon. Damn him – I wanted him to ask me out! I mean, I would have refused of course; I would have thanked him for asking but have told him the sex was – once again – an impulsive mistake. However, he made no presumptions nor advances. Which meant I had to.

I have seen him twice since we last made love. Neither of us currently has a book belonging to the other. Maybe Carl has a book to lend me. Because I am going to catch the tube, this allows me a little spare time. I know where to look for Carl. I live on one of the side streets that connects to a main road. The area Carl sweeps – I don't know it exactly, we've never discussed it, but certainly he sweeps these side streets rather than the main road itself.

Carl is taking a break, sitting on a wall outside an off-licence, chin on chest, reading, so he doesn't notice my approach. I sit next to him and look at the cover of his book. It's sci-fi, which is a genre I have never had any inclinations towards.

'Any good?'

'Not really. I have nothing else. Any recommendations?'

'I haven't read anything great since I last saw you. I've just reread *Perfume*.'

'No car today?'

'It's been stolen.'

'Oh. Sorry. What happened to your face?'

Phrases That Women Never Want To Hear: 'What happened to your face?' He's talking about the soreness, the slightly pink swelling caused by Richard kissing me without having shaved. Though Carl knows about him, I don't want to mention I've been kissing Richard; it isn't polite to remind him.

'I'm allergic to some soap I've been using,' I say, then . . .
– . . . – . . . (*Awkwardness*.)

Our last conversation, our last meeting, must have exhausted the subject of books without me noticing. And we have not yet established any other method of beginning conversations. In order to end the unease I must end the stalemate, which means either reverting to a contrived question about books or confronting the subject of us together: the future.

'I'd better go,' I tell Carl. It sounds very final. 'I have to catch the tube.'

'OK.'

All I know for certain is leaving now would be the end, because should I ever accidentally see him again it would mean having to pick up the conversation from where we left off and where we left off is having nothing to say.

'Are books all we have in common, do you think, Carl? If we don't talk about books, then there's nothing else?'

'We've talked about plenty of other things,' he reminds me. 'The problem is, it might be that we haven't *done* anything else together, I think. All we've done together is – gone to bed. We can talk about that, if you want. The ball is in your court.'

'Why is the ball in my court?'

'I have no one to answer to. You're the rule-maker because you're the one who has outside commitments – you're the one in a relationship.'

'And you're not?'

'Not now.'

'Not now?'

'I was. I broke up with her. After I slept with you that first time.'

'Why? I let you know I wasn't going to split up with Richard.'

'That has nothing to do with it,' Carl says. He looks very sad. 'I didn't want to lie to her.'

'Wouldn't it have just been easier to stay with her and not have slept with me?'

'That would have been far from easy.'

I take the sci-fi book off him so he has nowhere to divert his gaze.

'Carl, why are you a road sweeper?'

'Why?'

'Is it what you want to do?'

'I wish the money was better.'

'That's not a proper answer.'

'Does it bother you?'

'Why should it bother me?' These printed words do not convey the intonation. I am not being democratic; I am not saying it does not bother me a man I am attracted to is a road sweeper, I will respect him for his character not his job. I am saying, Why should it bother me, it's not as if we're together as a couple. However, Carl was there so he understood the true meaning.

'It doesn't bother me that you're a graphic artist,' he retaliates. He stands away from the wall and takes the sci-fi book from me, putting it into his overall pocket. He fiddles around in there for a moment, then produces a slip of notepaper. It has his name and phone number on. It is tatty.

'I've carried this around since our first ever meeting. Throw it away if you want. But I hope you don't. Phone me if you fancy a chat, or . . . Phone me if you want to borrow a book. You haven't seen my collection.'

I take the paper and carefully smooth it out, fold it and put it in the securest section of my purse; then kiss him on the cheek. Eight-fifteen.

I catch the tube at eight-twenty-seven. I arrive at the tube station newsagent at eight-forty-two. I browse but it has no book I am interested in. I have to run to work and I arrive at four minutes past nine.

Several months back I took a break from the day's routine and calculated exactly how many days I had worked at Ill Will. I took holidays, weekends, even days off sick into account and arrived at a precise – depressing – number. I intended to mark up the total as each subsequent day passed, but it became too oppressive. Anyway, in round figures I have certainly worked here for two thousand days. Two thousand times I have passed reception, passed the security man (only thirty times has he bothered to look up from the back page of the *Daily Mail*), caught the lift up to the eighth floor, entered Ill Will's offices, sat at my desk. Two thousand times. I stay at Ill Will inspired by a sublime lack of ambition. It is easy work and changing would be too inconvenient. After I had calculated how many days I had been there, I considered submitting an extremely optimistic pay claim. I wrote why I believed I am worth it, why the company owes me, how it would bind my future with them: all good, well thought out arguments. I filed it using my unique system for all problems I wish to delay dealing with. I kept it on my desk until it became lost amongst all the other papers, then, after a week or two, having had no reason to search through these papers – I threw away the lot. Though not a flawless filing system, it has always served me well.

FOUR

I have no explanation for how this could have happened but – I am twenty-nine. This means I'm too old to start big diversions in my life, like going to university, moving abroad or becoming a lesbian. Yet I remain convinced I am too young to draw a line under all I am now and announcing this is the way I intend to live the rest of my life. Once, people left childhood behind them when they took jobs; they fought in wars or lived through real political change, so by thirty they smoked pipes and knitted, simply pleased to still be alive. This is why the idea of being thirty and being old exists. The notion has been so embedded in the culture that it still persists even though in the world now, with late motherhood, pop stars living into their fifties and sixties, better diets and later mortality, thirty-year-olds can have the money of grown-ups yet the freedom to still act like kids. I am still young, I know this and know I should wish to celebrate the fact. I know I should do something more constructive with my spare time other than reading: something like rock climbing or skiing, something that requires thick socks. I am too old to have my eyebrow pierced like Jo yet I'm too young to tape and keep every episode of *A Touch of Frost* like Allan. At Ill Will Jo makes coffee; Allan takes around cards to sign for people on the same floor of our building who are marrying or leaving. I am in between Allan and Jo: I don't have to make coffee nor have I ever had a card signed for me.

Only once have I been on a night out with Jo. It was a Saturday night, and it was a rude awakening. She danced and took whizz and sweated away wearing fewer clothes than I wear to bed. I watched and was disapproving, bored and remote. People my own age were there, some even older than me. They did not seem out of place, they had no inhibitions. My inhibitions were common sense: the mortal enemy of fun.

34

I tried a little of Jo's whizz but its only effect was to accelerate my inertia. I despised everyone I saw and everything they did: their clothes, their hair, their expressions. Everyone and everything was an orgy of idiocy, a commemoration of The Worthless. Most disturbing was my envy of every couple I saw. I should be here with Martin, I kept thinking. I prefer that other world I lived in with him, where judgements of worth were not made based purely on surface trivialities. If I was with Martin I wouldn't have to condemn every other woman as competition, nor assess every man on suitability. If Martin was here – I kept thinking – he'd be in on the joke. I might have enjoyed this world even if I hadn't been out with Martin but knew he was waiting back at home. Music, lights, drink were no distraction from my life's lack of tenderness. This world offered nothing to interest me, and there was no alternative. When I returned home that night I made myself a Horlicks and watched the *Casualty* episode I had taped, wondering how and when this change had overtaken me. Up until that night only tiny incidents, small unimportant things, had separated me from the very young. That phase of my life, a phase I had actually abandoned of my own free will – dancing, heavy drinking, randomly screwing – had now gone for good. This was no longer open to me, I was excluded. At the places Jo took me, it seemed inappropriate and undignified for me to be there. On the following Monday Jo was enthusiastic about arranging another night out but when she later tried to fix a date I made excuses.

I do not understand why reading in a book that Martin is now married should have come as such a surprise. People our age are most often married. I should have reasoned this out years ago. Not that I believe *The Counterfeit Confetti* could hold the truth about him. Yet logically, somewhere, at some time, Martin will have – most probably – married. It would have been fascinating to have read more of *The Counterfeit Confetti*, even if it was just to discover more of these blatantly obvious truths. I wish there was hope of having the book returned. The depressing part of no longer having Martin to fixate over is that I have only Richard. He's not enough to be everything. I am immensely grateful to Carl for giving me his phone number. I'll never ring him, but nevertheless it's a security blanket.

Being the last to arrive at work this morning, Jo brings me a coffee straightaway as a reward for taking the heat off her – she was a little late herself.

'It's not often you get here after me,' she says warmly.

'I've had a bit of an exciting weekend,' I tell her.

She leans over me, staring at my computer monitor as if being consulted. This is in case Allan believes her to be skiving and gives her work to do. The deception would be more convincing if I had turned the computer on.

'Exciting?'

If Jo might be inferring I have had a weekend of nightclubbing, dancing and drug abuse I must now destroy her illusion with the truth. Though truth is relative.

'I went to a party on Saturday,' I begin. A party is sort of the truth. I'll bet in a really comprehensive thesaurus a wedding reception is synonymous with party. 'I got so drunk I had to leave my car. And it was stolen.'

Jo is sympathetic but not impressed. She does not ask about the party – guessing, I should think, it was not likely to be a party by her definition. To attract Jo's attention, Allan is leaning back in his chair. She returns to her own desk.

Whilst I drink my coffee I phone my insurance company and they arrange for the remains of my car to be taken away. As I am going through the details I fidget with the piece of paper Carl gave me. To phone him would be a serious betrayal of Richard. A far worse betrayal than the sex. A phone call is premeditated, the sex was spur-of-the-moment. *Moments.* I will not phone Carl even though Richard, after last night, may be history. And Martin, at long last, is also now history. I might phone Carl. Richard provides me with less than he does. I rarely converse with Richard; he will speak, I will listen; I will speak and he will listen; yet rarely will either of us speak as a reaction to something the other has said. We often hold two entirely different conversations running parallel to each other. Sex isn't much different – he does everything necessary, then I do the same for him. I will finish – he will finish. I enjoy it because even in its lack of intimacy at least I *do* get to finish.

Being with Carl is not like that. In spite of my complaint to him, our conversations have been rewarding for me. He will listen whilst I speak because it is vital for him to understand everything I am saying so he can formulate his response; and there is genuine joy when I express a view he can agree with or I share an experience he can relate to. His response will then elaborate on these and as a result our conversations are always complete. And sex is like this, too. Complete. His touches are for his benefit as much as mine. He relishes taking his time because it prolongs the touch. When we are together properly – by properly I mean naked – it seems less like fulfilling a mere simple biological desire and more like the creation of an experience separate from everything else in the world. With Carl, because I know there is no future, the excitement is concentrated in the present. I think. All I know for certain beyond any of this is that sex has only ever been this joyful with one other person before. Martin, of course. Carl isn't Martin, though. And even though we have talked about so very much I still know I only have inadequate knowledge of Carl and he of me.

When I come off the phone from the insurance company I finally turn on my computer. I have several items of work I should be getting along with. None inspires me, each is a task. Everyone in the office this morning seems subdued. Normally Allan attacks Monday morning full on – he will try to rouse us for the week ahead; he will tell us of his weekend and flit around the room as if delighted to be back. This morning he sits, leaning forward, head in his hand, running a pencil along a piece of paper, crossing out words or sentences.

Keith is reading a newspaper. No one else in the office could do this so blatantly and escape comment from Allan. Allan, though, is a little afraid of Keith. Not that Keith is intimidating; it's simply that he does not indulge in trivia – Allan's staple diet. If anyone speaks to Keith it has to be relevant or extremely interesting. Subsequently, I usually talk to him only when it directly concerns work. I used to regularly borrow his newspaper until I increasingly found myself as alienated from its content as if it had been printed in a different country or era – such was its irrelevance to me. Keith is forty-two and on his third marriage. Personally I have no idea how he ever convinced even just one woman to marry him. Though he is affable he seldom shaves before coming in to work and often smells of last night's beer. I can smell it on him even now and his desk is seven feet from mine. His complexion is purple and his eyes water; he holds a pencil in his hand as a substitute for the cigarette he would prefer. If he could arrange the world to exactly suit him he would smoke constantly. Smoking is now strictly forbidden everywhere in this building. It's not even permitted in the toilets. So unless Keith genuinely has a severe bowel disorder he breaks this ban as often as twenty times a day.

Mary is working. She compensates for her basic inadequacy for this job by working twice as hard as everyone else. Mary is married. I say this in the same way I would describe someone as being an albino. It is so fundamental to her identity that everything else about her is related to that fact. She is three years older than me. When I first joined Ill Will she was already married and had been here for three years. Within a month of me starting she took six months off to give birth and look after her first kid. She repeated this three years later. They have had no more children. The two photographs she keeps on her desk are regularly replaced with updated ones. Though I try not to dislike Mary she does not make this easy. She is smug about being married, as if it is an achievement on a par with winning a Nobel Prize. In all the time I have worked here, whenever I have broken up with a boyfriend she will listen sympathetically, biting her lower lip, tilting her head – it's as if I am telling her my flat has burnt to the ground. Even when I have dumped the guy she still makes me feel as if I've failed. Another of her supremely irritating habits is when she distances herself from Jo and Jo's age to lump herself in with me. When Jo had her eyebrow pierced Mary said it looked 'kinky' (her word) and said to me, 'Nobody had their eyebrow pierced in our day, did they, Tanya?' *This* is my day! I am not married, I am not a mother. I am twenty-nine, not fifty-nine. I am still young and irresponsible. If I hadn't been afraid of the pain I would have had my eyebrow pierced that very lunchtime. As it happens I went out and bought a book instead.

I have the same job description as Mary, more or less. We design – using Ill Will's own software programmes – greetings cards, wrapping paper, oddities like mugs and key-fobs and other bits and pieces the marketing people come up with. The majority of time we concentrate on greetings cards. Allan is the 'Artistic Director', assigning the work to us, rejecting or passing our designs or making suggestions for alterations. Technically, Keith is Allan's assistant, though he does exactly the same work as Mary and myself. Keith is the only one here who is naturally talented and would deserve Allan's job if he could ever force himself to give a toss. With Keith so blatantly failing to carry out his responsibilities as his assistant, Allan received permission to recruit another assistant. I was the only suitable candidate – Mary is useless. Though it would have meant a little extra money I declined on the grounds that I did not want the extra responsibilities. I was not entirely certain there were any extra responsibilities involved, but nevertheless I didn't want to take any risks.

Jo has the same job I had when I first started. She runs errands, makes coffee, does the photocopying, keeps all the stationery supplied and is occasionally given small design jobs such as pictures for corners of envelopes or inside cards. Also, she is the collator of all the gossip on this floor of the building. Though this is an unofficial role it is the one she takes most seriously and the job that consumes most of her time.

The only other person who works in this room is Troy, but he is freelance and is not required to work from this office. He is kept on contract provided he produces a specified amount of work per month – which he conspires with Allan to ensure he does. He writes and edits jokes for the greetings cards. His jokes are often very funny but I have never once heard him make a funny remark. Also, the sentimental verses he writes are completely at odds with his own personality. He is devoid of sentiment. Because Troy doesn't drive his wife collects him from work. I have seen her several times. Troy is thirty-five, a little overweight, always wearing combat trousers. Though he is not ugly he is certainly not handsome. Yet his wife is gorgeous. She has long, straight, fair hair, wears carefully applied make-up and is always immaculately, fashionably dressed. He once told me how they met – she approached him in a nightclub and chatted him up. I can only imagine the circumstances: poor lighting and far too much alcohol. This, however, does not explain why she continued the relationship; he's sullen and scruffy. It's not that I dislike Troy, it's just that I wonder why someone would marry him.

These people, who occupy one third of each working day of my life, are all easy to be around. I am familiar with their virtues and comfortable with their flaws. Change would jeopardise this ease. If I worked in a more competitive environment I might be expected to be competitive. I prefer to be left alone.

This morning it is Troy, unusually, who breaks the office silence.

'Greetings cards wishing friends about to go on holiday a safe journey?'

He directs the suggestion to Allan, who stops writing while he considers its merits. Keith's verdict can only be guessed from his actions: he squeezes his eyes shut tightly, then leans forward and sighs – as if he is passing a particularly stubborn stool. He recovers, folds his newspaper away, then turns on his computer.

'I'd send one,' Jo offers, beaming at Troy.

'No,' Allan tells Troy.

'You're right. Stupid idea,' Troy says.

This could be described as a 'creative' conversation, so Mary might think she should contribute. I watch her concentrate, desperately trying to force some idea from her barren mind.

'Should we have some music on?' she eventually suggests.

Keith quickly stands from his desk. He is over at the radio immediately. This speedy response is to prevent Jo making the choice of station. Keith chooses Radio 2; Jo would have tuned to some obscure dance station. When I was Jo's age I used to despise Radio 2; now I think it's excellent. Jo sulks.

'I'm off for staples,' she tells Allan and exits.

Keith begins drumming on his desk with a pencil. He picks

up another and uses both. He does not drum in accompaniment to the song on the radio – it is just a habit he has when concentrating.

'I have a headache,' Allan says to the office in general, though it is really aimed at Keith. Keith takes the hint and does a flourish to finish: a drum roll using the desktop as the snare, his coffee cup as the high-hat and the top of the computer monitor as the cymbal – then puts the pencils down. It is evident he is not in the mood for work when he resorts to speaking to me.

'When I had my car nicked, sorting the insurance was a nuisance, but after that it worked out pretty well. My old car was on its last legs anyway – I like to think it packed in on the thieves and killed them.'

'Whoever stole mine burnt it out.'

'Wankers,' Keith says. Though Mary is offended by this she keeps her attention on her work, hitting the keyboard just a little harder than usual. To my knowledge Mary has only ever sworn once. She had a spell of three weeks when every piece of her work was rejected by Allan. Finally, she redoubled her efforts for one last piece. Allan rejected it and I am certain I heard her mumble a solitary 'Shit' as she returned to her computer.

I intended to spend my lunch hour rushing around the two bookshops situated reasonably near the office – a Dillons and a Smith's. I do keep a book at work. Since starting here I have always had a book to read in emergencies such as this. I chose 'worthy' books, ones I wish to read because they are classics or they have a great reputation, but which I would not normally choose. By this method – a few pages per week – I have ploughed my way through Barry Unsworth's *Sacred Hunger* (overwritten), Victor Hugo's *Les Misérables* (keeps drifting away from the main story), John Irving's *Prayer for Owen Meaney* (too anecdotal) and John Kennedy Toole's *A Confederacy of Dunces* (too slow). I am currently working my way through Thomas Pynchon's *Gravity's Rainbow* (too stylised). This book is 887 pages long and has been in my desk for six months. I have only just reached page 109 – I may have retired before I get to finish the book. Instead of touring bookshops or reading *Gravity's Rainbow* I implement a more adventurous plan. I borrow Allan's A–Z and try to retrace my car journey of Saturday, from my house to St John's Church. For each of the possible roads we travelled I look through the Yellow Pages to see if there is a bookstore on that road. This method is laborious and proves unfruitful. My conclusion, at the end of my lunch hour, is that the second-hand shop must have opened only recently. I begin the afternoon hungry and still without the prospect of a book.

Allan's wife prepares his lunches for him. She makes enough food for an orphanage picnic: fruit, sandwiches, crisps, yoghurts, pies, biscuits. He is still munching at the end of the hour when Keith and Troy return from their pub lunch.

For her lunch Jo visited a nearby, recently opened noodle bar because she fancies someone from this building who eats there. The food cannot have been to her satisfaction as she is pouring the remaining crumbs from a packet of cheese 'n' onion crisps into her mouth. Mary does not eat during the day; she uses her lunch hour to shop. Today she has been out searching for tile paint and is ridiculously pleased with herself for finding some.

The only way I can divert my attention away from my hunger is to spend the afternoon working hard. The hardest work I can think of is to concentrate on those assignments I have been putting off and the ones I have previously attempted, then abandoned. The list of files is longer than I remember. I knuckle down and dive in. By four-twenty-five all files are closed. I finish printing off roughs to show Allan. He is surprised by my effort and rewards me by passing everything, then suggests I skip lunch more often. Keith notices me putting on my coat and so shuts down his computer; he quickly tidies his desk and puts on his own coat even before I have finished buttoning mine.

'Nothing to show me, Keith?'

'Tomorrow,' he tells Allan as he exits. Already he has a cigarette out of the packet ready to be lit the second he is outside.

Allan quickly turns his attention to Mary before she takes

it upon herself to switch her computer off. He asks to see her day's work. She sits in scolded silence whilst he dissects each piece, pointing out the many obvious flaws. He passes just one of her designs and this success is enough to permit her to leave the office smiling. Allan and I leave together. Jo and Troy are left in the office. Jo has been ordered to tidy her desk and Troy is not in a rush; his wife is taking their car to be washed, which means she will be picking him up later than usual. When Allan and I are in the lift neither of us speaks. It has been an unremarkable day at work. Most days are.

London is at its worst in the evening rush hour: its filthiest, most congested, rudest and most depressing; travelling on the tube concentrates all these flaws. I wonder if it is a characteristic only of the British that whilst we can simultaneously so completely ignore our fellow passengers we can also so articulately convey our feelings of hatred and revulsion.

I wouldn't be so bitter if I had eaten, or if I had the prospect of a new, good book to read. I face an evening of boredom. I metaphorically fidget with the piece of paper Carl gave me, which bears his phone number. If I phone him tonight it would make him believe I am keen on him. I have slept with him yet don't want to give the impression I'm eager enough to make a phone call – even irony as dense as this probably won't persuade me. I may yet phone Caroline, for a talk or a visit. I may yet forgive Richard and – if he has left an apologetic message on my answerphone – phone him back.

During the tube journey I think about food. I have nothing at home that can be cooked quickly and will satisfy my appetite. There is a takeaway pizza restaurant on my walk home. I call in and order a large mushroom and salami; then whilst I am waiting for it to be cooked I call into a nearby newsagent and buy myself a film magazine. This is how I decide to spend my evening: I will eat my pizza, have a bath, watch some soaps, then put some music on and read my magazine. I will even open a bottle of wine. Tomorrow I will make a determined effort to buy myself a book.

All goes according to plan. Except that I have no wine in the flat, and the pizza is too greasy, and the only drama the soaps seem to provide is who is sleeping with whom – which is very undramatic for anyone who is not a regular viewer and is unfamiliar with the characters. There's a new sitcom on, which I watch for less than a minute. I am not in its target audience – I have not suffered brain damage in a car accident. I begin to read the film magazine but even this does not hold my interest. It has started to disturb me that in recent weeks I have been content to let Richard make the decision on which films we see. Consequently, I have seen an abundance of films about explosions and heroes who drink too much with the only side effect being that they forget to shave. I wonder if gradually losing interest in the cinema is another symptom of getting older. Pamphlets should be issued by the Department of Health giving an indication of the signs.

I am left with no other choice but to dig through my books to find something to read. The book I choose is one I have owned for a decade but have never read because I have never before felt the interest. I own it from sentimentality; it belonged to my dad and I took it after he died to remind me of him. It's the only book I can ever remember him reading. It is *Groucho and Me*, the autobiography of Groucho Marx. My dad was a massive Marx Brothers fan and every time one of their films was shown on TV he would make me watch it with him, convinced he could convert me. But I never saw the joke and as I read the book now I only think that I dislike Groucho for being a blemish on my memory of how well my father and I were otherwise matched in those things that made us laugh. I put the book away.

With nothing else to occupy me I decide to make a phone call. I am not in a charming enough mood to make an obligation call to one of my diminishing number of friends and I have nothing significant to tell my mother. If I phone her out of the blue, with nothing extraordinary to say, she'll only worry. If I tell her about my car being stolen she'll send money. It's as if I'm still supposed to believe in the tooth fairy. Richard is arrogant enough to have not yet phoned and apologised, so the remaining option is to phone Caroline. This is a reversal of a five-year trend: I will be phoning a friend I like! It's not even eight-thirty. I could still ask her to come and collect me so I can view her posh home. The evening may yet be saved.

Annoyingly, as I'm searching for her number the doorbell

rings. I prevent myself from shouting 'I'm coming!' when I remember last night's skirmish with Mrs Davies. Now that she has been in my flat she may believe she has the right to make it a regular event.

Through the peephole I see Richard's distorted face. Five minutes earlier and – provided he was suitably remorseful – I might have been delighted by an unannounced call; now it's inconvenient.

'De-da!' he says to announce himself. I don't fully open the door and I don't smile. 'I should have phoned, I know, but you don't mind, do you?'

'I'm going to Caroline's.'

'Now?'

'To see her new home.'

'Oh. OK. Well, don't look so annoyed. Being your boyfriend is supposed to entitle me to visit you.' I say nothing. 'I came to say sorry to you for last night. I was so exhausted, that's all it was. I had been working, remember. Tanya?'

'You can't come in.'

'Are you mad at me?'

'No.' I do not want to let him in. If I do he might then offer to give me a lift to Caroline's, which I will have to accept and which will be a nuisance if she isn't in.

'Yes you are.'

Yes I am. I wish I had the available time to pursue this, to torture him. Regrettably, I don't. I have set my mind on phoning Caroline.

'No I'm not. Really, Richard.'

'Well, good. I'm glad. Here, I've brought you this.' He hands me a plain white paper bag. I mishear him and believe he has said, 'I've *bought* you this' and it is clearly a book so I am not delighted. Richard is the last person I want a book from; it will be a Joanna Trollope or a Monica Dickens.

'What's it called?' I ask.

'Huh?'

'It's clearly a book – so what's the title?'

'I haven't looked.' Such ignorance as this is promising – a book picked at random at least stands some chance of being readable. I remove the book from the bag.

It is *The Counterfeit Confetti*.

'Where did you get this, Richard?'

'You left it in my flat.'

'When? No, I didn't. I left it in the glove compartment of my car.'

'On Saturday night you brought it into my flat with you.'

'I didn't.'

'Obviously you did. You must have done. It would be burnt now, otherwise, wouldn't it? The state you were in – what do you remember about Saturday night?'

It's irrelevant how drunk I was – I know I did not take *The Counterfeit Confetti* into Richard's flat. However, the more I try to make a picture in my memory the more I become separate from the truth: the truth becomes different; the truth becomes me taking the book into the flat with me. This is not a genuine memory, but because Richard is not lying to me his truth becomes my memory.

'Thank you,' I tell him. 'I'd hate to have lost this.'

Though Richard isn't too pleased to be dismissed without a kiss or a quick cup of coffee, he accepts my excuse – that I'm going to Caroline's – and my gratitude for the return of *The Counterfeit Confetti* is genuine enough for him to think I still like him. Which, after all, I do; though I remind him it's very rude to call at someone's home without first phoning. I thank him again as I close the door.

Back inside my living room I make myself a strong coffee. I sit at the dining table. This is where I go when the reading is serious.

I approach the book like a normal novel, beginning at Chapter One, which begins with my father's death . . . which begins with the death of the father of the lead character. This quickly segues into other storylines, all about my life. Both the narrative structure and the style are erratic, yet I am so enthralled I read the first five chapters before I take a break.

Now I am scared.

FIVE

It was early evening and the pub was starting to fill. As he stood by the one-armed bandit whilst his friend fed the machine, Martin's attention stayed on Tanya. She was sat at a table, talking with a girl who was taking the same college course. Tanya had also noticed Martin. She told her friend to discreetly look over; the two wondered which of them held Martin's interest. From a smile she had ignored, Tanya knew it was her – yet agreed to go to the toilet to leave her friend alone, providing Martin with the opportunity to make an approach. The route to the toilet took Tanya past the one-armed bandit. Martin stepped forward.

'What do you care about?' These were the first words he ever spoke to her

. . . to me. I tried to act cool and not look as if I was thrown by his approach. I looked him over as if analysing whether he was worth the trouble. This was how I always behaved in those days: momentarily hard to get. This was a reaction to my early teenage years when I would go to the discos at St Martin's Church Hall, usually dressed in a rah-rah skirt, wearing an armful of bangles and pink and blue eye-shadow, always wondering why I only attracted boys I could never be attracted to. Eventually I began to question how they could so often talk me into bed. All women know that men prefer the conquest of a difficult woman rather than a pushover; I learnt that the trick is to remember this in the chaos of the moment, like remembering the crash drill on a plummeting airplane. Many times I forgot the drill, waking up and recovering in the debris, swearing I'd never fly again.

'Is this simply a cheap chat-up line?' I asked Martin, trying to sound sassy and even aggressive, just in case he was an idiot.

'It is a chat-up line. But not cheap. I've agonised over it.' The smile on his face flickered and he moved a half-inch closer to me. 'What it is, you see, I've never chatted anyone up before. With girls, I usually know them first before I . . .'

Looking far less confident now, Martin didn't finish the sentence. I smiled at him, positioning myself so my back was to my friend. Even after just these few words I knew I was interested. I could see he had promise. He had all the correct paradoxes: charm with honesty, confidence with nervousness, good looks with flaws. To make a favourable impression, I answered his question asking what I cared about by saying I cared whether people were happy and whether they had whatever it was that made them happy. And I also cared about smoky bacon crisps. This easy joke made him laugh – he was eager to please me. At this point I quickly left for the toilet. I'd read somewhere that the perfect moment to make your exit is when you've made the other person laugh. In the toilet mirror I checked out how I looked, wiping the sweat from my top lip. I wore the barest minimum of make-up. In those days I usually dressed better and took greater care with my make-up, yet Martin seemed attracted to this simplicity so I had nothing to worry about. When I came out of the toilet I walked towards him, not knowing if he would speak again. He handed me a packet of smoky bacon crisps. By now Martin's friend had come off the one-armed bandit and I could tell from his puzzled expression that Martin had not discussed me with him. I liked this. I seem to remember refusing the crisps.

'I'm with a friend. I really can't talk.'

'That's OK,' Martin answered. 'Can we meet up another time?'

'I don't even know you.'

Because Martin seemed to accept this and made no further plea, Tanya returned to her friend. As Tanya sat down, Martin sat alongside her. He had followed.

'Hello. I'm Martin,' he said to Tanya's friend.

'Hello,' the friend answered.

Though at first Tanya thought Martin was acting too cute, nevertheless she

I was impressed – relieved, too – by his determination. Martin continued talking to my friend, asking about me and explaining why he had sat down. I can't remember her name and *The Counterfeit Confetti* doesn't say.

'She doesn't know me. We've just met. It was my first attempt ever at talking to a woman I don't know. I found out she cares about happiness and likes smoky bacon crisps. Now I want to find out her name, then try and persuade her to come out with me sometime. Don't you think she should?'

I distinctly remember thinking Martin was faking a coolness so blatantly out of character that my friend couldn't help but wish to be his ally. I was delighted to have someone work this hard to impress me, especially as I could see how Martin was going against his nature.

'She's called Tanya. We were both wondering who you were looking at. I guess now we know. Yes – I think she should go out with you.'
'Hey! Don't I get a say in this?' Tanya protested. The protest was not sincere. Tanya wanted to try to understand him and have him attempt to understand her. It would be a relief to find someone who did.

So we went out. He took me for a pizza. This might have been the first time I had been taken out for a meal on a first date, I can't exactly remember. I preserve few memories of other boyfriends. On that first date all my pretensions dissolved in the face of Martin's honesty. I had no need to try to impress him – he was impressed enough. His own pretensions evolved out of his desire to succeed, then collapsed when I saw through them all. Even by our second date affection had developed. I think it was encouraged by our many conflicts – in no time at all we learnt how to quickly resolve them, how to compromise, then move on. We soon learnt that we had more to pull us together than push us apart. We were in fourth gear when normally I would still have been in first or even reverse. We rapidly had attachment and sincerity – following this we soon had new instincts belonging to ourselves alone. We had our own new jokes, then new shared experiences and, before we had a chance to stop ourselves – love arrived.

The Counterfeit Confetti then changes storyline, back to my father's death.

> Nothing triggered Tanya's grief. Her mother, Gary her brother, her father's two sisters, all had been home when her father died. The expectation of death had been drawn out, the preparation fully complete – leaving no element of surprise. She watched the last flicker of life and heard the escape of his last breath – yet neither of these experiences acted as the trigger. Her mother cried.

I would like to stop reading now, but it's too compelling. It's like finding personal diaries I had forgotten. When my dad died my mother cried. My aunts cried. Then Gary. When I phoned Martin and he came straight to the house, even he cried, too. Surrounded by all this misery, I knew I should also be crying, yet I could never achieve that same ultimate understanding that my father was dead. I did not accept that 'dead' could apply to him. My father was going to grow old alongside my mother, I knew this. Gary and I, already grown up and moved out, had freed our parents to begin the third and easiest stage of their lives together – the second era of being alone without having to consider children, easier now with securer finances. The bigger plan was that, after their working lives had ended, they would indulge in active, fulfilling retirements, enjoy the easy pleasures of being grandparents – then, eventually, many years into the future, they would die simultaneously before their bodies became too messy. This was the bigger plan I had been subliminally indoctrinated with. Therefore my father was not dead.

> The funeral did not trigger her grief. Relatives, friends, her father's work colleagues, all packed the crematorium. Those who die before their time are a crowd-drawing attraction. None of those present shared Tanya's disbelief; no one else expected her father to jump from the coffin to announce the successful conclusion of an elaborate practical joke.

Only as I read these words now, ten years on, do I remember having that thought. I could not connect the coffin to the reality of my father; I had to stare at it, sinisterly forcing myself to picture its contents. This failed. The best I could do was picture Dad asleep on the settee at home, motionless. I could not picture him as a corpse.

I take an aspirin to clear my head. I have to focus on these memories. As the definition of that day returns to me more sharply, I go back to the book. I have lost my page – when I eventually find it I reread that last paragraph before continuing.

> The funeral did not trigger her grief. Relatives, friends, her father's work colleagues, all packed the crematorium. Those who die before their time are a crowd-drawing attraction. To Tanya, this ritual could have no relevance to her father. Her father's coffin was remote to the reality of him. To shake some sense into herself she stared at it, sinisterly forcing herself to picture its contents – but failed. Tanya could visualise her father asleep on the settee at home, yet could not picture him as a corpse. The grief in the room, at the conclusion of the service, was tangible. It was audible, too.

The funeral was a nightmare for me, not of grief but of shame. Everyone else's grief deepened as the service progressed until at the conclusion it was oppressive. I remember how I tried to force tears, for the respectable show of it. I flashed back to images of national catastrophes, I thought of selfish, petty tragedies from my childhood. I focused on remembering my dad alive, and my relationship with him. Perhaps, I thought, regret would make me cry. Instead, the memories of family holidays, of Christmases, of the times he had taken me swimming, our shared obsession with old black-and-white horror films, repeats of *The Phil Silvers Show*, our abortive attempts to build a tree house when I was already far too old – all these failed to achieve anything other than to make me smile. A smile I failed to stifle and had to disguise by putting my hand over my mouth as if suppressing a sob. It was only when I began to concentrate on my mother

– distraught, helpless – only then was I sad. I assisted her in leaving the crematorium.

All I could conclude by contrasting my mother's misery with my vague melancholy was that sooner or later I would understand, as she did. Yet it did not happen. Instead I found myself growing impatient with those around me. The pointed attention from Martin began to irritate me – his vigilant tolerance made me want to test him more. If I'm honest, my mother angered me too. I had trouble playing along with the easy lapse into routine she was careful to orchestrate. Only two days after the funeral she returned to work. She continued the rituals of making dinner at the same time as previously – a time only suited to the return of my dad from his work. She continued to drive their secondary, inferior car. She even watched those same TV programmes she had complained about whenever my dad had been in charge of the remote. To me this behaviour seemed to deny my father's death; and yet when I came across my mother secretly crying this also annoyed me – it was a demonstration of the *ready acceptance* of his death.

Tanya could not know how many of her mother's tears were induced by retrospective guilt. As a couple her parents had remained in love though their marriage had not stayed clear of incident. Two years previously, after a series of moody rows, of silences and petty recriminations – the source of which had become an irrelevance – Tanya's mother slept with Mick, her husband's closest friend.

I have to put down *The Counterfeit Confetti* when I read this. I concentrate, trying to remember the words I had read seconds ago, questioning whether I had been distracted and read incorrectly. I am light-headed, as if ill. The book says Mick and my mum had slept together before Dad died.

Leading up to this, Mick and Tanya's mother had enjoyed a long-standing flirty relationship, an open joke about how she would have married him if she had only met him before her husband. There was no substance behind these jokes, no intentions or ulterior motives, yet it had been easy for Tanya's

52

mother to push the joke that extra step forward, to kiss him as if still just friendly, then pull him closer for him to take the next risk. They had been arousing each other for more than twenty years, since late adolescence, and that's how the sex was: full throttle, sloppy and robust. Parting from each other's damp flesh, each was repelled away from the other; each sat back to back, each on the edge of the bed, each with head in hands. Guilty.

'That was a mistake,' one said.

'How did it happen?'

They dressed without another word, left the bedroom, separate; washed away all symptoms of the sex and for the next two years feigned an indifference to each other. Tanya's father never knew of the incident. Then he died and the world turned upside down.

Two years before my dad died, Mick and Mum had fucked each other and in turn fucked him. I throw the book across the room, cursing it. I know everything I have just read is nonsense. If there was any truth to this, then the secret would not have been kept; someone would have been told, someone would have suspected. Such corrosive guilt would have eaten away at their deception until the recriminations flew. If it had really begun in this way, Mum and Mick's marriage would not have survived as long as it has. Relieved by this thought I pick up the book to have it confirmed, but the damn book says nothing more about this incident now, instead returning to me and my stupidity, my petty confusion at not being devastated by Dad's death.

Mum, insisting she was fine, more or less ordered me back to my own flat. On my first night back there, my belief that nothing fundamental had changed in my world seemed confirmed by everything looking, being the same. The only difference now was that Martin said he should stay permanently. This was in case I finally broke – he believed he should be with me so he could comfort me. I was happy to have him stay for whatever reason.

That first evening was fine, I remember we were comfortable together. We ate, read for a while, watched a film on TV, then went to bed. There I kissed him and touched him.

53

He withdrew. I tried again – he removed my hand. I asked him to explain. To him, sex would have been inappropriate. Making love was an act of disrespect to my dead father – apparently. I don't remember if he actually said that, and *The Counterfeit Confetti* only prompts my memory with general details, missing out this dialogue. After Martin had removed my hand I got out of bed, went to the kitchen, poured myself a glass of milk, then found myself crying. The tears came out in an explosion. I covered my head with my arms. I bounced around the kitchen, finding nowhere to shield myself. When Martin rushed in and tried to hold me I screamed:

> '*Fuck off!*' *Tanya lashed out at his head.* '*Get out! Fuck off out of my home!*'
> '*Someone has to be here with you.*'
> '*I don't need anyone. I've told you to get out!*'

He left me in the kitchen. I think I scared him. The anger had flushed me clean. I shook myself free of the possession and wiped away the remains of the tears with a kitchen towel, then listened for Martin to leave. When I went into the living room I found a note saying he would call around the next evening at six, but if I needed anything in the meantime to please phone him. 'I LOVE YOU, TANYA' he had printed at the bottom. I had never seen the sentiment written down. He had even used block capitals. I tore the note up.

'I told him I don't need anyone. He must think I'm dependent on him,' I screamed loud enough for my neighbours to get the message.

She turned the TV on, then watched it through the night. Next day she skipped college – staying at home, reading all day. A joke in a book made her laugh. She forced herself not to care that laughter, so soon after her father's death, could be thought of as peculiar behaviour. It was natural – so therefore healthy. Instinctively she marked the page to show the extract to Martin; then quickly removed the mark as she remembered her resolve not to open the door when he called that evening.

He called at six. She opened the door. Determination to ignore him had transformed into a decision to test.

I was deliberately luring him into a trap. How nasty was I? How stupid, how cruel? I was thinking that the supposed trauma of Dad's death would give me licence to act hatefully. I thought if Martin saw I was capable of such behaviour, yet persevered with me regardless, then this would demonstrate his love was more profound than those superficial platitudes of 'love', which I heard from others. It was that time in our lives: everyone we knew believed they were in love or about to fall but I thought they were all wrong. I believed a future life together where one day, inevitably, one died leaving the other alone, was worth the risk only if Martin's was a love by the same definition as mine. So I began a test. Quiet please, no conferring.

'I don't want to see you, Martin,' she told him.

'Not tonight? I'll call tomorrow then. But you're OK?'

'Why shouldn't I be OK?' she laughed.

'I'm worried about you being left alone. Have you spoken to your mother today?'

'No.'

He could think of nothing else to ask. This was the first time any silence between them had mattered.

'I'll call tomorrow at the same time. Maybe you'll let me in then? I'd like us to talk about this.'

'About what?'

'Well – your father.'

'This isn't about my father.'

'It isn't? What is it about then?'

She signed wearily, as if he was stupid for not guessing the problem. In truth – of course – there was no problem.

'I'm closing the door now,' she told him, spitefully.

'I'll call tomorrow then?'

'Suit yourself.'

He dare not kiss her in case she moved to avoid it. He left with neither of them saying goodbye.

Tanya, satisfied, went into the kitchen for a drink. She took a glass and

I hesitated, then decided not to bother. I returned the glass to the cupboard. Then I looked through my kitchen window, leaning forward, straining to see if Martin was still on the street. When I didn't see him I went back to the cupboard and reached for the glass again before remembering I had abandoned that idea. Before I had a chance to prepare myself I experienced a repeat of the previous day's scream of tears. They flooded out of my soul, frightening me because absolutely nothing tearful was in my thoughts. Clearly, rationally, methodically, as I sat down on the lino, curling myself tightly into a ball, all I could think was why this only seemed to happen in the kitchen.

Tanya unplugged her phone; she did not answer the door. Three nights running Martin came. Each time she ignored him. On the fourth night Martin came armed with Tanya's mother.

'We're worried about you, Tanya,' her mother called. 'If you don't speak, then we're left with no choice but to break down the door.'

'I'm fine. There's nothing wrong with me. I'm not going to open the door.'

Tanya stood behind the door, heard her mother talking to Martin. Though she could not decipher clear words the tone was relief.

'Why won't you let us in?' Martin asked. Tanya remained silent.

'Why won't you let us in?' her mother asked. Tanya moved back into the living room to answer.

'I don't want to see anyone. There's nothing I want to see anyone for.'

I believed if I saw no one, then my callous lack of grief would not be detected. No one would see how spiteful, how selfish I was. Besides, when alone I did experience some of the desolate emptiness I had expected from the death of my father. Being alone was my grief: boredom was comforting, hopelessness reassured me. If I had no real grief, I'd manufacture it. If I could control unhappiness it could not control me.

On the fourth day alone I remember wondering about madness. I spent three hours on the settee, considering whether I was on the first rungs of lunacy. There was an open book in front of me, unread. Days had passed. I forgot to wash. I didn't think to eat. Sleeping became difficult. Here I was punishing, with enormous relish, the two people I most loved in the world. There was no sense to it. How do the insane recognise their insanity? The truth, I told myself, is they don't consider it. This conclusion served to prove I was still sane. Yet I began to enjoy being alone. This, surely, was not normal. I'd always been taught to fear being alone.

I took a long bath. I put music on as I fixed my hair. I took care with how I dressed, then finally left the flat. Fresh air – only the sane can detect the difference.

> She was the only one in the cemetery. The gravestone her mother ordered, having first consulted Tanya and Gary on the wording, had not yet arrived. A plain black cross marked where her father's ashes were buried. It bore a white plastic plaque with his name, the year of his birth and this year of his death. Three facts summed up his existence. On all the gravestones around her lay dried, decaying flowers; some stones were stained with moss; some were chipped; many were leaning, ready to topple.

I examined those gravestones that were my dad's new, permanent neighbours and understood each to be as misleading as my father's simple plaque. You can't easily sum up a life, so all attempts bear some degree of insult. If I was beginning to experience sadness now, it was sadness at his life, not his death.

> For a long time there was an extraordinary silence. Then a plane flew overhead. The sound faded – silence returned. A dog barked; Tanya's eyes searched for it. A young boy threw a stick for the dog. The boy kept to the path, throwing the stick out into the graves. When the dog was at its furthest distance the boy hid behind gravestones. Each time the dog found him.

I left the cemetery disappointed. There was nowhere I could go whenever I wanted to be reminded of my father. That day taught me my family had disintegrated: Father was dead, my mother lived alone and my brother lived away. When I returned to my flat its condition appalled me. I tidied and cleaned; then I took my second bath of the day.

> She phoned Martin. He was there as quickly as possible. Tanya explained how she was not yet able to accept her father's death. Martin said nothing. They went to bed and made love.
> Martin stayed with Tanya every subsequent night. More and more of his possessions were transferred from his parents' home to Tanya's flat. He integrated his routines and habits with hers. Chores of cleaning and maintenance were shared; food shopping – due to the increased volume – became formal, done on one specific day following a list they added to over the week. They never quibbled over money nor complained over loss of privacy. In short – and this became a living joke between them both – they became their parents: an established, settled couple.

After Dad died and Martin came to live with me full time, and no one objected, I suddenly became conscious of being an adult; as if on that day I had been given a certificate of proof. From then on, through the months we lived together, making love with Martin had a sensual seal of legitimacy.

Yet no matter how wonderful it was I kept comparing it to how my mother and father had loved each other. They had once formally, religiously, declared their love in front of a congregation of witnesses, then proceeded to prove this love by living together and raising a family. They had spent nearly a quarter of a century together. My father's death had changed this. Love was destroyed. Overnight. Promises, commitments, intimacies had vanished.

Martin and I accepted that we loved each other. By definition I knew this had to be a less substantial love than that of my parents. If so – I thought – then how easily could this love be destroyed? It had come too easy for us, this was my worry. We had met and been too readily compatible, then circumstances had conspired to throw us together like this. Too easy. To arrive at certainty, we first had to pass through doubts.

I resumed the test. Paper II.

58

When Tanya asked Martin to move out she explained that she was worried they were living together from convenience rather than real love. She told him that, with the shock of her dad dying, she was unsure how she felt about everything, even Martin, and that some distance from him would let her pass judgement more rationally. To her disappointment he accepted without argument. He dared not pursue the matter in case he should corner her into a more extreme position.

He took his essential possessions back to his parents. They had not split up, he told them, even though Tanya had not assured him to the contrary.

He dared not phone her. Each time the phone rang Martin was there to answer it. Finally it was Tanya; she asked him to come over. Delighted, he ran like a child. When he arrived he was greeted by Tanya standing at the door with the remainder of his possessions. He had kept a smile on his face; now he had to phone his father and beg a lift home. He still dared not ask Tanya how their relationship stood. He risked a kiss. She did not prevent him. This gave him the courage to ask if he could visit her that evening. She said no. He told her he understood. This infuriated her so much she could happily have slapped him. Instead she shrugged her shoulders, indifferently.

Two days later Tanya wrote to him. She wished never to see him again.

There was no action he could take that would be constructive. If he kept his distance from her, then he would have no opportunity to ever plead his case. On the other hand if he pursued her he risked strengthening her resolve. He wrote to her. She returned the letter unopened, with no explanation.

I stand up from the table and circle, trying hard to remember my motives for returning Martin's letter unopened. To anyone with even the slightest amount of curiosity, when they receive a letter even from someone they care nothing for, it is too tempting not to open it. The thoughts of my twenty-year-old self have long since been lost to me, yet I never believed Martin would have written a letter reproaching me. The only motive I could have had to prevent me from reading his letter was sheer, vile spite. I sit down again and find my place in the book.

There was no action he could take that would be constructive. If he kept his distance from her, then he would have no opportunity to ever plead his case. On the other hand if he pursued her he risked strengthening her resolve. He wrote to her. She returned the letter unopened, with no explanation. The letter had only said he hoped she was fine and that if she ever needed him or wanted to talk, no matter how far into future, then to get in contact. Martin had been pleased with his restraint, yet now her ignorance of its contents was humiliating – she must have presumed it was a begging letter, pleading to take him back.

Martin waited. His plan was to let her calm down and grow to miss him. They would bump into each other accidentally. He would be civilised, he would show genuine concern for her, yet fall short of insinuating he wanted her back.

Tanya, however, scheduled her activities to keep her distance from Martin.

Three months passed with Martin and Tanya never meeting.

I believed Martin had failed me. I had set him a test, set him free with an expectation that his love would compel him to pursue me. Instead he had accepted the parting. Maybe, for all I knew, he had welcomed it.

Never fully understanding why, Martin believed Tanya's love had ended. Where previously he had hoped to bump into Tanya, now he dreaded this in case she hated him or she was with someone new.

After all the things I had said to him I don't know how he could ever have thought it was possible I could hate him. Except – of course – through my actions. How stupid was I?

Martin took a promotion that meant moving to Swansea. Being far from her would exorcise her; yet she was never out of his thoughts. His life seemed hopeless.

Tanya and Martin never met again. After marrying, Martin then settled into fathering two children. He continued to live in Swansea, working for the DVLA, and learnt to be happy.

Still, to this day Tanya never forgave herself

. . . I have never forgiven myself for making the mistake of forcing a test on Martin. Tests of love are ample enough without being contrived. That's how stupid I was.

Her love for him never diminished, extraordinarily – it grew. Time filtered out his imperfections, making him impossible to replace.

Everything I read, which I could verify, was true. The two things I could not verify were my mother and Mick having had sex whilst my dad was still alive and that sentence I had read previously about Martin being married and living in Swansea. He did work for the DVLA, and though I heard rumours he had moved I never thought of him as married. I genuinely hope he is happy.

SIX

'What exactly is wrong with you?' Allan asks, making no attempt to mask his scepticism.

'I don't know.' I had planned on telling him I have diarrhoea. This is common enough to be plausible yet vile enough to not prompt too many questions. I reconsider because diarrhoea would last no longer than a day or two. I cough down the receiver as an impromptu, generic symptom.

'I just feel tired and achy,' I continue.

'Like the flu?'

'I don't think it's the flu because I'm not . . . I don't have a headache or sore throat or anything.'

'Will you be in tomorrow?'

'I can't see it, Allan, to be honest with you.'

I have a six-day sabbatical planned to establish the meaning and potential consequences of the incidents I have so far read about in *The Counterfeit Confetti*.

'Maybe I'll be better by the back end of the week,' I lie as I hang up. Perhaps it is a consequence of feigning illness, but when I come off the phone I appreciate my good health.

The book exists. I mean, it's there on my dining table. I am not imagining *The Counterfeit Confetti*. On all verifiable facts it is my life story. Though not written in the first person it is ostensibly written by me – *Tanya Stephens*. It is my memories; as I read they come back to me, perfectly formed and vivid. Yet I did not write this book. The book contains enough accuracies about my life to convince me that *only* I could have written it; and yet it contains information which, although it may be true, I cannot know for certain. There must be an explanation for the book. It is not a gift from God due to the fact that there is no God. I'm an atheist of the practising, orthodox, fundamentalist sect of the faith. Of course *The Counterfeit Confetti* could be all coincidence – yet the mathematical combination of all those pieces of information matching so exactly the incidents, events, feelings I have had through my life make coincidence impossible. Even the coincidences of all those matching names is too astronomically far-fetched. The odds must be equivalent to winning the National Lottery without buying a ticket.

I do not believe in the supernatural – the paranormal is not the answer. I am not living in an episode of *Tales of the Unexpected*, nor are Mulder and Scully going to investigate this puzzle. I am a rationalist. The paranormal, like philosophy and religion before it, is an invention to occupy the unemployable. This real world, which I inhabit, is the only existence I am prepared to believe in. Yet it may be that there is no rational explanation. People still keep buying Elton John records – there can be no rational explanation for that.

I sit and begin a list of those sections of *The Counterfeit Confetti* that I need to investigate.

1. *Phone Mum and find out if she slept with Mick when Dad was still alive.*

Does it even matter if Mum slept with her second husband whilst she was still married to my dad? And if I confront her, she will want to know how I know – and that is not something I can reasonably answer. She will deny it and I cannot prove otherwise. The likeliest conclusion of such a confrontation is an impasse, perhaps leading to us never seeing each other again. It might be safest to do nothing. Unfortunately I am compelled by my own curiosity. When Dad was alive there were many times when I wondered if Mum and Mick were too friendly with each other.

2. *Does Martin still work for the DVLA, does he live in Swansea – is he married?*

It is easy to find the phone number for the DVLA; the snag will be getting through to Martin. I construct a story that will allow me to get past the DVLA switchboard operator. I will say I want to speak to a Mr Martin Heaton who I believe works for the DVLA and is an old school friend of mine. I will add that I have lost contact in recent years but need to speak to him regarding the death of a mutual friend.

Next on the list:

3. *Track down the bookshop where I found* The Counterfeit Confetti.

I need to be out of the flat anyway; I need to be away from the temptation of opening *The Counterfeit Confetti*. The shocks need to be rationed.

When I have only gone a few steps from my front door I decide to look for Carl. I want to have sex with him now Martin is history, just to see if the sex is better. Now I will only be betraying Richard. Sex will consume another hour of the day.

I keep the conversation brief, inviting him over during his lunch hour, making sure he understands it is only for sex and not to expect food or literary discussion. He looks a little disappointed, which is rather insulting, but after being so brazen I am aroused enough not to care. His disappointment will pass once we're naked and sweaty.

It takes me thirty minutes to walk to the district where I found the second-hand bookshop. I recognise the road immediately; there is the usual selection of shops: a Pizza Hut, a Benetton, a Dixons, but also distinguishing shops such as a specialist lighting store, a derelict restaurant and a toy-model shop, all of which I clearly remember from Saturday.

Yet no bookshop.

I remember this branch of the Holbeck Building Society. I remember gliding alongside it as we parked. The bookshop was next door. Next door – now – is a jeweller's. I walk further along, past a few more shops. No bookshop. I return and enter the Holbeck. There are no customers and the girl behind the desk smiles warmly, ready to help.

'Is this the only branch you have on this street?'

'It is.'

'How long has the jeweller's been next door?'

'I don't know exactly, but certainly since I've worked here – that's three years now. Are you looking for something?'

'A bookshop.'

'There's no bookshop around here that I can think of.'

I leave, freaked out, amused. This is from *The Twilight Zone*; I wish Rod Serling was still alive so I could phone him.

I look along the street, each side in turn, just in case I made a mistake about the Holbeck Building Society, though I know

I did not. I wish I could tell somebody about this who would not laugh or call me insane.

As soon as I am back at my flat I pick up *The Counterfeit Confetti*. It is taunting me. I skip through to the sections where my mother and Mick slept together for the first time.

Phone Mum and find out if she slept with Mick when Dad was still alive.

'Mum, it's Tanya,' I say the second she answers the phone. She begins a warm greeting, which I interrupt.

'I'm coming up late this afternoon. I need to speak to you. And to Mick.'

'Are you getting married?'

'What? No!'

'Is it bad news, then?'

'What I have to tell you is not good news.'

I hang up. I want her to worry. Maybe I'm pregnant, maybe I have cancer, maybe I have become a Born Again Christian. She deserves anxiety.

During the next hour, before Carl arrives, I prepare myself for him. Hair is purged, skin is moistened, some make-up is applied, teeth are rigorously cleaned. I put on perfume and consider wearing stockings, but they're uncomfortable and make me look cheap. Sometimes I like that – but not today.

Carl arrives at the exact time we agreed. He looks grimy and tired. I wish I had put on the stockings. Whilst he uses the bathroom I go into the bedroom and close the curtains.

'Are you off work for any reason?' he asks when he enters.

'I wanted to see you,' I say in a seductive voice, which I am never certain I pull off convincingly.

'Is that true?'

Whether it is true or not is irrelevant. I was trusting he would simply be flattered and abuse the opportunity I am presenting him with. Instead he stands, awkward, at the opposite end of the bed from me, as if he is at a job interview.

'You remember what I said, don't you? We're going to bed.'

'OK.'

I was trusting this directness would bring him to me in a passionate rush. To simply answer 'OK' and then not move is irritating.

65

'So shall we get undressed then? Carl?'

'Sure,' he says as if I had asked him if he wants a cup of tea.

'Carl – show some enthusiasm, please.'

'I am enthusiastic. I like making love with you. I'm glad of the chance.'

'I don't want to make love. I want sex. Selfish, hard, passionate, uncomplicated.'

'Fine. But is there a reason?'

'*Reason?*'

'There has to be a reason why you're not at work. There has to be a reason why you want us to go bed.'

'I've wanted us to go to bed before!'

'When it's happened before it hasn't been pre-planned. It just developed into sex.'

'All right. If you insist on knowing – I have some worries, that's all. I need a diversion. I can't go into a detailed explanation but . . . All I can say is, it's about my mother . . . It's about the past, and maybe the future . . .'

'That's quite a comprehensive worry.'

'There's nothing you can do about it. The best help you can give me is in bed.'

'OK.'

At last we get undressed and into bed. Carl puts his arm around me, I rest my head on him. He kisses the top of my head.

I have clearly been mistaking exhaustion for arousal. I want to sleep.

'Did I tell you about my dad?' I mumble. If there had been any other sound in the room Carl would have had no chance of hearing me.

'You told me he was dead.'

'Yes.'

Carl says nothing, perhaps not sure if he should. He gently fingers the lobe of my ear.

'What about your parents?' I ask.

'Both alive.'

'That's good.' It's good because I do not want to have to offer him sympathy. I am expecting him to begin kissing me, to caress me somewhere other than my ear. He doesn't. I hold him tighter.

'It's taken me nearly ten years to come to a full realisation that my father is dead. And really, even now I still have doubts. It's as if he moved abroad or something. Yet I'd accepted his death enough to be happy when my mother married again. The only thing is, I think she slept with her current husband whilst my dad was still alive.'

'What makes you think that?'

'I can't say.' I am not telling him I do not know, I am saying I am prohibited from telling him.

'I've discovered several other things as well,' I continue.

'For instance?'

'I've discovered that a guy I used to go out with is married. He's the only man I've ever loved. There's no chance I could fall in love again.'

I am committing a cardinal sin to be speaking of Martin to Carl. I detest being with men who continually talk of their ex-girlfriends, it's simply dull. When I am with a man, I make certain I never talk of previous boyfriends. Richard, for instance, knows nothing of Martin. And when Richard has tried to talk of his ex-girlfriends I have forbidden it. It is unforgivable to be boring Carl like this. More insultingly, I have more or less told him there is no chance I will ever fall in love with him.

'You don't love Richard?' Carl asks.

'God, no!' I surprise myself with the ferocity with which I say this. I do not understand why I continue to see Richard. I hold Carl tighter still. I kiss him on the chest.

'I think more about you than I do about Richard.'

'I wonder if that's true,' Carl says. It's not a challenge, so I do not respond. 'Tell me about this guy you loved.'

I sit up. Carl sits up. I hold the bedsheet over my breasts.

'I want to know what my competition is like,' Carl adds. 'I'm interested.'

I begin to tell Carl all about Martin, how we met, a few of the easier to explain reasons why I fell in love with him, how we had a short period of living together. Finally, a glossy version of how we split up. As I talk Carl puts his arm around me and we slip back down so we are lying on our

67

sides, facing each other. My nose touches his, I can feel the warmth of my breath reflected back. His eyes draw me into him. I tell him some real truths about Martin, about the intensity of my love and the foolishness of its longevity. When I finish I feel salt tears burn down my cheeks and drip onto the bed sheets. I wish I had not bothered with make-up. I am happy and free. In the past, whenever I have told anyone about Martin I have been apologetic, embarrassed by my continuing love. Carl does not speak, never takes his eyes away from mine. I palm away the tears.

'Wow, what an idiot I've been. What a waste of nine years.'

Once again I sit up. I let the sheet fall from me and turn my back to Carl.

'A waste?' he asks.

'I think even if he had come back, even if he hadn't married, he wouldn't have been the same person I fell in love with. And even if he was – anyone who hasn't changed in nine years is hardly worth knowing.'

'How have you changed?' Carl asks. I think he is missing the point if he thinks it is appropriate to ask this. He now sits up in the bed, close behind me, resting his chin on my shoulder and wrapping his arms around my stomach.

'That's the problem. I haven't changed enough. I haven't let myself change.' I can change my job. I can change my flat. I can finish with Richard. I can read less – be more sociable.

I stand and turn to face Carl. He is about to stand, too, but I prevent him. I wait until he starts to look at me, to look me over. When I see he is aroused I bend to kiss him, then I sit over him.

'Do you have to get back to work?'

'Yes,' he says. He falls backwards, pulling me with him.

Two hours later Carl dresses and leaves. I go to see my mother.

My home town. I make a return visit twice a year, on average. I never understood how pleased I was to be away from here until I first had to face the prospect of returning to visit. I do not *hate* the place; my feelings are so minor as to defy the attachment of an emotion. I do wish I could regard the town with some nostalgia. On previous visits I have tried to force a sense of loss or regret or whatever nostalgia is. Perhaps these attempts have failed only because there is nothing here that has changed enough for me to miss. The three schools I attended are still here, plodding on. St Martin's Church Hall where I first went to a disco is still here, still holding under-age discos. The shops vary little, there have been few new building projects, no historical landmarks have been removed. The most remarkable change that has occurred has been in the films showing at the local Odeon. Kids dress more expensively, act cockier – but that's not just here, that's everywhere. The only progression that ever happens is people leaving. My only thoughts, whenever I return, are that this place was where I was with Martin. This is its only significance.

I should feel nostalgia for the people I knew. Like teachers. I'm guessing other people feel nostalgia for teachers. I was an unremarkable school kid. If I was to appear on *This is Your Life* none of my old teachers could testify as to the kind of pupil I was because none would remember me. And in return no teacher made any significant impression on me. All I recall are physical trivialities, which even the most talented police sketch artist would scoff at. I remember Mr Chapman wore a blue leather bomber jacket. Mr Gray was a maths teacher with one joke in his act, repeated for each lesson: 'What does zero times zero equal? OXO!' Mr Mathews, from Yorkshire, was our English teacher and his one joke was: '"It isn't in the tin", or as I prefer to say, "tin tin tin".' Miss Thomas had pointy breasts; we used to speculate on whether she used yoghurt cartons for a bra. I remember Mr Betts by his limp. I remember Mr Booth by his Zapata moustache; and I remember Miss Ellis for the same reason.

I have as little nostalgia for the friends I had here as I do for good meals I have eaten. In middle school my closest friends were Janet, Margaret and Cathy. At my last school there were many more, the closest being Judith Goddard. For a year or two we were inseparable. We dressed alike, discovered boys together, went shopping together. Clothes, attracting boys and shopping used to be my only preoccupations, which is as it should be for teenagers. Our friendship

69

diminished when we entered the sixth form. We concentrated on different subjects; she became determined to pass exams; she wouldn't drink alcohol and refused to buy cigarettes, so I began to mix with those who did. On the last day of the last term I remember us swearing to each other we would keep in touch, make the effort to stay friends if our lives took us on different paths. I expect she still lives in this town. I hear she married Gerard Dunne who also went to our school. *Judith Dunne*, then? I hope I never bump into her, we would have to catch up on the missing years. I'd have to listen to her anecdotes about her kids, how well Gerard is doing; there might be a renewal of those lapsed vows to keep in touch. Torture.

I brought Laurie Lee's *As I Walked Out One Midsummer Morning* for the journey; it is one of the few books I read in the days before reading became so important to me. Inspired to busk around Spain, I asked Dad if I could learn to play the violin. He agreed to both paying for the lessons and buying me a violin. I took him up on neither offer and have not read the book again until now. As I read it once more it is remarkable how many passages still seem familiar to me, though I am not as taken by the prose as I was when I was a much younger woman, when busking around Spain seemed like an exciting idea.

I get a taxi from the train station to my mother's home. Once out of the taxi I do not hesitate, taking long strides to the door. Instead of walking in, I ring the bell and wait. I am ambushing them.

'Tanya!' Mum says, smiling – a smile that drops immediately she reads my face – 'Why didn't you just come in?'

I walk in past her.

'Is Mick home from work?'

'He's in the kitchen,' she answers, following me because I am already heading that way. I detect anguish and even a subdued anger in her voice.

Mick is sat at the kitchen table. He says hello, smiles and folds up his newspaper. I do not say hello back – I wait for Mum to enter. She begins to fill the kettle.

'That isn't for me, is it?' I ask. 'Because I'm not staying.'

'You're not staying?' – Mick.

'You're not staying?' – Mum, plugging the kettle in.

'No.'

'Why? Tanya, what is wrong with you?'

I want to sound indignant, outraged. I pause for effect and do it beautifully, with perfect timing. A split second before my mother cracks and speaks – I speak first.

'Did you and Mick sleep together whilst Dad was still alive?'

If this was a movie the soundtrack would come to a dramatic crescendo and the editing would cut from a close-up of my mother to a close-up of Mick. They both pass looks to each other so rapidly they must believe I do not see. In the movie version they would never cast my mother to play herself, she cannot act the innocent. She averts her eyes, then overcompensates for this give-away by looking at me directly, defiantly.

'What makes you ask that?'

'Your answer is yes, then?'

She looks at Mick. He looks down at his folded newspaper. Mum turns back to me. In spite of this virtual admission, she perhaps believes there is mileage left in avoiding an outright admission.

'What makes you ask, Tanya?'

'Just admit it's true,' I insist.

'What makes you ask?' This obstinate third repeat of the same question is nothing short of a confession.

I pause again. I never realised how good I was at these dramatic pauses. I should be in an American soap opera. I manage to squeeze every drop of suspense and drama from the silence. My only worry is that I am doing it too deliberately, that I am too pleased with myself; I have to struggle to avoid giggling. I answer the question by giving details of the facts I know; that is to say those possible facts I have learnt from *The Counterfeit Confetti*. I tell her of the circumstances and the context surrounding the sex, who probably made the first move, their inevitable sense of shame. I begin to sound like Columbo unravelling a mystery to confounded villains.

'Did your father tell you all this? Tanya, did he think we'd – erm – you know, slept together?'

'He didn't tell me.'

'Then how could you even suspect such a thing? What makes you ask it?'

'I can't see how that matters.' It would have sounded better, harsher, if I had said, 'I cannot see how that is of consequence.'

Mick stands and moves away from the table to be next to my mother.

'Tanya, your mother and I have done nothing wrong.'

I'm not going to listen to nonsense such as that. I have had sex many times, with – I suppose – a reasonable number of men, yet not once, no matter how drunk I've been, no matter how much I've regretted it later, no matter how inappropriate the person or circumstance or place, not once could I ever legitimately say *I never meant for it to happen*.

'What a fucking ridiculous thing to say!' I shout at him.

'Why? What are you talking about?'

I walk out of the kitchen, along the hallway, open the front door – all anticipating that either Mick or my mum will follow. Maybe one makes the attempt and the other prevents them, or both concede that Mick's protest was so stupid it deserved my response.

I leave their home, pausing just outside the door. The door has been painted blue for a decade but today I notice it has been chipped, the gash marked in rainbow colours from when Dad was alive and he painted the door every summer, a new colour each year; the mark goes right back to yellow, from when I was very small. I remember that year and my mother hating the colour.

Only when I realise I am smiling do I regret having acted as I just have. I wait for my mother to rush out to offer an explanation, so I can reassure her none is necessary. I dare not re-enter the house of my own accord; this would demonstrate contrition, which would demonstrate some doubt, which would put me on the defensive. I cannot be defensive when I have so recently been offensive; they would soon discover my source of information was suspect. The longer I wait the happier I again become that they have made no attempt to come after me. My family died with my father.

I walk away with the smile now returned. I walk along the street still expecting a call back. None comes.

I have to catch a bus back to the town centre; I wait forty minutes. At the train station I have another ten-minute wait. Due to my haste to flee this town these ten minutes seem like an hour. I reconstruct my exit, wondering how it must have appeared to Mum and Mick, the effect it must have had on my mother. I will never see my home town again. It's a great burden removed.

I have no past, no family, no religion, politics made negligible because I don't care enough any more, no great friends, not even any pets or plants. I am freer than anyone else I know.

SEVEN

It is mid-evening when I arrive home. The answerphone light is flashing. I skip through all four messages, winding forward each time, as soon as I hear my mother's voice. I wipe the tape clean; I want the tape blank of my mother so I will not be tempted to listen later. This is a complicated procedure; I have never done it before. I inadvertently wipe off my own answering message and have to make a new one.

I make myself a coffee, then abandon it. In its place I pour myself a Southern Comfort with plenty of ice. I drink the first glass even before the ice cubes have begun to dissolve. I look through the *Radio Times* to see if there is anything worth watching. There is a James Bond film, which is the kind of escapist nonsense I need at the moment, but its two and a half hour running time is too much of an ordeal to face. To fill in the time I could make phone calls – if I had anything new to say to anyone I know. I drink more Southern Comforts and go to bed.

I waste my remaining days off. I finish *As I Walked Out One Midsummer Morning*, then reread Voltaire's *Candide*, which is the first book I ever read in one session. I was twenty-one at the time. I was dressed ready for some big night out and had a quarter of an hour to kill so thought I would read the first chapter. I ended up staying in and reading the whole book. I now wish I had picked up a longer book to read because when it is finished, late on Friday afternoon, I close its cover and know I have to bow to the inevitable. I pick up *The Counterfeit Confetti* and open it at random.

friendship renewed, Caroline asked Tanya if she would like to give up her current job and work for her.

'Your idea for the Martians was so good,' Caroline explained.

'But what exactly would you want me to do?'

'The same as me. The planning. Ideas. Sketching. Some of the finished drawings, maybe. Plus there's a lot of work coming in for merchandise. You could do that.'

Tanya had no reply, so Caroline continued, enthusiastically.

'All in all, the money will be better than you're earning now.

And it will be good fun – won't it? – the two of us working together?'

Hold on. This extract is not about something that has happened – it's my future, isn't it? Unlike previous chapters, *The Counterfeit Confetti* is now telling me something that is *going* to happen. So *The Counterfeit Confetti* doesn't only know about my past or my present circumstances, it also knows about my future.

Trusting in fate, I drop the book on its spine, resolving to read whichever page falls open. I have to do this several times before it falls open at a page towards the back of the book, where incidents from the future are most likely to be written.

Leaving Ill Will was the wisest move Tanya ever made. She had never been happier.

There is my future. Caroline offers me work. I leave Ill Will. I become happy.

I have been at Ill Will for too long. Just because it keeps my life uncomplicated is not an adequate reason to stay. Complications drive lives forward.

I like Caroline. I want her friendship. I don't know, however, if I can unequivocally say I would like to work for her. At David and Rachel's wedding reception, though I know I drank too much, I clearly remember most of the details Caroline told me concerning her work. I think I became bored with her – she sounded too boastful.

I read to the end of Chapter Seven: the days covering the near future, leaving Ill Will. According to the book I am leaving – I have no option.

I do not drop *The Counterfeit Confetti* on its spine any more. I hate to maltreat books. I deliberately open it near the back half.

She had no qualms over her actions, only her technique. Her letter to him, never sent, had been abandoned due to its overuse of clichés and the brutality of finishing by letter rather than face to face.

Beforehand she had dreaded the confrontation, yet once it had begun she relished it. Richard was startled, never having imagined the relationship was in any kind of trouble, let alone to a degree where she would end it. Tanya enjoyed this powerful position and took sinister pleasure from his discomfort.

Looking back, the sex had been worthwhile and all encounters with other people are lessons that make us appreciate our own company better. Nevertheless, now, without Richard, she was happier. He was the last in the reign of boyfriends taken simply for the sake of having a boyfriend.

When it comes to breaking up with boyfriends I have been the world's biggest coward. If it is only a recently begun relationship I ignore phone calls and do not answer the door until they get the message. If it is a relationship older than a month I orchestrate an argument. This is never difficult. Men's behaviour is always as flawed as that of children, and women have reinvented themselves so many times in the last few decades that all couples have fault lines ready to exploit. We can accuse even the most perfect man of being too casual or too demanding, too weak or too arrogant, too nasty or too nice. However, I don't recommend finishing with a man by saying he's too nice; rather than taking it as a compliment they invariably go off in a frenzy of belligerence. 'We can't fucking win with women these days – you mad bitch!' was the response I received the last time I accused a man of being too nice. I guess women are no longer the closed books we used to be; they know 'nice' is a euphemism for dull.

I wrote the letter to Richard several weeks ago, waiting for a good cause to provoke its use. *The Counterfeit Confetti* – as ever – is right; a letter seemed too brutal. Here is the final draft. For reference purposes I later numbered the clichés.

Dear Richard,

This is the hardest letter I've ever had to write [1], but I don't think things are working out between us [2]. I want you to know that I really do care for you [3] and that I will always remember you [4]; but I think it's best for us both if we do not see each other any more [5]. This might seem out of the blue, but to be truthful with you it is something I have been thinking about for a long time. Phone me to arrange to collect the bits you have in my flat. I hope you do not hate me for this and that we can still be friends [6].
Love,
Tanya

After a beginning thick with clichés I lapse into sincerity (that part about how I have been thinking about dumping him for a long while), then recover and finish with the biggest cliché of all. I did consider leaving out 'we can still be friends' but its omission would simply be offensive. Though I put the letter into an envelope I never bought a stamp.

If *The Counterfeit Confetti* is right and I do break up with Richard and relish the confrontation – I think this will be regrettable. If the book is right when it says Richard is the last of the boyfriends taken simply for the sake of having a boyfriend – yippee! Sex is my weakness, the chink in the amour. Without the need for sex I am truly free.

I first met Richard, he first met me, when we were both drunk. Alison, who is a nurse, had phoned me four times, inviting me to a party some junior doctors were having in the hospital where she works. By her fourth call I had run short of excuses and going with her seemed the lesser ordeal. I arrived at her house at six o'clock. Some of her nurse friends were there with a bottle of vodka. Alison has two kids – both girls – and was keen to make sure we emptied the bottle so as not to leave any for the babysitter. I waited until we were

77

leaving her house before I gave her back a CD she had lent me. However, she insisted I took another, ignoring my protests that I might lose it at the party.

The party was held on the top floor of the hospital in a room adjacent to recently closed wards. I was still on my first bought drink when Richard approached. I saw him begin the journey yet didn't realise who he was walking towards until he had actually stopped in front of me, less than a foot away. Alison and her friends fell into mid-sentence silence to hear him speak; I was flattered he had singled me out. I would say I am attractive in an enigmatic way; although I do not usually turn men's heads in pubs, I am the type that more rational men seek out. Unfortunately rational men are seldom the type to approach women cold. Rational men meet rational women through work or mutual friends. Both these areas are wastelands in my life. Meeting suitable men by waiting to be chatted up by one is as fallible as choosing a second-hand car over the phone. Richard's opening line, apropos neither of us knowing the other and neither of us having given any indication of attraction, was:

'Hello.'

'Hello,' I said back. Drunk I might have been but a snappy answer seldom evades me. When I play back his 'hello' in my mind I hear how it was spoken: he believed he knew me. I see now he had made a mistake – I was not the person he believed he was coming to speak to.

'Do you want a drink?' he then asked.

An ad hoc bar had been assembled in one corner of the room. Though they were selling only bottled drinks, the selection was impressive. The future stars of the medical profession were repeatedly giving incorrect change and getting confused when orders exceeded two items.

'I already have a drink. But thank you anyway.'

This completely stumped poor Richard, I don't think any woman had ever before refused a drink from him. I knew I had to add more, to make sure he understood I was still interested.

'Besides, I've drunk too much tonight anyway.'

'How is it possible to drink too much?'

From this joke I instantly learnt all there was to know

78

about his character; it sealed my opinion of him from that day to this. For me, for my ideal, he was too much of a drinker, too much of a pretend thug; and yet he was able to laugh at himself, which was sweet and demonstrated that his worst side was not necessarily his true nature. How I knew I could tolerate him long term was from his eagerness to laugh. Those people who laugh so readily are often the best company.

He phoned on Sunday afternoon at the exact moment I was getting bored with the style of the book I was reading. He asked if I would like to see *Celebrity*, the new Woody Allen film. I think I replied yes more to the film than I did to him. On Sunday evening, as we were queuing for the tickets, he confessed he was not a Woody Allen fan but had guessed I might be. Later, reflecting on this, I felt vaguely insulted. Now when I reflect on it I wonder if he had made the guess because Gail had been a Woody Allen fan. Anyway, it worked out well as we both enjoyed the film. We came back to my flat afterwards and kissed for about an hour without any groping. Perhaps he thinks he's respecting me, I told myself. I was curious so agreed to see him the following Tuesday night. We went for an Italian meal, then he invited me back to his flat. Once there, he seemed to be in a rush, stirring my coffee as he brought it into the living room. His hand was in my blouse before the coffee had stopped swirling.

This was five months ago.

I do not wish to suffer any more prophecies from *The Counterfeit Confetti*, so I look through my books, desperately wanting to have another enjoyable reading experience, which means rereading a book I love. I start, then abandon H.E. Bates's *Love for Lydia*; I start, then abandon Virginia Woolf's *To the Lighthouse*; I start, then abandon Muriel Spark's *The Girls of Slender Means*. I abandon them because I do not wish to use them as a diversion. I do not want to read these loved books whilst my thoughts are elsewhere. So I forget reading and turn on the TV. On the local news there is an item about street cleaners. Apparently there's a severe shortage. I phone Carl to tell him, thinking he will be interested. When he answers he is so delighted to hear from me I let him believe I have phoned simply wanting to talk with no reason, which is sort of true anyway. We are on the phone for a hour and a half. We talk about children's TV programmes, fashions of the 1980s, Margaret Thatcher, discontinued types of sweets, children's comics, how best to depict Martians in popular fiction, and our favourite sex scenes from movies. Carl chooses Jeff Goldblum and Emma Thompson in *The Tall Guy*. I choose Jenny Agutter and David Naughton in the shower scene from *An American Werewolf in London*. Carl is the only person I have ever spoken to about Space Special and remembered it with equal fondness. It was a green-coloured pop, which I haven't had for years. In fact, I'm sure they no longer make it. At last I understand nostalgia!

EIGHT

Saturday. I shop for food. Though it is hard to resist looking for books I am determined not to let *The Counterfeit Confetti* beat me. I should finish that book before I start another. I have been treating *The Counterfeit Confetti* like a drug – not daring to exceed a specific dose.

When I return home the answerphone is flashing. Two messages. The first is from Richard. As his answerphone message starts, the phone rings. I try to stop the answerphone message as I pick up the receiver. It is Richard.

'Hi. It's me,' he begins. I have only succeeded in pausing the answerphone and it now clicks off pause and begins to play so I hear Richard live in tandem with his recorded message.

'Tanya –'

'Tanya, it's me.'

'Hello?'

'What's going on?'

'Are you there?'

Me this time: 'Hold on, Richard, I'm having problems.'

'I was phoning to ask if I could come over.'

Me – 'Hold on!'

'I haven't really seen you for a while . . .'

'I haven't said anything.'

'Or spoken to you for a while . . .'

'Have you fixed it yet?'

'And . . . That's it really.'

'That's the end, I think. Tanya?'

'I'll phone later.'

The answerphone clicks off.

'Hello? Me, now,' I tell him.

'I left that message earlier –'

'I gather.'

'Have you just got in?'

'I've been out. I've been busy.'

'Are you busy now?'

'Yes.'

'Oh.'

A long pause follows because it's my turn to speak and I don't.

'See you then,' he says, desperately trying to sound casual. An even longer pause now occurs whilst I am silently waiting for him to hang up and whilst he is silently waiting for me to speak and therefore prevent him hanging up. He hangs up.

I put the receiver down. It rings. He must have pressed redial.

'Have we split up?'

'OK,' I say.

'OK? What do you mean, OK?'

'OK, if that's what you want.' I hang up. I unplug the phone from the socket so I will not be tempted to speak to him should he ring back. I begin to play the second answerphone message, which is from my mum. I stop it halfway through when she lapses into bemused fury.

No Richard. No Mother.

It is Saturday night and, though bored, I am not happy that Carl has turned up at my flat. He did not first wait to be invited over. He clearly believes *he*, now, has earned the right. I might not object if he had phoned first. After all, I genuinely like Carl – I am genuinely attracted to him and genuinely interested in him. I want him in my life. But strictly upon my terms, and that is not fair or reasonable. I wish to be able to continue to call upon his services whenever they are needed. But only when it suits me. It does not suit me when I did not first agree to a visit.

'This is a surprise,' I say to him. He has made himself comfortable in my armchair.

'Good surprise or bad surprise?' he asks. I shrug my shoulders. Only as I make the gesture do I realise how cruel it must look. One day I phone him and we are like ideally suited lovers; the next he calls and I am offhand for reasons that I have no explanation for, except that, after my mother, then Richard, being nasty is addictive.

'Oh,' Carl says, clearly shocked. Though he stands up he does not move. 'Do you want me to go?'

I shrug my shoulders again, this time looking at him to soften the effect.

He sits.

'I want . . .' he begins, then stops. I am not curious so do not ask him to conclude. He stands again. Though he looks sad he manages to speak without sounding sad.

'I just thought I'd come and see you. No big deal. I'll go. I'll leave it for a couple of days and then phone you, or something. You obviously need to think things over.'

I accompany him to the door, expecting one of us to speak. Neither of us says another word. He leaves. This morning there had been no active plan in my mind to free myself of either Richard or Carl but now I have succeeded in alienating them both as if these conclusions had been predetermined.

I have nothing to read. Tonight, at least, I am not going to read any more of *The Counterfeit Confetti*. It's too confusing. I look through my books, fancying something non-fiction. I pick up *The Twelve Caesars* by Suetonius because it's an easy read and can be devoured in sections with long gaps in between reads, which I can do through those intervals when I have had enough of *The Counterfeit Confetti*.

After only the first chapter of this, I phone Caroline, to ask if she would like to go to the cinema. I tell her about my car being stolen.

'I've had a tough day,' she tells me. 'I'm fed up with *The Stink Monsters*. It's hard work.'

'Is this a new one?'

'I mentioned it, didn't I? *The Stink Monsters on Mars*.'

'You're rich enough not to work – not if you don't want to.'

'The richer you get the more expensive your tastes become, Tanya. I'm having to feed a more luxurious lifestyle.'

'Give yourself a break. It is Saturday after all.'

'I'm just bored with it. I need inspiration. I can't think how to draw the Martians.'

Martians! I have an idea about that, according to *The Counterfeit Confetti*.

'I was wondering if you fancied going to the pictures. Or something. What do you think?'

'Do you mean tonight? I would love to go!' she yells. 'But can't. I have a date.'

'A date? A *date* date?'

'Uh-huh.'

'Who with?'

'Can't tell you. Top secret.'

In the publishing circles that Caroline might – for all I know – move in these days it may well be that she has met some famous author. Maybe an author I admire.

'*Who is he!*'

She won't answer.

Alone and reluctant to read I regret how I spoke to Carl. I want to go to the cinema so I track down the piece of paper with his phone number. He'll know of some great little independent cinema I've never been to before and he'll choose a fantastic film I've never heard of but will love. Somehow I retain enough sanity not to use it; phoning him so soon after being rude might seem psychotic. He might ask for an explanation for my rudeness and the only truthful one I have might repel him – I am habitually rude. Besides, we cannot go on a proper date yet as I have just broken up with Richard; there's a respectable mourning period to observe.

Instead I do something even more psychotic. I phone Alison.

'Alison, it's Tanya. I still have your *Del Amitri* CD.'

Delighted though she is to hear from me, she only agrees to the cinema if I agree to having a drink afterwards. Alison has to arrange a babysitter and this makes her consider all nights out as a big deal; this means alcohol has to be on the agenda.

She asks me, not unreasonably, 'Which film is it that you specifically want to see?'

'I don't know. I just fancy going to the pictures.'

Bath. A little make-up; enough only to cover blemishes. I put on jeans so if one drink should carry over into several and Alison attempts to talk me into going to a nightclub, my jeans will make that impossible.

I wait outside the cinema for Alison. Couples meet up and enter. I am waiting for someone I do not want to be with. When she arrives, also in jeans, she launches straight into a depressed rant about her job: the awful hours, the money, the idiocy of some patients. Alison continues whinging even through the film itself. We receive heckles. Alison 'tuts' loudly, incredulous that these strangers should be more interested in a hundred-million-dollar movie than her anecdotes about bedpans and lanced boils, or whatever it is she has been talking about because, frankly, I have stopped listening.

Those women who keep on returning to their violent husbands are a mystery to me. To a degree I even believe that if they are that stupid they don't deserve sympathy. Yet here I am in the company of someone whose company I know bores me. It always has. And I know this. Yet I phoned her. I deserve no sympathy. I should have phoned Carl.

After the film, and dutifully fulfilling my contractual obligation to the letter, we have a drink in the cinema's own bar. She begins to talk about her two children. I buy another drink. I have finished my drink within three minutes of sitting down. It takes her twenty-five minutes to catch up. She is so self-absorbed, so wrapped up in her world and her problems that she cannot believe I could have anything to contribute. I do not care about the school her children attend, or the cost of children's clothes, or the trouble she has with her ex-partner, their father. I am nurturing a contempt for her, as if her act of boring me is out of vindictiveness, and this is not the truth. She simply believes I will be interested because I pretend I am her friend. It is nasty of me to have kept this deception going for so long. When I get back home – if I make it alive – I am going to throw Alison's phone number away. Better still, I am going to write her a letter, which will say I am no longer capable of being her friend. Because no one breaks friendships by letter this will make her understand such a precedent is caused by exceptional circumstances. She is not a bad person; I will be protecting her more than myself. I want no friends and admit I am only using her tonight. I want to remove the temptation from myself by evicting her from my world.

'Do you want another drink?' she asks.

'Better not risk it,' I say even though we've had just two, it's only twenty past ten and she's agreed to drive me home.

'Here's your *Del Amitri* CD,' I tell her, handing it over and praying she has nothing else to lend me. She hasn't, which means when she receives my letter the so-called friendship will finally be dead. She does not ask if I enjoyed the CD, and this is fortunate – I never listened to it.

'Is Trevor still living in the same flat?'

'Uh-huh.'

Each time I see Alison she asks this same question. She barely exchanged three sentences with Trevor when they shared an address, so to still enquire about him years later is perverse. There can be no doubt Alison is the loneliest woman in the world.

'Anyway – what's been happening to you recently?' she asks as we walk through the foyer.

'Nothing much.'

She drops me off at home and I promise to phone her soon.

I spend Sunday away from home. After finishing the other eleven of *The Twelve Caesars* I go to Southwark and walk along the banks of the Thames, looking around the second-hand book stalls before making my way up to Covent Garden to look at the bookshops there; then – in an attempt to stop myself from buying more books – I visit other shops. I end up returning to the same cinema to see the same film I saw last night with Alison. The cinema is a more fulfilling experience when the accompanying dialogue can be heard. This development is encouraging: if I can go to the cinema alone, then I need not have a boyfriend for that reason.

When I return home I am saved from the confrontation of *The Counterfeit Confetti* by finding an envelope, with no stamp, addressed to me, propped up against the door of my flat, which means someone – Mrs Davies being the prime suspect – brought it up and put it here.

Tanya,

Sorry I couldn't make it last night. I'll call for you at

seven to take you to my flat, if that's OK. There's
something I want to talk to you about.
  Love,
  Caroline

I hear Mrs Davies's flat door open. She will hope to use the note as a pretext for talking to me. I can guess this because it's a tactic I've used in the past. I had a crush on Darren Holden at middle school. He supported Sheffield Wednesday and, aware of this, I would scour the back page of my dad's newspaper for any references to Darren's team so that, armed with this information, the next day I would have material to begin a conversation. He soon learnt my trick and began to support Charlton Athletic – they're never mentioned any-where ever. I bought a Charlton Athletic scarf.

Desperate to avoid Mrs Davies, I find my keys, open the door and charge into my flat within seconds. I amaze myself. Darren Holden eventually began to avoid me with the same ferocity – quite literally turning on his heel and scarpering as I approached.

In the twenty minutes I have before Caroline arrives I must eat, wash and change. Although we are only going to her flat, I feel compelled to create a smart impression upon my prospective employer. I drink milk and eat crisps and ice cream – because none of these takes preparation and I can eat them whilst in the bathroom, washing. I change into jeans, a plain yellow T-shirt and a sweatshirt. I am ready at seven precisely and go down to meet Caroline so she will not have to come into the building. Caroline arrives at seven-twenty, apologising for being late, although offering no explanation. I tell her not to mention it, tell her how delighted I am to see her again and say, as a forerunner to accepting her offer, how I dread returning to work tomorrow. Already I detect a formality in my voice and wonder if she will notice.

'When did you post the note?' I ask her after we have been travelling for several minutes.

'Huh?' she answers, distracted from her thoughts.

'The note. When did you post it?'

'Oh. Today. I fancied a drive out. I was stuck again.' She is

87

referring to her work on *The Stink Monsters on Mars*. 'I hope it wasn't too short notice.'

'Not at all. It's great to see you.' This is shameless sycophancy. 'I wasn't sure whether to get dressed up – but you did say it was just a talk.'

'That's right,' she answers. She does not elaborate, concentrating, instead, on making a difficult right turn at a busy junction, then negotiating the car down a narrow street, through a tight valley created by parked cars and only narrowly missing the oncoming traffic. I make another attempt to coax her into talking about the job offer.

'So you work Sundays too?'

'Not often. I was bored.'

'Did you manage to get started again on *The Stink Monsters* after you'd delivered the note?'

'Not really.'

Last night she couldn't come to the cinema with me due to having a mysterious date. Though I ask again who he was, she still vehemently refuses to say. To ensure I do not persist with this question, Caroline turns on the car radio. She fidgets around, jumping from station to station in search of music she likes. The search still hasn't concluded by the time we arrive at her home.

Her flat is very American, very open plan and minimal. The windows take up the full length of the walls; it's glamorous yet lacks real comfort. The only room I truly envy is her studio. There is a large wrought-iron bookcase; its books are all large-format art books. She has a wooden unit with plenty of drawers, shelves for papers and a top made to hold brushes and paints; it is on castors and she tells me she had it made to her own design. The studio is exactly the kind of room I once dreamt of, when I was younger and had obscure artistic ambitions. Though I no longer draw recreationally I am convinced I would start again if I had these facilities. Around her desk are scattered sketches she has been working on for *The Stink Monsters on Mars*. I pick up a selection, looking through them carefully, using this as an excuse to approach the subject of Martians.

Being the Mistress of Subtlety, I begin with, 'These

88

sketches look fine to me. I thought you said you were having problems? Something about Martians, you said.'

She sorts through the sketches and hands me a specific one. 'What's the matter with it?' I ask. Though the Martian she has drawn is comic enough it lacks originality: it has a scrawny body with a large head and black slit eyes; the hands have just three long fingers and the head has antennae.

'I don't think it's original enough,' she tells me. 'Or comical enough. What do you think?'

'Maybe the problem is that you're trying to make it comical.'

'I don't understand what you mean.'

'Well, the *Stink Monsters* are comical monsters – right? So for comical effect you should juxtapose them with aliens who look like ordinary humans.'

Caroline studies this idea. She takes several minutes, in silence, to work out its consequences.

'That is an excellent idea, Tanya!' she eventually says.

We walk into her living room. She takes some of the sketches with her, yet once in the room casually discards them on the coffee table. She sits across from me, then stands to push her armchair closer to mine. We are facing each other, only feet apart. She smiles broadly without making any attempt at conversation. She is distracted and itchy, frequently adjusting her position. Deciding that I should make an attempt to look relaxed, as if I do not know she is troubled, I sit back and sip at my drink. I asked for a Southern Comfort with lemonade and lime – and she made it perfectly.

'Lovely,' I tell her, holding up my drink.

'Good.'

Though I like Caroline's flat I will decorate and furnish mine quite differently once I am on an equivalent income. If *Stink Monsters* earns me enough I might even rent the vacant flat opposite mine, for the extra space. Though I might be wiser to buy a house, I'm accustomed to my flat in spite of its flaws. Mrs Davies can't live for ever and moving all my books would be a headache.

'Shall we go for something to eat?'

She looks straight at me. The question catches me off guard. It was not in the book.

'Er – sure.'

'In a minute. Good. OK. First, Tanya, I wonder if you remember what I said to you at Rachel and David's wedding? I said it only as a joke, really – you know, about how great it would be for us to work together again? Do you remember me saying how much fun I think it would be?'

If she had said it I am sure I would have remembered being described as fun – it's not a word often used about me.

She goes on, 'Tanya – here is a daily routine I *would* enjoy. My alarm goes at seven-thirty. I get ready and leave the house by eight-thirty; fetch *you* back here to begin work at nine. We have coffee at ten-thirty, lunch at twelve. We could even nip out to the pub. Back here for one, one-thirty. Coffee again at two-thirty. Finish work at five. Or four. So it will only be six hours of work a day for you. That's a thirty-hour week. I'll pay you far more than whatever wage you're on now, plus a percentage of the book. Royalties.'

'You're offering me a job?' I ask, faking amazement.

'Why not? Your idea for the Martians was so good.'

My response to this – in the book – is something like . . . I can't remember the exact words and the longer I struggle to remember the more remote the words become. I would like to say something different, to contradict the book. In the end all I can do is speak the thought in my mind.

'Exactly what job would you want me to do?'

'The same as me. I've told you what I do. Planning. Ideas. Sketching. You could even do some of the finished drawings, maybe.'

Like replaying a vivid dream, as I hear her speak I know her words are familiar. She is exactly repeating those words of hers written down in *The Counterfeit Confetti*. And in reply I say . . . Nothing, I seem to remember. So I say nothing.

Caroline leaves her chair and comes over to me.

'What do you say?' she begs.

Caroline is so desperate to hear me accept I can torment her no longer.

'Yes,' I answer.

She hugs me. This is an American habit catching on in this country due to our overexposure to imported TV programmes. Habits like hugging do not belong here except at times of grief or perhaps when someone is released from prison. I would have preferred a smile and another drink.

'You'll have to work your notice at Ill Will, won't you?' Caroline asks. 'So do that; and then we'll begin. Now when I go to Los Angeles to advise them on the animated series, you can come with me. It'll be a great way to start our working relationship. Plus, it'll be a laugh. Think of it, Tanya! America! Hollywood!'

'Who will you tell them I am?'

She takes a moment to sort through the semantics of this question.

'You're my . . . Personal Assistant. No – that doesn't sound grand enough. We'll think of some flash, long-winded name. Executive in Charge of Image Co-ordination, or something. I can't wait to have you here working with me! You know what – apart from the money the truth is I only agreed to do this work so I could have some legitimate contact with Kenneth. I envy you for Richard. I wish I could go back to those days of just going out with someone for no better reason than I fancy them and they fancy me.'

'What makes you think my relationship with Richard is that simple?'

'Isn't it? Why, what's up?' She asks this too eagerly, as if hoping for controversy.

I do not answer because my answer would only confirm her assumption – it is, was, that simple. I would rather talk to her about her unrequited love for Kenneth. Pointlessly still loving someone after the relationship has long since ended is definitely something I can empathise with.

'It's tough – love,' I say, attempting to sound wise but only succeeding in sounding confused. 'If it's any help to you – and I know it won't be really – I'm finally over Martin. You know – the guy I held a torch for.' I wish I hadn't used that archaic expression; it sounds as if we were at the Olympics together.

'Do you love Richard?' Caroline asks.

'No,' I admit. This confession is becoming easier.

'Why, what's up?' she repeats. It is clear she suspects something.

I cannot stop myself: 'I've met someone else. I'm splitting up with Richard.'

'Someone else? Who?' Caroline is excited and I find this contagious.

'He's called Carl. He's good looking and smart and we have a great deal in common.'

'What does he do?'

To avoid making an honest answer I crack a weak joke: 'Everything!'

'So you've slept with him?'

'I shouldn't say anything else, I haven't formally split up with Richard yet. I told him we'd split up but that might not be enough.'

'You've split up . . . or are splitting up . . . with Richard to go out with this new guy?'

'No, not really. It just wasn't working out with Richard, that's all.'

It had been a foolish impulse to have mentioned Carl to Caroline. She pushes me for more details, making my regret deeper. I start to retreat, to sound less enthusiastic. The clumsy way I begin avoiding her questions might even appear as if I am inventing Carl. In a desperate attempt to change the subject I begin looking through more of her rough sketches for *The Stink Monsters on Mars*. She refuses to be distracted.

'Where does he live, what's his home like?'

'I don't know.'

'You don't know?'

'Is it important?'

'It's a bit important. How did you meet him?'

I no longer want to talk about Carl.

'How did you meet Ken?' I ask even though I know her answer. She worked with him.

As promised, Caroline takes me out to some newly opened fashionable restaurant in the West End. One of those restaurants that receive favourable reviews less for the food and more for the personality of the chef and the celebrity status of the customers. I learn every incident and anecdote she has from the story of *Caroline and Kenneth*. Caroline orders wine faster than we drink it, even though we drink rapidly. Some of the pleasure from the evening is taken in behaving inappropriately: we enjoy ourselves openly; we talk too loudly and laugh too extravagantly.

We stagger out of the restaurant at eleven. I am nearly indiscreet enough to reveal to Caroline I knew of her job offer beforehand; fortunately the spectacle of her being sick into a litter bin sobers me into silence.

'It must have been the food,' she suggests.

Back in my flat, though it is late and I have been drinking, I do not feel sleepy. I look over the letter I wrote to Richard – then tear it up. I begin to think about work tomorrow and how I will tell them I am leaving. Of course I *know* how I do it: I have read how I do it. I look through the books I bought today but dismiss all of them without real thought, wondering why I bought each. I pick up *The Counterfeit Confetti* and glance through the passages where Tanya in the book resigns from Ill Will. I read through today's events where Caroline offers me work. Written words match actual events far more closely than I remember. I wonder if this can be explained by my subconsciously imitating these paragraphs after already reading them. I abandon any attempt to undress. I collapse onto my bed still in my jeans and T-shirt. I sleep well.

I wake in the morning clear-headed and cheerful. There is a message on the answerphone from Mum. In my drunken state last night I didn't notice the light flashing.

'Tanya, please phone me. Please. I really want to talk to you. That's not unreasonable, is it? We've always had such a good relationship. Please phone. Tonight.'

I am glad I did not hear this last night when I was drunk. I might have phoned her and been abusive.

NINE

Monday morning. I pass the security man, who doesn't look up from the back page of the *Daily Mail*. I catch the lift up to the eighth floor, enter Ill Will's offices, sit at my desk.

Allan is already working.

'Hello, Tanya,' he says. 'Feeling better?'

I ask if he wants a coffee. He suggests I wait for Jo but I decline. She could be another half-hour yet and I need caffeine now. Besides, Jo never makes it strong enough and gives everybody two sugars according to the way she takes it.

'Did you have a nice weekend?' I ask. He'll say, 'Oh – so-so,' or maybe 'Nothing to write home about.'

'Oh – so-so. You?'

I answer in a similar nondescript way, cleverly adding that I was still recovering from my illness. Gradually everyone else arrives. When asked about their weekends Keith and Mary give their statutory ambiguous answers, Troy says his customary 'Did I bollocks' and Allan doesn't ask Jo. She tells me about it anyway: where she went drinking, which new nightclubs are good, which are boring, who fancies her, whom she fancies, the clothes she wore, new records she likes. The young are at the very cutting edge of triviality.

I have several items of work I should be getting along with. None inspires me, each is a task. This morning everyone in the office again seems subdued. It never used to be like this, least of all when Caroline worked here. The place has lost its vitality. It was once a young, vibrant company, developing new and adventurous products. Work was exciting. I often ended the working day with a sense of real achievement. These days I feel fortunate if I end it fully conscious. We go through the motions: steady, saleable, dull. Ill Will was started twenty years ago. Its inspiration was the simple concept of cashing in on that habit that close, British friends have of being extremely insulting to each other. The company produced greetings cards with obscene insults and offensive sentiments. The two guys who began the company sold it off to a larger greetings card company, which then kept this office, believing the independent style would thrive only in a small environment. Allan was a relative of one of the founders, and Keith was a friend. The rest of us are later additions. 'The Season of Ill Will to All Men' was the slogan on one of the earlier Christmas cards. And, though I think the card was never actually produced, the name stuck. That's the story of the company – though I no longer care.

Keith finishes reading his newspaper and excuses himself. He leaves for the toilet – for his first cigarette of the working day. When he returns he begins drumming on his desk with a pencil. He picks up another and uses both, then abandons this percussion, bored when no one complains.

'Greetings cards for pets' birthdays?' Troy suggests.

'Try out some ideas,' Allan tells Troy.

'Pets? People aren't that stupid,' Jo says.

We all stop work and look at Jo. We all have the same cynical expression. Compared to her, we are all old.

'Try out some ideas,' Allan repeats to Troy.

'Should we have some music on?' Jo suggests. Allan quickly stands from his desk but today Jo beats him. For the next hour we listen to monotonous, thumping, stupid dance music. The entire lyric to one song is: 'Left, Right, Mine, Yours'. *What the fuck is wrong with this generation?*

'I'm off for ink cartridges,' Jo tells Allan. The second she is out of the door Troy finds Radio 2 and the office breathes a sigh of relief.

Mary has just made a big mistake on her computer. I know the signs. I recognise the uncontrolled grimace, the furtive look around, the manual taken surreptitiously out of her desk and flipped through till she finds the troubleshooting chapter, which she hopes will bail her out. She could always admit she has made a mistake and ask for help, yet never does. I know for certain she has made a mistake because I read in *The Counterfeit Confetti* that she would.

'Close the file,' I tell her. I am standing over her. She looks up at me stunned, but does not ask how I know she has a problem.

'Why?'

'Just do it. But when it asks if you want to save the changes, click "No".'

She moves her mouse and clicks.

'Now open the file again, and you should be OK.'

She does. She smiles.

'How did you know?'

'Intuition.'

Troy is writing away furiously, presumably on his pets' birthday cards idea. He has periods when he works like a demon, then other days when he appears to do nothing.

Lunchtime. Troy and Keith – pub. Mary – shopping. Jo – collecting gossip. Allan – eating his massive lunch. I rummage through my desk, clearing out rubbish – old magazines, two old cups, discontinued stationery items. I throw it all away – even the cups, because they're filthy. There's nothing of value here.

The only way I can be diverted from my utter boredom is to spend the afternoon working hard. This I do, yet everything I produce is substandard. I have lost the will for invention and my only remaining motivation is to get home. Allan accepts all my work without comment. Keith notices me putting on my coat and shuts down his own computer. He quickly tidies his desk and puts on his own coat even before I have put both arms through mine.

I am the first out of the office at five. I travel down in the lift with people from other floors in the building. Though I have seen some of these faces hundreds of times before, I do not know their names nor even how their voices sound. It has been a very unremarkable day at work.

Walking along the street towards my flat I see Mick waiting. He can only be here with the intention of persuading me to see my mother. Maybe if he had taken me by surprise, caught me off guard, maybe that way he might have stood a chance of soliciting a positive response. Unfortunately for him the element of surprise has gone from his ambush: I have a walk of several hundred yards to prepare my resistance. It cannot help him that I have also been anticipating hearing his appeal on her behalf. Something had to give.

'Hello, Tanya. I wasn't sure what time you got home from work.'

'I start a new job soon.' Damn. I curse myself for offering this information. It has nothing to do with him.

'Really?'

I unlock the house door.

'I'm not going to invite you in, Mick. There's nothing for us to talk about.'

'Look, Tanya, somehow you've made a big mistake. Why are you doing this to your mother?'

'I'm doing it because ... If she now slept with *your* best friend, don't you think you'd be angry with her? I'm giving her Dad's anger because he's not here to give it himself.'

'Where did you hear this from? Your mother loved your dad.'

'Sure she did.'

'She did! And she loves you. You cannot imagine what this is doing to her. You're turning her into a zombie, she does nothing but ... ' He stalls, exasperated by my fierce expression of indifference. 'Are you really prepared to just cut her out of your life like this? Dead? Full stop?'

'Yes.'

'We did not sleep together whilst your dad was still alive.'

He really should have worded this better; such an adamant denial leaves me unable to reply, unless I wish to contradict him and begin a real argument. I do wish to speak but all that is suitable is conciliatory, and reconciliation so soon after such accusations would require more sensible explanations than I have.

Taking care to make no reply and show no expression, I enter the house and close the door on him.

I hear the telephone ringing even before I open my flat door. I let the answerphone come on in case it is Mum asking if Mick is here. When I hear Carl's voice I am so relieved I pick up without considering whether I might have been wiser letting him talk to the answerphone.

'I'm phoning from the call box near Asda,' he tells me.

Asda is less than a hundred yards away. 'Do you want me to hang up and go home?'

'Come over,' I say.

Damn. I do not want to *never* see him, I just do not want any big developments.

In the three minutes it takes Carl to arrive I tidy my hair, have a quick brush of my teeth, refresh my lipstick, clear away the most obvious mess in the living room and put on some music. The music is for him to hear before he enters, to convince him I am relaxed. I take it off when he knocks; this demonstrates how less relaxed I am with him here. A surprising amount of thought goes into achieving an effect I am not sure I want to achieve. I do not immediately ask Carl in, wanting to make him feel awkward. He smiles and says nothing – which succeeds in making *me* feel awkward. I walk away from the door, leaving it open. He follows, and closes the door. To make him believe I am startled – as if I had not intended him to follow – I quickly turn around when I hear the door close. He stands a foot away from me. Carl never looks worried or alarmed; nor does he look cocky or arrogant.

'I'm quitting my job soon,' I tell him. He smiles.

'Really?'

'Of course really. I wouldn't make that up. I'm looking forward to it.'

'It's an empowering feeling. I know. I've done it myself.'

'You've quit your job?'

'Not *this* job. The job I had before.'

'You quit a job to become a road sweeper? Christ – what job could be worse?'

'Ha ha,' he says. Carl understands I am being over-insulting, over-patronising just to annoy him. I go into the kitchen.

'Drink?' I call back to him. 'I've just got in so I haven't had one myself yet.'

He enters the kitchen, following me.

'Sure.'

I hadn't expected him to follow and my kitchen is too narrow for two people to be in at the same time. I keep bumping into him and having to squeeze past as I make the coffees.

'So what are you going to do?'

'Caroline has asked me to work with her.'

'Less secure.'

'More fun. Better money.' I leave it at that, finishing before I say, 'I'm too young to consider security,' as I am not confident of how convincing it will sound coming from my 29-year-old mouth.

'You seem happy about it,' Carl says.

'I am.'

'Good. I admire you for doing it.'

I immediately stop making coffee. The bag of sugar topples over on the kitchen unit, spilling. I stare at Carl as if he has materialised from nowhere. This is one of those rare moments you experience with other people where you are flung back to day one: the slate is wiped clean. I have to look at him intensely to force myself to imagine, after all, who he might be. *Carl admires me for quitting my job.* Richard would have said I was nuts. Mum would demand a fuller explanation, in writing. Alison hates her job, yet would never understand any explanation for forfeiting security.

'What's the matter?' he asks, worried by my silent staring.

I step forward so our faces meet. I kiss him, my fingertips on his face.

'I was a bit rude to you when you called on Saturday.'

'True.'

I finish making the coffees; we sit on the settee in the living room. Carl takes my hand even though all we now do is talk. The things Carl tells me about himself make me positive I want him around.

Carl's previous job was for a public relations company. He earned over forty thousand a year. When he resigned they believed he was probably leaving for another company, so offered him more money as an incentive to stay.

'It's such a worthless job. So redundant. I grew to realise how it's nothing better than prostitution. OK, so they might be the most expensive whores around, but it still means they'll do *anything* for the right money. That's bad enough, but the shame of it is they're so self-obsessed. They actually

99

believe they're doing something worthwhile, something useful. Even something creative! I found it increasingly difficult to maintain my pretence of giving a damn.'

'I fucking hate PR people,' I say, speaking without making the attempt to curb my prejudices or my language. Carl laughs because I don't even say it to him, I just spit it out uncontrollably.

'Even so,' I add, 'it's a bit of a step down – isn't it? – to, you know, to . . . Well, from a PR career to . . . sweeping roads.'

'Sweeping roads is one million times more useful.'

'You sweep roads because you want to be useful?' I ask, immediately regretting this scorn.

'No, I do it for the money, and I wish the money was more. But really, I'm fine. I have far more time to read. I have no pressures or stress or guilt. Once I'm home all the time is mine. My mind is free. It's the only important freedom.'

I tell him some of the hopes I had when I was younger. I tell him the hopes I have now, working for Caroline. I try to add some sense of ambition but fail to pull it off. Ambition cannot be faked.

'I don't see ambition as being a positive characteristic,' Carl says when I confess my failure.

'Personal ambition isn't. But ambition for your children, or for your country . . . ' I begin, then wish I hadn't. I don't want children and I have no ambitions for this country any more.

'Past generations believed in aiming for kindness, forgiveness, love. We've grown up during a time when personal ambition has become the greatest of virtues.'

'The only people I like lack ambition,' I say.

'I lack ambition.'

'I like you.'

If Mrs Davies had not called and interrupted I might have asked Carl to stay the night. Before she knocked on my door Carl and I had talked without stalling, but the conversation was slowing, considered silences punctuating the shorter sentences. We had drawn closer and eyes looked at lips.

'That was my upstairs neighbour,' I tell Carl when I return

from the door. I am pleased Carl was here when Mrs Davies called, his visit providing an excuse to be abrupt.

Carl has picked up *The Counterfeit Confetti* and is flicking through it. I wait for him to make a comment. He might at least say something about the author having the same name as me.

'Would you like to borrow that?' I ask.

'I'm always borrowing books from you,' he answers, which is the wrong answer.

'I'm hungry,' I tell him. 'I'm going to have a snack. Then I might have an early night.'

'You want me to go?'

'I'm glad you phoned though,' I tell him. He puts down *The Counterfeit Confetti* and walks over to me. We kiss, then kiss properly. Then I lead him to his coat and hand it to him.

'So I should phone again?'

'Um.'

Though I had intended the 'Um' to sound pleased and sexy it sounded only indifferent. To compensate, as I am walking him to the door, I repeat the news Mrs Davies gave me in the hope it will make me sound chatty and friendly, which is the impression I want him to leave with.

'The upstairs flat – next to Mrs Davies – has been burgled. Mrs Davies was burgled last week.'

'Did she tell the police?'

'Yes. But she isn't sure who lives in that flat any more, so they're trying to get in contact with Mr Ostryzniuk, our landlord.'

'Are you worried?'

'I don't want to get burgled, of course not. But I'll be fine. I don't have much of value. Just books. Even crooks don't steal books.'

When Carl has gone I put a frozen lasagne into the oven. The phone rings. It is Carl.

'You agreed I should phone again.'

'Not so soon!' I laugh and hang up. He must have rung from the phone box near Asda. This gag is corny but I enjoy it. Though I dislike myself for enjoying it and dislike Carl for making it. Maybe this is his flaw: his sense of humour. I never trust people who say the first quality they look for in other people is a good sense of humour. It's meaningless. An *intelligent* sense of humour would be a better boast.

Whilst I wait for my lasagne to cook I consider why I did not want Carl to stay. I do not have an answer. I eat the lasagne, remembering I do not particularly like lasagne, yet continue to buy and eat them. No explanation.

In too good a mood to read *The Counterfeit Confetti*, I begin to read Joyce's *Portrait of the Artist as a Young Man*. This is my third or fourth attempt to read it and this latest attempt again fails through lack of commitment. I do not want to invest the time in a real book so instead I begin to reread Vasari's *Lives of the Artists*, one of the very first books I recommended to Martin. I chose this because it can be read in chapters, left and returned to much later. When I first read it, in those days when I had the belief that my interest in art would somehow compensate for my inability to paint and lead me into being a successful artist, I gave copies to everyone. I even forced one on my mother who thanked me warmly but never read it. As I now read the book it saddens me to think how little I once understood myself. I now wish I had read *The Counterfeit Confetti*.

On Tuesday I pass the security man; he doesn't look away from the woman he is talking to. He is smiling and flirting – happily distracted from his job. If I was a terrorist I could easily bring a bomb into this building. I wish one would, I wouldn't mind a scare and an evacuation, just to break the routine.

Jo makes coffee. For a change it is reasonably strong, and damn it – she's made me accustomed to taking two sugars.

I have several items of work I should be getting along with. None inspires me, each is a task. Simply being here is an ordeal. The morning is a drag and the afternoon is tedious. I clock-watch. I've never done that before. I have decided that tomorrow I will definitely tell Allan I am resigning. I'll arrive early.

When I leave work I take the stairs as the lift is too slow.

How do those people who don't read books plug the gaps in their day? The journeys, the break-times, the evenings in when the telly is crap, the time in bed before sleep arrives? I used to hold them in contempt but now that I understand better I pity them. At the moment I am one of those people. I only have *The Counterfeit Confetti*. I cannot concentrate on anything else until I have finished that; after all, something so profoundly relevant to me demands my full attention. It's like receiving your exam results through the post – any delay in reading the information is pretence. That night when I dived in and read the first five chapters straight through was the largest single chunk I have taken out of the book, and it revealed enough enigmas to scare me off another substantial read. Tonight, however, I intend to indulge in another big session. No more glimpses, no more random openings. I want the full picture. If nothing else, reading it might cheer me up. Unless there is some catastrophe forecast in the book, which I have not foreseen. Hair loss, breast cancer, gas explosion.

I sit at the table, eat, then reach for *The Counterfeit Confetti* even before I clear away the dishes. I hesitate before opening the book. I haven't suffered anxiety like this since the days running up to my driving test. I passed first time, incidentally. Irrelevant information here, but I can never resist mentioning it.

I read up to and including Chapter Ten.

TEN

Chapter Ten begins with the phone call I made to my mother telling her I was coming up to see her. My being abrupt and deliberately ambiguous made her speculate on possible reasons for my visit, which then made her think back over my life and how little trouble I had always been, that I had always had robust health, learnt quickly and appeared happy. There is a section about how, as a small child, I played with Gary's toys far more than my own: the cars and the toy soldiers. My mother worried I might become a tomboy, yet was also hopeful that an aggressive streak would help me take care of myself later in life: I would probably be single-minded and worldly. The book reminds me how, at the age of ten, my interest in all toys faded. The only presents I requested on birthdays or for Christmas were tropical fish; they became a dominant interest in my life. I read every book the library had on the subject; I solicited for paid chores so the money could buy ornaments and equipment for the fish tank. This interest ended tragically after the whole family had been away for a weekend. A fuse had blown in the plug that ran the heating for the tank.

> Tanya's parents watched their young daughter wrap the fish in newspaper, then put the parcel in the kitchen bin; she then emptied the kitchen bin, returning to the house to empty and clean the fish tank – which she later sold. There was none of the sentimental ritual that is normal upon these occasions in a child's life and she never bothered with fish or other pets again.

I find it extraordinary how this incident with my tropical fish is written as if I didn't care that they had died. I've always worried that this is how my parents believed I felt, but in fact

I was furious with them. In the first place, I had had to persuade them to let me buy me the fish. They insisted I would eventually lose interest and the fish would be neglected. I was persistent enough to convinced them otherwise. I took immense care of those fish, feeding them every day, making sure the temperature of the tank was closely monitored, changing the water at regular intervals. They died as a result of Dad's carelessness. He had fitted the plug incorrectly – this is the reason it had fused. It wasn't that I was calm about their death, my silence was contempt for my parents.

The book then reminds me about my adolescence and how I developed the usual interests in boys, music, clothes and going out, even though I never seemed casual about my studies, and Mum and Dad hoped for high academic achievements. At varying intervals, I produced boyfriends for them to quiz; they were introduced, then vanished. My parents learnt – like veteran First World War fighter pilots with new recruits – not to bother memorising names; the boys were never around for long. When Gary was accepted at Oxford, even though by now I was all set for college, I announced I did not intend to pursue a university career. Mum and Dad asked me why and I told them:

'Because it won't help me be happy.' It was a stupid answer, yet an answer they had no way of arguing against.

It was whilst at college I met Martin. It took just three visits for Mum and Dad to lower their guard and begin to like him, though they attributed it to his influence when I started to behave introspectively in their company. The book reminds me of the style of clothes I began to wear.

Tanya wore utilitarian boots, T-shirts and jeans, the darker the better. At night her parents were regularly in bed long before she returned home. Her mother perfected an act of trust; but this was not the truth. It's a severance as significant as the cutting of the umbilical cord the day a mother realises her child is now an independent sexual being. You're no longer a fully valid parent after this. There could be no doubt Martin and Tanya were sleeping together; they never disguised their passion or intimacy. Wording the question meticulously, after planning the conversation through all potential hurdles, Mrs Stephens asked Tanya if she was having sex with Martin. There was a hesitation, whilst she considered the options of outrage or lying, before Tanya settled for honesty.

'Yes, Mum,' I told her. 'In fact, we've slept together several ... Frequently, in fact.'

I waited for her to be outraged. She wasn't. She might even have smiled, it's difficult for me to remember.

'OK ... You're careful, aren't you?' she asked.

'I've never cared for anything as much in my life.' I remember as I said this how happy I was to be having this conversation.

'You know what I mean, Tanya.'

'I do know what you mean, Mum. Don't worry about that. We don't want kids. We just want each other.'

When she comprehended how happy her daughter was, it dawned on her how their having sex was a positive development. It was mature, it was tender, it was exciting; she realised, also, just how jealous she was of this excitement.

'I'm happy for you,' she told her daughter, visualising the combined joy of being young and exploring sex with someone you truly care for. There could be no perceived boundaries; you cannot imagine repetition or boredom. When bodies are firm and minds are open, when rules aren't known and trust is a given, sex is at its most perfect; sex is not an act, it's the genuine article.

I put the book down and wonder about my parents' sex life and how it might be for anyone who has been with someone for so many years. When it comes to sex, silently wishing it was different is the most disturbing fetish; habit is the most obscene act; obligation is the most unpardonable perversion.

I will finish this chapter, there are ... five or six pages left ... then go to bed. So far, though of course I'm deeply interested, I cannot conceive of the purpose of the book. If it is to teach me something about myself – to perhaps, somehow, improve me as a person – then it's failing; every revelation about my personality or history is something I already know. It's taught me nothing. And why me anyway? *The Counterfeit Confetti* would have served greater purpose if it had landed in Caroline's lap. Or Alison's. Or Richard's. Or maybe my mum's.

When *The Counterfeit Confetti* reverts to the story of my mother it becomes dull reading. I preferred it when it concentrated on me, so I speed-read through to the last few pages, about how it was fortunate for my mother to have had Mick. He rescued her from depression after Dad died – a depression that he could not, however, rescue her from after I had confronted her about sleeping with him when Dad was still alive.

The rest of the chapter is about me again and I become so enthralled that when the phone rings I do not answer it. I hear Mum's voice.

I am reminded – it is the first time I have thought about him for years – that after Martin my next serious boyfriend was Graham. By this time I had left college and was living in London with no real wish for another boyfriend until I could understand why there was any need for one. Graham didn't answer that question, but he was pleasant, charming and persistent enough. I eventually agreed to go out with him and simply because there was nothing better to do we began to see each other regularly.

Graham was taller than Martin; I enjoyed the difference. He was more athletic. He took command. Whenever he asked me out he had somewhere in mind. Though he would ask if his suggestion was OK, he never once asked if there was somewhere else I would prefer to go. I liked this because it was in such marked contrast to the many debates I had held with Martin whenever we had gone anywhere.

Graham took great care with his appearance. Graham adored Tanya. Graham's parents adored Tanya. Tanya was bored. She had no courage to break up with him. She abandoned her first London flat, moving without informing him; she had to change jobs and leave no connections behind that he could later trace. She would have had to explain why she did not wish to see him any more and she could think of no good reason.

For her own ease of mind Tanya wanted an explanation.

What was love? The love she had had with Martin had come so young and so easy, was so bright and exciting that it had never occurred to her that it might never be repeated.

I remember now: I visited home, to ask my mum if there was an explanation for why I didn't love Graham. I went through all his qualities, then the reasons why I believed I could never love him: he had no enthusiasm for anything outside his own immediate experience. His political opinions lacked coherence. Graham had predictable interests in films. He didn't read. He was too fussy about his appearance.

My mum had no answers. Though she didn't exactly laugh at the trivialities of my complaints, neither did she fully understand my ultimate wishes. I wanted to know why it was considered a fault to not be able to love anyone. Why chase love when love inevitably ended in misery?

'Love will hunt you down, whether you want it to or not,' my mother told me. I remember thinking this was a ludicrous thing to say. It was no use discussing this with her; she was newly remarried so for her love again felt untainted. That moment was the first time I thought of escaping my mother. I considered whether or not to tell her my new address. Then, however – eight years ago – I was not cruel and reclusive enough. I could have walked away from my mother just as I had Graham. But I didn't.

Until I read his name I had almost forgotten about Graham. I wonder if he thinks I'm dead?

The last paragraph of Chapter Ten lapses into the present day and says I believe I will never see Carl again, which isn't true.

As a further step on her road to complete indifference Tanya continued a purge of her remaining human contacts. Richard was painlessly got rid off; she believed she would see neither Carl nor Martin ever again; Caroline had changed roles; her mother was cruelly dismissed. There were still lingering friends, but none who would cause her any real trouble. Except for Alison. No matter how infrequent and dull their meetings had become, Alison still existed in a world were the two of them remained good friends. Tanya had to rid herself of

Alison. A phone call could turn into a debate; a meeting might lead to abuse. Tanya wrote a letter. So Alison was now also gone.

Further on, the book describes how Mick came to see me, to plead my mother's case. It is exactly as it happened.

Walking along the street towards her home, Tanya saw Mick waiting. If he had taken her by surprise he might have stood some chance of hearing a positive response. Unfortunately for him Tanya had a walk of several hundred yards to prepare her resistance.

I finally finish Chapter Ten of *The Counterfeit Confetti*. However, before I go to bed I look back at Chapter Five because, when I think about it, there seems something inconsistent about Mick visiting me – his innocent attitude, his insistence that I was in the wrong. Chapter Five definitely, unambiguously, categorically and in lurid detail told me how my mum and Mick slept with each other whilst Dad was alive.

This is the paragraph I reread from Chapter Five:

Tanya could not know how much of her mother's tears were induced by retrospective guilt. As a couple her parents had remained in love though their marriage had not stayed clear of incident. Two years previously, after a series of moody rows, of silences and petty recriminations – the source of which had become an irrelevance – Tanya's mother had confided in Mick, going into details about the inadequacy of her sex life and how the marriage was lapsing into increasingly long periods of routine and tedium. Mick, who had never married, was of little help and was embarrassed to hear this of his friend, especially from the mouth of his friend's wife. She realised the awkwardness of the situation and apologised to Mick. Neither of them spoke of the conversation again. Then her husband died and her world turned upside down, letting loose all that clogged-up crap of unspoken sentiments and epic remorse. Mick became her sidekick again, the stooge to her mourning.

Oh shit. *Neither of them spoke of the conversation again.* It did *not* say that before. It didn't!

ELEVEN

Alison – in a desperate attempt to make me hate her even more than I already do – wakes me by phoning at 7 a.m., a full half-hour before I normally wake. As can only be expected, she receives sleepy incoherence.

'Hiya!' she booms.

'Whussot?'

'You're up, aren't you? I've been on nights and I have an hour before I collect the kids, so I thought I'd ring and invite you to come to the London Dungeon on Sunday. I'm taking the kids, and I thought you might like to come. What do you say?'

'Hyuh.'

'We're setting off at ten. Shall I book you a ticket, then?'

'Alison . . . Time . . . Seven!'

'You've got plenty of time before you go to work, haven't you?'

I cough and splutter.

'What do you say then? It's a great day out. You'll love it.'

'Yeah, but . . .' This 'Yeah' is in answer to her previous question, 'You've got plenty of time before you go to work, haven't you?'

'Great! See you on Sunday then!'

'No! No! Fuck it! No! Alison! . . . Bitch!' I scream down the receiver once she has hung up. It's a classic interrogation technique: deny your victim sleep, ask a quick succession of questions to disorientate them, then take their positive answer to one question in preference to a negative answer to another.

Having been so professionally ambushed, my senses are now fully alive. I hear a distinctive noise, far away. I look out my bedroom window and see the postman walking away from our door. I can fetch my mail without fear of meeting Mrs Davies – even she will not be up at this ungodly hour.

I take extra caution to sneak downstairs anyway. I have flung on an old beige raincoat over my T-shirt and knickers. As I descend the stairs I wish I had put socks on. The communal carpet is horrible, greasy and gritty.

There is a letter from my brother, Gary. I recognise his dreadful handwriting. This is the only letter I have and it can only be in regard to my mother, so the journey downstairs was hardly worth the trouble.

Then Mrs Davies appears. She is like a phantom, standing at the top of the stairs, looking down. She is fully dressed, which means she must have been out of bed at six. This woman is unhinged.

'Is there any mail for me, Tanya?'

'Nothing, Mrs Davies.'

'Why don't you ever call me Betty?'

Because I did not know she was called Betty; because I do not want to call her by her first name, as if she is the same age as me, as if we are the best of friends. And anyway – Betty Davies?! She must be having me on.

I climb the stairs. I fake a shiver.

'It's freezing, isn't it?' I say this in order to put a time limit on any discussion. If she yatters on incessantly I will be able to start shivering with increasing ferocity, until her humanity will compel her to free me.

'Anything nice?' she asks, looking at my letter.

'A letter from my brother, that's all.'

'I think I've seen him. He's called here, hasn't he?'

He's been here just once. Mrs Davies has information on me that any professional stalker would envy. It is civility and pity that keep me talking to Mrs Davies: two sentiments that are responsible for more misery in the world than hatred and vengeance.

With the knack of a genius in the field, Mrs Davies now increases my guilt by contradicting all my presumptions about her – she leaves me.

'I'll let you get dressed,' she explains. For me this is a lesson learnt; from now on, if I wish to fetch my mail without the fear of being stuck with her all I have to do is wear as few clothes as possible.

As I make myself a coffee I begin to read Gary's letter. I can hear his voice all the way through it: older-brother, bossy, condescending. He still talks to me as if he is thirteen and I am ten.

Dear Tanya,

Mick has been in contact with me, telling me that you have had some massive fall-out with Mum and asking if I will have a word with you. I've been meaning to come to London for a while so I will be coming down on Saturday, with the kids. We won't stay long, because there are plenty of other things I want us to do. But I will be interested to hear what it is that has made you so angry with Mum. Mick wouldn't specify. All he would say is that he's very worried about her because she's sleeping so little, eating badly and barely speaks to him now. Whatever the trouble is, I think it is very childish of you to behave like this. Grown adults do not just walk away from their families. When you have children of your own you will appreciate the trouble and sacrifice that all parents make. Are you now just going to act as if Mum made no sacrifices? You must have forgotten what you were like as an adolescent, and how you constantly demanded new clothes, whatever was in fashion that week – didn't she always do her best to get you them? You must have forgotten how Mum stayed up with you on those nights when you first started drinking, and you used to come home from nightclubs and spend the night curled up around the toilet, where you'd fallen into a drink-induced sleep; you must have forgotten the many times she cleaned up the purple vomit so Dad wouldn't see. Didn't she also pay – out of her own purse – to have our neighbours' car fixed after you rammed it on one of your first driving lessons? She did that to hide it from Dad – who would have rightly refused to pay for any more lessons. You must have also forgotten how, at school, she attended dozens of crappy school plays and other productions for no better reason than that you painted the sets! And finally, Tanya, what about the simple facts that she loves you, she is your mother, she gave you life and she protected you, fed you and guided you into adulthood? If you are sulking with her because you think she did a poor job of the adulthood thing, then you shouldn't. You are to blame for that. I suggest you grow up and phone her. This is what I will be telling you on Saturday, face to face.

Janet sends her love.

Gary

Janet is Gary's wife; and my vomit during those adolescent days was purple due to drinking either lager and black or – if I was acting sophisticated – rum and black.

Apart from Gary's tone and the arrogant way he assumes I will suspend all my other plans just to accommodate his Saturday visit, the part of his letter that angers me most is his insulting comments about Dad. Dad didn't care that I used to drink. OK, so I might have been a little under age when I started – but that's Britain. Everyone starts drinking early: prime ministers and their sons, bishops, royalty; and my dad. I remember several conversations I held with Dad when I had come home after my drunken nights out. He would come downstairs and wake me. Invariably, I would have made myself a cup of tea, then fallen asleep with the TV on and the tea still in its cup, stone cold. We talked about sex, and families, and politics, and music, and any damned subject that came up. He never criticised me or lectured me or patronised me. The only advice he gave – which was the smartest advice I have ever received – was to never listen to anyone's advice – everybody wings it.

I began to write my reply to Gary immediately.

Dear Gary,

How dare you write such a nasty letter to me? Do not come down on Saturday because I have no wish to see you whilst you are in such an insolent mood.

I am delighted by my use of the word 'insolent' but stall immediately after using it. I debate whether to use his letter as a pretext to also cutting him out of my life. With luck, if I carry on at this rate, I will have no Christmas presents to buy. I temporarily abandon the letter, deciding I will finish it at work. This is the plan for the day: write a letter to Gary, calling him an arse; write a letter to Alison, telling her to get lost, and write another letter to Richard formally dumping him – one that this time I will post. My main occupation will be to finally hand in my notice. That is the first letter I shall write.

The answerphone is still flashing from Mum's message last night. I wind the tape back and reset the machine. She might really be innocent of the accusation I made. I cannot clearly think how I could respond to this.

Wednesday. A different man on security, the other must be off ill or on holiday. He can take his break confident that his substitute is doing the work with all the established dedication. Except that the newspaper whose back page this one is reading is the *Sunday Sport*. The cover has a photo of a girl on all fours with her arse facing out. It's demeaning to women that this paper believes a woman's arse is more attractive than her face; it's demeaning for men to be presumed so base. Everyone deserves demeaning because this paper sells so well. This is the reality: we are a nation of arses who idolise arses.

The day begins as it will end. I have four new items of work I should be getting along with. Four letters to write. None inspires me, each is a task.

I think about the girl posing on the cover of the *Sunday Sport*, arriving at the studio, getting undressed, being told how to pose, listening to the camera click behind her. This is her job. She has friends and parents.

No one bothers me or comments on my lack of effort. This would not happen at most places of work. The work I do here is often dull, constantly repetitive and sometimes frustrating. Yet it is easy and relaxing; the office is informal and friendly; there are none of those big intrigues or politics so often found in other offices. This also means I can occasionally leave work early, it means I am not severely remonstrated with if I arrive late and it means – most importantly – work is an inconsequential part of my life; my real life is outside of work and work never interferes. I have little responsibility, no stress and am not expected to perform miracles. My concern is that I think if I was pushed into it I *could* perform miracles. If I stay at Ill Will I know I have thirty years ahead of me without miracles.

Maybe if I was working for Caroline she would expect miracles. She would certainly expect dedication. And I would be obliged to her; she is a friend and I would not wish to disappoint a friend. This said, I could not write down why I regard Caroline as my only true friend. I did not see her for years; she holds so many attitudes I disapprove of, opinions I disagree with – and she is one of those women I normally despise; she needs to have a man in her life, she feels inadequate and lost without one, even if it is a man she does not especially like.

I begin the resignation letter. It turns out phenomenally different to how I had predicted. It says:

Dear Alison,

We have been friends for a long time now. However, I can see no point in continuing the friendship. You have moved to another area of London; you have your children and you have interests in life that are nothing like mine. I do not care for going out, for socialising, for any of those activities that require friends. I will not be going to the London Dungeon with you and your kids on Sunday. I do not like the London Dungeon. Or kids. I have no need for family, lovers or friends. Not only is this the securest way of finding a continuing contentment, it is also the simplest way to have a quiet life, which is all I want. I am sure you understand what I am saying because I have insinuated much of this before. Now I put it in black and white so that you will clearly see that this is nothing personal. I am also finishing with my current boyfriend today. Life is as complicated as we desire it to be. I want it simple.
Yours sincerely,
Tanya

It is lunchtime when I print this letter. I put it in an envelope. As soon as I am out of the office I buy a book of four first-class stamps. I use the first on this letter. I hold the envelope in the pillar-box hole. Someone else wants to post a letter – this compels me to drop mine. I immediately look to see when the box is next emptied, just in case I need to beg the postman to hand me the letter back. Whatever time it says I immediately forget. Though it was a nasty letter to write I had no choice. Goodbye, Alison. I wish I could dispose of Mrs Davies so easily.

I avoid bookshops and end up buying myself a bottle of rum. I haven't had rum for years. Now that I am an independent woman living in London I am reluctant to mix it with blackcurrant juice – that seems too provincial.

I treat myself to a meal in a restaurant but when the meal arrives I find I am not hungry. I eat it anyway because I hate waste. I appear to be the only one in the restaurant eating alone. All the other diners are either couples or in large groups. Everyone is enjoying their meals; all have healthy appetites and are not short of subjects to talk about. I have eaten alone in restaurants before, but always accompanied by a book. Without a book it is a depressing, even humiliating experience.

Back at Ill Will I start the afternoon by ploughing into proper work, just for the show of it, just in case I am challenged by Allan. Within two hours I complete enough to demonstrate I have finished an average day's work. I face up to beginning the resignation letter but a disturbance breaks out, which distracts me. It is a one-woman commotion: Mary is pestering people, soliciting congratulations, shaking her head in disbelief, smiling and repeatedly thanking Allan.

'What's going on?' I ask. Oddly, Mary smiles less when I become involved. She sits on the edge of my desk. Although this will shortly not be my desk because I will be leaving, I resent her cellulite-blemished cheeks on it now.

'I've been promoted,' she tells me.

'Mary is going to be my assistant, Tanya,' Allan says. 'She has been here the longest, after all.'

'Oh, is that all?' I say. I roll my eyes to Keith and Jo, to show them how little I care. 'I told you, anyway, Allan – I wouldn't want the job.'

The smug smile drops from Mary's face. She crosses over to Allan. Whatever she is saying to him she is failing to hide her agitation. He must have told her she had won the promotion on merit or seniority rather than on the more credible criterion of her having been the only person who wanted the job. Having upset Mary, my work here is done: I write my resignation letter. I halt its printing when Jo takes a telephone call for me. I would not want to risk the letter being read before it is officially delivered. Typical of Jo's telephone manner, she did not ask who was making the call. As soon as I hear Gary's voice I prepare to stand my ground.

'Tanya, I'm sorry but . . . Mum died last night.'

My reaction is silence. I know this is not suitable.

'Tanya?'

At this moment all I can think is, armed with the news of my mum's death, I will be able to leave work early. However, I can hardly come off the phone and simply tell Allan my mother is dead – out of the blue. He will wonder why I didn't react accordingly during the call. I have to make appropriate whelps of horror.

'Tanya? Hello?' Gary says. 'I know it's a shock, but . . . '

'Dead?' I say, loudly enough. If Gary challenges me I will pretend my lack of emotion is disbelief, or shock. The word has the desired effect. Everyone in the office is listening. I see them exchange anxious looks – all very befitting.

'The funeral is on Monday,' Gary says.

Monday. My thoughts are: I need not have written that letter to Alison as I now have the perfect excuse not to go to the London Dungeon. I will be in mourning.

'I'm staying with Mick till then, so . . . Of course I won't be coming to see you on Saturday now. Not much point.'

This just gets better and better!

'The funeral is on Monday. At home . . . Tanya?'

'Sorry, I'm just . . .'

'It's OK, I know. It's a shock. She took some pills. It was just a simple, stupid accident. She hadn't been sleeping and –'

'Sleeping pills?' I interrupt Gary with this because I need these words to be said for the benefit of the office.

'I think Mick feels a little guilty because he called out the doctor who prescribed the pills, and then . . . You are coming to the funeral, aren't you, Tanya?'

By now Allan is so concerned he stands over me. The worst possible thing happens: I giggle. Allan smiles, comforted by this, believing I am all right in spite of the alarming words. I masterfully turn my solitary giggle into a rapid succession of giggles, in a manic, deranged way.

'Yes,' I tell Gary and hang up on him so he will not question my giggling. I stand and put my coat on. Allan asks for an explanation. I mumble my reply, knowing I have to take my departure as quickly as possible before the giggles return. I tear up my half-printed resignation letter, then delete its file. I shut down my computer and exit. Jo runs after me. I pretend I do not hear her.

TWELVE

I guess I came home by the usual route, yet I cannot remember the journey. When I reach my building, though it is two hours earlier than usual, nothing seems out of the ordinary.

Sickness prevents me from running upstairs. I am hoping there have been no new messages left on my answerphone. I am relieved to see the light on steady. I play Mum's message left last night.

'Tanya – are you there? I'm tired. You should phone me. You should talk to me. Er . . . I want . . . Never mind . . .'

There is a silence, as if she is thinking of something to add, then she hangs up. I take the tape out of the machine. I will buy a replacement when I remember to.

I spend the remainder of the afternoon rearranging my books. Though this is not a frequent preoccupation it is still something I do regularly. I once attempted to put them in alphabetical order, by author, but had to abandon this due to the difficulty caused when a new book had to be inserted into a long row. Grouping them into genres proved too complicated, so this time I am settling for simply putting the books into three simple categories: those books I will never read again and which I might eventually rid myself of; those books I like, yet have no immediate plans to read again; and finally, those books I certainly hope to read again. Sorting through this last selection I am sorely tempted to reread one of these now and abandon my vow of first finishing *The Counterfeit Confetti*. I resist. Due to the large number of books I own – maybe it's as many as three thousand now – the afternoon is fully over and I can at least feel as if I have accomplished something with the day. I will read all of *The Counterfeit Confetti*. I pick it up. I open the book on the last page, then change my mind. Instead I find the beginning of the last chapter and start from there. If I am to discover how my life turns out, I should at least have the full context.

Carl moved into the empty flat adjacent to Tanya's, anticipating their relationship could now only progress. Tanya had analysed the possibility of any potential problems, concluding all the risks were worthwhile. In many ways the move seemed the perfect compromise. It was living alone, yet with her boyfriend being so close as to be practically living with her. The best of both worlds, they agreed.

And for a while all went well. They did their shopping together, though with separate trolleys. This was fun. Tanya enjoyed criticising his choices and in turn defending her own. They both made an effort to spend their free time together. To her surprise, Tanya did not consider this to be an effort. Through the first weeks their sex life became exhaustive. No opportunity was missed, no spare moment occupied with anything other than sex. Weakened by all this physical intimacy, they succumb to the delusion of love – each had no one else. Like all such fierce passions, however, it could only fade. Neither of them fought against the relaxed schedule, both were old and wise enough to have anticipated it. Those evenings when they did not see each other increased; and when they did meet it was from a belief of obligation, to reconfirm their relationship.

There follows a slow descent into the inevitable. According to the book, I spend more time sketching and Carl becomes increasingly fond of reading, which – laughably – I resent as it means he spends less time with me. I also resent him for not earning as much as me. In fact the book becomes so absurd I am tempted to abandon it. In spite of everything else I have read, this last chapter nearly convinces me I have been wrong all along; *The Counterfeit Confetti* cannot be about me, I am not like this. I read more. I am angry with him when he forgets my thirtieth birthday . . .

Although many of her other childhood illusions had been happily shattered, the one that persevered in her subconscious was that thirty was the age when people were all either married or doomed never to marry. At thirty there was no turning back, nor looking ahead. Who you were at thirty was who you were likely to remain. To have the option of change closed off – even if only symbolically – was potentially depressing. Though she had no desire to discuss these worries with anyone, nevertheless she would have liked for Carl to have been instinctively sympathetic, to have showered her with affection, reassuring her how young and attractive she remained.

As I read this I understand I have been deceiving myself. Thirty is daunting, and I am not looking forward to this being added to how I am described. So then I start thinking ... I do, genuinely, dislike myself for wishing Carl had a better job. And if these things are true might it not also be true that if Carl moves next door – which is something I have only casually thought about – then the day might arrive where we see each other only because we believe the relationship obliges us to? Christ, how pathetic.

She knew enough about her previous boyfriends to have always held the suspicion she might become bored with even this new one, the best for so long; yet she had put aside those doubts trusting Carl had potential. She was soon disillusioned. He was not going to develop into the perfect partner for her. He had long since finished his developing; Carl as he was now was the complete picture. Unlike her other boyfriends, however, she was stuck with this one: his front door was three yards from hers. Although she was happy to have him near for sex, their sex lives had degenerated into routine and predictability. Any romance he might once have demonstrated was now dormant. Tanya, again, had not imagined this lapse could bother her. They were not even friends, they were civil neighbours.

After this our relationship degenerates rapidly. Then ends.

'Carl, I'm rude to you whenever you call,' she began when she saw him that night. 'I make ridiculous excuses to get out of being with you. I quite blatantly do everything in my power to avoid you. Yet you don't realise why. Do you? I don't want to see you any more. What I mean is, it's over. You and I are no longer going out with each other.'

The next day Tanya phoned an estate agent.

Within a year of Carl taking the adjacent flat Tanya moved out of the building. He would get over her, of that there could be no doubt. Whether he would find love again was not so certain. Carl was not stupid, and love belongs to the young or stupid.

Her life continued and resolved itself in much the way she had hoped. She bought a home on the coast in a small town with two good restaurants, an excellent independent cinema and a plethora of second-hand bookshops. The shore and scenic countryside were all within walking distance. She kept tropical fish as a hobby, then later bought a dog to walk and even grew fond of the thing. She called the dog Cooper, after the boxer. She continued illustrating children's books and even took up painting again, with plenty of suitable landscapes in the near vicinity. She painted Cooper regularly, too. And of course she read. There was no boredom in her life. After the first year of this life the absence of sex became of no consequence to her – she did not miss it.

Though she was relatively young when this life began and was content to believe she could live this way until she died, she had some concerns whether one day, when she was much older, she might look back and regret having cut off so many opportunities, which were open to her only at that young age, but she satisfied herself that such doubts could have no substance. She had seen all she wished to see of other people and experienced all she wished of excitement and passion.

And if she genuinely missed these things, she could always read about them.

If meant as a novel, this ending is a weak climax. If it is meant as a warning to me, then it is unnecessary: it only confirms my beliefs about how my life would turn out under those circumstances. Where it fails is that there is no possibility of Carl moving into the vacant flat opposite mine, not a chance of it. The ultimate ending, the home on the coast, sounds all well and good, but once again I cannot see how this could realistically happen. So here is my great relief:

The Counterfeit Confetti cannot be about my life or my future, its last chapter has proved this. Once I read this, fear changes to relief – like being half asleep and seeing a sinister silhouette standing over my bed, yet when the lights are switched on the shape reveals itself to be nothing more than an arrangement of clothes slung over a chair. Reading *The Counterfeit Confetti* – up until I had leapt to the last chapter – had made me afraid of something, which I understand now was only a deception.

In an act of impetuosity that is so foolish and unexpected I condemn myself even whilst I am doing it – I phone the DVLA. I have no idea how many people work for the DVLA and I doubt whether the switchboard operator has ready access to all their names anyway, so I am not hopeful of progressing further than an irritated 'Sorry, I'll need a department or extension number'. It's nearly six, so he'll have gone home anyway. I dial the number. The DVLA operator asks which department I want.

Before I even have a chance to touch upon my dead, mutual friend story, she has put me through. There is a clicking sound, the briefest of pauses, then –

'Hello. Martin Heaton speaking.'

– Martin. It's his voice. A ghost. Alive. Unchanged. My past: Martin. I dialled the numbers, told the switchboard operator I wanted to speak to Martin Heaton – somewhere in this process it should have occurred to me he might answer and I would be expected to reply. I have nothing to say to him! If I had been an irate customer wanting to make a complaint I would have been put on hold for ages, put through to numerous wrong departments, fobbed off on to underlings. The thousands of times I have had sense enough to reject my impulse to track him down, then I fail as stupidly as this.

'Hell-o?' he sings.

'Hello, Martin. This is Tanya.'

'Tanya who?'

My God, the bastard has forgotten me. I've drifted through the last nine years unable to dispel him from my thoughts, unable to persevere with any other relationships because I couldn't kill off the myth of him – and he doesn't even have the decency to be similarly obsessed. He chooses to insult me by being rational.

'Not . . . This isn't Tanya Stephens. Is it?' My prolonged silence has forced him to take this stab in the dark. I remember how I once phoned Martin after midnight when he still lived at home. His irate father answered and, afraid, I hung up without speaking. Forty minutes later I was woken by gravel hitting my window. Martin knew the phone call was from me and had come over to see what I wanted. I confessed I wanted nothing urgent. I went down and let him into the kitchen. We talked and kissed, then he left.

Another reckless impulse of stupidity makes me consider replying, 'I'm not called Tanya *Stephens* any more' – then giving another surname, as if I am married.

'Well, actually – it is. Yes.'

'Tanya! Hello! What a surprise! I don't believe this! I especially like the way you said "This is Tanya", as if it was only Thursday when I last spoke to you!'

'I suppose this is a bit out of the blue.'

'Just a little! It's been ten years, hasn't it? Something like that.'

To correct him and tell him the exact number of years, months and days would sound obsessive. I'm not so unbalanced – I do not know the exact figure by heart, but I do have the dates written down.

'Something like that. So I thought I'd ring and see how you were. Are.'

'I'm fine. You?'

'Fine.'

Bit of a pause here.

'Everything's going well for you?' he asks because he is too polite to ask what the hell have I rung for if I have nothing to say. I feel like an actor who has starred, from day one, in the West End's longest-running play; then one night, when the playwright is in the audience, I forget my lines.

'Great,' I reply. 'And you?'

'Great.'

So far so dull. It gets worse.

'How did you know where I was working?'

To tell him 'I read it in a novel' is not a viable option. He had always worked for the DVLA and I had heard second-hand, half-baked rumours of Swansea. But this is not convincing enough. So I invent a spontaneous story about bumping into an old acquaintance – whom I call Chris – who explained about Wales, wife, DVLA. There is no Chris but I tell Martin such an elaborate story he begins to believe Chris exists and he has simply forgotten him. The knack to telling a convincing lie is detail and consistency. Because consistency is not a problem here – I will never speak to Martin again – detail is my only concern. I describe how Chris looks now, how much he has changed: fictional Chris is married again after having been divorced and has two children from his previous marriage. His new wife is seven years his senior and a policewoman.

'Are you married?' Martin asks me. The only satisfactory answer to this question, asked by an ex-lover who is now happily married, is a resounding yes. Everything else sounds like failure, like a life lived in mourning for them. It is only a failure for women. Men saying it sound like successes; they have never been trapped, no woman has yet proved themselves good enough, their careers have been too important. As a woman I could have spent the last decade of my life first travelling to Mars, then home to become Prime Minister, yet if I have remained single it's a life unfulfilled.

In spite of the implication, at first I dare to confess the truth and say, 'No,' before I then chicken out by adding, 'Not any more.'

'Divorced?'

'Uh-huh.' A lie made up off the cuff really tests the imagination. I have used most of mine inventing Chris's life, and now I have to invent an ex-husband. Not only him, but the circumstances behind the divorce and the consequences for my life afterwards. I tell Martin how it was my husband – James – who instigated the divorce; he caught me with another man. I can't explain it, society ought not to work like this, but having committed adultery sounds hipper, cooler than any other reason for being divorced. I attempt to sound sad yet resolute. I do not know why I called him James. I hate that name. Jimmy, I should have said. He could be a lower-league professional football player.

Martin then tells me, with no shame, about his own marriage, his kids, his life with them in Wales. There is no regret or embarrassment.

Many times have I imagined the reunion conversation with Martin. In no version did it proceed like this. He is too relaxed about hearing from me, too content about his life without me, then far too casual about dismissing me.

'The office is closing,' he tells me. 'Phone again though. It's been lovely to hear from you.'

'My mum died yesterday.'

The second I say it I no longer want to speak to him; I am embarrassed at having phoned him and ashamed of having told him about Mum. He hasn't seen her in nearly a decade – why should he care?

'Oh – Tanya! God, I'm so sorry.'

'Not to worry,' I answer. 'Anyway, it was nice to hear from . . . To speak to you, too. See ya, Martin.'

I hang up. A phone call that should have been monumental was worthless, trivial. It wasn't sad or pathetic or wretched; yet now I really think about it, in every version I've ever imagined of this conversation, no matter if they've been loving or argumentative, sexy or vindictive, in every version it was Martin phoning me and not the other way around.

His voice has shocked me out of my coma. I know now – for the first time as an undisputed certainty – Martin has gone from my life. Finally. A reconciliation was never likely to happen – yet such logic was never good enough to wake me, sober me. Now I truly am without him. The sadness is only sensible now. He's gone. Married. He lives in Wales. I am genuinely pleased he has found happiness. Though I have now started to behave as if *The Counterfeit Confetti* is unquestionably about me, I can think of no other way to approach this.

I look at myself in the full-length mirror I have in my bedroom. I stand closer to the mirror. At either side of my chin, my cheeks are fractionally starting to swell, ready to slouch. This is where one day the baggy jowls will appear. I have fine semicircles of lines under my eyes. If I push my chin out and smile this makes the jaw firm and young again – but the lines around the eyes then become worse. My skin is no longer unblemished: the colouring is less consistent these days; the pores appear wider; my skin now looks less like clothing and more like insulation; one day it will look like lagging. Never before have I so clearly noticed these precursors to old age.

I dig out an old photograph from when I was at college. It was taken at a student union party I went to with Martin, even though he isn't in the photograph. I don't own one of him. I compare how I look in the photograph to how I look now, to more accurately judge how I have aged. In spite of my self-pity I am not doing too badly, really. The greatest alteration is in size; as people become older their faces and bodies develop a robustness, a thick-set solid construction, which isn't fat or muscle, but bones and hostility.

I replay a thousand times the telephone conversation I have just had with Martin – it changes every time. In my memory I am granted the freedom to be wiser. My chant for a decade has been, 'I need to do something to get him out of my mind' – then I phone him. If there was a Nobel Prize given for outstanding contributions to the world of idiocy I'd begin preparing my acceptance speech right now.

THIRTEEN

I phone Carl. He doesn't answer. I guess he has a social life I
know nothing about. He has friends and interests that don't
involve me. I dial Richard's number. I dial it maliciously; if he
answers quickly, then he is doomed. He is history. He
answers on the second ring. I would have given up on the
fourth.

'Not at work?' I ask.

'I've been home an hour. I was just going out,' Richard
says, hastily adding: 'Not that I don't want to speak to you!
I'm only saying that I'm glad you caught me.'

'I'd like to see you.'

Before I make phone calls I should rehearse everything I
intend to say and how I intend to say it. I *should* have said, 'I
think we need to talk,' and in a serious tone. However, such
severity would be redundant: he already believes we have
broken up. I have now given him hope of a reprieve.

'Great! We'll go out tonight, if you fancy it. I can cancel
my other plans.'

'No, Richard. I mean, I'd like to see you . . . I want to see
you because we need to talk.'

'Talk?'

'I'll come over now, Richard. It shouldn't take long.'

'Shall I come and pick you up?'

'No.' If the journey has already begun when I tell him we
are through, he could easily abandon me in the middle of
nowhere. Or if we have already arrived at his house when I
tell him, he might insist on driving me back home afterwards,
in which case we will have to fill in the silence of that journey
with polite promises we have no intentions of keeping:
staying in touch, friendship. I need to be at his home so I can
make an exit.

Out of sheer spite – I admit this – I put on make-up, fix my hair, put on that white V-neck T-shirt, which shows off my neck and breasts. I believe in looking good when I'm breaking up with a boyfriend; that way they are left with a positive image of what they will always be missing.

I scout around my flat and collate the accumulated rubbish Richard has left here. I put it all in a carrier bag. I catch the bus to Richard's home. As I am waiting for the bus it occurs to me *The Counterfeit Confetti* is not only wrong about my future but also about the present. It clearly said I *dreaded the confrontation* with Richard; yet this is not true: I dread nothing. I am not even nervous. It also said *without Richard she was happier than she had been for a considerable time.* I begin to rehearse the conversation I will have with him. I ask him why he even wants to go out with me – for this I cannot imagine his answer.

The bus stops almost directly opposite his house. I hesitate, cross the road and wait for a while at the opposite bus stop, perhaps thinking I might return home, then phone him to assure him all is well. I again leave it to chance. If a bus comes in the next few minutes I will board and go home. A bus comes. I take the bit between my teeth and do not get on the bus. I'm nervous, so that damned book is right: I *am* dreading the confrontation.

Richard is good looking. Let's be frank – looks count for a lot. We forgive the good-looking a great deal more than we forgive ugly people. And the sex is good. Again, let's be honest – sex counts for a great deal. I doubt, if I'm honest, I could sustain a relationship even with my perfect life's match if he was inadequate in bed. Though I've rarely met many men who are irretrievably useless. Most can be improved with the appropriate coaching. Given clear and specific instructions, most men – after they overcome their initial alarm – will come up to scratch. Only in extreme cases are actual physical speed traps needed. However, there's nothing better than a born natural. Though I cannot know if Richard was always a naturally good lover I do know he's damned good now. My belief is his good looks have sanctioned a long and extensive apprenticeship. Do I now seriously want to dismiss a lover who holds his City and Guilds in the trade?

The third reason for my hesitation over whether I want to

finish with him: I'm getting older. Even though I despise them, there is a basic authenticity in all those books and sitcoms and romcoms with the premise that good single men are hard to come by. I've never been a victim of this shortage because I've never judged men as being 'good' by the standard of being a potential husband. The trick is to view each new man simply as a temporary phenomenon as this way most are OK. When I am buying a car I want an attractive range of features plus a comprehensive warranty; if I am getting a taxi all I care about is basic roadworthiness.

It's only when I am back at the bus stop to return home that I remember Carl.

I ring Richard's doorbell. He keeps me waiting, no doubt employing a delaying tactic for a purpose I cannot imagine.

'Come in,' he says when he answers. He does not smile and tries to sound casual. He is smoking; this is a relapse after a two-month struggle. When I answer with a straight, dead no, however, he makes an effort not to flinch. He steps out of the house, I back away. I hand him the carrier bag containing his possessions.

'Richard – I don't want to see you any more.'

He shrugs his shoulders. Clearly he has thoroughly rehearsed the act of casualness and no diversion from his planned script can shake him from his adopted character. He says nothing. I have to choose whether to leave now, which would be impressive, or to wait – to stare him out and see who will speak first. The competition is soon won. Richard breaks; his shoulders slouch and his eyebrows droop into pathos.

'You said as much on the phone on Saturday. What are you here for then?'

'I came over because I thought you deserved to be told face to face.'

'All right . . . Tanya, I don't want us to break up,' he says.

'Sorry.'

'Tanya, I don't want us to break up,' he repeats with the exact same intonation as before. It's a curious mixture of arrogance and weakness – as if simply saying it again will reverse the fact of us ending. This is ridiculous; it's as if he's on the *Titanic* and yelling at the iceberg to move.

'Sorry,' I repeat, and I also use the same intonation as before. I wonder if he will despise me for making this into a joke. He doesn't even notice. He steps back into his house.

'I didn't –'

He stops to let someone exit from the building. He smiles and exchanges a nod of recognition, then waits until they are out of earshot before continuing.

'I didn't see this coming. Up till the other day I thought everything was fine.'

'It wasn't.'

'Has something happened?'

'No.'

'Have I said something wrong?'

'No.'

'Have you met someone else?'

'No!' This is the first no I say with indignation because it is the first no that is a lie.

'Why then?' Having now fully abandoned the pretence of casualness, Richard sounds weak and pathetic in a way I would never have expected from him. *The Counterfeit Confetti* is bang on the money here – I am relishing this.

'You must have realised it was going to end sooner or later, Richard.'

'No. Why should I have?'

'We're not compatible.'

'We're very compatible.'

'In what way? Name one thing.'

'S—'

'Not sex. Besides sex.'

After a considerable pause: 'Loads of things.'

'*One* thing, Richard.'

'The pictures! We both love going to the cinema.'

'Our tastes in films are diametrically opposed. And besides, something as trivial as that is no basis for a long-term relationship.'

'Who's talking about a long-term relationship? I just want to keep going out with you. I don't want us to break up.'

'We're breaking up. Why do you even like me? I'm bad-tempered and rude. Do you go out with me just because I look like an ex-girlfriend of yours?'

He allows a pause before he submits to honesty:

'To begin with I wanted to be with you because you do look like her a bit – yes. I was mad on her – this is a long time ago, so I can't explain why I still think about her . . . Now, though, I want to keep going out with you because you don't ask anything from me. You never go on about ex-boyfriends, you never pester me to see you. You're easygoing and funny and . . . We don't make plans, we never talk about the future, we never discuss our feelings for each other. I thought this was all wonderful until now. Do you remember a while ago I told you how I'd met up with an ex-girlfriend and arranged to go for a drink with her, just as friends? That was a lie. I wanted to see if you'd try to stop me. When you didn't I was just happy that you weren't the jealous type. Now I guess I understand why you've never tried to discuss feelings. You don't have any.'

Somewhere inside, I'm an insanely jealous bitch. Before becoming involved with me, Martin had been going out with another girl for several months. Though this was whilst he was still at college, she was not a student. She worked in a local travel agency. When I pressed Martin on why he had finished with her he admitted the only reason he had gone out with her for any length of time was that she had taken him up to Edinburgh during the Festival – courtesy of the company she worked for – and so he felt some obligation towards her. He still dumped her sooner than he had anticipated, however. He could tolerate her no longer; she was too desperate, too demanding of his attention. I saw evidence of this when she continued to look for excuses to see him, even after he had started going out with me. She kept appearing at places she anticipated he would be, not caring whether I was also there. Martin often broke away from me to say hello, even though it was patently obvious he was genuinely bored with her and was always quickly dismissive. I never even slightly doubted him; I already knew enough to trust him completely.

I went to where she worked. I sat in front of her console. I told her if she ever looked for Martin again I would knock her out. I asked her if she took my threat seriously, because if she didn't I was prepared to do it right there and then in front of her colleagues. She believed me and *I* believed me. The only fight I have had in my entire life was with Nicola Robinson when we were both eleven; I remember a lot of screaming, some slaps any robust fly could have shrugged off, then a twenty-minute stalemate clutch of each other's hair.

I left. I sulked with Martin for a few days, retaining enough sense to never explain the cause.

'We can go to bed one more time, if you want,' I tell Richard. I hadn't planned on saying this; because he looks so pathetic, I fancy Richard less than I ever have before. If he has any self-respect he'll say no. But he's a man.

When we are in bed I refuse to let him kiss me because his breath smells of cigarettes.

I ask, 'Why have you started smoking again?'

'Why not?'

Believing astounding sex might grant him a reprieve, Richard's performance is selfless and athletic. The trouble is, he tries too hard. He is down on me for so long I even become a little bored. I look down and see him looking up. His eyebrows are moving in motion with his jaw. It's horrible. I want to stop him. I will tell him about Mum . . .

'Use your jaw less – more tongue,' I say instead.

'What?' he says. Then he coughs and splutters, nearly choking on a half-swallowed hair. I pull him up so he is facing me. He enters me.

'When you come, shout "Gail".'

'What? Why?'

'It's who you want to be with.'

'It isn't. I want to be with you.'

'Say it or get off me now.'

I stop him saying another word. He carries on; he comes and shouts her name. I jump out of bed and dress as fast as possible.

'It's over, Richard.' I say this at the door to the house. He has followed me downstairs, having quickly put on his jeans and a T-shirt.

'I don't want to be with Gail. She's married now. Don't go, Tanya, please!' I hear him shout behind me. I have genuine disgust for him, for the use of the word 'please'. I would have been happier to have dumped and walked away from a boyfriend who hadn't sounded so destroyed.

'Bye-bye,' I add, maliciously.

I walk to the next stop to deter Richard from following. Once on the bus I am immediately bored. I have no friends. No family. I have finished with Richard and I have no intentions of pursuing a pointless relationship with a road sweeper, which I know ends in unhappiness.

I go to Carl's flat, not sure if he will now be home. He is. He is surprised to see me, of course. Perhaps he does not remember telling me his address. I do not allow him the chance to ask me in.

'I can't see you any more.'

'Oh?'

'I don't want to see you any more.'

'Oh.'

'For God's sake, is that all you have to say?'

'Would anything I say make you change your mind?'

I do not respond to this. I just go. When someone is dumped it is customary for them to ask for an explanation, or at least to attempt to persuade the dumper to change their mind – it's only common decency. Finishing with Carl was not fun. It was frustrating. Nevertheless it has made me absolutely confident it was the right thing to do.

I am reluctant to return to my flat. I want to go to the cinema. A reconciliation with Richard, simply for a visit to the pictures, is not a serious consideration. Richard is gone for good, and I am relieved. I could phone Alison . . . She won't receive my letter until tomorrow . . . But, no.

Of course I do have a friend. I have Caroline. I have been reluctant to phone her only because she is the sole person with whom I might be inclined to talk about Mum. I want to discuss her death with no one, I will have to deal with it in my own way. Though I don't necessarily go along with that British notion of the stiff upper lip, I do believe a suppressed emotion is an emotion that dies. An emotion that is flaunted flourishes.

Immediately I am home I phone Caroline, having thought up the pretext of telling her I have already quit Ill Will and can start work for her as soon as she wishes. The problem is, her phone is engaged. I return ten minutes later and it is still engaged. I leave it for half an hour, then it is only her answerphone.

Being alone means never having the trouble that comes with other people, yet on the other hand it means having to deal with being alone even on those rare occasions when having someone would be handy.

London is for going out. I go out. I will have a walk around the West End. Millions of tourists every year find some thrill in this, so maybe I have been missing something.

First, I find a hairdresser's that is still open. I state that I fancy a change – something bold. Afterwards, when I am outside, I hunt down a reflective shop window to hastily repair the worst of the damage.

I walk on. Thinking. Gate-crashing thoughts crowd my head in spite of my protests for them to leave. *Dad. Mum. Martin. Carl.* For a moment these thoughts become so intense they take up all my brain capacity; I stop walking. I am stood in the middle of the pavement, breaking the flow of people.

I rerun my break-up conversation with Carl and curse myself for not wording it differently, then curse myself for not persevering with the conversation until he made a plea for me to change my mind.

I rerun the conversation I had with Gary on the phone.

I rerun the day I went to confront Mum and remember how I left her house, having taken such great joy in hurting her.

I need alcohol – this is the answer.

In some West End side-street bar I sit and order a drink. Rum and black. Some young upstart fancies his chances and stands next to me. I am guessing he is in his late teens or early twenties, but immature: far too clothes conscious, too careful with his appearance and far too sure of himself.

'Are you waiting for someone?'

'Yes.'

'Can I sit with you whilst you're waiting?'

I sigh deeply to demonstrate my annoyance.

'How do you know it's not a boyfriend I'm waiting for? Someone who'll beat the shit out of you?'

He grins broadly, arrogantly; then sits anyway, pulling a chair next to mine so the arms are touching.

'I'll take my chances. Besides, I can take care of myself.'

'So can I.'

This makes him laugh.

'OK. Fair enough. We're only talking, aren't we?'

I sit back in my chair to show him I am confident and I am not intimidated. I look at him directly.

'What can we talk about? What do you think we might have to say to each other?'

'You can tell me your name.'

'Jo,' I say without hesitation, even though I had not been preparing the lie.

'I'm Chris. What's Jo short for – Josephine?'

'Yes.' Jo at work is actually called Jody. I refuse to be named Jody even to someone I have never seen before and will never see again.

'OK. Nice name. So what are you doing here? Let's take it as read that you're not waiting for someone.'

'I'm *not* here wanting to get picked up.'

'I can tell.'

'How?' Though I am careful not to show it on my face I am angry at myself for asking this. I want him to know I am not interested, not even in an innocent conversation.

'Because – and I don't want to sound cocky – but I'm good looking, I get more than my fair share. But you're still being a little snotty with me. That shows you're not wanting to meet anyone. I can also tell because you haven't looked at anyone. Before I came over to talk to you, you just kept looking down into your drink.'

'I was thinking.'

'What about?'

'Alcohol . . . I came out for a walk; the West End seemed the safest place to be. But I forgot how boring it is if you're not a tourist. So I came in here for a drink. After this I'm going home.'

'I won't ask you where you live, that'll sound too creepy. But you can come home with me, if you like.'

'Sorry? Just exactly why would I want to come home with you?'

'For whatever reason you want. I'd prefer it to be sex; but we can get something to eat, get some drinks. I have some dope, if you like that.'

Though I carefully write the outrage on my face I avoid all the obvious verbal reactions to his proposition. I do not holler 'I hardly know you!' or 'You could be a serial killer for all I know!' simply because they are too clichéd. I admire his directness, his cheek; yet like all women I've had a lifetime of indoctrination not to take up every offer that tempts. I finish my drink. At the very end of my life I might look back on this and remember it as my last ever chance of having sex with someone as young as him. Perhaps if I had not so recently had sex I might even accept his offer. The hard fact is I am not interested in anyone, least of all annoying strangers.

'No thanks. I'm going home,' I tell him.

'That's a shame.'

'You'll get over it. If you're as irresistible to women as you think you are – you'll get someone else. I admit it, you are good looking. You have a disarming charm.'

'You're not tempted?'

'I didn't say I wasn't tempted. I was very careful with what I said. I just said, "No, thanks".'

I have finished my drink; I should now be indignantly walking away.

'And I was very careful what I said,' he answers. 'I said I was good looking and that I get more than my fair share. I didn't say I always get the ones I want.'

'Why do you want me?' I ask.

'The smartest answer to that would be a lie. The truth is, the real truth . . . I've never had an older woman. You're older but still lovely.'

Every instinct I have, my whole life's experiences of men in the pursuit of sex, tell me he is certainly lying, that every word and sentiment is carefully constructed to seduce me into bed. And, more importantly, I do not want to be in bed, not with him or anyone. The fact that I get some perverse kick out of being considered – for the first time in my life – as an 'older woman' is, however, keeping me interested enough to stay. I want to see how this works for me – I may enjoy it.

'So have I ruined any hope of you coming home with me?'

'What do you think of my hair?'

'I have no choice but to say I like it. I can see cuts of hair on your neck, so you've just come from a hairdresser's, right?'

He continues to persuade me to go home with him. The more he speaks the more his chance diminishes – I have to shut him up before he completely talks me out of sex. I tell him to write his address down and give it to the barman, explaining this by saying we have been waiting for a friend and so if someone comes in looking for Chris, then this is his address. This is my way of guaranteeing Chris will not now dare murder me. The barman is a witness. We take a taxi and I take care to remember the address Chris had written down to make sure it tallies with the actual address.

He begins by offering me a drink. I decline, reminding him of the reason we are here.

Due to his confidence and obvious experience, I had expected him to be far better at sex than he is. The poor sex is partially my fault: my participation is passive. The foreplay is perfunctory, his nails are too sharp. When he is on me he doesn't support his weight well. As he jerks up and down his head bangs sideways into mine; then as he finishes he shoots his arm out forward. I yell because he has caught his wristwatch in my hair. He then removes the condom, ties a knot in it to prevent spillage, lobs it towards a bin and cheers when it hits the target.

I walk home wishing I had extra legs so I could walk faster and still have the spare capacity to kick myself to death. It's dark, chilly, lonely. London is for staying in.

Because I have taken the tape out there are no answer-phone messages. The relief of this persuades me to unplug the phone completely. I drink a few glasses from the bottle of rum I bought today. I look through those books I have selected to read again. I cannot decide between Allan Massie's *Augustus* or Charlotte Bronte's *Villette*. I settle on *Augustus* because in this melancholic, sentimental, self-pitying illness I am suffering from, there can be nothing about the corrupt, depraved Roman emperor that I can relate to myself or my life. I want escape not empathy.

The alarm goes at seven-thirty because last night I forgot to turn it off. Allan won't expect me at work for the rest of the week – I am grieving. I could sleep in today if I wished, but I force myself out of bed. I need a bath. I take the sheets off the bed, too; I will do a wash later. Before my bath I have breakfast whilst watching TV. One programme blends into another and I lie on the couch flicking through the channels, all through the morning.

Of the one thousand eclectic thoughts I have, there are only two that make sense to have had. The first is a memory of my mother coming to fetch Gary and me from the kitchen, when we were still kids living at home, to sneak into the living room to spy on Dad. He was listening to The Who's 'Barbara O'Reilly' with him playing the role – full on – of Keith Moon doing his most exuberant drumming. Dad stopped 'drumming' only when he was alerted by his family's hysteria.

The other relevant memory is of my only trip to London before I came to live here. Dad wanted to come down to see some exhibition; he chose to make the trip a family event. Mother persuaded him to go to the exhibition alone and took Gary and me on a tour of the sights. Tower Bridge, Houses of Parliament, Trafalgar Square, Piccadilly Circus, the Tower of London. That day was the first time I ate pizza – I saw London as exotic and thrilling. I was only nine, wondering why all adults didn't choose to live here. Except, I wondered, if they lived here how would they do any work with all this excitement going on around them?

I have another thought – it doesn't relate to my mother but it's interesting because of all the possible connotations, it is the first time I have explored this one: how might my life have worked out if, after splitting up with Martin, I had not left my home town and if Martin had stayed there too? Our home town is of the size where within a year you are guaranteed to have seen all its residents. So I would have bumped into Martin. He would have been polite, he would have asked how I had been keeping. The conversation, after this . . . I have no reasonable idea how it might have developed. I would have had to answer Martin; I could have been polite, or flirty. Or honest. Or else I might have perpetuated the lie that I did not want him back. No matter how miserable I was after losing him, even though I might have been aware that here was my only real chance to win him back – no matter. I might still have remained defiantly stupid.

In the afternoon I put the sheets back on the bed after finally realising I am not going to do the washing today. I eventually run a bath. I am in for over an hour, until the water becomes so cold it causes discomfort when I move.

I do not continue with *Augustus* but instead watch TV all evening. Its noise prevents me thinking.

Though I did switch off my alarm, I instinctively wake at seven-thirty. This is a measure of how much Ill Will is in my system.

The remote control is in my hand all day, except at teatime when I have to wipe it free of sweat. I cannot recall one moment from all the TV programmes I have watched for the last two days. My mind has hopped through all channels, never staying on one memory long enough for it to make sense.

I take a bath. Was it just yesterday when I had my marathon bath? I have no idea. I have had the phone unplugged, I haven't answered the door, I've had the curtains drawn, I've eaten rarely and I've watched so much crap on TV my mind is a mush. I read the first sentence only from a whole, random selection of books, becoming immediately bored each time. I think I need to sleep; my eyes ache and my body is as numb as if I have been in a fight. Yet all the time – in my head – there is so much junk whirling around I anticipate sleep is not a possibility.

I am remembering random incidents from my life, ridiculous, trivial things, which could have no relevance or significance no matter how much dream-study and psychology they were subjected to. I remember being at a fair with my parents and being put on a ride that made me sick, and the sick flying out and hitting people standing around the edge of the ride. I remember the headmaster at my middle school hitting a boy in our class, hitting him across the head and knocking his glasses to an angle; I remember an eighteenth birthday party I went to in a nightclub and kissing three different men in one night – I can even exactly remember the dress I was wearing. I remember the father of a school friend I had – I forget her – who used to grab my arm when he was talking to me and would stroke the back of his fingers on my breast. I must only have been thirteen or fourteen, I knew he was wrong to do this and I hated it – yet I said nothing to anybody. I remember carving my name on the thick wooden desks in the chemistry labs. I remember being taken to tea with an auntie – she told me off for stirring my tea for too long! I remember Mum. Her fault was she tried too hard.

FOURTEEN

It's my mother's funeral today. Wearing grey is acceptable, and I have a grey skirt. I do have black shoes, though not a black or even a dark-coloured coat. Owning only inappropriate coats is not excuse enough to miss my mother's funeral.

Saturday passed. I stayed at home, not bothering to shop for books. On Sunday I plugged the phone back in. Mick phoned to confirm the funeral arrangements. Even though I was offended when he questioned whether I was coming, I assured him I was and gave him my condolences. He did not return them to me. I unplugged the phone again, after that. I did no reading. It was a waste of another free day.

I put on a white blouse with the grey skirt. It's an awful blouse, which I don't remember ever liking. My motives for buying it, I seem to remember, were that it was cheap and it would be suitable for work. I am not concerned about anyone's opinion there. I have had it two years and Mum's funeral will be the first time I have worn it.

I anticipate their questions and rehearse answers to those people who will attend the funeral. I abort this and instead consider whether I should phone Allan and explain about the funeral and why I will not be back at work today. I hold the phone plug over the socket, practising sounding distressed. I anticipate questions he might ask and how I should respond. In the end I do not phone. He should be able to figure out for himself how a funeral naturally follows a death.

My white blouse sags out of my grey skirt like a beer gut. Though the skirt is too long if I pull it further up my waist, the belt will make my bra redundant.

I will have to sit with Mick and say suitable things; I will have to talk to Gary and act as if we are close.

Mum never went out much, her friends are few and far

between, and the remains of her family are too remote for even death to warrant a trip.

There'll be few mourners, which will focus attention more closely on me. I will be the star guest. I could attend my own mother's funeral and not cry. Or worse, I might once again succumb to giggling.

I am dressed uncomfortably. I try not to think of Dad's funeral, but I have no choice. Though I know this is a day I should not be having selfish thoughts or acting out of anything but the interest of others, I change out of the funeral clothes and dress in a T-shirt and jeans. I sit on the couch and turn on the TV. Each channel is flicked over a dozen times, nothing of any substance is on offer. I turn off the TV and pick up *The Counterfeit Confetti*.

> The compelling banality of daytime television could not help Tanya divert her thoughts from the memory of her mother, or from the continuing belief that had it not been for her actions, then her mother might still be alive. She considered the consequences of attending the funeral and having this accusation made directly to her by either Mick or by Gary.

I put the book down. I do not need to be reminded about my mum today. It's perfectly obvious people are going to think I contributed to her death. If I hadn't argued with her she might not have had a problem with sleeping, and consequently the accident would not have happened. More significantly, there are malicious gossips in the satellites of my immediate family who will no doubt say it was not an accidental death – it was a suicide. 'What could have driven her to suicide,' people will ask, which is when my name will be mentioned.

I go downstairs to Trevor's flat with the intention of rerouting some of my anger onto him. I intend to tell him once and for all that I have had enough of his music; he plays it far too loud and far too late into the night. The anticipated argument never happens, however. Trevor is out. To capitalise upon my effort, I decide to visit Mrs Davies and impress her with my plan to confront Trevor – even though the plan was foiled. She will be delighted by my visit and by having a confederacy against Trevor. This will provide me with credit for when I make a point of avoiding her in the future.

She is not at home either. I shouldn't be as surprised as I am; I have seen her leave the house before, and not just for church on Sunday. She has to shop for food the same as normal people. She wears a very thick, wool coat, whether in the dead of winter or the height of summer.

I am in the house alone. Logic decrees this must have happened many times before; the difference is this is the first occasion when I am aware of it. There are two unoccupied flats in this house, possibly three; the recently burgled flat opposite Mrs Davies was supposed to be occupied, but the tenant was never seen by even super-sleuth Davies. The flat opposite me has been vacant for five months; the last tenants were a young couple who never made any noise: no music, no love-making, no television. I exchanged hellos with them once, and then they vanished. The ground-floor flat opposite Trevor is the one that has been vacant the longest, empty since Alison left. No one wants it now because the kitchen is so tiny and the bathroom is damp.

It shouldn't make any difference being alone in an empty house. I have been alone many times before – I like it, I prefer it. I return to my flat and lock the door.

I sit in silence. I do not read. I am startled by a knock on my door. I rush to open it, then halt myself in case it is someone who has come about the funeral. Although it is still far too early for any of them to realise I am not attending, someone may have been given the job of transporting me there. Relatives are sneaky like that.

There is no second knock and I hear no movement outside. I go to the window to see if I recognise any of the parked cars. I see the van Richard uses. I see Richard coming out of the house and getting into the van. Pete, in the driving seat, points up to me. I duck away, instinctively; then sheepishly look back. Richard does not get in the van. I wave him up. He says something to Pete, then re-enters the house.

I open the door of my flat to confront Richard but am embarrassed to find a carrier bag propped against the door; inside is a colander, which I lent him months ago.

'I thought you might want that back,' Richard tells me

when he is halfway up the stairs. He slows his ascent and stops three steps from the top.

'Thank you. I'd forgotten about it. Is that all you came for?'

'I promise. I like your hair, Tanya. So ... er ... Did you call me back for a reason?'

'I didn't get the chance to open the door when you knocked,' I lie.

'I didn't expect you to be in. I thought it would be best to return it when you were out. It's nice to see you, but I didn't want you to think the colander was an excuse.'

'My mum died.'

'Fuck off.' Richard and the sensitive art of condolence. He climbs the remaining steps and comes to me. '. . . Shit. Really?'

'Really.'

'Are you on your own?'

'What do you mean?'

'Well – shouldn't you be with your family, your brother or someone?'

'I don't need anyone.'

'I know you don't. Not all the time. But sometimes ... Times like this. You're not as hard as you make out, Tanya. I can tell Pete to work alone, if you don't mind me staying.'

'You can't do any good. It won't make any difference.'

'You should tell Caroline, she's your mate. She can . . .' He doesn't continue. He cannot think of how even Caroline could help me.

Calling me hard has made me think of how, at Ill Will, we always used to laugh at Mary when she maintained she had been on a diet and lost weight. To us it was clear she had not lost weight, yet she would remain adamant she had. Though Richard and, for all I know, everyone else sees me as hard, it is not how I really see myself. I have no desire to be hard or nasty, even if that is how I act. All I simply want to be is happy.

'Go back to work, Richard. I'll deal with this on my own.'

'Can I phone you? I mean, to check that you're OK?'

'I'm always OK. Thanks for the colander,' I say. Then, as an afterthought add: 'Sorry about Wednesday.' Then I wonder if it was Wednesday when I went to his home. I cannot think straight.

'You were wrong about Gail. I was not with you because I thought of you as a substitute for her. I treated her like crap. You wouldn't have put up with any of the stuff I put her through. Only later did I realise how much I thought of her and regretted blowing it. The difference with you is, I don't know what I did to put you off me.'

After I close the door I return to the living-room window, careful not to be seen. Richard is quickly out of the building and the van drives off without either of them looking up. Richard never even met my mum, so why did I tell him about her dying?

I go out.

Troubles are best overcome by indulging in the activity that gives most pleasure. For me, book shopping is the best therapy. Browsing in a second-hand bookstore is both spiritual and materialistic; it can give sensual and physical pleasure.

On those occasions when I have been able to indulge in a lengthy browse I have a continuing quest to find three books. All serious readers have at least one elusive book they pursue. The first of my three is a novel called *Gentian Violet* by Edward Hyams, which is about a man who is simultaneously elected as both a Labour and a Tory MP. I read about it in a book of British social history and the premise seems brilliant. However, I've never yet found a copy. The second book is *Beam Ends*, a novel by Errol Flynn. Martin was an Errol Flynn fan and would have been delighted to receive this as a present. If during the last nine years I had found a copy, I would have bought it and sent it to him anonymously, care of his parents. The third book is the latest addition to the search: *King Jesus* by Robert Graves, a book Carl told me he hunts for. It's the book I look for first in each of the shops I visit. I find none of these three books. I am careful not to buy any other books; if I do then the temptation to officially abandon *The Counterfeit Confetti* might be too strong to resist, even though I know its ending and that it cannot now complete its promise of being about the real me. The restraint has become too much; I resolve to finish reading *The*

Counterfeit Confetti in one long stretch, just to free myself of it. In fact I would go home right now if I could be sure either Trevor or Mrs Davies had returned to the house. Today I do not feel like being alone.

It's twelve-thirty. I go to work.

The usual guy is back on security, only this time he is reading the *front* page of the *Daily Mail*. This epiphany is probably due only to the later hour of my arrival; plus, the leading front-page story is about some dopey television presenter screwing some dopey footballer. And this is front-page news. The world must be a wonderfully peaceful place.

I return to him and pull down the brim of his newspaper so he can see me. He is alarmed at first, then irritated.

'Hello,' I say. 'I'm Tanya Stephens. I work for Ill Will on the eighth floor.'

'Yeah, I know.'

'You knew my name?'

'I know you work here.'

'How do you know? You've never stopped me once.'

'Is this some kind of test?' he asks, straightening his tie and glancing around in case I have an accomplice.

'I wanted to say hello,' I say, trying to sound friendly. This does nothing to ease his fears. I belatedly wish I had not made the attempt; friendliness is not in my nature. Or at least it is not my nature to initiate it; I can be friendly enough when people approach or speak to me first.

'Are you just returning from dinner?' he asks.

'No, I'm late.' I tell him. 'It's my last day.'

I catch the lift, enter Ill Will's offices and take off my coat. All done before, but today done with resonance. I am conscious of everything. My desk has poignancy.

Silence greets my entrance due to the fact that everyone is comatosed by their work. I puzzle over why I should be nervous. I should be elated. Maybe I am confused – maybe it's excitement not nervousness. I think a lack of recent exposure is making me fail to recognise excitement. Allan is sat at his desk with his chair facing away. Some of his substantial packed lunch remains untouched.

I sit at my desk. Keith notices me first, then Troy. They do not say hello. I wonder if they are punishing me for being late. Allan temporarily abandons a *Penguin* biscuit; he has seen me.

'You didn't come into work this morning, Tanya,' he states.

'No.'

'I thought you might phone.'

'I meant to.'

'We're all very sorry about your mother,' Mary says. This seems to exorcise the uneasiness. Everyone returns to their work. Jo enters moments later. She comes over and hugs me without speaking. The hug is uncomfortable and awkward because I am sitting and she is having to bend. She insincerely compliments me on my hair, then leaves the office again.

I begin my resignation letter. I will finish and print the letter, hand it to Allan later, before everyone leaves, then stand back to witness everyone's reaction. I do not wish to make the dramatic gesture of resigning without an appreciative audience. As I write I am fully conscious of a thought in my mind, somewhere up there, pestering me, yet never managing to be a real consideration . . . The thought is that I might not resign. But I will. No, definitely. I have no intention of staying. I'll never have another opportunity like this. I never take chances these days.

Jo – on some far-flung gossip-collecting mission – is gone for so long Allan is forced to make coffee. This is so rare it can only be a sign he is in a good mood. Which is a relief. I want him in a good mood so he is more likely to try to persuade me to stay. I have invested a considerable portion of my life here; I want my leaving to be a thing for their regret. If Allan was in a bad mood he would say nothing in reaction. He'd sulk. He'd act betrayed.

'Can I speak to you, Tanya?'

Allan stays at the far end of the office by the kettle. I am being summoned, so I walk to him. To make sure of discretion, I delete the file containing the new resignation letter.

The kettle steams though it is still well short of boiling. He adds coffee and sugar to the cups. Just one sugar to each: to suit his taste and my former taste before Jo corrupted me.

'You take milk, don't you, Tanya?'

All these years and he doesn't know this rudimentary fact about me.

'Yes, please.'

'Say when,' he says. He pours the milk.

Allan talks about the ongoing events on *Brookside*, *Emmerdale*, *Coronation Street* and *Neighbours*. He doesn't watch *EastEnders* on principle. I've never asked him to explain this principle. Maybe it's something to do with the BBC. Or cockneys.

'Did you want to speak to me?'

'I've had a word with . . . I know you were upset about Mary getting her promotion.'

'No I wasn't.'

'And it's terrible about your mother . . . You're a valuable asset to the company, and you are appreciated. You put in a wage claim some time ago, remember? Well, keep quiet about this because although technically Mary is senior to you, you will actually now be on more money. As from this week.'

So I did submit the claim. I have no memory of anything other than writing it out.

I thank Allan and return to my desk. I will be earning more money than Mary. Well, zippety-fucking-doo-dah.

I have several items of work I should be getting on with, but what's the point – none inspires me, each is a task, everything is worthless. I start a new resignation letter. I am unsure whom to address it to, so again put 'Dear Allan'. That's as much as I manage to write before Jo interrupts me. She is excited after her date last night, a first date with some young bloke she's fancied for ages but who – until recently – she could never cajole into asking her out. Here's the bottom-line reality: these very young, modern girls – for all their piercings, tattoos and girl power – are no different from women my age or any other previous generation. The idea of women doing the asking, of making the first move on men, certainly happens, but as a mass movement it's still largely a myth of perfume ads and magazines articles.

'We went to the pictures,' Jo adds.

'Why?'

'To see a film.' Good answer, but it misses the point of my question. The whole point of a first date is to find out about the other person, to see if they're interesting and to judge compatibility. This is something that is hard to do at the cinema: questions cannot be asked, opinions cannot be spoken, jokes cannot be cracked. I have nothing in common with Jo. Today her smiles and cheery whistling make her seem like a child. She has a trust in men that is still to be shattered, and an optimism for the future that is borderline insanity. Without Jo I have no friends at Ill Will. Allan is my boss, I dislike Mary, Troy is impenetrable and Keith's only friends are alcohol in any form and King Size Embassy Regals.

I finish my resignation letter, adding an attractive, decorative border – then remove it. I change the font, then revert back. I think about adding a graphic image, but cannot find one suitable.

I print off my resignation letter. I have kept it simple and short. It is so formal and stiff the tone might be interpreted as anger. Good.

Mary works. Jo has disappeared. Allan busies himself with old invoices. Keith has done some work, executed the regulation drumming and now returns to his newspaper.

'Greetings cards welcoming new employees to a firm,' Troy suggests. There is only me listening and I tell him my opinion, that it is a silly idea.

Ten minutes before home time: I hand Allan my resignation letter as I prepare to leave the office.

'What's this?' he asks, opening the envelope. The seal parts easily because the glue is still moist.

'You're resigning?'

Mary, Keith and Troy are quickly stood around him, gazing down at the letter. Jo enters and is soon involved in the intrigue.

'You're not really leaving, are you, Tanya?' Jo asks. She is the first to break the silence.

'Good on yer!' Keith says. He gives me a friendly punch on the shoulder, the most tactile he has been in all my time here.

A barrage of questions follows. They gather around, wanting to know my plans, where I'll be working. I tell them about Caroline and the work I will be doing with her. For some reason this does not impress them as much as I had hoped. They ask only how Caroline looks these days and how she is, insisting I pass on their regards. I tell them I am looking forward to working with her, expecting this will reintroduce my future into their thoughts. It doesn't. Everyone returns to their work, eager to wind up for the day.

'I suppose this is a bit out of the blue,' I say. No one replies. Only Jo continues to ask questions. Not far beneath her surface misery lurks her ulterior motive: she is only considering the future here, the future without her only ally. She whinges about isolation and victimisation as if Ill Will was the Foreign Legion.

'Look on the bright side,' I tell her. 'With me leaving you'll get promotion. You won't be the office dogsbody any more.'

'Yeah? . . . But I will honestly miss you.'

She gives my shoulder a squeeze as she returns to her own desk. Moments later she makes an excuse to leave the office, no doubt to pass on the news of my leaving to those of her gang who are interested. I hear her outside the office, whistling.

I take Allan to one side.

'Allan, I've been wondering about my holidays.'

'What about them?'

'I know I have to give two weeks' notice, so I was wondering if I could bring my holidays forward.'

'Take your holidays as your notice? So *today* will have been your last day?'

Allan makes a phone call.

'OK then. Your wages will be paid into your bank next week.' He pauses to add weight: 'Of course, you realise your pay rise won't now be included in your money?'

He then makes the announcement to the rest of the office. Though they are all suitably distressed, it is now five o'clock.

'If you're leaving – we should arrange a night out. A goodbye. We should all go for a meal,' Allan suggests. This is not met with any enthusiasm because we have never been the type of office to socialise together. We have attempted Christmas drinks in a local pub on two occasions. Each time has been strained and dreary, the most interesting part of the ordeal being who could come up with the most plausible excuse to depart early. Mary won on both occasions with the most pathetic, saddest reasons possible – child-related. The others only agree to a farewell meal because no one wishes to offer the insult of refusing. I feign delight and tell them I will arrange it and phone with the details. I imagine only Troy and Keith are astute enough to guess this is a lie.

I travel down in the elevator with Mary. She is the most self-involved person in the world. She yatters on about her sister-in-law who is visiting from Nottingham. By no stretch of the imagination could Mary possibly think this might interest me. Mary, however, has no imagination to be stretched. A farewell meal would be marginally interesting; I'd like to see her husband, to see the kind of man who could be attracted to Mary and sustain any interest in her.

The rest of my journey home is not euphoria but its close cousin, relief. Relief as if my head has been held underwater for a tortuous length of time, then released.

I approach my home cautiously, in case Gary or Mick have driven down to lynch me. The only welcoming party is Mrs Davies and Alison. Mrs Davies is in tears!

'Alison, hello. Hello, Mrs Davies. Are you OK?' I force myself to ask.

'Tanya ... Oh, I'm sorry, Tanya, love, but now *you've* been burgled.'

I can't help thinking that if the intention of *The Counterfeit Confetti* is to be of any meaningful use it might have warned me of this. At least I have a marker to remember the day of my mother's funeral: I resigned from Ill Will and I was burgled.

Alison does not seem confrontational so I wonder if I did not post the letter I wrote to her. The memory I have of holding it above the letter box and looking at the collection times – this is all fake. Alison carries a large, full carrier bag.

'I didn't come to embarrass you,' are the first words Alison says when we enter the building. 'I was a bit bemused by your letter.' That's the trouble with nurses: every day they witness so much undiluted honesty they think it's normal. 'It came out of the blue, didn't it? Anyway, it's your decision. I came because ... Well, it doesn't matter now, you have bigger worries. It'll have been stolen with everything else, but you borrowed a necklace of mine once. Remember?'

It was on the night I met Richard: I was at Alison's home; she had a silver chain necklace with an Egyptian hieroglyphic medallion, a bird. On a whim, I borrowed it.

'It wasn't stolen. Here.' I have been wearing it. I have worn it constantly since that night. Though I am reluctant to part with it now I am relieved it was not stolen – this way my debt to Alison is completely cleared. I had grown so accustomed to wearing it I had genuinely forgotten it was borrowed.

'Oh. You like it that much?' Alison asks.

'It's yours,' I tell her, forcing it into her hand.

'Keep it. I came here and . . . When Mrs Davies told me about your burglary I went back home and got these few things for you.'

Alison searches through the carrier bag. She has brought me a portable gas ring, a tiny television and an electric kettle. We are still in the hallway. I have not yet seen the extent of my burglary. Mrs Davies's tears and Alison's monumental pity do not bode well.

'I won the TV at Bingo. I've never used it.'

'They've stolen my TV?' I ask. Mrs Davies and Alison exchange indiscreet looks and do not answer. Mrs Davies makes an excuse, that she needs more Kleenex, and leaves.

'I have to go,' Alison says. 'I've left the kids with my sister. If you find it difficult in your flat . . . I can get the girls to share a room. What I'm saying is, I can fix a spare room up for you.'

Alison is forgetting my horrible letter. She is being generous and warm and kind whilst all I am is a cow.

'Alison, my mum died last week.'

'Oh God! Tanya, I'm sorry.'

I do stupid things sometimes. I wish I had not mentioned my mother.

'I do stupid things sometimes. I wrote that letter to you on the spur of the moment . . . I don't know what I was thinking.'

Alison makes me promise to consider staying with her. All through our short conversation the prevailing thought I have is the urgency of investigating the extent of the burglary to see how bad my predicament is.

I take a moment to look through my mail; it is still on the hall table. My telephone bill has arrived. I look through if to see if I recognise the DVLA phone number. It is not there. Closer scrutiny shows the period for this bill ends before I made the phone call. Even so, I begin to wonder if I made the call and whether I spoke to Martin in reality. I know I have spoken to him many times in my imagination.

FIFTEEN

When I first came to this flat the most time-consuming and infuriating part of the move was clearing out the trash left by the previous tenant: a ripped, vinyl armchair, an ancient music centre, a rug, a greasy-glued gas oven, a decrepit Formica dining table, a million damp newspapers and a substantial collection of clothes that held enough wildlife to warrant a visit from David Attenborough. Clearing all this took a full day of hard work, thirty bin liners and a lorry from the council. Life would have been easier if I could have found the flat as empty as it is now. Nothing remains: no furniture, no carpet, not even food. It's as if the thieves set themselves the challenge of taking everything: clothes, curtain rails, light shades. Only a healthy team of burglars could have done the job, working intensely, confident of not being disturbed. The policeman who came agreed. He even went so far as to take notes before he left. When Mrs Davies came down again I told her how this policeman, like hers, had also expressed doubt whether the thieves would be brought to justice. When he told me, 'We'll do everything we can,' there was definitely a smirk. He asked if I had any family I could stay with.

Voices echo in the room, now. Footsteps clod on the bare floorboards. I suspect it was only to avoid flooding, but they did leave the central heating radiators; I have them set on high, yet a draught numbs the air. The flat is as forbidding as a railway station waiting room at midnight.

Mrs Davies refuses to leave me alone. She repeatedly apologises for being out of the house – as if I had employed her as a security guard.

'I haven't had bagels for donkey's years,' she explains, 'so I decided to have an adventure and go seek some out. Proper ones, I mean, from an authentic baker's, not supermarket ones . . . Then I did my main shopping . . . Even so, I wasn't gone all day. They must have been in here the moment I left the house.'

'They can't have been, I left the house *after* you. I went up to see you.'

'You did?'

'Not a bad job, really – clearing the whole flat like this. They're wasted; they should be professional removal men, they'd make a fortune.'

'You don't sound as upset as I would be, Tanya. Well – you know, don't you? – you know how I was when I was burgled, but compared to you they hardly bothered taking anything from me.'

'I'm insured.'

'Insurance doesn't replace everything. Think of all those things that have sentimental value.'

I do not care about sentimentality, I do not care about possessions – even my books can be replaced – and there is even some relief in the permanent banishment of *The Counterfeit Confetti*. However, the real upset, the disruption that will really piss me off when I finally grasp the totality of having had everything stolen, is simply the sheer inconvenience. To say I am insured is an easy answer – I cannot unequivocally say which company I am insured with. So many other vital documents have also gone. I will have to go shopping to replace everything – furniture, clothes, books . . . In the meantime I need blankets . . . and a cup . . . and a toothbrush. A pillow and a telephone.

'Is there anything I can do for you, Tanya? Anything.'

The consequences of not permitting her to help is a night trying to sleep on bare floorboards, in these clothes, with no blankets and no pillow.

'Could I use your phone, Mrs Davies?'

'Of course! You don't even have to ask!'

I follow Mrs Davies upstairs. I instinctively lock the door of my flat.

Mrs Davies makes me a coffee and I am happy to share her bagels. To fill them she has bought coronation chicken cottage cheese from Marks & Spencer's, which shows such superb taste I can only imagine she has stolen the idea from a TV show. Her coffee, however, is grey.

'You know where the phone is, don't you?' she calls to me from the kitchen as she clears away the coffee cups.

I do not phone anyone. I hold the receiver and put it down as she re-enters the living room. I have not phoned any of my family (this is how I will explain if she asks) because I do not wish to worry them further, after our recent bereavement. If I tell her of my mother's death, however, her pity will be heaped on me double. I could tell her I do not know the phone numbers of any of my friends off by heart. I will tell her I have not phoned my boyfriend because I no longer have one. Or two. I have not phoned Alison because she is too kind – it embarrasses me.

'It's all settled,' I lie. 'Thanks for the bagels.'

I go to her door.

'Who did you phone?'

I did not anticipate such a direct question.

'Just someone I know. I'll go wait for them. Bye, Mrs Davies.'

'Bye, Tanya. So you're staying with them tonight?'

'That's right.'

I open her door.

'Are they coming over for you?'

She'll offer to come outside and wait with me. Or else she'll simply spy.

'I'll take a taxi,' I say. I attempt to put a note of annoyance in my voice, the idea being that she should realise her questions are annoying me; the effect, however, is to make it sound as if the thought of getting a taxi is the annoyance.

'Do you have the money for a taxi?'

'I . . . Er . . . '

'Or is your friend going to pay at the other end?'

The hole I am digging for myself is getting increasingly hotter as I approach the earth's core. She is going to ask me questions about this fictional helper, where they live and how long I can stay there. She will lend me money for the taxi, then stand outside waiting until it arrives. To make the lie seem like truth I can visualise having to phone for a taxi and then spending this night in some dreadful B&B.

158

I close her door.

'I didn't phone anyone, Mrs Davies. I don't like to trouble people.'

'Tanya – you're silly. People like to help.'

'I'll manage in my flat. I've slept in worse conditions.'

Oh-ho. Please don't ask me to elaborate, Mrs Davies. I once went to a party in Norwich with a gang of friends and seven of us ended up trying to sleep in the back of a transit van. Another time I slept in an allotment greenhouse with Martin, waking up half frozen and having to sneak back into my home before my parents woke.

'If you could lend me some blankets, Mrs Davies, that would be a fantastic help.'

'You can't sleep on bare floorboards! And what about washing? Tanya – I want to help. You can sleep here. You can sleep on my settee. It's not ideal, but I'll keep the fire on, and with a pillow and a quilt you'll be fine.'

Sleeping on Mrs Davies's settee is preferable to my floorboards. It means, however, an evening in her company, then waking up to her company. It means being indebted to her; it means future obligations.

'*I can't see you any more.*'

'*Oh?*'

'*I don't want to see you any more.*'

'*Oh.*'

'*For God's sake, is that all you have to say?*'

'*Would anything I say make you change your mind?*'

Carl did not make any indication of being saddened nor did he offer any argument. He gave me nothing to cling to, no straw to clutch at. I cannot give him a second chance now – he did not ask for one. If I phoned and asked for help he might believe I was using him out of desperation. I could use the death of my mother as a context to dumping him: I was going through a dark period of madness. Or I could tell him I regret finishing with him! No – I'll do neither, I have to draw the line.

Mrs Davies isn't too irritating; we watch TV together and her comments are sporadic. During a documentary about Hitler Mrs Davies comments that one of the interviewees should have made more of an effort with his hair if he knew he was going to be on TV. She condemns a cookery programme on the grounds that some of the ingredients used are too exotic. We both sit in agonised silence through a crime re-enactment programme, where one of the items is about rape and the victim was buggered. When I was a kid at home and an embarrassing sexual programme came on I would pretend to read, or clean my nails, or appear very, very bored. Happily, this programme is followed by a book programme. Afterwards I have a real brooding for a book. I browse over those Mrs Davies owns. There are a lot of Colin Dexter, Hammond Innes, Dick Francis and so on, yet amongst all these is a copy of Zola's *L'Assommoir*, which I read many years ago and remember liking, but can now barely recall. Mrs Davies explains that Clement was the reader, but she never bothers. She insists I keep the book.

'It's an odd book to have in amongst these others,' I comment.

'It's French, isn't it? He must have got it by accident.'

Mrs Davies lends me a nylon nightie, which I am reluctant to accept; then she presents me with a cup of cocoa, makes up the settee so it is comfortable; finally she leaves a small table light on and wishes me goodnight. It is ten-fifteen.

There are three contributory factors to the thrill of opening the book. It's an old-time thrill, which I seldom experience these days – I read too many books; beginning a new one has been too common an occurrence. These altered circumstances are part of the thrill tonight. Also, it is a release from the burden of *The Counterfeit Confetti*. Finally it is the book itself: I went through a long phase of exclusively reading classic French novels. I am infuriated to realise my own collection of Zolas, Balzacs and Flauberts are now in the possession of some scumbag thief.

I become even angrier when I remember that, besides *Groucho and Me*, the only other book I treasure for sentimental reasons is now also gone. When I was young Dad used to read Clement Freud's *Grimble* to me. He would finish it and I would make him begin again, over and over. The only joke I can still recall from the book is when Grimble finds a biscuit left by his mum and dad, with a message written on it in green ink. The message is: Do not eat this biscuit as eating green ink is bad for you.

Reading *L'Assommoir* calms me down. I am comforted by holding the book, the ease of its read; the story is comforting – it reminds me to put my own troubles into perspective. I am not going to starve to death.

I suspect it is past midnight when I turn the table lamp off. There is a moment when I struggle to make myself comfortable; but next all I am aware of is that it is eight hours later and I am woken by Mrs Davies desperately trying to move around her home without making any noise.

I suffer no bewilderment in these new surroundings; I remember exactly where I am and I'm alert enough to immediately establish my getaway excuse:

'What time is it, Mrs Davies, please?'

'Morning, love. Did you sleep well?'

'I slept like a log. Am I going to be late for work?'

'It's eight-fifteen. I've made you a cup of tea.'

'Lovely. I'll have to hurry for work though.'

'Couldn't you phone and explain about your burglary?'

I have no work. I have quit Ill Will. I have told Mrs Davies yet another lie. In fact, I cannot recall anything I have ever said to Mrs Davies that has not been a lie.

'I want to go to work, Mrs Davies. It'll help me take my mind off things,' I tell her.

I drink half the cup of tea and take a slice of toast to eat on my way to the work I have quit.

Today I will see Caroline and give her the magnificent news that I am free to begin working for her immediately. I will also beg for a shower; I couldn't bring myself to take a bath in Mrs Davies's home and the nightie she lent me, whilst being perfectly clean, has left me scratching my body even though there are no itches. Dressing back in the clothes I had on yesterday – including knickers and bra – increases the urgency for a shower.

As I approach Caroline's home there is a man at her door, waiting. Caroline answers, giving a pantomime performance of hatred at seeing him, even before the man speaks. Then, when she sees me, she launches into an extravagantly fussy welcome, complimenting me on my hairstyle. I tell her it is better now I have altered it to my liking. The man says nothing, until I look directly at him and Caroline is forced to introduce us. This is Kenneth, the writer of *The Stink Monsters*. His face is too red and blotchy, he wears a goatee, which he has not maintained properly, and his two front teeth slightly cross each other. Maybe this has happened overnight – it is the only explanation I can think of for Caroline's attitude. Didn't she tell me she loved him? Caroline uses my presence to ignore him, reiterating how delighted she is by my surprise visit.

'I called earlier. Where were you?' Ken asks; Caroline ignores. 'Whose bed did you spend last night in?'

These tactics finally rouse her attention.

'It's none of your fucking business who I'm fucking,' she tells him. There is real venom in Caroline's voice; Kenneth is shocked by her admission. He smiles too broadly whilst he attempts to recover enough to say something else . . . then fails to do so. Caroline gives a sly wink to me, in triumph.

This is not the relationship I had been led to believe existed between these two. I had understood that Caroline was still obsessed with Kenneth and that he was no longer interested.

'What are you doing here anyway?' Caroline demands of him.

'. . . Sketches . . .' is the single word he manages to mutter.

'I've said – you have nothing to worry about! Didn't I tell you everything was on schedule?'

'I still have the right to an input, don't I?'

Caroline disappears, never thinking to invite me in. Kenneth and I both struggle, wondering if small talk is possible. We mutually decide it is not. Caroline returns and shoves a handful of sketches into his hands.

'Your input is the writing. I don't interfere with that so don't you try and interfere with my art. I'm sick of it. So fuck off,' the artist says.

Kenneth does not move, defiant, yet avoiding eye contact with Caroline. After a while he smiles at me and mumbles how it was nice to meet me, then tells Caroline, politely, he thinks the sketches are good and he'll phone her tomorrow. Caroline shrugs her shoulders. As he is leaving I signal wildly to Caroline, doing my very best to mime drawing; I even mouth 'Tell him I'm going to be working for you!' Caroline, bemused, remains silent.

'Kenneth, er . . .' I say before he has walked too far. 'Can I just ask . . .'

'Yes?'

'What would you think about Caroline getting some help?'

'You mean like a psychiatrist? I'd say it was long overdue.'

Caroline nudges me on the shoulder, guiding me inside.

'I've asked Tanya to come and work for me. Nothing to do with you; it won't affect you at all. OK? Bye!'

The door is closed: us inside, Kenneth out.

'Caroline!' I protest.

'What? Don't worry about it, Tanya. It's nothing to do with him who I work with. He'll be pleased. He's so fucking anal about deadlines, any help I get will let him relax a little.'

We walk up to her studio.

'I thought you loved him. I thought you were mad about him. This is what you told me. That's changed, I'm guessing.'

'I never said I loved him. Did I? I did still fancy him – but that has definitely changed.'

'How come?' I ask.

Caroline grins.

'I'm seeing someone else.'

'Really? Who?'

'Telling you is a bit awkward . . .' she says. She begins to gather other sketches together. I follow her around. I quickly sift through the available evidence to decipher why it could be awkward for Caroline to tell me whom she has been seeing, whom she had sex with last night. The only probable candidate who could induce awkwardness between us is her ex-boyfriend and my ex-boyfriend, Richard. I keep the puzzled expression on my face whilst I decide whether there can be any profit in pretending to be angry with Caroline, my new employer. Though it isn't really a betrayal she has committed she might be persuaded to believe it is.

'It's Richard,' I say, straight-faced. 'I'm guessing.'

'Are you angry?'

More pieces fall into place.

'I phoned you last Wednesday night and you were out . . .'

'I was with him,' she admits.

'You went out with him on Wednesday night?' The significance of this is it was Wednesday when I officially broke up with Richard.

Then another thought occurs to me:

'On the Saturday you said you had a date . . .'

'That was with him.'

They went out together on Saturday, yet on Wednesday he was still keen to take me back. We had sex on Wednesday.

'Tell me about that Saturday,' I ask.

'What happened was . . . He phoned me, to ask if I had any explanation as to why you'd finished with him.'

'What did you say to him? Apart from asking him out.'

'I didn't ask him out! He asked me. What happened was . . . I agreed to go for a drink, to sort of console him.'

'I'm sure sleeping with him consoled him plenty.'

'Who said I slept with him!'

'I'll bet you did though.'

'What happened was . . . By the end of the night I thought I might as well sleep with him. I mean, I've slept with him before. Why are you mad, Tanya? *You* broke up with *him*.'

'I'm not angry,' I say indignantly – which is a form of anger by those feigning superiority. 'Just explain Saturday night to me. He asked you to go for a drink so you could talk about why I'd finished with him – and you agreed?'

'I want to be honest with you, Tanya. What happened was . . . Well, I knew all along what was going on in his mind. Men don't need discussions, they don't need post-mortems on a relationship. The only comfort they need is sex with someone else.'

'And so he phoned you.'

Caroline comes to me and holds my wrists; when I don't respond she lets go. She sits.

'I don't care, Tanya. We live for moments of happiness. We live from one moment to the next; the best you can hope for is that the moments aren't too far apart.'

I have heard this somewhere else. Maybe she has said it to me before or maybe it is something I have read.

Caroline continues, 'I just get a bit lonely. And I miss sex.

You probably won't understand. What's the longest period you've ever had in your life without sex?'

'Eighteen months.'

'Bloody hell!'

The eighteen months happened three years ago. In that time I had no boyfriends, casual or serious; no flings, no dalliances. Though this initially pleased me because being happy in your own company is the only true measure of happiness, Alison simply assumed I must be looking for someone and tried to set me up on blind dates. When I ferociously declined she made distinct overtures to assure me how liberal-minded she was in case I confessed to being a lesbian. Modern thinking considers celibacy a failing not a discipline. The reaction is not Well done, but What's wrong with you then? I am not immune: I spent an increasing amount of time wondering what was wrong with me, and a decreasing amount of time thinking about sex.

'Well . . .' Caroline continues after she has recovered from the shock of my revelation, as it negates the point she was hoping to make, 'the longest period of denial for me was up until Saturday. Nearly six full months I have gone without sex. I don't want to sound like an addict or something, and I know technically it's not a definite biological need, but I desperately wanted, well, a good seeing to. And I got one.'

'At David and Rachel's wedding you told me it was *two* months since you last had sex.'

'No I didn't.'

'You did, Caroline. It was with some ex-boyfriend, you said.'

After a moment of concentrated thinking, Caroline remembers.

'Oh God – him! I'd forgotten about that. He doesn't count. He was useless.'

Nothing for a second – I try to stay blank – but then I cannot restrain my laughter. Caroline laughs, too, and before we know it all differences are forgotten and we laugh more. I sit with her and she tells me how happy she is. I tell her a little about Carl. I have not forgotten that I have broken up with him, I am simply using his name so Caroline will understand

I no longer want Richard and therefore her happiness can be unrestrained.

'I feel comfortable with Carl because I've never yet had to explain myself to him. He understands why I read so much, he understands my lack of ambition. But there's more to it. I sometimes say clumsy, rude things to people, my irony is sometimes heavy-handed, my sarcasm is vicious and there have been times when my sense of humour is the most hurtful kind of insult. And he's always understood this without me ever having had to explain. I like that he has passions that don't make his character extreme. I like talking to him and listening to him. What it is – and this is remarkable for me – I don't resent any time I spend with him.'

Caroline has been listening patiently, pretending she is civilised.

'Is he good in bed?' she then asks.

'I actually think what makes the sex so good is that I . . .' I can't say I love him because I don't love him, yet there is no other compromise word that can suitably convey how I do feel. The word *love* is so remorselessly abused by drunks, lyricists and lazy people who work for greetings card companies, and *like* sounds too trivial. For Caroline's convenience I simplify all this by concluding the sentence with '. . . we get on so well.'

Caroline asks questions about Richard, which I have surprising difficulty in answering; I never took enough interest to discover answers. To shut her up I consider telling her about my mother, even though Richard must surely have told her the news. Instead I tell her about being burgled. She offers the correct sympathetic noises. When I finally tell her I have resigned from Ill Will, she screams in delight – then metamorphoses before my eyes. She even visibly backs away from me.

'Good. Excellent,' she says. There is a determination, even an urgency, to set the correct tone for how our new working relationship will begin. Her smile has no genuine warmth now; this Caroline is not tactile or chatty, she is stiff and uneasy. Putting aside the way she is dressed, this is Caroline as if she had been raised within the royal family.

Her Majesty announces: 'Then, let's see, if this is the first day of your employment with me, it might prove more productive to spend my time setting out the workplace so that we can start as soon as possible.'

'That sounds sensible.'

'But coffee first – don't you think?'

'I'm gagging for a coffee. I haven't had one yet this morning. Caroline,' I add her name as an afterthought. Saying her first name sounds slightly inappropriate, even insubordinate.

Caroline makes good coffee, which is promising. We even have doughnuts, too. After we have successfully negotiated who will have the third doughnut (we cut it in half – though she takes the half with the jam) I ask her more about her and Richard. I am asking only out of politeness, making a supreme effort to make the enquiry sound casual. I have barely thought about him since we broke up. It is a little sad to have him so easily dismissed from my immediate circle of concerns.

All Caroline now has to say about him is:

'He mentioned your mother, Tanya. About her – you know.'

'Oh,' I say. *Mentioned*. They must have been stuck for conversation. 'I have nothing to say about Mum. I just want to get to work.'

I follow her back upstairs and into the studio.

She shows me around, forgetting she has done this before. She sets out three projects to start work on. The first is to add shade to an already completed illustration; the second is to simply ink in a pencil drawing, and the third is a section of text with a note, handwritten by Caroline for her own benefit. She tells me to read the note and illustrate this text myself, imitating her style as closely as possible. Clearly these tasks are meant as tests. I am listening to her yet also, audibly in my head, talking to her about my mum. I think if I had a friend whose mother had just died I would feel compelled to ask questions. If she seemed reluctant to talk I would still insist on offering sympathy. Caroline is selfish. I know I am too, but at least I can show the courtesy of feigning interest. We work in silence; there is not even a radio for accompaniment. Though I can understand how some concentration is needed, we are not designing the re-entry mechanism for the space shuttle; surely a little distraction could be permitted? When Caroline suggested I came to work for her she talked about fun, she talked about it being a good laugh. As the morning progresses Caroline becomes increasingly oblivious to my presence.

I have to admit her sweatshop conditions succeed: I do the shading in in less than a quarter of an hour, the inking in takes an hour and I make several rough sketches of my own original interpretation of the text within half an hour. I cough and hold up the sketches, startling Caroline. Though she seems pleased enough she offers no comment. Under these circumstances I cannot find a way to steer her into inviting me to stay the night.

I should say something, make comments about whatever it is she is working on just to break the silence. I should insist we have a radio. If I work through this first day without establishing ground rules, then tomorrow will carry on the same; any suggestion of change will then be answered with, 'Well, why didn't you say anything before?'

'Do you have a radio, Caroline?'

'A radio? What for?'

Because I want to adapt it for transmission to signal for a rescue.

'It's just so quiet. I thought a little music might be nice.'

'I hated the radio when I was at Ill Will. I couldn't concentrate for the noise!'

She hated the radio so much she used to listen to a Walkman.

She goes back to work. More silence. Discussion concluded. No radio.

'Coffee?' I suggest.

'Again?'

It's now been over two hours since our last coffee. If this prolonged denial had happened at Ill Will, Keith would have been rolling on the floor in cold turkey agony with caffeine withdrawal symptoms. Troy would have made comments about how dry the office and his throat were. Allan would have sacked Jo. Mary always brought a flask of coffee, to save herself money; always decaffeinated to save herself from any stimulation.

'Show me what you're working on,' I say.

'Done now,' she says and puts the drawing in her desk. She stands and approaches me. 'What about lunch?'

'Great.'

'Have you brought anything?'

No I haven't. I haven't made a packed lunch since my school days.

Oh balls. I have made a massive mistake. At Ill Will I had a steady little job, which I did not hate and which I had grown accustomed to. I had gained a certain seniority there, a certain respect for the years I had put in. There was music and coffee, and at lunchtimes I could nip out and eat in a choice of restaurants, buy a hamburger or sandwiches. I could have a quick snack and tour nearby shops. Caroline is expecting me to bring a packed lunch. My life has degenerated so quickly I yearn for the job I was doing only yesterday.

'I've made a lasagne,' Caroline adds. 'I took it out of the freezer this morning and it's been slow-cooking in the oven. Do you like lasagne? Say no if you don't.'

'I love lasagne!' I don't, but this exclamation of pleasure emanates from relief.

I tell her more details about my burglary. She expresses some sympathy. Whilst Caroline sets the table I am permitted to phone my bank, which has the details about my home insurance. I phone my insurance company, and then the police again, and the worst of the problem is sorted out in fifteen minutes – which is about ten hours faster than I had expected.

During lunch Caroline's Jekyll and Hyde behaviour continues. I eat lunch in the *real* Caroline's kitchen; she is so warm and friendly I am nearly fooled into confiding to her about that truculent bitch I have begun working for. The subjects of my burglary and my mother are not mentioned again. The lasagne is nice; we have one glass of red wine and I once more ask about her and Richard.

'Back to work, I think,' is her reply.

The afternoon proves to be a great relief. Caroline guides me through each of the individual characters in *The Stink*

Monsters, pointing out the idiosyncrasies that distinguish each character from the rest. She shows me sections from previous books, concentrating on the illustrations she is especially pleased with, yet also mentioning those she wishes she could do again.

She tells me, 'Illustrating children's books isn't as easy as people imagine; and it certainly isn't as easy as I sometimes make out. I think I only got away with it at the beginning because Ken knew even less about it than me; and I did try especially hard to impress him.'

'You know, this morning was so odd. I can't understand how your attitude to him has changed so quickly.'

'It's just one of those things. Anyway, try a fuller illustration of that text, then we'll see what it's like when it's inked in. I'll go make coffee.'

She leaves and does not return for forty minutes. She returns with coffee just for me, and it is cold. She picks up the new, fuller sketch of the illustration I have completed whilst waiting for coffee. She is standing above me and makes no comment. I am about to stand so I can point out some of the details to her – I have added little touches, background jokes that are not immediately noticeable. There is no need. She grins.

'Yeah, I see what you've done. This is good work, Tanya. Let's call it a day, eh?'

'Fine by me, Boss.'

Caroline laughs at this.

I walked here from my flat this morning and now make the return journey again on foot as this bookends the day. I need some structure to my life at the moment, no matter how artificial. Besides, I am in no hurry to return home to my empty flat.

It would not take too much change to the world, I would not be asking for too much, if I could be returning home now, still as it is, but facing the prospect of having a really good book to read, one that genuinely enthrals me and which I am eager to continue. This is all I ask to make me happy. I remember fondly, painfully, when I was reading David Nobbs's *Second from Last in the Sack Race*, my attempts to read even whilst I was in the bath. I was so involved not simply because the book was funny but because it was insightful and true in a way that winners of prestigious book awards seldom are. I bought three copies of the book; the first two were ruined by being dropped in the water.

SIXTEEN

It's one of those London early evenings that command an easy anticipation: the sun is preparing to set and the traffic is dawdling. On any other day I might be relaxed. It is the type of evening walk where a diversion off the normal route might be interesting. However, as I have not yet established a route, all are diversions. I reach home at six. Alison, in uniform, is waiting outside the house. I reward her with a generous smile.

'I knew you weren't in because you have no curtains and I can see there are no lights on. I didn't knock because I didn't want to be stuck with Mrs Davies.'

This makes me laugh. That is to say I laugh internally as I do for ninety per cent of the time; but I make an attempt to give this laugh a voice just so Alison can see how I sympathise with anyone wishing to avoid Mrs Davies.

'It's nice to see you,' I say. 'Have you just finished work?'

'I had a bit of time to spare because my mum has taken the kids to the pictures. It's funny, but the number of times I pray for a few moments of spare time on my own, then when I get the opportunity to have it . . . I just want to see the kids. Oh, guess what? I spoke to Trevor. He remembered me.' Alison has lowered her voice, in case Trevor can hear through the walls of the house. 'He asked if I wanted to come in and wait inside his flat.'

'Why didn't you?'

'To be honest . . . Don't laugh, but I sort of fancy him.'

I do laugh – and this one I keep firmly internalised. I have always suspected Alison of this eccentric perversion.

'So why didn't you go into his flat? It would have given you a chance to talk.'

'I never saw inside his flat when I lived here, and it might be scruffy or filthy. I can't fancy someone who's happy to live like that, and I like having Trevor to fancy. There are so few people around for me to fancy these days. Does that sound odd?'

'No. I like having a small clique of people to fancy. Everyone has one, don't they? The clique becomes smaller as you get older. It's one of the great shames of getting older; you become less fanciable yet you become choosier at a time when the choice diminishes. Or is that just me?'

'I know what you mean.'

'Do you want to come in? But my flat is still – you know.'

'I came to ask – you can say no, I won't mind, I won't be offended – but I thought you might want to have tea with me and the girls. You can hang around and watch telly with us or . . . it's up to you, it's just a thought.'

'I'd love to.' I take no time in making this decision because – kids or not – the prospect of my alternative evening is far worse.

Alison's mother arrives at her home just as we do. I am introduced to the mother, who is suspiciously eager to abandon the children and make her escape. Though her children seem harmless they are at such a young age no jury would dream of prosecuting them for their actions. I am immediately at ease in Alison's home because Alison has too much to occupy her to make a fuss of me. She begins to make the tea, whilst continuing to (remote) control her children. The TV is turned on when the children demand it. They watch for two minutes before their interest turns to fighting each other, then to playing. One girl colours in a colouring book, the other plays with a hand-held computer game. I am the guardian by proxy: the only adult in the room whilst Alison is in the kitchen. The children take no notice of me, which is both reassuring and also a challenge.

'What's your name?' I ask the girl who is colouring in. I already know the other kid's name.

'She's called Chloe,' Charlotte says. Chloe says nothing – clearly, of the two, she is the tougher nut to crack.

'Can I help you colour in, Chloe?' I ask.

'You can do the tie,' she tells me. I sit next to her. The picture is of a circus bear, on a ball. The bear wears a striped tie. I pick up a red crayon.

'Not red!' Chloe yells. She hands me a brown. She has already coloured the bear green, so brown will not clash. I begin to colour one of the stripes of the tie. I take a disconcerting amount of satisfaction from not going over the line, and ponder whether to inform the girls drawing is the way I earn my living. We sit, colouring in, in silence for several minutes. I think of questions I might ask, then keep them to myself. Somehow my guardianship seems more successful if we all remain silent. To confirm this Alison comes in from the kitchen.

'I wondered what was going on. They haven't been this quiet for this length of time since they were babies. You obviously have a way with kids, Tanya.' Alison returns to the kitchen: 'Tea won't be long,' she calls back.

'Have either of you any idea what we're having?' I ask the girls.

'Mum sometimes makes stew,' Charlotte tells me, screwing her face up. 'Or salad. I don't like celery though.'

'It'll be something with chips,' Chloe adds.

'And you'll get coffee or tea. We have pop. Milk sometimes.'

'I've had coffee.'

'Liar.'

Alison calls us into the kitchen; she has set the table and the food is ready. Tea is chips, fish fingers and peas. Still full from Caroline's lasagne, I do not eat much. Alison asks the girls about the cinema. Their film criticism leaves a lot to be desired; both summarise the film with, 'It was all right.' Alison persists, asking the girls about their day at school. Charlotte goes into a long, detailed description of her English lesson. She has been told by her English teacher she is doing very well, especially with spelling. Connected to this, in Charlotte's mind at least, she adds there is a boy in her class who cannot pronounce the word biscuit. Kids can say something that is both malicious yet innocent and produce a combination that is implausibly hilarious. I am in uncontrollable hysterics at the manner Charlotte tells us about the biscuit boy, and only calm down when I realise for the others the humour is less obvious. I think that out of these two children I probably prefer Charlotte, though Chloe will turn out to be the kind of adult I prefer.

When the meal is finished the kids, with no prompting, know they have jobs to do; each takes their plates and cutlery to the sink. They then clear away everything else from the table, putting the salt and pepper in the appropriate cupboard and the tomato sauce in the fridge. This ritual has been drilled into them by their mother and it inspires me, for the first time I can ever remember, to admire Alison.

Once excused, the children rush back into the living room to continue playing, arguing or watching TV. I remain with Alison whilst we finish drinking our cups of tea.

'You have two nice kids there,' I tell her. Parents like no better compliment than to be told how great their children are.

'Yeah, they're no problem. It's not easy on my own though.'

'They do as you tell them.'

'I don't mean discipline. I mean money and . . . No, not even money really. As a parent you have to wing it, you make all these daily decisions even though you've had no experience or training in bringing children up and . . . I got an instruction book when I bought a new toaster, but nothing for either of the girls. It's a lot of responsibility. Sometimes I wish I had someone just to share the burden with, someone I could blame when things went wrong.'

'But you don't want their father back?'

'He was an idiot. Still is, whenever he decides to visit. You never met him, did you?'

I never met him as such, only seeing him when he used to visit Alison in their pre-children days, when she was still living downstairs from me. He was in Alison's life less than a year: enough time to impregnate her and for her to give birth to one kid before abandoning her when she became pregnant with the second. That which he lacked in commitment he made up for in speed.

As we wash and dry the dishes Alison elaborates on her sex life since he left, an elaboration that contains only disappointments, betrayals, frustration. Alison expected different – this is her downfall.

By the time we enter the living room the girls have abandoned all other occupations and are lost in some shoddy American TV animation. Alison turns the TV off.

'That's enough of that. I'm going to run your bath. If you have any homework, I suggest you start it now, because you have less than an hour after your bath before you go to bed.'

When Alison is upstairs I finish colouring in the bear's tie, then help Chloe finish where she left off: the ball the bear is balancing on. The two girls obediently run up to the bathroom when their mother calls. I am left to fend for myself, so I turn the TV back on and watch the news. This is escapism for me, hearing of events in a country that does not concern me any more; neither its celebrations nor its tragedies interest me. I am relaxed enough to take off my shoes and put my feet up. Alison, exhausted, comes down as the news finishes.

'They're getting into their night-clothes. They have no homework so I've told them they can watch a *Mr Bean* video. Do you mind?'

'Actually, if it's not a bother, whilst you're watching that I wouldn't mind having a bath.'

'A bath? Of course you'd like a bath! Why didn't I think? Come on, I'll show you where everything is.'

Alison runs me a scented bubble bath and it is relaxing and glorious. I fall asleep.

'Are you OK, Tanya?' Alison timidly calls through the door some time later.

'Huh?' I wake. The water is cool. 'Has the video finished?'

'The thing is, I want to put the girls to bed and they need to use the loo.'

'God, I'm so sorry! I fell asleep.'

Once out of the bath, I dry myself quickly, wrap myself in a towel and pull the plug. As I open the door the two girls rush in, shouting about how they are busting and begin an argument about who should pee first.

'Charlotte first,' Alison tells them.

'Why?' demands Chloe.

'Because she really wants to pee. You're just putting it on.'

This settles the argument, though I have no idea how

Alison could have developed this ability to know who is faking a need to pee.

Alison lets me use her bedroom to dress. When I am done she enters and, realising I am having to wear the same clothes, offers to lend me some of hers. I am pleased to abuse Alison's offer. All that prevents me borrowing more is the logistical problem of transporting this lot home tonight.

Alison puts the girls to bed. I wish them goodnight. Charlotte waves goodbye.

When Alison comes down she collapses into an armchair.

'It's not even eight o'clock and I'm knackered,' she tells me. 'I try and stay up some nights, maybe watch a film or something, go to bed at a reasonable hour – eleven or eleven-thirty, just to remind myself I'm an adult. But it never works. By ten I fall asleep. Always. I'll make a coffee, eh? To keep us awake?'

Alison tells me more about the girls' father. Theirs was one of those catastrophic relationships where one is devoted and the other is so uninterested they have no fear of being callous. Most of Alison's anger is now aimed not at him but at herself, for being so gullible, so easily manipulated.

'When we finally broke up,' she tells me, 'I was so devastated I was petrified I would develop a real yearning for him, you know? I don't know if you've ever done this, but when you break up with a guy you'd had big plans for, you can then spend months, maybe longer, missing him, thinking about him, obsessing about you and him together in the past. I genuinely feared this was going to happen. The shock was I shrugged him off and then only felt foolish for ever being conned by him.'

I should have eaten more. I have an ache in my gut from hunger.

I ask Alison, cautiously, 'Could you imagine having a guidebook to tell you how you're supposed to behave? You know, something that would tell you the right decisions to make?'

Alison laughs falsely, imagining I am proposing the idea as a joke. I say nothing, to show her I am serious.

'Well – not really,' she begins. 'It would be awful, if you think about it. Who would the book help? When you're young half the pleasures of being young come out of acting stupid, behaving irresponsibly, making silly mistakes. Would you really have liked to have lived your life without having done those things?'

'Well, the book could come to you when you're older, when you're smart enough not to make mistakes.'

'Then it would be redundant, surely?'

I think out my response before I speak it aloud. 'The purpose of the book . . . Its purpose could be to put your life into perspective. Give you a structure to prepare for a worthwhile ending. It could also remind you of your old self, to remind you that beneath your acquired habits and caution there are still your old instincts.'

'You've lost me,' she confesses. The confession is fair enough – I wasn't entirely convinced myself. She asks if I want another coffee.

'I have to get off, Alison. I've enjoyed this evening, I really have.'

If Alison is disappointed or feels snubbed she is careful not to show it. She puts the clothes into carrier bags so when the taxi arrives they are easy to load. My abrupt departure is made easier by Alison's admission that she intends to watch an hour or so of TV whilst she does her ironing, then go to bed.

I ask the taxi driver to stop off at a cashpoint, then I pop in at a mini-market to buy my own kettle, a telephone, then some coffee, sugar, milk, snack food and a sleeping bag. At home it takes two trips for me to carry the four bags up to my flat. On the last trip, as I am struggling to take the last of the bags of borrowed clothes upstairs, I hear Mrs Davies's flat door open. I wait for her, so I can ask for *L'Assommoir*, which I have left in her home, and to inform her I will be sleeping in my own flat tonight.

'Are you coming up, Tanya?' Mrs Davies asks. I explain why not. She is not pleased. She has bought lamb chops.

I make a coffee, then take a bite out of a Cornish pasty I have bought. The inside is a grey pulp; it tastes of dishcloths and newspaper. I pick up *L'Assommoir* and read a paragraph; then I read a bit of the blurb on the back cover. I read another paragraph, then glance through the introduction.

Then I plug the new phone in and consider phoning Carl to ask if he has ever read this book. I am not certain about his number; I mean I can remember the numbers, though – except for the first three – not exactly in the right order. Three or four attempts would find him. I have mentioned the death of my mum to Martin, Richard and Alison – so the desecration is already done; once more is of no significance. I broke up with him in a deranged state of grief, I will say. I could go over to Carl's house, eat properly, sleep somewhere comfortable, talk to him about her.

Then I am ashamed to be even having these thoughts. I am ashamed to have told Richard about my mum. I am even more furious for using my mother's death to have Alison absolve me of my sins. My mother's death changed nothing; it is the cause of nothing. If she had lived, the future would have been for me to carry on seeing her occasionally though increasingly rarely – with only Christmas guaranteed. I would have continued to remember her birthday, there would still be phone calls, year in, year out, as we each watched the other become old. Though it's depressing for children to see their parents getting old, it's not such a tremendous shock – we've always seen them as old. The other way around, however – parents seeing children growing old – must surely be distressing. Mum is saved from that. We are both saved from a relationship bound together by sentiment and memories of a long-gone, closer family life. Mum will never see me old.

My mother was always in the house. Though she worked full time just like Dad, I was always aware of her presence. She would issue the instructions, lay down the rules about behaviour, bedtimes and curfews. Dad was our advocate; he pleaded for liberty, gave extra spending money, permitted ridiculous clothes and tolerated mutinous attitudes.

I know my mum is dead; it is not going to dawn on me with a shock. I am not in mourning because I always suspected I would live to see her die.

I think about the poem 'This be the Verse' by the only poet whom I have ever read and actually enjoyed, Philip Larkin; this is the only poem I have ever learnt by heart. When I read it I understood it and connected to it even though it did not directly relate to any experience in my own life – just as, rarely, great novels can do. The first lines are, *They fuck you up, your mum and dad/ They may not mean to, but they do.*

I watch a few minutes of TV. The tiny screen hurts my eyes and magnifies the worthlessness of the programmes. I turn it off and force myself to continue with *L'Assommoir*; here is remorse, here is guilt and regret. I cannot become engrossed in this new book because I have not finished *The Counterfeit Confetti*. I do not impose many rules on myself – it is only reasonable to try to obey the few I have.

I press 141 before I attempt to dial Carl's number; then hang up before I even complete dialling it.

Immediately the phone rings. I can only think this might be Mick or Gary, which will be a confrontation. It's a confrontation that is inevitable so I might as well have it over and done with. Unless, by some fortunate miracle, I am blessed and they have agreed a pact to cut me off.

'Hello, Tanya Stephens.'

'Tanya. This is Martin. Martin Heaton. I'm in London.'

I think about, remember, when Martin was on holiday from work and came to my college to have lunch with me. A guy – I can't remember him at all now – came over to speak to me, thinking Martin was only a friend, and asked me out. I teased Martin by flirting with the guy, taking his number and telling him I would consider phoning him. When the guy left, Martin took the number off me and ate it.

I think about, imagine, a future where we reunite and we are pestered by his ex-wife, who remains in love with Martin. Eventually I have to confront her, telling her the full story of Martin and me and how it was always inevitable we would get back together. Except it isn't inevitable, it's impossible.

SEVENTEEN

I read in *The Counterfeit Confetti* – it has gone, of course, so I don't have it here to confirm this, yet I know I am not imagining it; in fact, I remember this so clearly because it jarred a little, even though I had long since accepted it as a fact – it damned well said, *Tanya and Martin never met again*.

I always imagined that Martin would just appear at my door.

'Hello, Tanya,' he'd say. No matter if we had wasted nine months or nine years apart, I would have said hello back and we would have embraced. The time apart would have immediately been immaterial.

'It's a stroke of luck that you reverted back to using your maiden name,' I hear Martin say on the phone now, 'otherwise I would never have been able to find your number.'

I begin to envisage the scenario: I meet up with him; I have to persevere with the story about my divorce. I have to meet the only man I have ever had any genuine feelings for – now nine years older. We have to make promises to keep in touch as if we had drifted apart accidentally. The only missing ingredient preventing such a meeting being an out-and-out disaster is if I had any genuine expectation of renewing my previous relationship with him. He is married, he lives in Wales. I no longer think in terms of permanency, we may both have fundamentally changed. So if there is no chance nor hope nor desire for a resumption, where is the benefit in meeting him? I do not want to see this older version of Martin; the young version is my untainted ideal. A meeting would be awkward, disappointing, disastrous. I pray Martin will not suggest we meet.

'Hello?' Martin says. I must learn not to have these

protracted internal debates whilst I am on the phone; the silence they cause leads people to believe I am rude or deaf. 'Are you OK?'

'I am. I hardly know what to say. What are you doing in London?'

'I get down regularly,' he boasts like a 1970s DJ. 'I have to meet a junior transport minister in the morning.'

'Wow – you're a real bigwig at the DVLA now, huh?' Saying this to anyone else would be perfectly innocuous; it might sound like a genuinely impressed question. That word 'bigwig', however, was one of our shorthand derogatory terms for an individual who took their work too seriously or boasted over the slightest responsibility or perk. I didn't mean to say it; I forgot whom I was speaking to, forgot it was *he* who was the only one who ever shared this joke with me. He will think I am a bitch, that I am ridiculing him, his job, his life now.

'I'm in London fairly often, as it happens. Though I usually try not to stay over. I've met seven different cabinet ministers since I was promoted.'

Martin doesn't remember our joke. He *is* a bigwig in its ludicrous sense – and proud of it.

'You're probably going to say no, and I'll understand if you do . . . '

Here it comes. I'll tell him I'm seeing my boyfriend tonight. No, I'll tell him I *live* with someone.

' . . . I was wondering if you fancied a drink. If it's not too late. Or even going out for something to eat. I'm on expenses whilst I'm here, but I have no one to abuse the privilege with.'

I am hungry, I should have eaten more at Alison's. I abandoned the so-called Cornish pasty in an act of solidarity with insulted Cornish people.

I want to read *L'Assommoir*.

I have to adjust my seating position, my leg has gone numb.

Or I could watch TV.

If I met Martin I could tell him about my burglary, I could tell him about my new, impressive job. It would put a damper on the evening if I reminded him about Mum; and he might think I am cold-hearted for going out for a meal only the day after her funeral. Worse still, talking about her death might make him recall the circumstances surrounding our break-up. I will meet him. I would like to explain that break-up; perhaps I might even apologise and explain I had not fallen out of love with him.

'I can't, Martin. I live with someone.'

'Oh. Are they there with you now?'

'No.'

'Can't you tell them it's just a meal between old friends? Have you ever mentioned me to him?'

'Yes, I've mentioned you.'

'Mentioned I'm married. I have children.'

'It's not that simple.'

'Oh.'

His 'Oh' is a recognition of the severe restrictions some relationships place upon the people involved. He believes I have become involved with some guy who lays down the law, who makes rules I must obey. Martin believes it is possible I have changed so fundamentally to have permitted this to happen.

'The trouble is I . . . The flat has been burgled. Cleared out. I have no make-up. I'll look a mess,' I lie, 'I have no change of clothes.'

'I don't care about that. Do you think I'd give a damn about that? I haven't changed *that* much in nine years, Tanya. I don't care how you look.'

'That's not the point. Men always think women are bothered about their appearance because they want to impress the man. I'm bothered about being scruffy because I don't want to be . . . scruffy.' This is a weak argument; then I make it weaker by immediately contradicting my earlier point: 'I don't want to see you after all these years and not look sensational.'

'We'll meet somewhere where it's dark, then. Tanya, I promise you – if you have alopecia, if you have eczema, if you have been horribly disfigured in some horrendous car accident, I won't care.'

Alison has lent me a reasonable selection of clothes. It would be a challenge to conjure up a wearable combination. I should take a greater interest in clothes; I am a woman, it's supposed to be a part of my natural character. I'm not entirely useless; I can make an effort, for a special occasion, and I wouldn't leave the house unless I felt comfortable in the clothes I was wearing; I always like to dress appropriately. In an ideal world, however, there would be no such concept as clothes fashion. Mao had it right: we should all dress exactly the same. We should dress as they do in bad sci-fi films; that way we could concentrate upon important things like not being stupid. Stupid people have fashion to give themselves a subject of conversation; it's the same reason old people have gardening.

This long silence I disguise as a continuing hesitation:

'Don't you have any qualms about us meeting up, Martin?'

'Why? I think it will be fun. Say yes.'

'Don't you think it's a mistake to rake up the past? I have some fond memories of you; meeting you after all this time might ruin those memories – and I don't want to run that risk.'

'And I have some "fond" memories of you, too.' His voice has gone deeper and the way he emphasises the word 'fond' is to show irony, I think. Fond isn't an adequate word – it's rather insulting, really, when you consider all those other things we once said to each other.

He continues: 'That's why I think it would be great to meet up. It's not a question of raking up the past. Nothing is going to be destroyed. It's just a meal between two people who once meant so much to each other and now they're older they want to be . . . to be friendlier to each other . . . I have – *of course I have* – I have thought about you a great many times since I last saw you. I was devastated when we broke up. And when you phoned me the other day, out of the blue, so much came flooding back to me . . . All good memories, Tanya. I'd like to talk about those memories with the only other person on this planet who shares them. So whaddya say? Please. Come on – it can't be that complicated.'

The goddamn second I put the phone down I know it is a ludicrous proposition I have agreed to. If *The Counterfeit Confetti* did any good it was in making me understand Martin was gone, dead, buried. I have just agreed to having a meal with a corpse.

I wish I had not changed my hair, it was far better before; and I wish I had taken greater interest in the clothes I borrowed from Alison. She has lent me a wide selection; to compensate for wearing a uniform she has nurtured a taste in informal evening wear that is flamboyant, even ostentatious. I will be too self-conscious in any of these clothes and self-consciousness is a trait that cannot be concealed. The skirts are too short, too split; tops are too low-cut, too bright. All the dresses she has lent me are too showy. I am well equipped for a game of charades but not for a date with an ex-boyfriend.

However, I systematically try on everything, varying each combination to try to inspire a compromise. I want to be smart, with style; I want sexiness and sophistication. I want to look young yet elegant. The least promising item proves to be the most successful. It is a simple black evening dress, not too short, with full-length sleeves and a neckline that remains on the discreet side of revealing. My initial reluctance to try it on was caused by a gaudy red ribbon tied in a sort of floral design above the right breast. This, fortunately, is only tacked on, and the stitching is easily removed, leaving no trace. The shoes Alison has lent me are black, too – though unfortunately they are flat. Martin is my height; I would like to wear heels in order to tower over him. I even find my new hair being extremely obedient tonight, brushing smooth and shiny.

I need some make-up; I need some disguise on minor blemishes; I need lips more clearly defined and my eyelashes need to be painted so they can be seen. Though I hate to make this effort, because Martin will believe I have done it for him, without some make-up how plain I look will preoccupy me all through the evening. Appearance gives confidence to women in the same way alcohol gives it to men, the difference is our ability to produce a literate sentence increases as theirs diminishes.

Mrs Davies accepts I am in a hurry and is delighted to let me use her make-up. My visit makes amends for not sleeping in her home again tonight. She takes me to her bathroom where she has a surprising selection; everything I need is here. The only quibble I have concerns her chosen shade of red lipstick. I would prefer a subtle red, a red nearer to pink. Her red is blood red. Once on, however, it looks less bloody. (Being a very nasty, superficial person, before I use her lipstick I surreptitiously wipe a layer off with toilet paper.) Her foundation is too dark for my colouring. Thankfully she has moisturiser – I blend the two to produce a subtler shade.

'Where are you going?' she asks after I have told her about Martin's phone call.

'I have no idea. I'm leaving it up to him.' I am compelled to qualify this answer to show her I am not entirely passive: 'He's paying, so it's only fair.'

'Is it a special occasion?'

'This isn't my boyfriend. This is an old boyfriend. He phoned out of the blue. A very old boyfriend. I mean, he's not ancient – I mean he's from my distant past. I haven't seen him in nine years, that's all. We're just going out to catch up. I still want to look nice. Even though we're just friends.'

I apply the lipstick as I talk to Mrs Davies. My hand starts shaking so much I have lipstick smudged around my mouth like a four-year-old after a jam sandwich. Mrs Davies sees she is disturbing me so leaves the bathroom. I wipe the lipstick off, apply a second coat and remove the excess. Mrs Davies owns a small hand mirror with a magnifying mirror on the reverse, designed especially to make applying make-up easier. When I stare close into this, my eyes look puffy, my skin looks blotchy in spite of the foundation; rather than disguising blemishes it has emphasised my pores into a pox. Mrs Davies has no concealer, but even concealer would be inadequate. I need Artex. I am tired. I am miserable. I am old. Dressed as I am is the best I can do and the result demonstrates a desperation. I look ridiculous, scruffy. Without make-up I look like an exhausted nun; with make-up I look like a decrepit tart.

I agreed with Martin to have him pick me up in taxi. As I wait outside my house the skin on my face hardens in the evening cold. The taxi pulls up and Martin is sat in the back. He leans forward a little, enough for me to see it is him. No adverse changes. Hello, Martin.

I am so conscious of my body it's as if it had been transplanted onto me this morning. My hair itches. I suck in my cheeks biting the insides because – suddenly – I am convinced my face is swollen. I stick my chin out to firm up my jawline. I climb into the taxi conscious of how my every manoeuvre is fake. I move like a female impersonator with first-night nerves.

'Hiya,' he says.

'Hi.'

The driver moves off without hearing further instructions from Martin – the arrangements must have been made on the way to my home.

'Wow. I can't believe how fantastic you look.'

'Thank you,' I answer. I don't believe a word, yet to disagree would sound as if I am fishing for further compliments. I tell him he looks very grown up. I mean it as a sort of joke; he does not react. Instead he continues to stare at me, grinning. In fact, he is staring at my breasts. Though this dress displays them more than I would normally choose, nevertheless Martin was never the leering type. I hunch my shoulders. I begin to touch my chin and shoulder, crossing my arms.

'Where are we going?' I ask, slightly stooping so as to catch his eyes. He is forced to look away from my chest.

'It's a French restaurant in Knightsbridge. It was recommended to me by a colleague. He says it's top-notch.'

'Oh, how super,' I say in my best upper-class twit voice. Though he smiles, aware that I am attempting humour, he makes no attempt to escalate the joke. Martin might look the same but this cannot be him. I do not belong in posh restaurants, I do not want to belong in posh restaurants. I only want to go to posh restaurants with people who – like me – believe they are a joke. Once upon a time Martin would have been that person. He's not in on this joke, he *is* the joke.

When I first began drinking with Caroline she asked me to suggest a nightclub instead of us always going to the ones she liked. Months earlier I had been to a club that I eulogised over. When we went there, however, it contradicted everything I had told her. To me it had become quiet, dull, expensive, snobby, scruffy. The problem was I had put too much store by my own recommendation so I took every fault as a personal insult and on that night all its previous virtues seemed negligible. I can only think something similar has happened now, because every quality I had attributed to Martin no longer seems to exist.

The rest of the journey is taken up with answering questions about my burglary. His house in Wales was burgled several years ago, he tells me. He holds the burglars in contempt, he holds the police in contempt, he holds Wales in contempt. Mrs Davies would like him. He only holds back from exulting in the severest of penalties because he reveres – in my presence at any rate – his old, liberal self. Martin is as nice as pie to the taxi driver and tips him well. When he drives off, Martin complains London taxi drivers talk far too much and are far too expensive. Our driver said nothing.

We are seated immediately and I order quickly. I do not bother with a starter and will skip dessert. I want the evening ended. I pull the shoulder straps of my dress closer to my neck and pull the dress down at the back – this helps cover more of my cleavage.

Martin orders wine and I drink a glass in three quick swigs. I suspect it is an expensive wine ordered to impress me. He shouldn't have bothered as all I know about wines is that some are red and some are white. His French accent was impeccable when he ordered the bottle so I presume the wine is French, unless his showing off is raging out of control. All that has impressed me about him so far is the possibility that this persona might be attributable to nervousness; at least that would be slightly endearing.

'I like that dress,' he says, pointing to – nearly jabbing – my tits.

This cannot be Martin. I hate him. For nine years I revered him, I wrung every second of memory out of our time together, I made a virtue out of all his faults. Every touch, kiss, every word he spoke has passed through my mind a thousand times, sifted of impurities and cherished as perfection. He is my paradigm. Never in all possible futures we might have had, all those paths we might have chosen, in none did Martin develop into this. I know I have changed, too. *He* began the change. I am darker, cynical, solitary – but my humour and my ironies remain intact. My wit and vision might have been thrashed out into a resentful bitterness – but they are still there. He has retained none of his charm. He is brash and showy, he is lecherous and snobby. Worse, much worse than any of this, he has perpetrated the greatest violation of all: he is boring.

And in his presence I am boring too. This is perhaps my greatest disappointment. I know my old self remains in me. When I have imagined our reunion, he has not changed and in my fantasy this consistency resurrects my dormant personality. Once more I am that open, gregarious, vivacious young woman. I crack wild, impulsive jokes; I am openly insulting about people and about ideas I barely understand; I flirt and flaunt my sexuality merely for the fun of the tease. Tonight I had expected her to re-emerge, but she is not inspired to. She stays away, turning down the invite on the grounds of disdain.

I hate this Martin because he must hate this me.

'Very fruity, very full bodied,' he says. He means the wine though his attention remains on my breasts. I now brazenly hike up the front of my dress to hide them. I fill another glass.

'What do you think, Tanya?'

''Sall right,' is my opinion. I quickly finish this glass of wine and pour another. My new plan is to reach the end of the evening having so thoroughly destroyed my inhibitions I will be incapable of restraining myself from telling Martin how I now regard him. Finally, at long last, if I am abusive and insulting enough, Martin will really be gone and this thief in his body will not dare imitate him again. I can only pre-plan rudeness when I know I will be drunk.

Throughout the meal the conversation spirals so rapidly into tedium that Martin is reduced to making comments about the china. His reward is my silence. I consider trying to talk about books, asking him if he still reads as often and what he is reading now. But if this has also changed, if he never reads or has developed appalling taste, maybe only reading fantasy or detective novels, I will have to abort the evening with violence.

'Do you remember how we used to shop for food together?'

'What?' I ask because this question relates to nothing that has yet been spoken aloud.

'In that flat we had. You don't remember shopping together?' he perseveres. 'I do. We were being very adult; we had a list and we bought vegetables.'

Even though I do not want this subject continued, I have to contribute to the conversation because his memory is so flawed.

'We bought junk most of the time, I seem to remember. Crisps and biscuits.' I enjoyed the trips to the supermarket. Martin pushed the trolley, I examined the produce. We had long debates over practically everything we bought.

He corrects me, 'You're talking about the first time we ever did it together. The first time we were experimenting with being independent. I'm talking about later, when we got into a routine of shopping.'

'Our experiment in independence failed when we decorated the kitchen. We thought it would be done in a day and ended up with half of the plaster from one wall coming down on top of us.' I say all this in spite of myself. Martin laughs. This is his first laugh of the evening. It is so strained and false I wonder if it is his first laugh in nine years.

'And fusing the lights in the whole flat!' he adds.

We had two nights of pitch darkness due to neither of us knowing how to mend a fuse box. I don't speak this thought aloud because I do not want the conversation to thrive. But Martin does.

'How did we fix the lights in the end? I can't remember.'

I tell him I can't remember either. In fact I remember perfectly: it was the last time my dad ever came to the flat; Martin was not legitimately living with me. My dad fixed the lights and also ended up re-plastering the kitchen wall.

'Decorating is fun the first time you do it,' Martin continues. 'Even having mice was fun. Do you remember the mice?'

Of course I remember. I had never seen a mouse up until moving into that flat; then I saw a half-dozen within a week. It felt as if I was living in a horror film from the fifties.

'We had a competition to invent a mousetrap,' I remind Martin. 'Your ludicrous idea was to put an empty milk bottle on a slope, with a bit of cheese in the bottom and butter around the inside rim.' It was clever in theory: the mouse is tempted into the bottle by the cheese, but once it has eaten the cheese it can't climb out of the buttery bottle.

Martin adds, 'It didn't work – I guess – because mice are smarter than I gave them credit for.'

'I won the competition with my idea of a bucket of water, a ruler balanced from the table top onto the run of the bucket, with cheese on the end of the ruler. If you remember, the mouse walked along and toppled into the water.' I had Martin fish the dead mouse out. I wanted him to think I was squeamish of dead mice even though I wasn't.

'Your prize was to cut my hair. You'd been nagging to do it since we met,' Martin says, closing his eyes and shaking his head in mock horror at the memory. In fact, we cut each other's hair. We cut each other's hair twice in the time we were together. I liked the way Martin cut my hair. I had begun to cultivate a new image of too-short, dishevelled hair. I remind him of that, and of how I used to dye my hair jet black.

'It's how I remember you, how I still picture you. Jet-black, very short hair.'

He looks at my hair now and I expect he is mentally comparing the before and after pictures, a competition the *after* has no chance of winning. At least he is no longer looking at me in a lecherous way. This look has fondness in it, and regret. The waiter comes and Martin asks if I want a dessert. We both order the same.

'Do you remember that time we were stranded in Shef-field?' I say this out of the blue after searching through the back catalogue of my memories, editing out all the ones with sexual attachments. This struck me because, as clearly as I remember most things, I cannot for the life of me remember why we were in Sheffield.

'Of course I remember it,' Martin answers. 'It was before you had the flat, wasn't it? I remember because we couldn't get home – you were petrified of what your mum would say. We had five hours outside Sheffield railway station, freezing and shattered.'

'But what the hell were we doing in Sheffield in the first place?'

'We'd gone to see The Beautiful South –'

'That's right!' I interrupt. I remember the concert so clearly. Somehow I had separated the memory of that from the memory of later. The group came on late and went off late and so we missed the last train home. Martin – scared of recriminations – talked me out of phoning my dad to drive up and collect us. At dawn, as I tentatively walked up my garden path, I saw the light in Mum and Dad's bedroom go out before I entered the house. The next day they both pretended not to have waited up. This was one of those rare times in my young life when the approach of adulthood made a tangible leap forward.

'I remember us staying in my uncle Graham's house here in London,' Martin says. He adds nothing else and I start to tire of sentences that include the word 'remember', so contribute nothing to this memory. The house was in St John's Wood. Martin's uncle was in Mexico; he had asked us to come to London to keep an eye on the house for a weekend; we were his protection against burglars. The house had a jacuzzi and a leather sofa – we abused both. Every time I pass near St John's Wood I remember that weekend.

'That was our first – you know – full night together,' Martin says, eventually. He avoids eye contact and I wonder if I should let it pass. Unfortunately I cannot resist correcting this major error:

'No it wasn't. Our first time together was in Great Yarmouth. I told my mum and dad I was going there with Gill, from college.'

'Which one was Gill?'

'I made Gill up in case they tried checking. I guess they suspected the truth, though they never said anything.'

'Great Yarmouth. Yes. I hadn't forgotten. Great Yarmouth always makes me think of you. And fireworks night makes me think of you, because of that night we spent just walking from one dying fire to another, right till about three in the morning.'

I try to think of something else but something else refuses to come to me. I think of Great Yarmouth, 4 March, ten years ago.

We went to Great Yarmouth for one purpose only – to

have sex. I can't imagine anyone had ever done that before. Both of us were experienced enough to want something different for *this* first time, the first time with each other. The words had not been used and never would be banished due to their sentimentality, their banality – but already we understood how this – us – was *different*, this was *special*. No, more than that – this was unique. Having sex somewhere unusual, somewhere not home, would guarantee the event its uniqueness, preserving a fuller memory. As short of funds as we were, the bed and breakfast place we found was basic: the room had not been decorated in our lifetime; there was a sink without a plug; and the shared toilet would have been a disgrace to an open-air rock festival. The sheets on the bed were clean, however, and the bed was the only purpose of our visit.

We arrived in Great Yarmouth at one in the afternoon, found the B&B at twenty past, unpacked our single change of clothes and were out exploring the town by two. We walked around shops, along the shore, then ate fish and chips; we bought a bottle of Martini and a bottle of lemonade, then headed back to the B&B. We had little past to regret and a future as directionless and flimsy as a papier-mâché canoe. Even though it was still only five-thirty when we arrived back, the room was so cold we decided it would be smartest to dive straight into bed. The Martini and lemonade were drunk from the single cup that came with the kettle, and a glass, which was on the sink. We talked about the virtues of living on the coast; we discussed – even though we had discussed this before – our first ever experiences of sex. We had not turned a light on in the room, to let the darkness deepen naturally.

Though our abstinence up till then had been determined it had nevertheless been frustrating; so there was a desperate urgency to finally make love, yet we delayed the penetration until it was inevitable, until our limited repertoire was exhausted and we knew of nothing else to do. I was glad I was not losing my virginity; if this had been my very first time ever, then the sex we had would not have been perfect, it would have suffered the blemishes of inexperience and pain. As it happened I can remember it for ever as our vows: a promise between us never to be with someone else in that same way. That is probably the only promise I have ever kept.

When Martin looked at me that time in Great Yarmouth, I saw in him, reflected in his eyes, how I, in turn, was looking at him – and expressing everything we both sensed. That night, when we finally separated, Martin said to me:

'We've done it now.'

I replied: 'I know. No turning back.' The sex was like taking vows.

Martin is the only man whom I have kissed in order to take chewing gum from his mouth. The only man who knew when my period was due. The only man whom I have asked to point out facial spots. He is the only man I have ever been sick over, though this was an unfortunate accident rather than any demonstration of intimacy.

I eat because I do not want the conversation to continue; it is turning away from event memories and towards affection memories. I do not want to talk about Great Yarmouth or anything else that reminds me of him in the past. Nothing more is said until we have finished dessert and ordered coffee.

'Was I fun, Martin?' I ask him.

'Everyone is fun at that age.'

I was fun then. I was no longer fun after Martin.

I tell him, 'Christmas reminds me of you. That one Christmas we had together. We made each other presents, do you remember? You made me a picture frame from plaster of Paris, with my name embossed on it. I still had it, up to the burglary. I made you a novelty paperweight.'

'It was a house brick you painted red.'

I laugh before I realise Christmas will not remind him of me. Christmas will make him think of his children. Naturally.

'Do you remember that time we went horse riding together?' Martin asks. 'I nearly broke my neck, and you got covered in mud. I haven't been on a horse since that day. You?'

'No,' I tell him. The coffee arrives. I do not tell him I have never been on a horse in my entire life. He is mistaking me for someone else. My memories of Martin are sacred; they are never contaminated with memories of other boyfriends; they are never confused by the passing of time or the accumulation of other memories. Martin is always separate and precious. For me.

I cannot remember anything about my first London flat, not even the address. Yet I remember the home Martin lived in with his parents. I could not recall most of the conversations I have had in just the last few days – yet I doubt whether there is anything Martin ever said to me that I have forgotten. I have no substantial memories of past misery, pain, of any sensation other than love for him.

The horse story has exhausted his reserve of *remembers* and I want no more of mine defiled, so the conversation stalls.

I have no option but to take the risk. 'Do you still read as much as you used to?' I am hoping for a conversation like we used to have: heated, enthusiastic, eager. He would extol the virtues of one of those many books he used to press on me, such as Jack Kerouac's *On the Road* or William S. Burroughs's *The Naked Lunch*, books I could never finish because – in my opinion – the writers wrote with an elaborate style contrived to parade their ideas, even at the cost of story. This was at a time when I was going through a stage of reading novels from the sixties, such as Stan Barstow's *A Kind of Loving*, Alan Sillitoe's *Saturday Night and Sunday Morning* and John Braine's *Room at the Top*. Martin, furious, would be outraged at my opinion and insist I read the complete book. Sometimes I invented dismissive arguments simply because I liked to see him so passionate.

'I do still read,' he answers now, 'but I don't get as much time as I used to.'

We finish our coffees. His eagerness to ask for the bill is proof enough he has tired of me.

'I shouldn't have had a dessert,' he tells me, adding his wife nags about how he so easily puts on weight. I see it now, around his neck, his hands, his forehead – he is larger. He might one day die of a heart attack. These high-flyers who take their work seriously and eat rich food are susceptible to those horrible sudden deaths. His wife and children will grieve and his colleagues at work will pay suitable homage. I will still mourn a little, though far less than if this night had not happened.

We stand at the doorway of the restaurant whilst a taxi is summoned. Only one taxi.

'You haven't changed a bit,' Martin says to me in a tone of voice I haven't heard for nearly a decade. Inside the taxi I try to provoke an argument.

'It's kids that age people. Once you have kids you're forced into a position of authority, shouting orders, being bossy – which is exactly what being old is.'

'So you still don't want kids then?'

'Never.'

'What does your partner think of that?' Partner. Partners are in business together; it is not an appropriate word for any relationship where money does not exchange hands.

'Martin . . . I know I told you I lived with someone, but I don't. It was a lie because I wasn't sure what you were expecting from this meeting. It was also a lie because even I can't escape the implied failure of not having someone.'

Martin takes my hand. This is done casually, whilst I am speaking, and my fervour is such that I did not immediately notice.

'What are you doing?' I demand. I do not withdraw my hand, though I know it is giving him a false impression. I have been naive. Married or not, he expects to sleep with me.

'You've had it tough, what with your mum and then the burglary. The DVLA keep a flat in London, which is where I'm staying. It's nothing much, but if you've been completely cleared out, then it's bound to be an improvement on that. Come in with me and have a look, and if you like it you can stay for a couple of weeks.'

Though I have no intention of sleeping with Martin, I am not sure how to end this evening without it being the final conclusion of a past era. I withdraw my hand from his. The taxi turns off the main road. I say nothing. When it stops I will let Martin get out and I will continue home.

'So . . . OK, come on, tell me then, Tanya. It's been so long, it's not a big deal any more, but I would like to know, it's always bugged me . . . Tell me why you dumped me.'

The taxi stops. Martin doesn't move, waiting for my reply. To avoid making one, I get out.

The flat is three floors up in a large, white terraced building. He takes me to the main room, the living room, and sits me on the settee. He returns from the kitchen with an open, half-full bottle of red wine and two glasses. I cannot accurately calculate how much I have already had to drink tonight, yet no matter how foolish my actions I do not have the excuse of drunkenness. I am excessively sober.

Though Martin has turned the gas fire on full, a chill remains in the room. The furniture has been selected by someone who knew they would not have to live with it; it is hard-wearing and practical. The prints on the wall do not infringe any tastes. I am here and letting Martin head for his fall because I want him to fall. This is my latest plan: I want him to take me for granted so when he makes his move the shock of my rejection will make him aware of my contempt far more than if I should run away from him now.

He hands me my drink and sits next to me. Our thighs are in contact and I return his smile. We take sips from the drinks, then he puts his on the floor. Without asking my permission he takes my glass and puts it next to his. He moves to the edge of the settee, one hand on the back-rest, supporting his weight for when he leans in to kiss me. Instinctively, I wet my lips.

He does not kiss me, stopping short – shocked as if I had slapped him, even though I have been careful to express no emotion. He picks up my glass and returns it to me. He sinks back, slouched on the settee, and holds his own glass up to his lips but without drinking. I wait for him to explain.

'I was going to kiss you then.'

'I know.'

'I was hoping I might convince you to spend the night with me.'

'What stopped you trying?'

'This is horrible, isn't it?' he mumbles without looking at me. I am not sure if he is referring to the drink, so I make no reply. 'Us in a room neither of us owns. Why does it seem so uncomfortable?'

I lean back to help me hear him better.

'It wouldn't have mattered at one time. How does this change come over people, Tanya? There must be a cut-off period when situations like this no longer seem romantic. We're neither of us particularly old, you're not even thirty – so why does this seem tacky? If we were both twenty-year-olds and we met up and fancied each other, it wouldn't matter where we made love, it would be fun. Think about us, remember some of the places where we did it! In bathrooms, in fields, in sheds.'

'It's not the location, Martin. It's the predicament. You're married.'

'I'm happily married. I would never betray her.'

'Wouldn't she consider us sleeping together a betrayal?'

'She would. I wouldn't. I could never explain this to her or to anyone else in the world; but *me and you*, Tanya, is a separate thing from the rest of my life. I've mentioned you to my wife, in relation to different things . . . but I've never really explained you to her. I once even told her she was the only woman I have ever loved. If I even attempted to talk about the truth . . . No, that *would* be a betrayal. It might even be a divorce! . . . Tell me you've thought about me, Tanya?'

'I have thought about you, Martin. Of course . . . And you? Have you thought about me?'

'Do you want me to be honest?'

He is going to tell me he rarely thinks about me, or when he does he rapidly dismisses every thought.

'I've thought about you every single day, Tanya.'

I believe him. Those are words I have longed to hear. I want to be away from him now.

'You still haven't explained. You have to tell me why you dumped me.'

I take his glass. To prevent him speaking I give him a little kiss. He stops me.

'Tell me why you dumped me.'

It will serve no good purpose, but I have no choice:

'If you really must know . . . I broke up with you all those years ago as a test. I expected you to pursue me, begging; to demand that I come back to you. I wasn't surprised when you didn't. I understood how the tactics you chose were smarter. But they only strengthened my resolve, so I made the test harder by deliberately avoiding you. Then you were gone with no chance of coming back and the mistake I'd made began to punish me. Since then I've got on with my life and I am not dissatisfied with the result. I like the fact that I am alone and prefer being alone. It's contentment. I've had a steady stream of boyfriends, each relationship starting by accident and developing naturally. But they all end when I realise there's no point. I know it will never again be as wonderful as when I was with you. That relatively short period in my life I've revisited and analysed more than I dare tell you. I want that love again, with someone. And I know it's not possible.'

He is surprised. He does not reply immediately, not daring to let his delight show in case I read it as him being too cocky, too pleased with himself. Then we kiss. This close there is no difference any more; there are no nine years apart and no wife; he is no longer dull and changed.

I take his hand and lead him off to the bedroom. This fails because I do not know the flat's layout and so lead him into a cupboard. He shows me the bedroom, leaving me there whilst he returns to the living room to turn down the fire and turn off the lights. I do not begin to undress, hoping that on his return he will make some gesture to create an illusion of sensuality. He doesn't. He says nothing. Rather than undressing me, he begins to undress himself. I undress, keeping my knickers on. I get into bed. He follows. We kiss and we begin to embrace and touch. Each response I make is phoney and each caress I initiate is coldly calculated.

'Shall I turn the light out?'

In the darkness I become aroused. Martin's lips are warm again, his hands and body return me to a joy I had forgotten. Sex in love. We never speak, realising the illusion depends on silence. Then I am happy. An old happiness, a happiness that is a physical state. And memory.

EIGHTEEN

I take a calculated look at Martin, asleep. This is going to be my very last look at his face, this face that has embedded itself in my consciousness throughout my third decade of life. I was sure I knew it, I believed it held no surprises; and though I see nothing I could not have expected to see, the longer I stare the more unrecognisable he becomes until I reach a point where I wonder how I could have believed there had been no adverse changes in the last ten years. The only possible explanation is that his hair has not altered: same length, same colour, same style. Changed hair dates people – especially men. Apart from his hair, he is a completely different person: uglier, stupider, older.

The sex was discomforting. Last night, without speaking, I learnt about the years that have passed and those fundamental changes that have overwhelmed us both; but I could still sense the Martin of old. Yet as the sex progressed I had to try harder to envisage Martin as he was and forget about this guy who was with me now: this man who was awkward and had no stamina, who performed sex as if it didn't matter. His climax accelerated my nausea; as he finished all I could think about was how I wanted him off me. My revulsion was uncalled for and I fought it, I really did. I stroked his back until he could recover enough strength to roll onto his side; when he did I caught the lines of his profile in the narrow band of light seeping around the curtains' edge. He looked nothing like Martin. I was horrified for a second; I had been duped and molested. All that stopped me screaming out was a tiny morsel of sanity, which reminded me of reality: of course it was Martin. I forced a fake sleep so successfully that I fooled myself. Then I woke, ill with disgust. He was too old for me. I know I will never see him again because I never want to see him again; nothing remains of him.

Nothing remains of me, either. Nothing of the Tanya who enjoyed the passions of sex with a relish dangerously close to nymphomania. This is my greatest regret. I had expected that past self to still be in me. Whenever I imagined reunions such as this, Martin had not changed and this consistency resurrected my dormant sensuality. I would attack Martin, I would shout instructions, I would invite his fantasises. I would be liberated and inexhaustible. It's not that I have lost passion or any willingness to experiment; the difference is that these days sex offers no surprises; there are no freedoms to explore because my travelling companions know the routes all too well. In bed with Martin I had hoped some of our old delights would consume us. Instead he followed motions he had rehearsed on someone else; and I had accepted this, making neither complaints nor suggestions.

He wakes. In spite of the long separation, and flying in the face of every thought in my head, we easily renew our old waking-up-together rituals. We face each other and say a sleepy hello, there is a kiss and mutual smiles. I turn around so my back is towards him and he can curl up to me. It is not until we become thoroughly reaccustomed that we recall how the routine progressed: we would have sex again. I wish I was still asleep. Somewhere else. Martin kisses me on the back of the neck. My sudden stiffness alerts him. He dare not kiss me again; his right hand, which has been stroking my arm, stops. I now straighten out my spine and lift my arms up to my head in order to make his hand fall off my arm. We are in a stalemate: there is going to be no more sex; any resemblance to how things were a decade ago has ended. I want to get out of bed, get dressed and leave.

'What time do you start work?' he asks. The alarm clock is on his side of the bed.

'Eight,' I say. Hopefully it is seven-forty-five and I will have an excuse to dash away.

'You have ages yet,' he mumbles. 'It's only six.' Damn.

'I have to get home first, though.'

'I'll drive you. I have to get into work early anyway.'

He's never mentioned having a car here! That's not fair. If I am expected to lie convincingly he has an obligation to first furnish me with all the pertinent facts.

'I don't want you to drive me. I have to go now,' I insist. 'I'll get dressed in the bathroom.'

I am at the wrong side of the bed. To get out I have to climb over him, which will be too provocative. Fortunately, he solves this dilemma by getting out of bed first. He stands naked, unashamed. I grab a pillow and hold it to me as I scuttle past him and charge into the bathroom.

From the bathroom I shout:

'Can you hand me my clothes, please? They're on the chair.'

A moment later I hear a knock on the bathroom door. I open the door and put my hand out. He gives me my clothes.

'Tanya, is something wrong?' he asks. I close the door. I dress quickly; then for several moments I have to lean over the toilet bowl, though I am not actually sick. For fifteen minutes I do nothing, dreading going back out. Remembering the sex, I condemn myself – because there is no one else to do the job and I deserve condemning. Only parents retain the right to condemn the morality of their adult children. I no longer have any parents who can condemn my morals; I am free of that threat now. I could be a guest on *Parkinson* and say fuck. I could appear nude in *Playboy* though I doubt they would pay me much. Besides, the fine sculpting of pubic hair would be too much hassle.

As part of my self-condemnation I prepare a speech to make to Martin, which, if it contained every one of the thoughts running through my mind, every truth and revelation I have to tell him about the past and this present, would last for hours, but in a nutshell is: Martin, you remain the only man I ever loved *but* . . .

. . . *But* when I finally leave the bathroom he is not there. He has left a brusque note telling me to lock the door after I leave, then to post the key back through the letter box. This is no problem – the note says – because he has taken the spare key. It ends with, *I understand. Goodbye.*

Though the letter frees me from an embarrassing farewell, of my having to lie to him or him to me, nevertheless it is an insultingly inadequate goodbye. I look around to see if perhaps this is only a secondary note and he has left another, full of melancholic affection and tender sentiment. There is no such note. I look in the bin to see if there is an earlier, longer draft. When I do not find one I scrutinise the finished note, checking whether there are euphemisms and metaphors I did not immediately spot. I find none and realise I have no time for these paranoias; I am in Holborn. I have to return to my own flat, change, then arrive at Caroline's flat in Islington before nine. I am in a desperate rush.

I am in far too much of a rush to begin looking through his possessions.

There is a suitcase under the bed. Empty. In the bedside cabinet there is an empty spectacle case and a photograph in a silver frame. The photograph is of Martin with a woman and two children. The woman looks nothing like me. Good looking, though – in a Welsh sort of way. There is also a tatty copy of Keith Waterhouse's *Billy Liar*, a book I believe should have the same prestigious cult status in this country as J.D. Salinger's *The Catcher in the Rye* does in America. After I had phoned him a memory must have been triggered, which made him dig this book out. It is a copy I gave him ten years ago; in the inside cover are two words I wrote in large capital letters: READ THIS. The duplicity of Billy's life struck a chord with me then, as it must with most young people, about how to cope with clinging to your hopes whilst also having to accommodate the demands of the real world. I can't remember if, at the time, Martin ever shared his verdict of the book with me. Maybe this is his first reading.

I am dressed in evening wear so would look too much of a prat using public transport. I am forced to call a minicab.

On my way home I remember how, when we were first together, I used to look at Martin asleep and often (I have no explanation for this) feel sorry for him. Though he had not led a hard life, he had not suffered any traumas or any measure of misery, I hated that he could have any troubles – no matter how slight – and wanted to make sure he had even fewer in the future. I wanted to be around to help him cope, to fend off worries with my assistance and love. When I looked at him this morning, my conclusion had been that all the troubles he might now suffer he has brought upon himself; if he is unhappy it is of no consequence. Everyone is unhappy.

I arrive home at seven. There is a cheque waiting from my car's insurance company. I no longer posses my bank book so in order to deposit the cheque I will have to visit the bank in person and explain. I run a bath and relax, even though I have no soap and have to take care not to wet my hair because I have no towel. I wipe off the excess of water with my hand. Waiting for myself to dry I become bored. There is no food, no worthwhile TV, no books. I choose something to wear quickly, as the choice is minimal; then I leave – there is nothing else to do here that could occupy my time. I cannot return here tonight; I must ask Caroline about staying with her.

I set off to Caroline's with time enough to walk. Today I have to start getting my life back into some kind of order: I will have to buy a flannel.

I arrive early at Caroline's. She has not yet set off to pick me up, her car is still outside. When Caroline opens her door, instead of greeting me with a smile, as I might have anticipated, she instead asks what I am doing here, in an outraged way – as if I had turned up at a funeral carrying a shovel. She does not immediately let me in.

'Richard is here,' she eventually says. 'Do you want to wait until he's gone before you come in?'

'Why?'

'In case it's awkward for you.'

'Awkward?'

'Oh – I don't know! I just thought . . . Well, come in, then.'

Richard has his jacket on, ready to leave. He now delays leaving so as not to appear as if he is avoiding me. Any awkwardness I suffer is due to Richard's smile, the way he keeps his eyes on me, how he inches his way towards me. Caroline seems oblivious to this, caring only to make a show of how she has him now and I do not.

It has been nagging away at me, I have not granted it too much thought in case I was wrong, but now I see how Caroline has changed in the years between when I knew her before and now. The change is her desperation, her attitude to men. She always wanted boyfriends, she always enjoyed men and sex; she was always open about this; it was one of the things I enjoyed about her company. Before, however, it was fun; she did not hold any individual man in high regard. Maybe it was Ken who changed her, but I see she has become not just a woman who needs a man but one of those women who is prepared to mortgage her entire character simply in the pursuit of landing herself a man who'll stay. It's degrading.

When they begin to kiss goodbye I go into Caroline's kitchen to make coffee. Five minutes later I hear Richard shout 'Goodbye, Tanya' before Caroline comes into her kitchen, grinning. She drinks her coffee, offering me a Danish pastry – which I take gratefully.

When we begin work the immediate routine, established yesterday, starts again. After Caroline talks me through those projects she has set out for me, a silence develops, which is so dominant it survives the full morning. To announce its breaking, and to avoid startling her, I first cough. I have her attention.

'Caroline . . .'

'Huh?'

'I was wondering about Ken . . . About Richard. Does Richard know about Ken?'

She looks up from her work. She frowns elaborately, completely out of proportion to any offence the question may have caused.

'What do you mean? Of course Richard knows about Ken. How could he not know about Ken?'

'I mean . . . You know, does Richard know how you feel about him?'

She puts her pencil down. She stands! This is ludicrous anger now. I have clearly hit a raw nerve.

'I don't feel anything for Ken. For Kenneth.' Saying his name in full emphasises her lack of emotion. 'All right, so I went out with him for a while – but big deal. Am I supposed to still be completely in love with every one of my ex-boyfriends?'

'I was just asking. I was just wondering.'

She does not immediately sit. I stay silent and return to work; until then, like a child with a scab, I have another pick:

'Ken was different though. Right?'

'Tanya, you're talking as if you were around when I was

seeing Ken – but you weren't. Richard is "different", not Ken. Ken is a nuisance. I don't even particularly like him, if you must know.'

'You're right, I wasn't around when you were seeing Ken –' (Caroline sighs heavily, irritated by my perseverance) '– all I have to go by is what you told me about both of them. Richard, you said, meant nothing, and Ken, you told me –'

'Don't quote back to me anything I might have said.' Though she now returns to her chair, she remains indignant. 'When you found that photograph of me with Richard, I wanted you to think I didn't care about him – so I pretended I still liked Ken. But I don't. I can't see why you're going on about it. What's the big deal? I don't see Ken any more – I see Richard. And I'm happy. It shouldn't worry you. Not unless you still have feelings for Richard that you aren't admitting to.'

'I don't.'

'Maybe it's Ken –'

'It isn't. Ken?!' There is more revulsion in the way I say his name than I have any right to express. 'It is possible to be concerned about someone without necessarily fancying them.'

'All right, so come on then – out with it – who is it you're "concerned" about?' Caroline sneers.

'Richard.'

Again she puts the pencil down; again she stands. I stand too, now.

'I knew it!' she hollers. 'You still fancy him! You want him back!'

'I do *not* want him back. I've told you – I have someone else.'

'This "Carl" who you've talked about – is that who you mean? This Carl who I've never seen and who Richard knows nothing about.'

I sit down and make an attempt to sound superior, more dignified than her. I do not wish to be drawn into the subject of my relationship with Carl, not least when I remember I do not have a relationship with Carl.

I say, 'All I care about is that you're going out with Richard for the wrong reason.'

'And what is this "wrong" reason, then, exactly, in your opinion? Tell me – I'm fascinated.' She stands even closer to me now. With her standing over me I have to bend my neck backwards to see her. I am aware of how vulnerable this makes me.

'I think you might be using Richard. I think the reason you're seeing Richard is to make Ken jealous.' I don't really think this, I am protecting her feelings. Really, I think Richard is using her.

'What is wrong with you?' she sneers. 'Why don't you listen? I do not want Ken back. I want Richard. I like going out with Richard. I'm even beginning to think I might be falling in love with him.'

I laugh. It's a phoney laugh designed to show contempt:

'You treat love like other people treat service stations – you pop in whenever it's convenient. You loved Ken. He dumps you. You sleep with Richard and now you love him.'

'Stupid bitch,' she says, not venomously yet nevertheless taking me by surprise.

'Don't you call me a stupid bitch!' I yell. 'Bosses can't talk to their employees like that.'

'Oh grow up. This is hardly an argument between a boss and employee, is it? Don't talk crap.'

'It's you who's talking crap, not me!' I retaliate. We continue arguing. It's petty and childish, degenerating into whoever can think of the best abuse. I call her fickle and weak; she calls me hypocritical. I am a hypocrite because she is clinging to her initial theory that I am objecting to her seeing Richard only because I still want him. The fact of me dumping him has been overlooked. So I remind her of this and accuse her of stupidity in neglecting to include it in her theory. She concocts another theory, that my motive for dumping Richard was to force him into moving in with me, or even marrying me. I accuse her of projecting her own inadequacies and obsessions onto me.

The argument might have turned vicious if it had not then been interrupted by Kenneth arriving. When Caroline returns upstairs accompanied by him, she is silent and evasive. Though our argument was building to a nasty climax, she now only sits quietly. She draws, ignoring us both. Kenneth

says hello to me, has a quick look at some of the drawings I
have been working on, nodding approval, then looks down
at Caroline. He waits.

'Caroline?'

'What?'

'Well . . . '

'Well, what?'

'You know what I'm here for.'

'No. What?'

'The revisions we talked about on the phone. You've done
them, right? So where are they?'

Caroline puts her pencil down and freezes into an
expression of extreme annoyance.

'You haven't done them!' Ken quickly deduces. Caroline
said nothing to me about any revisions so I am free to enjoy
Ken's anger with impunity.

'Caroline, I don't set deadlines for nothing,' he tells her. 'I
set you deadlines because *I've* been set deadlines.'

'I've been busy.'

This complacency infuriates Ken.

'I know only too well what's been keeping you busy!' he
retorts. 'You're more occupied with spending time with this
new boyfriend than you are with your work.' If Ken is
jealous, then it is subtle and easily buried under the extremity
of his anger.

Caroline answers: 'One thing has nothing to do with the
other – so shut up.'

'Don't you tell me to shut up!' he shouts back. As the
momentum of his anger increases I begin to unravel the
mechanics of their working relationship: only when he is
angry is Ken confident enough to express his power.

He goes on: 'If we miss the deadlines set by the printers we
miss shipments and the books don't make it into the shops in
time.'

'Oh, relax, won't you? It's no big thing. We'll get it done
tomorrow.'

Though Caroline is continuing the argument with the same
apparent viciousness, her voice is less forceful and she keeps
an eye on how he responds to her, just in case she crosses the
line. She is his subordinate. I pretend to be concentrating on

my work. I doubt if I am fooling them, and if they checked they would notice the lead on my pencil has broken off.

'Tomorrow is too late! This is how you earn your living, Caroline.'

'Work is not the only thing in my life, as it is in yours. You need to loosen up a bit and go out one night and try to get laid.'

Kenneth laughs. Though the single laugh is sincere and natural, I have no idea how to interpret it: maybe he *is* seeing someone who demands a punishing sexual schedule, so his laugh is irony. It might be a laugh of contempt for Caroline's corrupt priorities; or his laugh might simply be a dismissive end to the childish debate. This seems increasingly likely when he does not pursue the argument; instead he calmly issues an ultimatum.

'OK. It's clear to me we can't hope to have a professional relationship if you refuse to respect me and respect the deadlines we're given.'

'Respect *you*!' Caroline yells. She points at him, looking at me to be her accomplice. I see real desperation in the gesture and I pity her. I have been erasing a non-existent pencil mark; I blow away the rolls of rubber.

'You're not the only freelance illustrator in London, you know,' he tells her. 'Not by a long chalk.'

'What's that supposed to mean? Is that a threat?'

'People buy *The Stink Monsters* for the story. I can easily find . . . I'm not threatening you, but if you don't start taking our work more seriously I'll have no option. I will get another illustrator.'

Caroline replies, 'Go on then.'

This is a revelation to me. I didn't know Caroline could be sacked. How could the circumstances have arisen where I accepted a job from someone who could be sacked? Caroline picks up her pencil and returns to drawing as if nothing adverse has been said. Even if she was capable of pulling off the illusion of recklessness, am I supposed to be impressed? She is being reckless with my job, too. She has forgotten she now has an extra mouth to feed. To illustrate my concern and to gain his attention, I look at Kenneth with an outrageously melodramatic expression: a charades mime to portray a beggar. Kenneth notices.

'It doesn't mean you'll be out of work, Tanya,' he tells me.

Caroline gives no indication of hearing this until I speak.

'Thank you,' I answer. I smile at him.

'You are unbelievable!' Caroline yells at me, as suddenly brought to life as an animatronic clown. She turns to Ken: 'How can you employ her – you haven't even seen her work!'

'I've seen some. You thought she was good enough to take on. Are you saying your judgement can't be trusted?'

Unable to answer this she turns back to me: 'How ungrateful can you be?'

'What the hell am I suppose to be grateful for? You've had two days of hard work out of me, I haven't seen a penny. You've been thoroughly miserable throughout that time – and I've supplied you with a boyfriend. And today – because of Richard – you've suddenly decided I'm the enemy.'

'I knew this had something to do with Richard! You were flirting like crazy with him this morning, did you think I didn't notice?'

'Are you mental? I. Dumped. Him. I do not want him back – and if I did I would take him. It would be easy.'

After silence and a frozen expression, Caroline retorts with:

'He only got with you because you look like Gail.'

'He only got with you because I no longer want him.'

Ken guides me out of Caroline's home before the argument turns violent.

Caroline shouts down to him:

'What about me?'

'We'll talk. Maybe we can still work together. But you need to grow up, Caroline.'

Outside Caroline's home Ken asks for my phone number and address. We discuss nothing else. I feel as if I have given my phone number to an attractive man, way out of my league, whom I have met casually and whom I have no reasonable expectation of ever hearing from again. He plans to still work with Caroline. His offer of work to me was only retaliation. I know this.

I walk around London, not arriving home until eight. I

think about last night with Martin. How stupid I was for letting it happen. After the reality of seeing him again I am now no longer free to indulge in fantasies of a reunion. With that illusion shattered, I am empty. I had the reunion and it stank. When I repeat his words, 'I've thought about you every day, Tanya,' I see only the face of the young Martin. If I have to remember him now, I hear those words as a lie; there can be no way he got married yet still obsessed about me with anything like the same intensity I obsessed about him. My real truth is that I did not think about him every day – it only feels as if I did.

I hear my phone ringing as I mount the stairs up to my flat. I do not rush to open the door. The phone continues to ring. I am forgetting this is a normal phone, not my answerphone. I answer it and I am not at all surprised that it is Richard. Before I tell him to drop dead I allow him a chance to explain why he is phoning. As if I do not know.

'I wanted to find out how you are,' he begins. 'We didn't get a chance to speak this morning.' I wait. He continues, 'I hope you don't mind me phoning.'

'Which one of your ex-girlfriends does Caroline look like?'

'Caroline was a mistake. She's already become a nuisance – phoning me every chance she gets. I've just finished with her.'

'Why have you done that?'

There is such a prolonged silence I am unable to prevent myself from adding: 'You know there's no chance of us two ever getting back together, don't you?'

'I'm not happy with the explanation you gave me for breaking up.'

'What? There's no tribunal you can take this to, Richard. If someone finishes with you, you have to grin and bear it. It's the way of the world. You act as if you've never been dumped before.'

'I haven't. Caroline says you've met someone else, that you were seeing him even when you were seeing me. Is that true?'

'Ah – that's what this is about. You're not bothered about being dumped, you just don't like the idea that I could have met someone I prefer to you. Well, I have some bad news for you Richard – I prefer *everyone* to you.'

'What are you being so nasty for?' he whinges. This makes me want to sound even nastier.

'If you had been reasonable about this I might still be friendly with you and I might think you warrant an explanation, but now you deserve all you get. Yes, I have met someone else. I've met someone who's exactly what I'm looking for. He is exactly everything you are not. He reads. He's smart. He's interesting.'

'Caroline told me he's a road sweeper.'

Now I become really angry: 'So what? So fucking what? What the hell makes you so superior? Sweeping roads is an honest way of making a living. Straightforward physical labour – entirely justified. Would it be preferable if I was seeing some ponce in an overpaid, worthless, redundant non-job: a market researcher, an image consultant, a press agent? And what job do you do that gives you the right to sound so superior? You're a carpet fitter. That's hardly rocket science, is it?'

'What are you getting at me for? I never said anything about his job! I was just telling you what Caroline said.'

I am not listening. My anger has rapidly given way to boredom.

'Whatever you might think of him, Richard, just remember – I dumped you for him.'

'He sounds like a cunt,' Richard says. He knows he has lost. I have told him 'cunt' is the one swear word I object to.

'Richard, never phone me again. And if we should accidentally meet sometime in the future, don't acknowledge me, don't speak. In fact –'

I hang up. The phone rings within seconds. I know it is Richard, determined to have the last word.

'Are you completely fucking deranged?' I bellow.

'God, I'm sorry, Tanya. I shouldn't have called, right? You never wanted to hear from me again, did you?'

It is Martin. I am standing in the middle of my gutted flat, on bare floorboards, still in my coat. It is cold and I will have to sleep on the hard floor. On top of all this I have just made an idiot of myself to him, The Only Man I Have Ever Loved – and I know I will never refer to him in that way again. The title is an anathema to me now; it is as obsolete and as insulting as calling Mohammed Ali Cassius Clay.

'It's all right, Martin. It was a joke – I've just got off the phone to a friend and I was having a laugh with her.'

'I tried phoning earlier. Several times. Were you out?'

'Why have you phoned, Martin?'

'Because I don't want your lingering memory of me to be hatred.'

'I don't hate you,' I tell him; then realise this is not so. These newer memories are something like hatred. Without telling me, secretly, deceptively, behind my back, he changed. I remembered the note Martin left for me. Maybe if he had signed it *Love, Martin* it wouldn't seem so abrupt.

'Martin . . . Come over.'

I have had two phone calls: one from Richard, one from Martin. Both ex-boyfriends – even though they are at opposite ends of the spectrum: my first and best experience to the latest, the one I feel nothing for.

I've never been the type to keep on a friendly basis with ex-boyfriends. I usually try make it known the end is permanent. I have never regretted this policy. Until now. I wouldn't mind another phone call, this time from Carl but similar to the one from Richard: asking why I had ended the relationship, expressing dissatisfaction with my explanation. I could back-track, give further reasons that invite debate and eventually lead to my having my mind changed, followed by a swift and happy reconciliation. However, Carl doesn't ring and I have to prepare myself for Martin's visit. My intention is to look my very best. I rummage through the carrier bags and choose, from Alison's clothes, trousers and a sweater that will make me look far sexier than last night's attempt.

I go see Mrs Davies. I explain I would like to borrow her make-up again. I prepare lies, in case she asks about where I stayed last night. I cannot tell her the truth – I am so accustomed to lying to her that changing the policy now runs the risk of arousing her suspicions. It's all academic; the sad, lonely old cow is just delighted to have any visitor, no matter how briefly and for whatever reason. To compensate for my flagrant abuse of her hospitality I permit Mrs Davies to sit in whilst I apply the make-up. I grant her the freedom to talk about her favourite subject – loneliness – by asking how her husband died. She may have told me this before, I forget. It's not as if I take notes. It's not as if I listen. The answer is – he died due to being old.

'I get so very lonely. Don't you get lonely, Tanya?'

'Me? I think loneliness is only a symptom of boredom. I'm a bit lonely at the moment because it's easy to get bored in an empty flat. Books are the antidote to loneliness.'

'Books? Oh no, I don't think so. Only a husband is. Would you like to get married, Tanya?'

'I don't know.' This is my answer under circumstances such as these. If I begin a longer debate with Mrs Davies I could never win, she would never be able to comprehend my arguments. Hers is that rare experience of marriage – a fluke of happiness.

'You should think about it,' she advises. 'It's the most wonderful thing.'

Already I can no longer resist the temptation to argue:

'It's a wonderful thing – if you're lucky.'

'Oh luck – yes, of course, luck is part of it. You have to work at it, too, though. It's not all an easy ride.'

'As it so happens, the man who's coming to see me tonight is the only one I've ever considered . . . or imagined what it would be like to marry.'

'Is this the same man who took you out last night?'

'Yes.'

'Oooh!' she exclaims. I add nothing to prevent her thinking she might have a wedding invitation in the post. She continues: 'Is there any reason you didn't marry him when you knew him before?'

'It was a long time ago. It probably wouldn't have worked. He was my first love!'

'I met my first love at school but we didn't start courting until we'd left. We worked at the same firm and he was always dropping notes off for me. We started going dancing together, but always in a big group of us; he didn't really like dancing but he was always there; he'd come and talk to me whenever I stopped to get my breath back. Then we started going to the pictures together. The first film we saw was *High Society*. Then he came home to meet my parents.'

'What happened to him?'

'We had an engagement party in a social club, and a year later we were married.'

'So Mr Davies was your first love? You never loved anyone else?'

'I never went out with anyone else.'

'That's sweet and everything,' I tell her, considering how best to ask the next question, 'but don't you ever wonder if you missed out? I mean, when you were married and you lived through all those changes in the sixties, with the permissive society and everything ... Didn't you ever wonder ...'

She proudly tells me she has never wondered. I do not question her, though I believe her answer to be a falsehood. Anyone who orders a meal in a restaurant stares in regret and jealousy as other diners are served better, more appetising meals during their wait. I live and have grown up in a different world to Mrs Davies. Most women under fifty have had sexual partners prior to their husbands; the vast majority of us could not imagine *not* experiencing a wide selection, to gain a feel for the market, to see everything on offer and view all potential opportunities before we settle on a final selection.

I achieve a far subtler effect with the make-up than I did last night. These clothes free me to be less self-conscious than the dress, consequently my confidence is about as high as possible under these hurried circumstances. Mrs Davies shovels on compliments. When the doorbell rings I tell Mrs Davies to keep her door open as I would like to introduce Martin to her. She is so delighted by this treat it is as if I have invited the Prime Minister around.

Martin holds a bunch of flowers: inconvenient because I have no vase and, anyway, flowers are never any use. Professionally, I give him warm thanks and invite him in. He has a taxi waiting, so dismisses the driver. It suits me that he has not come in his car.

'You look great,' he tells me. This compliment is made as we climb the stairs, and his only real view of me is my arse.

'I want to formally introduce you to my upstairs neighbour,' I whisper to him. 'Take the flowers, so she will see you've bought them for me. Humour me here, Martin – it'll give her a thrill.'

We pause before we mount the final flight of stairs. I kiss him on the cheek, to force him to lower his guard.

He repeats, 'You do look great, you know. You look nicer now than you did nine years ago. Do you believe me?'

'Yes.'

Mrs Davies is bowled over by Martin's charm. He apologises for intruding, he flatters her on her home, he makes jokey references about me, suggesting that somehow we are a real couple.

'She's a lovely girl,' Mrs Davies tells him. 'She looked after me when I was burgled so I'm glad she has someone to look after her now.'

'I'm going to do my best,' Martin coyly tells her, handing me the flowers again.

'He has a company flat here, Mrs Davies. He's suggested that I stay there until I sort my place out.'

'That sounds nice,' Mrs Davies says, nodding to Martin.

I continue, 'Problem is – we'll only end up sleeping together. Again. Which I don't want. I don't want it – and I'm sure his wife would want it even less.'

A very British silence follows: a silence whilst both Martin and Mrs Davies compose themselves so they can act as if they heard nothing. Martin is wide-eyed and shaking, as if he has been slapped.

'There's no point,' I tell Martin. He pulls a deliberately puzzled expression. I know I should try to expand upon this but *there's no point*. I give him back his flowers.

'It was nice to meet you,' Martin tells Mrs Davies as he reopens her living room door to leave. We have not been there long enough to take up her offer of a seat.

'Yes, and you too,' Mrs Davies replies. She smiles at him, regardless.

Martin's eyes are on me for a second, then he exits. This is a humiliation he could never forgive me for. He will never again contact me, and should I ever – in some disturbed, nostalgic state – try to contact him he will surely tell me to go to hell. I also embarrassed Mrs Davies – which was a bonus. I apologise to her anyway.

'My mother died, Mrs Davis.' That seems to explain everything.

To encourage sleep, I strategically place in my head the image I have of Martin from my living-room window, stood on the edge of the kerb, still carrying the flowers, as he attempts to get his bearings. He looked up and down the street, and by chance a taxi came by. It is not the catastrophic image I would recently have anticipated. I cannot keep the image, it fails to interest me.

Instead I construct an identikit picture of Carl's face. I see the completed picture, but know it is inadequate. Nevertheless it helps me sleep soundly.

Martin got in the taxi. The taxi went.

The End.

NINETEEN

Of my stolen books the three I will miss most are all by W. Somerset Maugham: *Of Human Bondage, The Moon and Sixpence* and *The Razor's Edge*. They are perhaps the three books I have reread the most, though it has been several years now since I last read them so I can no longer remember the names of the lead characters. In *The Razor's Edge* the main character returns from the First World War having seen such futile waste of life he cannot ship back into the pattern expected of him and so goes in search of a greater meaning. Meanwhile, the girl he leaves behind marries a man who genuinely cares for her, yet she cannot forget, and always remains in love with, the main character. In *The Moon and Sixpence* the main character is a respectable middle-aged businessman who simply abandons everything, job, wife, family, to pursue the life of an artist, in Paris. In spite of this desertion, and his often-stated complete indifference to the fate of his wife, she continues to be in love with him and would take him back. *Of Human Bondage* is, in my opinion, the truest love story in fiction, the most insightful into the true character of obsessive love. The main character pursues a woman who cares nothing for him and is even openly hostile to him, using him only when it is convenient for her; and even though he knows how she feels, it makes no difference to his love for her.

I can easily replace these books with new editions but I will miss the familiar covers, the smell of old paper, the tattiness caused by having been held in my hands for hours.

In the morning I leave my flat as soon as I am washed and dressed. I go shopping. I need to own something to store food in, to cook food on. I need my own clothes. I have made a rudimentary list of those items I really should buy, and now have the added benefit of a new credit card, which arrived today. The house insurance is in the process of being paid and eventually I will buy carpets and furniture. Many people might actually even envy my derelict position if they are lumbered with furniture and a decor cobbled together over the years. They would rejoice at having the slate wiped clean and the chance to start again. However, for me, my first port of call is – inevitably – a bookshop. I need books! Though this is a weakness I am also here with a purpose; I go to the appropriate alphabetical section and by sheer good fortune find myself in front of *King Jesus* by Robert Graves. I have been assured it is out of print, yet here it is. The £3.99 price suggests it is old stock. It is the only book I buy this day.

I next go to Marks & Spencer's. I choose a blouse and a cardigan, which I immediately put back. I once experienced an epiphany: I went from wearing fashionable clothes to choosing predominantly dark clothes, T-shirts and jeans with boots. But the cancer, the change to wearing cardigans and blouses, grew slowly, malignantly, till I stopped regarding it as an illness and gave up the search for a cure. Being reminded by *The Counterfeit Confetti* of how I dressed when I was with Martin has persuaded me to never buy blouses or cardigans again.

In Carl's opinion, the most beautiful woman in the world is Juliette Binoche, the French actress. When he told me this he added he liked the way she could dress simply, how she could look both casual and elegant at the same time.

With elegance, simplicity and Frenchness in mind, I go into an out-of-the-way clothes shop I have passed before yet never entered because it looked expensive. Inside I find a high-necked, dark-blue wool sweater. I find a short-sleeved, beige viscose top with a crew neck. I buy these and a pair of straightforward black trousers.

I buy fish and chips and go home. I will read *King Jesus* before I finally phone Carl. This present will be my apology and my pretext for phoning.

After eating the fish and chips I have to wash my hands free of grease before I begin reading; and as this book is going to be given as a present and is a paperback, I will have to try my best not to crease the spine.

Though I attempt to adopt a comfortable reading position,

sitting on the floor because of my lack of furniture, each new position rapidly becomes awkward, numbing an arm or buttock or leg. Pretty soon the ratio becomes seven new positions per chapter. Keeping tally of my movements is a measure both of my discomfort and also of how little *King Jesus* enthrals me. However, I persevere reading for two hours.

Then I take a bath. When I come back into the living room I notice the smell of the fish and chips, persistent because the papers were rolled into a ball and left on the floor. I have yet to acquire a new bin. They stole my bin and the rubbish in it. I try on my new clothes. I am pleased. Carl would be impressed, I think. I put on my coat, with *King Jesus* in the pocket, and take the fish and chip papers to the outside dustbin. Mrs Davies has her flat number stencilled on her bin so other people's garbage does not contaminate hers. As I am disposing of the fish and chip papers, Ken pulls up in his car. I greet him warmly but resist expressing relief. I want him to believe my talent is so huge I could be offered similar work anywhere else at any time. He has brought pencils, inks and papers. Together we take everything up to my flat.

'I brought all this because you'll be working from home and I knew you were burgled. I hadn't quite expected the burglary to be this thorough, though,' he says, frozen in the centre of the floor. He refuses coffee.

Ken explains how he has begun a new children's book. He shows me passages that describe its characters and the story's setting. The story concerns a little boy who converses with inanimate objects and has an imaginary friend whom we can see though the grown-up characters in the book cannot. This 'friend' is no more than three inches high but otherwise I have carte blanche to draw him how I please.

'The trouble is, Tanya, I'm a little stuck on the story. It has no title yet, though I'm probably simply going to call it *George* – after the main character. I've mapped it all out, I know how the middle progresses and even how the story ends, but I'm hoping that if I could have a few illustrations of the characters, for reference, then I might understand the *tone* I'm looking for. If that makes any sense to you.'

'Clear as day,' I tell him. I have read enough books to understand something of how the writing process works.

'Then . . . You're all set,' he tells me, preparing his exit.

Because we do not yet know each other, the formality between us remains an obstinate barrier. I cannot be hospitable because I am living like a refugee. Small talk would emphasise the formality, setting it in stone. All we have in common, before a bond of work develops, is Caroline.

'I was taken aback by the way Caroline talked to you. I'm convinced she still cares for you.' I say this even though I am convinced of nothing of the sort. I am interested to see how he will respond to something so personal.

'Well, she's . . . Even when I was with her she was . . . She's hard work.'

He looks around the room as if searching for somewhere to sit. Then he fidgets with some pencils. He coughs to clear his throat, as if about to speak. Then he stops fidgeting and remains silent.

'I think she was never sure how you felt about her,' I tell him, challenging him. His response to this challenge is to leave. He gives me his phone number so I can contact him when I have completed a substantial body of work, or in case I have questions. The anticipation of beginning this work is so urgent I let him see himself out.

Through the remainder of the afternoon I make many attempts at drawing George's imaginary friend, but am dissatisfied with each. I wonder if Ken will consider having the imaginary friend as a pig? I am superb at drawing pigs. My mind's image of George is one I steal from a photograph I have ingrained in my memory of Gary and myself when we were very small. In the photograph we are holding hands and Gary is looking down at me with a grin that is both benevolence and mischief. This, I decide, is how George should look, though he never comes fully alive until I dress him in a trench coat. Because he is a small boy the trench coat seems entirely inappropriate; it makes him look as if he has something to hide. This work is fun. I am concentrating so hard that when I break away from my work, at 7 p.m., the late hour amazes me. The natural light seems to instantly diminish and I am exasperated when I remember the bare condition of my home. I have no chairs or table so have been sitting on the floor and having to bend over to draw. My back aches. Then I am hungry.

I need to rest and to eat. I will go see Carl, face to face. I'll offer to take him out for a meal to celebrate my new job. I'll present him with *King Jesus*.

Again, as I am leaving the house Ken arrives.

'I was just wondering how everything went. No problems?' Having had first-hand experience of how uptight Ken can be, I prepared an exhibition. I have hidden the finished drawings of George and the failed attempts to draw his imaginary friend. I show Ken only the many rough sketches of George – concluding with the first full-length picture in a trench coat. I do not show him the full extent of my afternoon's work in case he consequently always expects this prolific standard. I explain how each piece was developed, and he is more than delighted with the results.

'I had an idea of how George might look, but you've brought him to life. This expression, his cheekiness, his innocence, it's exactly the character. I can hear him speak now. This is fantastic work, Tanya. This is better than all my expectations. And I had high expectations. I'm tempted to tell Caroline she's lost the work on *The Stink Monsters*. After the way she spoke to me the other day . . . But she's all set to go to America and everything. And besides . . .' He lets this fade without explanation; he knows none is necessary.

It is eight-thirty by the time Ken leaves.

I am alive now because I am sad. With Martin gone for good, for the first time in my life I know loneliness. It is not Martin I want.

If it's over between me and Carl now, permanently, there are not enough acquired memories to begin, then sustain, an obsession about him. I never gave him a chance. With Martin forgotten, now is my opportunity to take a risk on Carl.

I go to Carl's home without having the guts to risk phoning first. I have a present for him which should excuse my inconsistency. He says hello when he answers the door but even face to face, looking at his expression and into his eyes, I am unable to judge how he feels. I ask if I can come in.

When we are in his flat, because I am too proud to just kiss him, as I wish to, I hand him *King Jesus*.

'Wow!'

'Do you like it?' The most stupid question I could ask. Carl grasps the book in both hands, mesmerised by the front-cover illustration. He turns the book around, he looks inside the cover.

'I've missed you,' I tell him.

'I've missed you, too.' He is already skimming through the pages of *King Jesus*. As he has missed me as much as I had hoped he would, I should be insulted that a book has become his priority; instead of being insulted I recognise a fellow sufferer. So now I kiss him – off guard.

'This is great, Tanya. I can't thank you enough.' He's still talking about the book.

'I'm happy we're back together,' I tell him.

'I'd have waged my home against you ever coming here to see me,' Carl says.

'Well, there you are then. You don't know me as well as you think,' I tell him. He nods – which can only mean something nice. I add, 'I'm pleased I did come.'

He holds me. 'So we're *back* together? I ask this because I was never really sure we were ever together. You've been seeing someone –'

'That's over now.'

'And also . . . You were never fully sure – no matter how much you liked me – you were never entirely sure if you wanted to properly go out with me. A road sweeper. I'm right, aren't I?'

'Yes,' I answer. I am trying my very best to match his directness, his honesty. 'I don't care now, though.' I force this out: 'I guess I mean it doesn't bother me as much. But you bother me. If anyone asked me why I wanted to be with you I would tell them you bother me more than any other man has in a decade.'

'*Bother?*'

'It's a good thing, Carl. Trust me. I kind of hope people do ask me that. I'd enjoy telling them.'

Though we kept the intention to have sex, we then talked for too long; we fell asleep. I wake up alone and frustrated. Carl has abandoned me because he had to go to work. The sex would have been full-throttle, reunion sex. Reunion sex is a big deal; it's the only derivation of straight sex that even the sharpest entrepreneur in the extremely accommodating vice industry cannot provide. We missed out on this because I talked to him about work, my ideas for *George*. Then I talked about my mum. I talked about the accusations I had made, the stupidity of ignoring her phone calls, the circumstances behind her death. Carl should have shut me up to demand sex. Instead he again told me about his hopes of selling this flat for a profit and renting somewhere smaller. As he talked I fell asleep – eased into the bliss of self-admonishment.

Though I am keen to be home so I can continue my work, I decide to eat here because Carl's fridge is stocked with everything needed for a full nutritious breakfast. After breakfast I still do not leave. I am tempted to properly rummage around Carl's flat. I am considering investing a significant proportion of my future in him; such an outlay permits me to investigate his suitability. Though, unless there's a dismembered corpse in the airing cupboard, there's little I can think of which, if discovered, might persuade me to drop him again. Just as a precaution, I look in the airing cupboard. Blankets, towels, toilet rolls. Three full bin liners. I prod one, but it is too soft to contain a corpse. I poke a hole – patterned fabric – women's clothes. These must belong to Lydia, the girlfriend Carl dumped when he met me.

There is a knock on Carl's door. Not sure how I might explain who I am, I do not answer. Our relationship is still so new it is unknown to most of the people who know Carl.

An envelope is slid under the door. To my surprise it is addressed to 'Carl and Tanya'. It is an invitation to a wedding. Lydia is getting married. Next Saturday! I have a split second to decide – before she has left the building – whether I would like to meet her or whether to take home the invitation and hide it. Perhaps, after more considered thought, I might not want Carl to go to the wedding of his ex-girlfriend.

'He's at work,' I call down to her. She is at the house doorway, so returns to see who is speaking. As she ascends each step I see the realisation dawning on her – I am Tanya, Carl's new girlfriend. She is brave enough not to let her smile alter. She is around my age, with long, straggly hair; a face so strictly devoid of make-up she looks pale and earthy – like a new potato. She wears an ankle-length skirt and an elaborately patterned jacket. She is sort of hippyish in a different-century, half-baked way. I cannot imagine what she might think of me. I would have preferred her first sighting to be on one of those rare occasions when I look sensational. That would have really pissed her off. She introduces herself and explains why she delivered the invitation by hand.

'I was sort of worried about him . . . Not worried, but . . . I haven't heard from him.'

'Were you expecting to hear from him, Lydia?' I ask, almost friendly. Having said her name, seeing her closer, I have to accept that my summary dismissal was unfair. She has a natural prettiness, which is probably best served by wearing no make-up; she looks sweet yet corruptible – a combination some men would kill for.

'Not really,' she admits. 'But I thought I'd come in person . . . I was thinking he might not want to come to the wedding because he might feel . . . I don't know, maybe awkward or something. You know? I mean, Carl's a friend . . . I guess he isn't really a friend, we ended on bad terms . . . But I wish he was a friend. What I'm making a mess of saying is . . . I wish it could have ended more amicably. There's no reason why we couldn't be friends. Or friendly. Don't you think?'

She stumbles through this, choosing each word cautiously, fully aware I will be passing the message on and – as her potential enemy – corrupting everything she says to make Carl believe his ex-girlfriend is mental and he, therefore, had a lucky escape. It is evident that she still has strong feelings for Carl, which have little to do with being friends; perhaps she still loves him. Her smile fights on. She blushes in response to my apparent calmness. I am the one who prevented her having a life with Carl. She does not know, but I most certainly do – I am not deserving.

'Do you want to come in?' I ask.

'I'd better not. I have to get to work. If you'll just tell him I called. Tell him he doesn't have to phone me, or anything. I just wanted to . . . What I mean is, he'll feel obliged to call and . . . Well, you know Carl.'

She says goodbye and leaves. I think about the ingrained melancholy in those four words, 'Well, you know Carl.' There was tenderness and humour; she knows Carl will wish to call her now, from courtesy, yet will be cautious not to offend me. Lydia knows – and was sharing with me – Carl is considerate and selfless and sweet.

I return into Carl's flat and put my coat back on. I am outside his home when Carl appears, stealing a break from work. He has brought me flowers.

'What are these for?' I ask, surprising myself at how pleased I am to receive flowers from *him*. It makes me feel like a woman, a girlfriend – descriptions I have to be reminded of.

'This is the first time . . . You're the first woman I've ever bought flowers for,' he tells me.

'This is the first time anyone has ever bought me flowers,' I answer – cursing Martin for buying me flowers on the night I humiliated him and therefore making this a lie.

When I return home Mrs Davies is at the door; her face lights up when she sees me. She is eager to pass on the news of some excitement I missed by sleeping out.

'You'll never guess what happened last night, Tanya!' she begins. 'Trevor came home and found his flat being burgled!'

Judging by Mrs Davies's delight I make the guess the police were called and the burglars arrested.

'Not exactly,' she says; then, realising how inappropriate her smile is, wrestles it away and lowers her voice. 'They . . . er . . . sort of beat Trevor up. He's in hospital. The burglar was Mr Ostryzniuk's son. Mr Ostryzniuk has come to some arrangement with Trevor to stop the police getting involved. I told him all I cared about was having everything I had stolen returned. There are workmen here now, bringing everything.'

I see the van outside the building. A man is taking cardboard boxes down from the back. Another workman comes down from Mrs Davies's flat and she speaks to him. I open my mail. The cheque from my home insurance company has arrived – paid in full.

When the workman joins his colleague, Mrs Davies continues:

'His son has a lock-up garage where everything he couldn't sell was stored. They have some of your stuff too.'

Mrs Davies is having all her possessions returned whilst I am only getting my books back. Everything else of mine has gone. Mrs Davies, having already bullied the workmen into taking her possessions up to her flat, now begins instructing them on taking up the boxes, which contain my books.

'*All* these boxes are books, Tanya?'

'Yes, I think so.' I stop one of the workmen as he passes. I open a box. Books. Another – books. 'Yes.'

'*All* of them, though?'

'Yes.'

'Like reading, do you?' one of the workmen quips hilariously.

Small boxes have been used because it does not take many books to make a heavy box. Consequently, the number of boxes is tremendous. I tip the workmen generously.

'Like reading, do you?' the same workman quips absent-mindedly.

Before Mrs Davies leaves I ask more about Trevor. She is returning to visit him in hospital later this day with some pyjamas that once belonged to Clement, and some Lucozade and grapes.

'I hope he never finds out what I used to think of him!' she laughs. 'I couldn't have been more wrong. He's so nice. But very shy. I've always thought he was rude, but that's not it at all. He's very softly spoken. You wouldn't have guessed any of this from his music, would you? And he works for the government!'

'Really?' She makes him sound like James Bond.

'He's a civil servant at the Ministry for Agriculture, Farming and Fisheries. I have to go now, Tanya. I don't think he has any family in London, and he says his friends aren't the type of friends who'll visit him in hospital.'

She has a mission now, so does not hang around.

The amount of boxes is unfathomable; whole walls have

been constructed into mazes and partitions. My living room resembles some low-budget children's adventure park. To gain access to the kitchen I have to climb and deconstruct. No one should be this preoccupied with their hobby; this is only one single page short of insanity.

To forget the chaos of my surroundings, I dive into work. Having settled on this course of action, I make a coffee, clear a space and work using boxes as a work surface. In two hours I do enough to convince Ken, should he check up, that I have worked solidly all day. Because Ken cannot draw, like all other people who cannot draw, they cannot quantify the ability, so are susceptible to whatever lies we able people tell. Nevertheless, I work all morning and all afternoon.

As darkness falls and I begin to pack up the drawing equipment, I remove my coffee cup from the box I was using as a rest. The coffee spilt a little. I part the box flaps to see if any has dribbled onto the books.

The Counterfeit Confetti is the top book. There is a garden, twenty or so houses down from where I live, with a large dog tied up in the yard, which barks each time I pass. I should have learnt now not to be startled by it – but I always am. This is how it feels each time I find *The Counterfeit Confetti*. I have finished drawing for the day and have nothing else to do. For a while I had forgotten the book. Now, again, it is the most dominant thing in my world. I am obliged to open it, I am the only participant in this metaphysical mess.

I find my place in the book. I have already read the last chapter, which leaves just the four preceding ones. I am disappointed that the first three of these simply cover my recent past: Mother dying and other events concluding with last night, my reunion with Carl and Trevor being beaten up. Three uninformative chapters.

The penultimate chapter concerns Carl and some of his history. It retells, from his point of view, that day when we first slept together and how he subsequently finished with his girlfriend.

It occurred to Carl that Tanya had no reason not to be at work.
Maybe she had taken the day off especially.

Granted permission to touch and with her willingness to believe in his sincerity, he dared to kiss her. She warned that if they slept together it could be nothing of significance. She had a boyfriend already.

Carl knew exactly what to do now: put on a show, convince her how he was a great lover even in these casual circumstances. Once thoroughly satisfied she would later begin to imagine how sex might be under more permanent conditions. He gave a spectacular performance.

When he left her that day he knew he had begun the process. She would want him again. He borrowed three books – three she said she treasured – which guaranteed another meeting.

They did meet again and although the progress was slow, nevertheless he became convinced of her enough to terminate the relationship he was already in. This was neither easy nor painless. They had been seeing each other for some time, each had routines built around the other. Carl simply told Lydia the relationship wasn't working and refused to elaborate. He was sensitive enough not to mention Tanya. Being dumped for someone else was bad enough, being dumped only in the hope of someone else was simply insulting. They parted on bad terms; she left his flat so quickly she did not even take all the clothes she had stored there.

This confirms the degree to which Carl manipulated my responses to him, a manoeuvring I have always suspected. It is flattering to be wanted so much that a plan is contrived to win you.

There's a frustrating section next, which *speculates* upon the reason Carl became a road sweeper. It reiterates information I already know from Carl, about his past job and some of his motivation for leaving it, yet provides no other insights into his thought process. If the book knows everything about me and my life and the people closest to me, it should be able to clearly inform me of Carl's full character and why he lacks ambition so thoroughly that he deliberately put his career and prospects into reverse. This glaring omission inspires me to puzzle over why the book is so suddenly badly informed; then I try to assume an opinion for myself; but Carl – in this regard – remains an enigma. This chapter concludes with an analysis of why Carl likes me. Its addition can only be to act as the precursor to the last chapter where Carl moves into the adjacent flat.

> Carl was attracted to Tanya. There are a million attractive women in London so the explanation for his fuller interest had to be more complex. She was insular and unsociable, though he was convinced some of her militant solitude was a defence born not of a genuine desire to be alone but more from a dislike of so many other people. He understood. Tanya was difficult. There are people whose nature is so peculiar they inevitably tire of the misunderstandings it causes. Reserve is too often seen as aloofness, irony is heard as sarcasm, opinions are regarded as arrogance. Being alone becomes preferable to this unease; being alone comes with no confusion or conflict. It is too wearing to maintain your guard and disguise that side of yourself that too easily and too often offends. Only shallow people can show all of their personality and fear no retribution. He believed Tanya was waiting to be allowed to be a nicer person. Her snobbishness was being chipped away, her evangelistic isolation was being subverted.

As I read this I do recognise how I *might* interpret these descriptions as the truth about me. Though I can no longer unequivocally testify what is the truth. For instance, before *The Counterfeit Confetti* I would never have phoned Martin. I was happy with casual boyfriends and loyalty to a memory. Until the book came into my possession, contacting Martin was only a possibility in abstraction. It will be interesting to see how that final chapter will now read. Before, it confirmed all my instincts; I believed it to be the likeliest, the most accurate prediction of how my life would evolve, having a boyfriend living next door to me. My instincts about Carl, however, are now very different. If Carl lived across the landing we would be closer. I want that. I understand how nothing good can come from rereading the last chapter of *The Counterfeit Confetti*. More than ever before, I know my own mind. I attempt to try to remember more than the briefest summary. Carl moved in next door, all went well for a while, before all my worst expectations came true and we split up. Yet now my expectations are completely different. I see the future clearly – it could easily be Carl and me, together, happy; we become old in each other's customs so each has an ally against the onslaughts of the modern world. There is nothing wrong with this future.

I am exhausted and imagine I will sleep well. However, after maybe an hour of tossing and turning I am so wide awake I have no choice but to occupy myself again until sleep is possible. I search through the boxes until I find Albert Camus's *The Outsider*. Based only on vague memories of it from one reading, many years ago, I believe it should have increased significance for me now. Instead I am detached from enjoying the story because I find, now, the style is too cold.

As I again try to sleep I think I should have gone to my mother's funeral, in retrospect. How could I explain not going to Carl? He'll think I'm a cold-hearted bitch. I would have liked my mother to have met Carl; she would not have cared about his job because she would immediately have had the full measure of his character. She would have loved his kindness and consideration.

I went to my first funeral of the age of eighteen. I had sex with my cousin Philip afterwards. We did it in a relative's house, in a child's bedroom. The only clothes that were removed were my knickers, whilst all he did was lower his trousers around his thighs; afterwards he took several flushes of the loo to get rid of the buoyant condom. I remained captured in the bedroom whilst an aunt came up to ask if he was having problems with the lavatory. I do not like to think of the thought process that makes a man bring condoms to a funeral.

I wonder if Carl has ever been sad. I would like to know. I wonder how he anticipates coping with the difficult process of not simply liking my peculiarities but learning to have to live with them. It will not be easy.

It is Friday evening, nine-twenty-five. I haven't seen Carl this week, I have only worked, though we have spoken on the phone each night. Tonight I prevent myself from talking about my work even though there are so many subtleties and hidden jokes in my drawings for *George* I like to have someone to tell. Instead I tell Carl about my latest car, a second-hand Volkswagon Beetle. My parents used to own one. Then I tell him about our invitation to Lydia's wedding tomorrow. I left it to this last minute before telling him in case he is reluctant to go. He simply says nothing. So, quickly, before he can articulate any objection, I tell him I miss him and have been thinking about him. I tell him to be ready when I collect him tomorrow.

Saturday morning. As I exit from my flat Mr Ostryzniuk is unlocking the door of the vacant flat opposite to let an old lady enter. I presume she is a prospective tenant. I use the word 'old' as a generic term for anyone over the age of sixty. My first thought, when I see her, is Mrs Davies will enjoy having someone of around her own age in the building. It might be company for her, which would divert some of her attention away from me. On the other hand I may have *two* Mrs Davieses to be pestered by. Wouldn't that be fun!

I am introduced by Mr Ostryzniuk as her new neighbour.

I tell him, making an effort to sound permanently terrified, 'I came out because I heard a noise. I thought it might be another burglar!'

Mr Ostryzniuk hurries the old woman into the flat. Before I can leave the building I hear Mrs Davies hiss my name. She walks downstairs carefully, keeping a keen eye on the door of the vacant flat.

'She might be moving in. What do you think of her?'

'She seemed –' is all I manage to say before Mrs Davies interrupts.

'She is awful. He can't let her move in here.'

'You know her?' I ask. Mrs Davies confesses the full extent of her familiarity with the woman is having briefly met her when she first made an enquiry about the vacant flat. It was enough to condemn her.

'We have a nice mix in this house. We all get along. I think she'll interfere with the balance.'

Disregarding simple facts like how, until very recently, Mrs Davies hated Trevor and, anyway, the mix of tenants is hardly likely to be explosive when there are only three of us, all I can assume Mrs Davies means is that the balance of the house relies on having just the one interfering old bat in residence.

'Carl, my boyfriend, is selling his current flat,' I tell Mrs Davies. I say it simply as an academic exercise, to test her reaction to having my boyfriend as a new tenant.

'Tell him about this flat, Tanya. And ask Mr Ostryzniuk. I'm sure he'd rather have someone like your friend than *her*. You're a good tenant, aren't you? Mr Ostryzniuk likes you.'

'Carl is a road sweeper.'

A smile rises and falls within seconds. Incomprehension, then condemnation. Tough, she must learn to fight her petty prejudices just as I did.

Hearing Mr Ostryzniuk and the old woman prepare to leave the flat, we do not attempt to continue our debate. Mrs Davies scurries back up to her flat; she is fast when she has to be.

If Carl should move into the adjacent flat, forgetting all those predictions I read in *The Counterfeit Confetti*, it will annoy Mrs Davies. It's worth thinking about. I have pretty much, almost irrevocably, decided upon how I want my life to work out, whom I want in it and how the future should shape up. And this isn't like when I wanted to be a pilot. I won't be deterred by any obstacles as simple as being afraid of heights or bemused by machinery.

I have dressed in the 'French' clothes I bought especially for Carl. When I pick him up, he notices and compliments me. We are going to attend both the service and the reception: a full, drunken day.

Lydia's wedding is in a registry office. I sit through the service listening carefully to every word that is said. The couple make their responses oblivious to anything other than the face of the other. Their friends are all like-minded people, incapable of formality. They applaud when the ceremony ends, then swamp the couple with affection. For me, the most fascinating aspect of Lydia is that she is another side to Carl's personality. I cannot see how their relationship ever worked. He was in PR, she's this hippy type.

The reception lasts all day and well into the night. The food is all vegetarian yet at least the bar is well stocked. Though I offered, Carl bought the first drinks.

'I'll get these,' he insisted, with a tiny facial expression that would have been indecipherable to anyone other than me. I, however, have already learnt this secret language – it is ours only. We accept that I earn more money, and I have spent far more than Carl today, yet Carl has enough male pride – despite his protests to the contrary – to go through at least some of the rituals of a man and woman out together. For example, though I have bought most of the drinks Carl always insists on going to the bar. Emmeline Pankhurst might not understand why this should be an issue; it is only a minor obstacle on the road to the perfect world of equality.

Carl and I have been left alone. We know only Lydia at this reception, and she talks to us just once, and briefly. I detected only happiness, no malice or secret longing. I've never understood hippies. As Carl talked to her, he took my hand. Lydia split from Carl, then started seeing this new man, whom she is now married to, all within months. It reeks of panic – though she displays only joy. When she has gone, Carl is interested in me alone. When I try to force the issue, and ask if he thinks Lydia will be happy, his reply is to say he hopes so. Which I cannot argue with. Carl talks about us, how happy he is to have won me. I concentrate, knowing I should not be thinking about my work on *George*.

As we become drunk and affectionate, Carl breaks from a kiss and – making this question significant by beginning with a pause – asks: 'Are you OK, Tanya?'

'Me? I'm fine. Why?'

'I mean . . . I'm asking if you're OK generally. Everything's OK? It's just that . . . Recently . . . Have you been working too hard, do you think?'

'I have been working a lot but that doesn't mean I'm stressed out by it – if that's what you're thinking. I'm enjoying it.'

'The reason I ask . . . Don't be angry, but I bumped into Ken coming out of your flat, and we started talking.'

'Why should I be angry? What did he say?'

'He's pleased with the work you do for him. Surprised by how much you do and how quickly you work – but pleased, still.'

'Well, that's good, isn't it? What made you contact him?'

'I haven't seen you all week.'

'So you were being selfish?' I tease.

'I was worried. On the phone you sound tired. You only talk about work. And sometimes you just ramble.'

'Don't worry about me,' I say angrily, then decide against pursuing this. 'Thanks for worrying, but . . .'

It is only because it is so new to me, being at the early stages of genuine, creative work – this novelty is why I am so preoccupied. Carl need not worry.

I, too, had a long conversation with Ken the last time he called. Because I have been considering Carl moving into the adjacent flat I asked Ken how he made his decisions; did he rely entirely on his own experience, or instincts, or did he talk to friends and family? He didn't even answer the question, he just returned it to me. I didn't mention *The Counterfeit Confetti*, instead I told him I once had my dad to talk with, then Martin. When Ken wondered why I had put the question to him, I realised there was no sensible answer. He told me I looked tired. He suggested I take a break from work for a day or two. Though I may look and act tired I am neither.

I ask Carl, now: 'How do you make your decisions? What do you rely on – your instincts, your experience? For instance, when you decided to quit your PR job, did you talk to anyone first?'

'No,' Carl answers. 'I knew what I had to do. I had no reason to do it any more. I told Lydia only after I quit. She was very supportive.'

I dare not say this to him, but I cannot be certain if – in a similar position – I would have been equally supportive. I am glad I met him *after* he had made the decision; this way I have the finished result rather than a work in progress.

The night ends with the DJ playing 'Song for Whoever' by The Beautiful South and Carl asking me to dance. I refuse. I am too near thirty. Many years ago, as a student, I remember the spectacle of watching older people dancing, being quite oblivious to the fools they were making of themselves. I vowed then I would never dance once I was thirty. Of course, predictably, I do not feel changed; I feel no older than the day I made that decision. I do not, cannot feel thirty. We watch others of our own age and assume the act they pull off is genuine. I have learnt we fulfil our older roles only as a masquerade. The most competent of airline pilots, the most consistently successful of micro-surgeons, the most articulate and witty of orators, all perform their duties shitting themselves, ever aware of a voice in their heads, warning that it is only a question of time before the world detects that they are a fraud and that they will be denounced for not being adults but only kids play-acting. Yet we view with envy these frauds, squandering years of our lives wishing we were more like them, praying for better things for ourselves, bigger breasts, better jobs, nicer people around us. The big fat waste of all this is that big-titted, well-paid, well-loved people all suffer the same envy – oblivious to their own good fortune just as we, every one, every damn single one of us, are also unaware of *our* good fortunes. Everyone wants the very same thing from life – something else.

So Carl dances on his own, becoming lost in the crowd. All the other dancers are in couples. Alone, peering down the neck of a Pils bottle, I think about 'Song for Whoever.' It was one of Martin's favourites. I am not reminded directly of him; instead I realise how little thought I have given him since I humiliated him that night. I know if I ever saw him again I could not think of anything to say. I would be civil, though instantly bored should he try to prolong the conversation. Any mention of the past would embarrass me. The years I spent obsessed by his memory were cowardice.

I keep having a glance at Carl through the bodies. Dancing alone. To hell with past resolves, I think – and so I dance with Carl.

'Today an old woman came to look around the vacant flat across the landing,' I whisper to him as we dance.

'She'll be company for your upstairs neighbour.' Carl humours me, wondering why I should be telling him this now, perhaps thinking I am rambling again.

'Mrs Davies doesn't like her. And I'm not sure I'd want her moving in either.' Clearly this is a wide-open invitation to ask why I have formed this opinion, or to ask whom I would prefer instead. Carl does not accept the invitation. Instead he tells me he has visited another estate agent and has been looking at property prices in newspapers, just to gauge how much his own flat may be worth.

'I think I might get more than I initially hoped,' he tells me. 'I'll need it, renting is so expensive. I'm going to have to start looking for somewhere soon though, I suppose.'

Frustrated by his inability to take the hint, I spell it out. 'Carl, shut up. Were you even listening to me?'

'When?'

'How did I begin this conversation? I reminded you about the vacant flat opposite me. I told you I don't want some old lady renting it. And you'll be my neighbour. That'll be fun, won't it?'

At long last we go home, to his home, to enjoy reunion sex. I once believed sex the first time was the best kind of sex – not the first time ever, but the first time with someone new. Then I fell in love and believed that was the best kind of sex. I now know for certain the best sex is when the emotions are genuine and you reunite with someone you nearly lost.

For a few hours I repent everything I have learnt to be fact, and have faith that life is simple.

TWENTY

I spend all Sunday with Carl, never leaving his flat. We talk, cook, make love. I am learning how, during sex, Carl follows a natural sequence, employing a rotation system so I am able to anticipate where his hands and mouth will be next. When I begin to rely on these moves, however, he often thrills me by heading somewhere surprising. In the evening, before I leave, we watch a sitcom on TV. It is terrible; we make it tolerable by guessing the punchline to jokes or anticipating how a set-up will be paid off. As I am leaving Carl tells me he hasn't yet figured me out, which I like hearing. I tell him how much I have enjoyed the day. I was happy to have spent the whole day with him, to compensate for not seeing him last week. However, Carl cannot have failed to have noticed how frequently I have been distracted. I kept having to make excuses to use his bathroom; there I scribbled down ideas for use in *George*.

My reason for not spending Sunday night at his flat is that he rises too early. I need a good night's sleep to produce a good day's work. When I arrive home I immediately make a more permanent record of the scribbled ideas I had during the day.

I wake at seven and work till eleven, pausing only once, which I had reason to regret. It was strange. I wasn't dizzy or weak, but I can only account for my peculiar actions by attributing them to not having eaten breakfast. I went into the kitchen to make a cup of coffee. I put the kettle on, then put coffee, sugar and milk into the cup. When the kettle boiled I poured the water straight down into the sink. I realised I should not have done this. I put the kettle back on – having forgotten to refill it. It coughed and spat in alarm.

Slightly amused, but nevertheless wishing to clear my head, I put on my coat and left the building. Once outside, however, I simply could not remember why I had come outside. I went back inside my flat. Finally, I successfully made a cup of coffee. I laughed at myself, then opened the windows for air.

After this, and simply to give myself something to do as a contrived distraction from work, I ring my home insurance company to inform them my books have been returned. They sent an itemised statement of value, so I know exactly how much to return but I simply want to check the procedure. *My mother answers the phone.* I wonder if I have inadvertently phoned her by mistake. Though this would hardly matter: Mum is dead, and the woman who answered told me the insurance company's name and asked how she could help. I do not answer.

'Hello? Is anyone there?' she asks like an amateur medium. It is certainly my mother's voice though. I hang up, unable to reply.

To remove the voice and the shock from my head, I try to resume work. I cannot draw anything that resembles anything else. I have lost the ability. I keep having to refer to previous sketches to remind myself of the work I am supposed to be doing.

I think about the day John Lennon was shot. I was nine years old and I had never heard of John Lennon. My mother called up to me, telling me to either get out of bed immediately or be late for school.

'And by the way,' she added, 'John Lennon has been shot dead.'

I can hear Mum's voice, as clearly as if she was telling me that news now. I consider phoning the insurance company again in the hope of once more hearing the woman with a similar voice to my mother's. It would not be a shock this time, I could enjoy it. I consider phoning Mick. He will probably be at work and there may be a chance he has not yet changed the answerphone message – I will hear Mum again.

The best way I can take my mind off her is by making another, harder attempt to work, armed with a shot of strong coffee. I go into my kitchen and begin to fill the kettle. I rush out before it is filled, dropping the kettle into the sink. The tap is left running. It is as if I was grabbed by a ghost. I was about to be knocked over with grief. Again in a kitchen, just like after Dad died – I don't understand that! I knew it was coming and had to run.

My mother would understand. We had a secret pact. We knew all about the deal between us: she could holler at me, she could threaten and shout and berate me; I would reiterate with my typical guerrilla tactics of sarcasm, sulks and impatience. Yet all through that short period when the worst of my adolescence made me a bitch, and Dad scowled at or avoided me, Mum and I kept the negotiations open: I never complained about my share of housework, she was always complimentary about my paintings. She never warned me about how boys might wish to abuse me, but offered immunity if I ever had good cause to stab one. When things went wrong, whenever anything had let me down or disappointed or hurt me – and there are a million of these shocks at this age – she never used this to her advantage, never warned me how I might have avoided this trouble had I listened to her.

'Be truthful to your instincts when you're contemplating doing something sordid,' she had told me when I flirted with the idea of having a tattoo on my hand. Or it might have been that brief spell when I wanted to be a journalist.

So I know Mother would not be condemning me for not having felt open, demonstrable grief over her death. She is as omnipresent as any God when it comes to understanding me; she will know I will develop well-paced grief for her, lasting for the rest of my life with no climaxes nor any gradually getting accustomed. One day I may succumb to the inexplicable flood of tears I only just managed to avoid today. One day something may remind me of Mum – like the insurance company woman's voice – and my first thought will be only a sensible acknowledgement that she is dead. I know she is dead, there is no confusion. It is only that my instincts need reprogramming. I should have attended the funeral.

Deliberately, I do no more work for the rest of the day. I construct an armchair from the boxes of books, then simply think, remembering things I was reminded of by *The Counterfeit Confetti*. I make a point of remembering how life is good for me at the moment.

The next morning I again rise early, with purpose, to begin work. I am expecting no further blockage – this will be a productive day. For a while I cannot concentrate because I think of Carl. I appreciate him, how fortunate I am for finding someone who perseveres with me. And I enjoy my work. And so, really, if I cannot identify a reason who's to say I am unhappy? If you were continually happy how would you *know* you were happy? You would have no other experience to compare it with. I am asking too much.

Yet I have been happy. I was happy with Martin. I have learnt he was the main ingredient to the happiness I enjoyed then, but other contributory factors were being young, discovering love, experimenting with sex and having optimism. This is why I clung on.

I was content with that straightforward life of work, having a boyfriend, but taking all my real action, pleasure, enjoyment from reading books. If I ever began one that failed me, bored me, irritated me, I could discard it and move onto the other million on offer. Easy.

As these thoughts float around in my head I realise I have been drawing, detached from everything – subconscious doodling. Nothing I have drawn is of any use for *George* – they are pictures of fish, money, a penis, my car, a house – which I see is the house I lived in with my parents. I have drawn portraits of Carl, and Martin – young Martin.

To help concentration, I first need a distraction. I hit upon the idea of taking a drive: a recreational, nowhere drive around London. Because this is London, however, the ride is no more rewarding than being stuck in a warm box smelling of exhaust fumes.

A car horn sounds behind me, alerting me to the fact that the traffic ahead has moved and I have not. I still do not move the car. This is not defiance or lethargy, there is simply nowhere to go. The car behind accelerates past, its driver giving me the finger and mouthing inaudible obscenities.

I park the car and walk. After fifty yards, because I have no memory of getting out of the car, I have to look back to see if it is really there. It is. I enter a shop. I leave.

I see my father. I am in a clothes shop when through the shop window I see a man pass who looks exactly like my dad. Though I know it cannot be him I am compelled to look more closely to ensure the mistaken impression is thoroughly dismissed from my mind. I rush outside and follow him. From the rear view the resemblance is uncanny: his walk, his clothes, his build. I follow closer until I begin to walk alongside him. Glances to the side of his face only scare me more. It is Dad. I walk ahead, then, feeling sick. Each time I look back and see him square on, the knot in my stomach tightens. Dad is alive. I turn, face him and stop walking. He is forced to look this obstruction in the eye. I am completely lost in joy. He changes direction to avoid me, without betraying any sign of recognition. I catch him up.

'Dad?'

He only pauses when he realises he is the only person near enough for me to be addressing. He shuffles past and carries on walking.

'Dad? Hello,' I insist.

'Sorry?' the man says. It is not Dad's voice, and when I hear this wrong voice all the rest of the resemblance crumbles. In fact his face is too long, his eyebrows too fair, his nose too broad. He shares some of the features of my dad, but on his face they fit together differently. I apologise to the stranger and walk away with sweat clinging my T-shirt to my back. I am wondering how I could be confusing reality with daydreaming, with my imagination. This isn't as if I have read this, or been told a story I have then begun to believe actually happened to me; this isn't even as bad as when I heard the insurance company woman and thought it was my mother's voice. I know my father is dead, yet this bitterly learnt lesson was forgotten in the sight of someone who resembled him. I was prepared to forget all the grief and guilt – just so that, for a few moments, I could delude myself.

I find, in the seat pocket of my jeans, several scraps of paper, in my handwriting – though I have no memory of writing any of this. I read: *He's smiling, but evil in his eyes, thick eyebrows*; on another: *In silhouette it looks to others like a gun, but it's a banana, or something less obvious but funny*; another: *He throws his coat over the thief, then trips him*. I cannot think why I should have written these things or had these thoughts.

I go to a tube station and buy a ticket . . . then remember my car. Outside the station I have no idea where I am or of the direction to walk to find my car. I walk anyway.

Only when I see my car – by accident – do I remember I have been looking for it. I get in and concentrate. I have to drive home without letting my thoughts drift. I have been working too hard, that's the problem. I am not unhappy, I am exhausted. London can only make the exhaustion worse. I will take a break from work. Be with my friend Carl. Make love, talk, relax, think of the future. I am free to think of the future unhindered – that's how happy I should be.

A horn sounds from a car overtaking me and I realise how slowly I am driving. I speed up until I become aware I am rapidly approaching a junction – so then brake. A car rams into the back of me. My car spins – a car going in the opposite direction catches the front of mine. I am sent spinning faster. There are more thuds as cars smash into me. I sense that I am about to pass out. I don't, however. For a few moments I do not know where I am and do not accept that anything has happened. First thought – I am now Britain's most uninsurable person. Second thought – I must be hurt, so why aren't I in real pain? Third thought – get out of the car and begin the embarrassment and inconvenience of apologising and sorting this mess out. Fourth thought – nothing has happened, everything is fine, this is not real life, this is someone else's anecdote, this is something I have read in a book.

My car door is opened from outside. Reality.

'Are you OK?' I am asked. Not a dream, though very dreamlike. I know to answer – but do not, unsure of how to begin. I know how to behave rationally, I have not forgotten. It's just that it seems such monumentally hard work.

I suppose I must be insane. My only worry about admitting this –

'Are you OK? Hello?'

– is that insanity is a weakness, capitulation. Insanity is for those who care too much, who take minor things too seriously; it is for those who use such weakness as a device to attract attention. It's for those too scared of a fight.

'She's in shock,' someone says. This shocks me.

243

'She's bleeding – look,' another voice. This slaps me sensible. A man has said this – a man in the crowd. Questions are asked too rapidly for me to single one out to answer – this confusion must make me look deeper in shock. They look at my head. I put my fingers to my forehead. Some blood, not much. The crash might have caused the shock or the shock might have come from the realisation that I am ill. I am mentally ill, or something.

I answer questions from a police officer. I refuse to go to the hospital – I tell him this before hospital is mentioned. He confers with a colleague. I tell an ambulance man I *will* go to the hospital. I was making a spectacle of myself by refusing to go. I was able to grasp some sanity, step back and see myself – the nutter with blood on her head refusing to go with people trying to help. London is full of nutters.

The journey to the hospital is in the back of an ambulance, accompanied by a bored paramedic and a police officer desperate to take my statement before we arrive so that he will not have to accompany me inside.

At the hospital the police officer makes an indecently fast getaway and the paramedic hands me over to a nurse. I am placed on a seat. Abandoned.

The nurse passes to and fro, not seeing me, providing me with no information. I feel fine. There is nothing wrong with me. Though my name will have been logged down some-where, this need not necessarily deter me from leaving before I am seen.

In the A&E there is a loyal gang of five lads hanging around another who has an injured arm. They all look callous and shifty.

Two tramps ramble to each other to pass the time with noise, away from the cold.

Scruffy individuals slouch, malinger, waste doctors' time.

Carl does not own a car. I wish I had given him a set of spare car keys, then he could drive my car over to collect me.

My car is crashed. I remember.

I am not injured. I can find my own way home. There cannot be anything to be gained from phoning Carl. All it will demonstrate is further weakness that I need someone.

When Carl answers his phone he asks which hospital I am

in. Ludicrously, I now insist I am fine and there is no need for him to collect me. His insistence is far more forceful. I am pleased I phoned him.

He arrives in a taxi. I have been waiting outside – and now feel like a fraud; my cut is insignificant.

'Tanya, do you have any money on you?' Carl looks ashamed. 'I don't have enough for the fare.'

I tell him not to worry. I want to hold him and thank him and be good to him. To be going home now on my own would fill me with dread. Carl is with me and with him I will not again stagger into random, confused thoughts. He is keeping me sane in this packed, grimy, shitty city.

'London is handy for hospitals,' I tell him.

'Well ... Yes,' he answers, not clear why I should be saying this.

'And it's handy for the tourist sights ... and theatres. When was the last time you went to a tourist sight or the theatre?'

'Tanya, is this your way of saying you'd like us to go to the theatre? OK, great, we'll go to the theatre. It's years since I've been. Do you have something in mind that you want to see?' I don't answer. 'I'm still not a real expert at reading every thought of yours, I still sometimes need you to tell me what you're getting at.'

'London ... Its attraction fades the longer you're here. Don't you think?'

'Do you mean that? I love London.'

This is not the answer I had hoped to hear. We arrive at my flat. Carl insists I need looking after. I kiss him to prove differently, then tell him to come around later anyway. So, one way or another, I still go home on my own. No dread here after all.

Those scraps of paper I found in my jeans pockets were the rough notes I made for ideas for *George*. I throw them away so I will not be similarly scared if I should find them again.

I catch up on my ironing. I do not put the TV on, nor music. Instead I think. This noise is so deafening I wonder why Mrs Davies does not register a complaint.

Disordered snatches of ancient conversations pass through my mind. There is no reason. I remember a conversation I had with Alison – though it may have been another female friend. I told her the musicals *Kiss Me, Kate* and *West Side Story* were both based on Shakespeare plays. She told me the TV series *Mork and Mindy* was a spin-off from *Happy Days*, which in turn was inspired by the film *American Graffiti*. This is the closest I have come to a conversation about literature with a female friend. After college I never had a friend who read sensibly.

I remember a conversation I had with a boyfriend, not Richard, though let's say it was Richard for the purpose of simplicity. We discussed which should be put on chips first, the salt or the vinegar. We discussed the signature tune to *Cheers*, the American sitcom. Apparently two versions were used, one shorter than the other. He challenged me to name the three actresses who played Catwoman in the Batman TV series from the sixties. I knew only Julie Newmar and Eartha Kitt. 'The other was Lee Merryweather,' I was told by him. After Martin and until Carl I never had a boyfriend who could talk sensibly.

When Carl arrives he is wearing a new shirt and brings a bottle of wine.

'You OK?' he asks. I tell him I am fine. I even tell him I am happy because I don't want him to think otherwise. Meanwhile, my thoughts again have no coherence. I think about how Mick and my mother might have carried on had Mum lived longer. This leads to wondering the same about my mother and father if Dad had lived longer. Then I begin to think about Carl and myself in the future. Then I begin to think about my brother and his children, and how they might turn out. I have been an atrocious aunt. If they saw me in the street those kids would not recognise me; and if they did they would not be interested in me.

'You were lucky, I think. Being an only child,' I say to Carl.

'You think so? Didn't you have a happy childhood?'

I tell him the truth, that I did. How my memories, for the most part, are happy. I then have to explain that I do not hate my brother. So I have backed myself into a corner; why do I envy someone who was an only child? I have to make up a reason because I have nothing true to say.

'It must have been nice to have your parents' undivided attention, all their love.'

Carl takes this as an invitation to tell me more details about his childhood, which I am pleased to have him reveal. As he talks I can let my mind wander back to those random thoughts, which make no sense yet are nevertheless reassuring. I think about the first time I wore high-heeled shoes, forced into walking with outstretched arms. I think about how, between the ages of eight and ten, I obsessively collected pencil cases for no good reason. I think about a doll I had, which remained with me even after I had disposed of the others, which I took to my first flat but did not bring to London. I think about a teacher I had at school who told me how well she thought I would do if I went to university – and how this planted the first thought in my head of not going. I think about my cousin Susan; her wedding was the last family event I attended. I think about the day we moved into the family home we lived in through most of my life. I was six at the time and tried to help by carrying a cushion, or a lamp, or a photograph frame. I think about my parents. I miss my parents. Without wanting to speak to them now or see them now or have to consider them in any substantial way, I miss my mum and dad.

TWENTY-ONE

Every night since my accident – except last Tuesday – I have seen Carl. Though he came to see me on Monday night he didn't stay – we discussed him moving into the vacant flat across the landing. We have both told each other how eagerly we are looking forward to our lives afterwards.

On Tuesday I met up with Keith, from Ill Will. I had phoned the office and he – unusually – had answered. I thought it might be interesting, after all, to arrange the farewell meal I had talked about. I have been trying to regulate my work schedule into proper office hours. Sanity returned with reduced routine – such routine, though, makes me desire some recreation afterwards, something to separate my private life from my work life. I rely too much on Carl's company. After speaking with everyone in the office, Keith phoned me back. No one could meet up with me this coming Friday night, as I had hoped. He suggested I arrange a later date. I told him I would, then asked if he might want to go for a drink. I wanted his opinion of my work for *George*.

Keith chose the pub. Though I tried to make him interested in my work we were interrupted by his frequent trips to the bar. When he did glance through the sketches he made no constructive suggestions. He liked them, yet had nothing else to contribute. As I talked more and more about my work, about *George*, I could tell I was boring him so I thought it best to change the subject. I asked him about his wife as I could think of nothing else.

'We're having a bit of trouble at the moment. Well, *I'm* the trouble – if I'm honest. She's wants me to move out.'

He went onto explain the problem – his drinking. I asked about his other two marriages. The only one he talked about was his first.

'She's the one I should have made an effort with. She's the one I should have been good to. She made me happy.'

'It sounds as if you still love her.'

'I wouldn't call it love. She married again after me, so there's no chance of us getting back together; but if there was a chance . . . I would never again say I loved her. I said that to her a million times, then look how I behaved. And I wouldn't care if she never told me she loved me. All I'd want, all I'd try to achieve is that one day she'd tell me I made her happy; or maybe she'd tell me I was her best friend. Those things are more important. A reconciliation is out of the question – but I like having her as a sentimental benchmark. It's romantic to have this one great relationship that failed. I like the self-indulgent melancholy it permits me whenever I get a chance to talk about her. Everyone has one of those relationships, even if they're currently in a happy, successful one. They still have someone from the past, of whom they can say, "If things had worked out differently, *this* person is the one . . ." You have one, don't you, I'll bet?'

I told him about Martin, and enjoyed telling him. However, the melancholy and sentiment were now marbled with pretence. The pretence collapsed and I began to tell him about Carl. Once more I bored Keith. He made an excuse to leave. I suspect this was the first time he has ever left a pub before the bell rang for last orders. I bored him. Carl thinks I am interesting and fun. I was alone in the pub for only a few moments, thinking of and missing Carl even though I saw him only last night. This change frightens me, whilst also offering reassurance.

As I was leaving the pub, Alison entered. With Trevor. She was clinging onto his arm and chatting away, so did not notice me. I had to speak to her; for my own benefit I had to know how these two finally ended up together. Though Alison insisted Trevor bought me a drink, I refused. Understanding this meant a time limit before I left, she raced through the story of how Trevor had asked her out. When he was in hospital recovering from the beating he received from Mr Ostryzniuk's son, she left her own ward to make a point of visiting him, and in return he offered to take her for a meal as a thank-you. As she told me this, Trevor nodded in agreement whenever Alison consulted him, yet still said nothing. Alison apologised for not having phoned recently, telling me this is due to her seeing so much of Trevor. I would have liked to have kissed Trevor in gratitude.

I gave them a quick glance back as I left the pub, but they had already forgotten me. Both are desperate to be with the other.

Because I have not yet bought my third car of the year, I caught the tube home. The carriage was entirely empty. I read the advertisements for shows, for the Samaritans, for tourist attractions, for dating services. When I left the tube station I ran home, then phoned Carl straightaway – even before I took my coat off. My call woke him, yet he was still pleased to hear from me. I told him how right he had been, that even with this more relaxed schedule I have been concentrating on work too much. I asked him whether, if I rented a car, he might want to travel to Great Yarmouth with me this Saturday, to stay over and return late on Sunday. Sentiment and nostalgia have nothing to do with choosing Great Yarmouth, I know the motorway turnings to my home town and Great Yarmouth is on a straight line from there. I have never been an adventurous driver and do not wish to jeopardise my two days away with Carl arguing because we have ended up in Cumbria when we had planned on going to Brighton.

On Wednesday Carl came over to my flat. We argued over the fate of our books. Carl told me he has now begun packing his possessions into boxes, ready for the move. This – his books in boxes – has made him aware, just as it did for me faced with the same phenomenon, how many books he has. Together with mine, the shared quantity would be preposterous. Carl's initial suggestion was to find out which books in our two collections were duplicated, then sell only the spares. I suggested selling the whole damned lot: a cleansing of the past. Carl was never fully committed to this idea, so I concluded the debate by phoning a book dealer to arrange for him to pick up both collections. I then tell Carl something I may never fully believe:

'There's more to life than books.'

I have bullied him into submission. I like going out with

Carl. We made an agreement to each select ten books from our separate collections to grant an amnesty. We then made love before I flung him out – he has to rise too early to stay the night.

Last night, Friday, I picked up the rental car and drove to Carl's flat with my shoulder bag, ready to set off for Great Yarmouth early this morning, as soon as the book dealer has been. I brought the list of my ten books. We spent most of the night selecting Carl's ten. Post-war multinational conferences have divided up whole countries with far less debate. I maintained the pretence of a determined bad temper when actually I enjoyed the argument. I watched Carl agonise over his choices. My selection had been far more random and Carl raised no serious objections to most of them. The only one that he was curious about and continued to quibble over was *My Wicked Wicked Ways* by Errol Flynn. I had the wonderful enjoyment of telling him about the qualities of those books in my list that he had not read, *Billy Liar*, *Grimble*, *Of Human Bondage* and *Candide*. I envy him for having these books yet to read. Out of Carl's ten I have read nine. I would have kept none of his choices even if we were permitted to spare a hundred. The only one I had never read nor even heard of was *The Blinder* by Barry Hines. But it is a book about football.

With the twenty books pardoned off death row agreed, we went to bed and made love. The book dealer will first pick up Carl's collection, then drive to my home to collect mine. Somewhere in my boxes probably remains *The Counterfeit Confetti*. Just because it is being sold does not necessarily mean I will never see it again, of course, though I am convinced it has now gone for good. After all, I have read every page. I understand now. Nothing else can be served by having the book ever returned to my possession.

When I awake Carl isn't here. A note explains that he has gone jogging. His alarm clock says 8.30 a.m., and then his phone rings until I have to get out of bed to silence it. It is Carl.

'I found this little girl out on her own,' he tells me. 'She's lost. I think she's about four or five.'

I ask why he is phoning me. 'Take her to the police and come home.'

'She's upset. I don't want to be seen taking her. I'm a man, Tanya. It's an awful world, and I don't want to be accused of anything. Do you see what I mean? If I'm intercepted on the way they might not believe I was taking her to the police.'

I can now hear a child in the background, weeping. I understand his predicament. I tell him I will be there as soon as I can.

Carl does look very suspicious; he is in shorts and is sweaty; his eyes dart around as he shuffles nervously. I have to increase my pace, encouraged by his wild gestures to hurry. The child, when she sees me approaching, hides behind Carl's legs. She has her fist jammed into her mouth. She stares.

'She's called Josie,' Carl tells me. I try to walk around Carl's legs to say hello, yet as I do so she circles so his legs are always between us. This is the calming effect I have on children.

'Come on then, let's take her to the police.'

Carl entertains the girl with a step-by-step narrative of the journey. He comments on the shops we pass, fly posters, a flock of birds, a noisy bus. Josie becomes relaxed enough to slip her hand into mine. It is wet with her saliva. The journey is concluded with the little girl skipping along, occasionally taking slow-motion jumps suspended in the air held between our hands.

We do not even have to report to the desk when we enter the police station. Mother sees daughter, daughter sees mother. The little girl forgets us immediately. Though Carl crosses to the woman and attempts to offer a few words of explanation, she is too preoccupied with hugging and kissing the little girl. When Carl returns to me I ask if he was even thanked.

'She was too relieved to think straight. It's touching, isn't it?' Carl asks as we witness this pantomime. He is sincere. I would like to laugh at Carl for being so gullible, then shout at the woman that if she was so concerned about her kid, how come she lost it in the first place? But I bite my tongue.

As we walk out of the police station Josie waves at me. For

a split second I revoke some of my most extreme anti-child feelings. They immediately return when I remember the repugnant feel of dried spittle on my hand. My qualifications for motherhood are zero.

The book dealer is at Carl's flat when we return. Between the three of us we load his van with Carl's books. Carl showers and changes whilst I drive home, followed by the book dealer. We then finish loading his van with my books.

I drive back to Carl's home, thinking how much I wish I had never suggested Great Yarmouth.

I make the mistake of letting Carl drive the rental car. This is the first time he has driven since his career change forced him to sacrifice owning a car. Subsequently, I am given a running commentary of his driving – such is his thrill. Once out of London I tell him to shut up and let me read in peace. For a few miles silence is maintained, until he again begins to comment on turnings, other road users, upcoming junctions; every single road sign is read aloud.

We pull in at a service station; then, when we resume driving, the moment he speaks I put a finger in both ears and yell, 'I am not listening!' This finally does the trick – he shuts up. This is not a promising start to our break.

I holler a deliberately childish 'Are we there yet?' when I first see the coast. I am forcing my good humour so Carl will not suspect the contrary.

After we find a suitable hotel, we unpack and shower. We agree to have a meal in the hotel and maybe take a walk later, before we return and go to bed.

Carl is quiet throughout our meal. We are by far the hotel's youngest guests, a generation separating us from the next-youngest. There is no music playing and the other guests are couples who have been together for so long they no longer have anything to say to each other. This hard-core silence is mob rule; so after a brief discussion about the food and after the waiter has gone, we join everyone else and shut up. It's a hole which once you've fallen into is tough to escape.

To break the deadlock after the meal is finished, I tell him: 'Kids are the end of life, not the beginning. I would sooner put my breasts in a food blender than have kids.'

'You don't ever want kids?'

'No. But clearly you do.'

'I guess I do. If things work out between us, it's nice to know how we stand. These things should be talked about,' he says, solemnly.

Up in our room we get straight into bed.

'I've always thought I would like to be a father. I do want kids,' he tells me. 'But I want you more. If being with you means never being a father, I'll have to get used to that.'

We make love. The sea air always makes me frisky.

Breakfast in the hotel is triangles of cold toast, a bowl containing three mouthfuls of cornflakes and a glass of yellow orange juice. We haven't yet discussed how we intend to spend the day. The reason for this, I suspect, is that I have been too preoccupied and Carl has been reluctant to set an agenda. He may believe he has no right, because I'm paying for this. There is no scope for exhaustive debate; we are not in Disney World; the options for an exciting day are limited in Great Yarmouth.

'Shall we walk along the front?' I ask as I lead him in that direction. 'I fancy a walk, don't you? A long, exhausting walk.'

I link arms with him as we stroll along the front. I let him talk on without making any contribution to the conversation. Away from home the idea of us as a couple has a comprehensible definition. I can see us as others might; we do look comfortable and content together; it seems clear there is some rapport between us guaranteeing a future ahead. Unlike last night, Carl talks seamlessly, occasionally in reference to Great Yarmouth, the shops, the view, the people. Often he talks about himself and sometimes about us; for a while he talks about music, his favourite bands and favourite records. He tells me about his time at school and some of the years he spent in his previous job, laughing at himself now for his warped priorities.

'You're very quiet,' he tells me after a couple of hours. 'Am I boring you? Have I been yattering on?'

'I'm not bored, I've been listening.'

For a while we sit on a wall. We have long since walked out of Great Yarmouth itself and have come to rest on a slight hill with a view of the sea. I take Carl's hand and nothing is spoken. We look at the view: someone on their own could not bear the brunt of the sea's history. On your own an opinion would have to be formed.

'Shall we head back?' he eventually says. 'Are you hungry?'

'Let's carry on walking. It'll be an adventure.'

At first our adventure does not take us away from roads where traffic is any less than frequent. We walk through villages that bear no visible names, along hamlets that boast timeless facilities like horse troughs and converted gas lamps; then pavements lapse into footpaths. As we carry on I cannot help wondering if the track we are now on is public or whether we are trespassing. On one side woods dominate; on the other there are only open fields of rapeseed.

'Shall we continue walking?' Carl wonders. He is not reading my thoughts, he is simply deducing that the only sensible idea I could have would be to turn back. I am thirsty and hungry; my feet ache.

'Which way, which side do you think the coast is on?' I ask.

He points to the same side I would have, the side where the woods are. I suggest we enter the woods, trusting this will turn out to be a short cut. I suspect this is the kind of badly informed logic many previous adventurers have made – the type whose tragic deaths are immortalised in local papers. Carl, perhaps having been drained of the survival instinct, shrugs his shoulders in exasperated agreement.

The woods are not dense and we soon find a stream to follow; its sound is reassuringly cautious. We see no one else. As we walk further the woods thin out up to an incline of yellowing grass and bluebells. In the sky above this, in the near distance, seagulls circle. Carl agrees to my suggestion of walking over the incline to see if the land on the other side might help us navigate a route to salvation. As we ascend, a house comes into view; it is a cottage, really, though two storeys and built in red brick with a black tile roof. We look towards this cottage, and in turn it looks towards the remote view of Great Yarmouth. The cottage is surrounded by a loose circumference of hedges, which hold back the woods; several hundred yards from this is a road. No traffic passes on this road; it is brought to our attention only by a wooden gate. We head for this, our route taking us nearer to the cottage. A 'For Sale' sign is posted at its gate, destined to be seen only by those who are lost.

'Shall we ask if we can look around?' I suggest.

'What for? Anyway, it looks empty to me. No, come on, let's try to find civilisation. If that fails, let's go back to Great Yarmouth.' Pleased with his gag and suddenly much relieved, he kisses me, then – as if the decision is made – for the first time today he walks ahead of me. I dawdle, hanging back to take a more considered look at the cottage. The garden has been well cared for, designed to make maintenance easy; shrubs and bushes are far more prominent than flowers. The cottage is less than a hundred years old, I should guess, designed for function rather than quaint beauty. Built in so remote a spot, it can only have been constructed on the orders of someone who had the authority – money – to demand it, like a folly built on the whim of an eccentric industrialist. It is not fashioned to please others nor large enough to accommodate a family. Its clear purpose is a private sanctuary.

Out of idle curiosity I jot down the number of the estate agent. The cottage is an anachronism, peaceful yet peculiarly urban. I project into an imagined future, an unremarkable sunny day like today, and think how much I would like to sit in this garden and paint this view. This is my first unprovoked artistic thought in more than a decade. I catch Carl up.

'Wouldn't you love to live somewhere like this?'

'Who wouldn't!' he says as he climbs the wooden fence, which takes us onto the road.

The road in one direction is long and straight, in the other it disappears around trees – this is the direction we walk. The road bends and folds towards the coast. Five minutes later we reach the shore, then fifteen more and we are back on the front at Great Yarmouth. It is not yet 1 p.m. We decide to eat in our hotel so we can wash and change immediately after.

In our hotel room, after we have eaten, Carl is the first out of the shower.

'What are we doing this afternoon?' he asks as I undress.

'The beach.'

With both of us in sunglasses and hats, we take our books down onto Great Yarmouth's pebbles. We rent deckchairs and I prepare to indulge in a few hours of sunny nothing.

Carl is reading *Of Human Bondage* but making hard work of it. I think he is reading it simply to please me after I forced it upon him, assuring him he would enjoy it. Maugham goes in and out of fashion; his novels are story- and character-driven, his style designed to help these qualities. Some people see style as being the most important quality of prose. To me that's as absurd as saying the most important quality of music should be the innovative arrangement of notes rather than the beauty of the melody. Fortunately these people will not ruin the world of literature as they have art; too much time is required to read a novel when all you need for a piece of art is a few seconds.

Carl never settles. Forty minutes after we have found a suitable spot, he leaves to fetch me an ice cream I have not requested. For a change, because I wish to be in a light-hearted mood, the book I selected to bring belongs to that prominent modern genre of single women in their late twenties, worrying about career, weight, men. In spite of the bright, colourful cover and the splattering of quotes from rave reviews, it achieves the opposite effect to the one I had hoped. I yawn more times than I laugh; its clichés alienate rather than connect with me. The emotions, experiences and concerns of the main character are so remote from my own I can only conclude either I or the author is completely at odds with the reality of the modern world. I have to concede the fact that the book has been a best-seller.

Bored with it, and alone, I take stock of my indolent neighbours; they are mostly elderly. They occupy themselves with magazines, flasks and flattened, gritty sandwiches – tranquillised with a heavy dose of lethargy. Separate from everyone I notice one man who is sat motionless, facing the sea, with nothing to occupy him. I noticed him before, when I was reading, but each time I looked up to catch his eye he was always looking at the sea. As I stare at him now, however, he looks over without flinching. Perhaps he finds me attractive. He is in his sixties, I should think; he wears a polo shirt, a sports jacket and a trilby – consequently much of his face is in shadow. He stands, then begins to walk over to me, grinning! All I can think is how, exactly, do I rebuff the advances of a pensioner? Is there an etiquette to it? Is it rude to point and laugh?

Closer, though, I stand to meet him because I now recognise him. This is no pensioner, this is a man in his fifties, prematurely aged and possibly only wanting to tell me he hates me.

'I thought it was you,' Mick says. His smile stays and there is no malice in his voice.

'Hello, Mick,' I say. 'Hello,' I repeat after I fail to think of anything to add.

'Did you recognise me?' he asks.

'The sun was in my eyes.'

'Who's that with you?' he asks, waving in the direction of the promenade, where Carl was last seen.

'A friend. Boyfriend. He's gone for ice cream. We're just here on a break. We leave later today. I didn't recognise you at first. But now . . . Obviously. So what are you doing here? Sit, by the way.' I offer him Carl's deckchair. I am rambling because I am afraid. I am scared in case Mick should wish to talk about my mother. And of course he will, he must at least mention her. Then he might ask why I did not go to her funeral. Or he might bring up the subject of the way our relationship ended. Or how she died.

'I live here now,' he begins. 'I've only been here for a couple of weeks. I was offered early voluntary retirement from work. So I got a lump sum; then there was money I got from your mother, and I sold the house. So, I'm fine, really. I'm all set up. It's only a bungalow, your mother would have hated it – but it suits me.' Mother has been mentioned, the taboo breached. Still no malice, though.

It is my turn to say something. Encouragement, congratulations for moving on with his life; delight that he should seem so content. I say nothing. Anything I say will grant him permission to ask about my life and I'll rest easier if he has no information. Not that there is much for him to know; though I might, if pushed, tell him about the great success I am predicted to have with *George*. Maybe Mick senses that I have nothing to say, maybe he catches me glancing behind him, looking to see if Carl is returning. I wonder this because he then speaks urgently, as if seizing an opportunity he can sense passing.

'Tanya, I'm sorry to have to ask you this, but did your mother ever say anything to you about me? I mean, about how she felt about me?'

He removes his hat, wipes his forehead and then rotates the hat in his hands, avoiding eye contact with me.

'Didn't she ever tell you she loved you?' I ask.

'Just because someone tells you they love you, it doesn't always follow that they're telling the truth.'

'She loved you, Mick. I know she did. I never had any doubt about that.' I say this in a stern voice, as if I am a little angry at him. He can choose to believe I am angry either because he is doubting my mother's sincerity or because he is so foolishly insecure. Mick has aged badly in the time since I last saw him. He has lost energy and will. Even so, I am quickly becoming his contemporary because he speaks positively begging for reassurance, just as children do to their parents. He wants me to comfort him. He wants someone to listen who knows the characters in his story.

'I was never loved by her in the way your father was. He was my greatest friend, but I can't help resenting him for being her only true love.'

Carl chooses this moment to return. He has finished eating his own ice cream and the one he presents to me has been switched from his left to his right hand because his left is soaked – the ice cream is melting rapidly. I introduce Carl to Mick, then falter as I try to explain who Mick is; this is the Mick who was married to . . . He is my stepfather, I say. This is the first time I have really thought of Mick like this. My stepfather.

Carl lets Mick remain in the deckchair, whilst he sits on the pebbles, leaning against me. Before long Mick is again talking as if he had not been interrupted. Though I make many attempts to concentrate, my attention wanders every time, like a child watching *Panorama*. My ice cream commands more of my interest than Mick. He continues telling me how much he misses my mother and how his life and plans changed so fundamentally when she died. If it was ever true that he slept with Mum whilst Dad was still alive, I now see how such a mistake was an irrelevance. There can be no doubt about my mum's love for my father, and any lapse she may have made I can understand. I understand accidental lapses and I understand premeditated lapses. Without ever making such lapses, we are flawless human beings and flawless humans are insipid fakes.

As we leave I take Mick's new address. I might wish to visit him occasionally, or phone to say hello. We might meet regularly once I live here.

TWENTY-TWO

The good news is that, after having lived with me here in Great Yarmouth for one month to the day and, frankly, getting on my nerves, Carl has now found a job – so once again I will have my days returned to me, to work.

Financed by a generous advance from the first *George* book, we are living in the cottage we saw. For three months I lived here alone, waiting for Carl to join me. Though we talked on the phone every night, I could never succeed in making Carl understand the joy I felt when I had completed the renovation of the kitchen, or finished decorating one of the bedrooms, or my pride after I had sandpapered, then varnished the floorboards. So I longed for him to be with me so he could see for himself and understand how happy I hoped we would be here. The agreement we had come to was for him to stay in London to show potential buyers around both our flats, deal with the surveyors, the estate agent, solicitors and so on, then to quit his job before he moved. Carl has never become entirely happy at the prospect of living in a home that is in my name alone; but he genuinely wanted to be with me.

My first month here was spent in worry leading to regret; I became convinced I had misunderstood my own desires and began to deplore my decision to move from London. And I missed Carl.

The second month I began to acquire more comforts and these were fewer jobs that urgently needed doing around the cottage, allowing me more time to pursue my real interests, and to work.

The third month was all I had hoped this life would be, to be living surrounded by such remote and beautiful countryside. My routine became to never work in any disciplined way, which is the method most other professionals use, but to work only when inspired – which was often. I regularly worked without thinking to eat or barely noticing the silence long after a CD had ended.

In the last month, since Carl arrived, I have not had one of these long sessions of work. Whenever I'm working he will repeatedly interrupt to ask if I want a cup of tea, or he will stop me because a meal is ready. Carl's cooking, just like sex with him, is always enjoyable and satisfactory, though afterwards I am often left with the thought that these things are not quite worth the effort and the mess.

Before he arrived my assumption was that with two of us together life would be twice as simple; there would be half as many domestic chores for me and somehow, as the result of this equation, I would have twice as much time to work. But these mathematics don't translate into real life. Though Carl cleans and shops, things that before would have consumed hours of my time, I now find every hour I do have has minutes eaten away in my attempts to accommodate how he wishes this house to run. For instance, whereas before I might have had a quick bath, then dressed within twenty minutes, a bath now seldom takes less than an hour because I have to be meticulously clean, then dress presentably, and also keep the bathroom tidy. He doesn't protest if I leave a mess, but when I next visit a room I messed up I find it spotless. Shame forces me to constantly clean and tidy after myself, even when I think it unnecessary. And I always think it unnecessary.

In his first week here he changed where I kept the cutlery; to this day I still instinctively go to the old drawer. He often moves my ornaments, thinking I won't notice, like the two cuckoo clocks, which went missing from either side of the fireplace. He constantly moves the soap from the side of the bath onto the sink so that whenever I take a bath I have to get out to retrieve the soap. He begins novels that I am still reading, so I then confuse his bookmark with mine. He keeps the bathroom window open all the time, so there is a constant draught in the house. He has filled the house with plants, and keeps used tea bags steeping in a jug of water, which he uses to feed the plants. All of this behaviour annoys me.

I have completely lost the evenings, any chance to work

past five o'clock. This loss happened following his arrival and as a result of wanting to keep him company; this then became our routine – even though we seldom do anything at night but read. I am again reading as much as I ever did when I lived in London.

Since coming here, incidentally, I have reread *Laughing Out of Context* by Janet Greenhough. In the book the lead character walks into a travel agent's to confront the ex-girlfriend of her current boyfriend. As I read this I clearly remembered that episode from the first time I read the book. So the incident was not a story from my life – as I had believed. I never confronted Martin's ex-girlfriend. She just faded away. I had incorporated this fictional story into my real life.

This morning Carl returned from his routine jog to find the letter telling him an interview he had attended had been successful. He will be back in PR, working for Great Yarmouth Tourist Authority. I didn't confront him on the apparent hypocrisy of this U-turn just in case he agreed and refused the offer.

Though I had a rare chance to work unhindered today I sacrificed this to prepare a surprise dinner, to celebrate him finding a job. This is only the fourth time I have cooked since Carl arrived. He enjoyed the rare pampering I gave him as I ordered him to sit, then served him the meal. We talked and teased in a relaxed manner we have not experienced in a month. Our good humour even survived the food. Carl could not know my happiness has been renewed mainly by the prospect of having my home, at least by day, returned to me. Though my days will not be as productive as before he arrived, with him at work I will at least have eight hours of freedom. I talk enthusiastically about the sketches I have been trying out for the next *George* book, and he listens, as ever, dutifully.

But then he makes the shock announcement:

'The best part of this Tourist Authority job is that most days I can work from home.'

'Home?' I ask, a glass of wine poised near my mouth. 'You

mean you'll be working here, working from *here*? From here?'

'Not every day, but most.'

'No,' I tell him before I can stop myself. 'I mean, you won't like working from home.'

'Won't like it? I can't imagine what would make you think that. It's perfect. You're spilling that.'

Wine has dribbled from the rim of the glass. I get up and walk away from him, ostensibly to dry my hand. I use the opportunity of having my back to him to ask a direct question.

'So this job will make you happy? You're not happy now, then? You're not happy with me?'

'What? Of course I'm happy. I'm surprised how happy I am.'

'Surprised? Why?'

'I wasn't entirely sure about the risk, you know, whether it, *we*, would work. Moving. Quitting my job, changing my whole life! And ... Logically, knowing myself as well as I thought I did, I had great doubts about how I would feel living with you when you earn far more than me, far more than I'm ever likely to earn. And finally, well – *you*, Tanya. I always thought I was as independent as anyone could get – then I started to get to know you. I always thought your independence would drive us apart. This is what I believed and was certain about. That is, until you lent me your book.'

'Which book?' I ask because over the time I have known him I have lent him many.

'The book. *Your* book, *The Counterfeit Confetti*. When I took it I thought the author's name was only coincidence. Why didn't you tell me you wrote it?'

I quickly return to the table, pulling my chair close to his. There are so many possible things I could tell Carl now, explanation and exclamation. I could tell him I didn't write that book or I could explain that I have no explanation for its existence or for why it tells my story. I could even tell him that my memory is perfectly clear – he was curious about the book but never actually borrowed it so there can be no feasible way he has read *The Counterfeit Confetti*.

'Describe the book to me.'

'You should know what it's about. What's the matter?' he asks. He is puzzled by the urgency in my voice so I quickly make an adjustment, as if I am only casually interested.

'No, it's OK. I wasn't asking you to describe the story. I want you to describe the cover.'

'It has no dust jacket, but . . . Puh, I don't know. Shall I get it for you?'

'You've got it here?' The adjustment has gone and the astonishment has returned in full voice. 'Tell me exactly what it says that persuaded you to take this gamble on us. Show me.'

I follow him upstairs. He quickly finds the book. I recognise the distinct olive-green cover. The silver lettering of the first C is flaking and one corner is dented from where I dropped the book. He begins to search through to find a passage that will illustrate his assertion that we – as he believes – are going to be happy together. I now stop this pointless search; I know the book does not end this way.

'How can you have this book?' I demand. 'Think. Even if I really did lend you it – which I didn't! – we got rid of all our books except for ten. And this wasn't one of the ten. So why do you have it? Why is it here?'

Carl has no answer. I then permit him to read the last chapter of *The Counterfeit Confetti* after first explaining all I can about the book's impossible existence. He naturally listens to everything I say with massive scepticism.

'Just read the last chapter,' I tell him. I find the page. 'From here.'

I present him with the open book, turned to the first page of the last chapter. Then I leave so I do not distract him whilst he is reading, and to prevent him making contradictory arguments as he reads the same words I read, about how if we stay together we would fail. Even though the book did not say we would live together in Great Yarmouth, the principle remains.

Carl reads fast so I return after I believe he has had sufficient time and find him flicking through the whole book.

'I didn't *write* the book,' I tell Carl. 'But everything in that book is true to my life.'

I tell him the brutal truth of how happy I was before he arrived and how he has mostly annoyed me since.

'What does that have to do with this book?' he asks after he has recovered.

'Because the book is true. I ignored it and I shouldn't have.'

Carl looks bemused. 'But if it's "true" where's the problem? We live happily ever after, according to this book.'

'You haven't read it,' I tell him angrily.

'We stay together, eventually marry. We have children –'

'Children? What children? You haven't even read it, have you?'

'Stop telling me I haven't read it!' He controls himself: 'Please.'

Carl turns to the last chapter, then speed-reads down the pages, looking for the relevant passage. He begins reading:

After Tanya and Carl had lived happily together for a year –

'Give me that here,' I shout at him, snatching the book. I am thinking how tiresome it is of him to be making a joke at this moment. I look down the page to confirm that no such sentence exists. None does. I am about to reprimand Carl when I see from his expression there has been no joke intended. He is waiting for me to explain because he is bemused, or hurt. I look back to the page, reading more slowly, in case I missed the sentence. I don't see it – I turn back a number of pages. The last chapter now begins differently.

After they had lived together in Great Yarmouth for one month to the day, it was good news for Tanya when Carl found a job. Once again she would have her days returned to her, to work.

Nearly four months had passed. Financed by a generous advance from the first *George* book, they were living in the cottage they had seen in Great Yarmouth. For three months Tanya had lived here alone, waiting for Carl to join her, though they talked on the phone every night, and Tanya would update him on the progress she was making on the house and he would update her

Carl puts his hand on the page.

'Why are we looking at this book, Tanya? I'm thoroughly confused.'

I remove his hand and quickly turn several more pages, nearer to the new ending.

In the first month of his arrival Tanya worked far less than before due to Carl's constant interruptions. She also found each hour of her day had minutes eaten away in her attempts to accommodate how he wished the house to run.

Instead of reading further, which will be too dangerously close to the very end, I keep my finger on this sentence – like an over-officious postman asking for a signature – and demand Carl reads it. I want no mistakes or misunderstandings.

Carl told her he was not surprised that she made a good mother, he reads. *She loved their children, they made her laugh and the responsibility of protecting them and forming them made her –*

I snatch the book away and look further into the new last chapter. I look for a passage describing how our relationship has deteriorated. I find this:

To her annoyance he changed where she kept the cutlery; she cursed him each time she instinctively went to the old drawer. To her annoyance he repeatedly left the soap on the bathroom sink; she cursed him each time she had to get out of the bath to retrieve it. To her annoyance he continually began to read novels she had not yet finished; she cursed him each time she began reading from the place where he had left off.

'Here,' I demand of Carl again. 'Read.'

'Tanya, why? I don't get it.'

'Read. Please.'

On their wedding day –

'That's enough,' I tell Carl. I take *The Counterfeit Confetti* from him.

At last I finally understand the purpose of *The Counterfeit Confetti*. There can be no final chapter where we marry, and if children are involved he reads of a future designed to accommodate his desires, not mine.

My instincts are not Carl's instincts; my reactions and my nature are not his. Our predicted happy futures can only ever be different.

'Still confused!' Carl laughs. His laughter abruptly stops.

I stare at the book, concentrating, wondering about its greater purpose. I look at the title, trying to work out its significance. I open it at random.

After marrying, Martin then settled into fathering two children, I read again. This time it has no effect. I am only relieved he has someone to give his attention to so he will never bother me. I read more.

> Tanya had learnt how her decade-long obsession with Martin was only her cowardice; it provided her with an excuse to not seriously concern herself with other men. If she had an ideal, then no one could match him. Tanya and Martin were a phoney marriage – she always belonged to him because that life was the securest.

After Martin – now I have had time to think of him in the past sense – the happiest period of my subsequent life was with Richard. I was with someone it was easy to care little for; and I had the comfort of Martin in memory, along with the unspecified hope that came with those memories. Hope was then shattered and where else could I shelter?

'Tanya!' Carl shouts, demanding my attention.

I read the last paragraph of *The Counterfeit Confetti*. This is how the book now ends:

> The nine years she had been asleep, after losing Martin, were only a waste because she had been young and had not understood how people change. So when he returned, she found she had been mourning the death of a complete stranger.
>
> Once she had left London she woke; she was alive now because at last she had freedom and understood herself perfectly. She never had to do anything she did not wish to do. She missed Carl sometimes, even longed for him.

This remorse comforted her, and was all the comfort she needed.

'Please, Tanya!' he demands. 'What is it you want to happen?'

I think I am lying to Carl when I tell him everything that has happened between us has been too fast, too hasty. This seems inadequate so I fall back on an old anti-marriage standby:

'Whom do you know, which couple do you know who are happy? I mean, happy in a way you'd like to be happy?'

'Who cares about other couples? All I believe, Tanya, is that if we stay together we have a real shot at happiness. Genuine, joyous happiness. We might be a real example of how it's supposed to be – two people together as lovers, as close friends, as . . . '

He loses momentum here, witnessing my blank expression and stalling beneath the burden of the waste. I understand everything he has been saying and agree. It is a real chance, which I am turning my back on. I know this but cannot begin to explain to him why I am doing it because once I begin the explanation, he will believe there is still hope, and I do not wish to mislead him.

Carl says, 'You want us to break up then? I go back to London. You stay here. You want it so that we never see each other again?'

'I can't think how else to be happy,' is all I dare say.

'And me?'

'You'll be happy,' I tell him.

'I can only be happy with you.' This is the nonsense he is too intelligent to really believe but says out of desperation. 'Tell me you don't want me to leave.'

My refusal to answer is the answer.

'But I moved here for you. You made the decision without consulting me – yet I still came. I was even prepared to go back into public relations. I love you,' Carl tells me. First time. It makes me sick with despair. It's a punch to the gut.

'It doesn't make me happy to hear you say you love me,' I tell him instead. My intention is not cruelty though it wounds him nevertheless. Carl deserves more. A fuller explanation will have to be improvised. Inspiration escapes me; I have nothing else to add, nothing creditable.

Carl does not move. He waits. He throws down the final ultimatum.

'You're telling me to go?'

'Give me a minute,' I tell him, suddenly petrified. I hold *The Counterfeit Confetti*, ready to open it. I change my mind and the book stays closed. *I do not need the book any more*. I have made my decision free of influence. All that the book confirms is all it has ever confirmed, my intuition. My instincts are my true desires.

'Can't you answer me?' Carl asks. 'I've made sacrifices so I could be happy.'

'I'm making my first,' I answer. 'You have to go.'

'You don't want us to be happy?' Carl asks.

I tell Carl, answering a question he didn't ask, 'I will be happy.'

EPILOGUE

For the last hour we have been sitting in the living room, me on the couch, Carl in the armchair, both facing the TV. The hour might have passed more quickly if we had spoken or if the TV had been on. At regular intervals I hear him sigh. When I dare to look at him he doesn't notice; or he sees but it does not register – he is in such deep thought.

'I'll go then,' he eventually challenges. As soon as he has spoken it is as if the hour has not passed. I am determined not to return to that heated momentum, so I sound as consolatory as I dare.

'If I can help you out with money, I will. We'll begin packing in the morning.'

'No, no, you don't understand. I'll go. Now. It won't do any good . . . I don't want to be in the house with you for another night. I'll walk into Great Yarmouth and see if there's a late train to London. If not, I'll book into a bed and breakfast.'

He leaves the room swiftly, hoping to force me into saying an endearment hastily, before I have a chance to think of consequences. I keep silent, which is the nastiest response imaginable.

I pick up the *Radio Times* for when he returns, so he will see his leaving will not disturb me.

He comes back into the living room to fasten his coat. He pats the pockets down, then takes out his wallet and looks through it, counting the notes. Only after he has delayed his departure long enough for me to have intervened, then realises I am not going to, does he leave. He doesn't look at me, acknowledge me, say anything. I am proud of my restraint.

I wait a few minutes before I look in the kitchen. I prepare a look of annoyance, which I will then replace with anger. I

271

enter – he's not here. He is not here! I wait a few minutes more before I open the outside door, fully expecting him to be standing there. The fucker really has gone. It is a very still night. The silence and darkness are absolute and no matter how hard I concentrate I cannot break them. Carl has gone! In that time before Carl lived here, it never occurred to me how isolated I am. There's a silence and a darkness I have never been previously aware of. The inconvenience of this rushed departure can only mean I have hurt him so badly he now holds me in such contempt that he genuinely cannot bear to be around me any longer. I hadn't meant for such hatred.

My life cannot be dissected into analysable incidents. My memory is vain, as all memories are, giving me an exciting life by focusing only on the dramatic. My father dying made an impression on me – though really I was a fairly miserable person before this catastrophe. Losing Martin might have warned me off attaching myself fully, emotionally, spiritually, to one other person, yet having met him again I learnt I had used him only as an excuse; the truth behind my resistance to men is that I had never met another one who was worth the trouble. That is until I met Carl. His bad luck was to have met me when the person I had practised becoming was ready for a full performance. I'm like one of those actors – if this syndrome is real – who have played soap opera characters for so long they actually adopt their soap character's behaviour and personality in real life. I am this misanthropic because it is the natural conclusion to the persona I have coveted.

I think about Carl's smile. I think about his eyes. Carl's eyes – uniquely – are sexier, prettier when he is serious. I think about his smell – how it had never registered with me that he had a distinctive one, until he came to live here.

Back inside my home I immediately begin to plan new routines and new schedules. I do this deliberately because if I have a set plan for tomorrow I can also have the pleasure of abandoning it to simply do whatever I wish.

To occupy myself through the temporary loneliness I feel at this moment, in this house which has lost the noise of voices, I set out pencils, inks and papers so I can work. Lack of concentration handicaps any progress, even when I force guilt by reminding myself about how little work I have done recently.

This loneliness will not last. It is as artificial and deceptive as the weight and pressure still felt after a plaster cast has been removed. I permit myself to slide into despondency only because in future I will never have this feeling again and might question its existence, so I need a recent, distinguishable occasion when I can tell myself that it was a horrible feeling to have had and an unavoidable feeling, once you let someone penetrate your protective instincts.

When I snap out of these thoughts the ink has dried on my pen and will not mark the page. I scar in some dry lines; I write his name.

The sound of the kitchen door slamming shut startles me. Then Carl marches into the living room. I cannot be sure exactly how much time has passed but certainly he has not had long enough to have walked into Great Yarmouth, then returned. In this situation Caroline would run to embrace him. Alison would profusely apologise without the thought that she might have been in the right. Myself, I deliberately look alarmed, to put him on the defensive.

'Don't say anything,' he begins. 'Just listen.' His voice is neither raised nor angry, only measured and hard. He is determined to be heard.

'I thought you'd come after me, that's how stupid – naive – I was. I had the hope, somehow, that this was some sort of game you were playing. The last time – in London – you dumped me and I did nothing. But this time is different. I can't get it into my head that this is the end. I can't let it be the end.'

'You don't have any choice.' This is me speaking.

'Shut up, Tanya. Shut up and listen. Everything you've wanted from me I've given. I haven't spoken up or fought back. *Now* I'm going to fight back. I've never wanted anything as much as I want you. So you're going to hear me out.'

'It won't do any good, Carl.'

'Shut up, I said. Shut the fuck up.' The swearing and the

force of his voice surprise us both. Carl is embarrassed by his loss of temper whilst I am delighted.

'You've turned my world upside down, then you expect me to return to a city that is a million times larger than when I left it, now that it no longer has you; to return to no home and no job. I let you become all of my world and now you expect me to leave. I need you.'

'Carl, is there any chance you would believe me if I said I really didn't want to hurt you?' This is a sincere sentence. I can't imagine how it slipped out.

'I'm not actually surprised by this, Tanya. I might not have expected it or seen it coming, but I'm not surprised. If you were constant, reliable, perhaps I wouldn't have fallen for you. If you only wanted the ordinary, unexceptional things from life, I couldn't have kept such an interest in you. If you . . . You're bored, aren't you?'

The expression I pulled, which he read as boredom, was in fact sorrow. My eyes closed and I sighed because as I listened it occurred to me just how much he does love me and how easy it is for me, even though I love him in return – and in contradiction to the last thing I told him – to willingly hurt him. In an attempt not to look bored I smile, then immediately try to remove the smile because Carl may read it as enjoyment of his humiliation. Not only have I lost control of the words I speak but it seems my facial expressions are also running wild.

'How will you know you're alive, Tanya? You're smiling now, but what will be the point of smiling when you're here alone? You believe you back away from people because you see other people as being trouble, or a responsibility, or a risk. So you now have none of those things; but also no fun, no joy, no pleasure. I'm not perfect and neither are you. If people were perfect there'd be nothing for others to accustom themselves to. Only when it's unconditional is it love.'

So far I have agreed with everything he has said, except for this. Love is often, perhaps even always, conditional. The conditions are to be loved back, to have respect, to know trust. All of these I have with Carl.

He continues, 'I'm talking too much now because I daren't stop. This might be easy for you but for me it's a nightmare.

I'm not sure how you expect me to walk out of here alone. You have to understand things from my perspective.'

'I do understand things from your perspective!' I shout, far louder than I had expected. 'I understand because *your* perspective is *my* perspective. I know how important love is. Christ, how could anyone living in this shitty culture not understand? How many films have love as their theme? How many pop songs, how many novels? So – right – it has to be the most important thing in the world. I know. I do know. Trust me, I know.'

I am stalling whilst I think. Carl was doomed from day one, when my intuition first guided me into being *alone*. I maliciously broke up with him, now I irrationally want him back. Or maybe it's this: I irrationally broke up with him, now I maliciously want him back.

I try to explain, speaking rapidly, without taking a breath. 'I know the secret about me that you don't, Carl. The secret about me is that no one should love me because I'm not worth the trouble. And when I think about all the nonsense I've put you through, I see what a fucking horrible person I really am.'

I take a breath after this, long enough for him to interject with a fierce, lovingly loyal denial. He doesn't.

'You shouldn't love me,' I say now, speaking most slowly but with emphasis. 'When my dad died all I could worry about was myself and why I didn't seem to be grieving like everyone else. The truth is, I didn't grieve because that's the kind of nasty person I am. Then I stopped speaking to my mum for some stupid, ridiculous reason. Then she died and I didn't even take the trouble to go to her funeral because I was bothered about what people might think of me. I don't give a toss about my brother or his kids. I used to be polite to Mrs Davies but only because I didn't have the guts to tell her I wished she was dead. When I met you it didn't matter how much I fancied you or how much I liked you, or how smart you were, and how well read – all I could think was that you were a road sweeper and so I was better than you! *Me* better than *you*! The friends I had have become bored with me because I never had time for them. Those that persevered, like Alison, I ended up being openly nasty to; and the one friend I

275

had who I liked, Caroline, even her I learnt to hate because I began to think she was as stupid as everyone else in the world. She was stupid because she wanted love. That's how arrogant I am, Carl. I think everyone in the world is stupid and weak and –'

Carl hears me clear my throat. Carl sees me bow my head so he cannot see my eyes. I stop breathing so he will not notice any sharp intakes as I try to suppress a sob. I hope Carl believes my crying is born from a decent emotion like sorrow, but I know it is self-pity. Until now I never really realised what a true cow I was. Carl – however – completely misunderstands my tears.

'Are you crying, Tanya? I didn't mean to come on so strong.'

'If I'm crying for any reason . . . If there is a reason it's because I see what I've done to you and yet you come back. I didn't want you to go. I don't want you to stay. Either way seems like a failure.'

If I'm crying now, how would I react if we had had years together and he then died? I would be like Mum, rushing into the arms of whoever was most convenient, or I would be like Mick, wasting my remaining years in pointless paranoias; or, worse, I would be like Mrs Davies, unable to live any life because she has forgotten the definition of herself alone; she can only categorise herself by being half of a couple, and without that other half she is nothing.

'I'm crying because . . .'

Whatever else I might have to say is lost as my voice is stifled, as my mouth is buried in Carl's coat as he hugs me, consoling me. He strokes my hair, enjoying himself. I keep within his hold but push him back. His smile is restful, he looks at my lips. He believes we are going to kiss, to reconcile. Now that we have both said our piece and I have rid myself of any superfluous emotions that might otherwise have clogged up my mind for months, it would be better for us both if he was no longer here.

'You see, I know I have to be on my own. Everything I have learnt has taught me that's the best way. Everything I read in *The Counterfeit Confetti* –'

'Where is it?' he interrupts. He pulls away from me and begins to search around. As he looks I hear him muttering:

'That book . . . It's only a damned book.'

'What are you doing?' I demand when he finally finds *The Counterfeit Confetti*.

'You'll see. This book . . . I don't know what you think this book told you but I'm going to show you how worthless it is, how books aren't meant to be so significant that you . . . You . . . Uh!'

He is too angry to be able to think of the end of this sentence. In the kitchen he puts *The Counterfeit Confetti* into an earthenware dish, forcing it in so that the corners of the cover are bent and the book is lodged. He then searches under the sink for the turpentine. I make no comment and do not try to stop him because I see no point; also, I'm quite interested in seeing him act out his anger. Until tonight I have never seen Carl angry. I really have pissed him off – I'm quite proud.

He sets the book alight. He holds the dish out towards me, as if to provoke a reaction. The fire is intense and the kitchen smoke alarm sounds.

'Take it outside,' I tell him. 'I'll take the battery out of the alarm.'

He does this. Then he walks back into the kitchen, halts to look at me, then exits upstairs. I wait.

He comes down with an arm full of books. I can only guess, but I should think he has picked them up at random. His anger is defiant now, continuing only because he has no idea how to stop.

'What are you going to do with them?' I ask. He stops to look at me, then takes them outside. I follow. *The Counterfeit Confetti* still burns but the flame is weak. He holds one book, pages loose, over the flame until they catch alight.

'What are you doing?'

'I hate you,' he answers, then lights another book.

'What?'

'I wish you were dead,' he spits.

'No you don't.' A small fire rages; he begins to drop books onto it, one at a time, staring at me.

'I love you,' he now says.

277

'You just said you wished I was dead.'

'Every thought I've had for the future has included you.'

'But –'

'Shut up, you selfish, hard-faced bitch.'

'Carl!'

'What are you feeling now, Tanya? Confused? Sad? Afraid? Angry? A mixture you can't figure out? Tell me then, which book have you ever read that has captured how you feel now?'

He's right. I have never read a book in which the main character, faced with such confrontation, feels as I do now. I want to giggle. I don't know if this feeling manifests itself on my face in the form of a smile – I don't think it does – but Carl grins. I form a fist and hit him before I even think about making a fist or violence. I haven't put much force behind the strike and have swung my arm too wide, so, unhurt, his grin turns into a deliberate, patronising laugh. I put more effort into the next punch, hitting him on the forehead. His 'Ow' is still mockery, yet to protect his face he turns his back on me. I launch myself at him, jumping onto his back, an arm around his throat, swinging my free arm around to try to hit his face. He grabs this arm, then carries me back inside the house. I struggle but cannot escape. Carl carries me as if I were no heavier than a coat. I want to hurt him even more now, for turning this – my supreme act of anger – into a piggyback ride. He carries me upstairs; by now I am trying to strangle him and scream how happy I will be when he has finally gone. He has trouble bending, but manages to scoop more books under his free arm; then he carries me back downstairs and outside. He puts me down; then, as he tosses more books onto the fire, he holds me back. I smash at his outstretched arm, unable to reach him. I stop only when I am exhausted. This exercise would never make it to video but has done me more good than two hours of aerobics.

'You're burning books! *Books!*' I shout at him, denouncing him for this most uncivilised act of vandalism. I might have kept the moral high ground if I could have resisted adding, 'You fucking wanker!'

'I get it, Tanya – just like you – I do understand the pleasure of books. But they aren't the same pleasures as *experiencing*. Real love, real fear, real anger, real joy – reading is only spectating. Let me stay and I promise to make you feel love and joy. As well as anger and sadness.'

I refuse to laugh at Carl's attempt at a joke and so, to provoke any reaction, he once again drops books onto the fire.

'Why are you doing such a thing?'

He only shakes his head. Only three books remain and I recognise one, it's a book I have been looking forward to reading, holding it back in reserve because I feel so certain I will enjoy it.

'Not that one!' I tell him, reaching out to take the book off him. He gives me the book before he drops the remaining two into the fire.

No one else I have ever met, perhaps no one else in the world, even if they shared this same affliction – reading too much – no one would have given the book back to me. As hopeless as he believes the situation to be and even though it undermined his grand gesture of burning books to prove a point, Carl still understood and spared the book I asked for.

The fire burns slowly, steady in the still night, illuminating Carl's face in warm colours of charm and caring.

'I do actually think that you love me,' he tells me. 'So don't get rid of me because of some deranged, romantic notion of being a martyr to love. That's fiction. Then again, if I've said or done anything to change your mind, don't have me back unless you're pretty certain you're going to make a real effort at making this work. I don't want to ever feel like this again, Tanya.'

I rotate the book in my hands, working out how to speak. My knuckles hurt from where I hit him.

'Is there anything I could say that will make you change your mind?' he asks. This is a similar question to one he has asked before. It haunted me. He rubs his forehead. I want to apologise for hitting him. I need to learn how to apologise.

The happiness I experienced alone in this house came from being supremely content. There is a more substantial, rewarding happiness, which comes from work, and compromise and anger. It's the happiness that comes as a reward for tolerating the flaws of one other person. And there is no one else for me but Carl.

He still believes it is necessary to speak. 'Part of why I love you is because you want to be alone. Unlike most people – who don't care enough – you want to be alone so you can't disappoint. Tanya, you could never disappoint me – so tell me your decision.'

I toss the book I hold onto the fire. It smacks up smoke and ashes, which a sudden wind blows upwards. The smoke makes our eyes water and we cough. We need to wash our faces. Carl is temporarily blinded, so I take his hand to lead him. We walk into our home.